Library Use Only

Crime Files Series

General Editor: **Clive Bloom**

Since its invention in the nineteenth century, detective fiction has never been more popular. In novels, short stories, films, radio, television and now in computer games, private detectives and psychopaths, prim poisoners and overworked cops, tommy gun gangsters and cocaine criminals are the very stuff of modern imagination, and their creators one mainstay of popular consciousness. Crime Files is a ground-breaking series offering scholars, students and discerning readers a comprehensive set of guides to the world of crime and detective fiction. Every aspect of crime writing, detective fiction, gangster movie, true-crime exposé, police procedural and post-colonial investigation is explored through clear and informative texts offering comprehensive coverage and theoretical sophistication.

Titles include:

Maurizio Ascari
A COUNTER-HISTORY OF CRIME FICTION
Supernatural, Gothic, Sensational

Hans Bertens and Theo D'haen
CONTEMPORARY AMERICAN CRIME FICTION

Anita Biressi
CRIME, FEAR AND THE LAW IN TRUE CRIME STORIES

Ed Christian (*editor*)
THE POST-COLONIAL DETECTIVE

Paul Cobley
THE AMERICAN THRILLER
Generic Innovation and Social Change in the 1970s

Michael Cook
NARRATIVES OF ENCLOSURE IN DETECTIVE FICTION
The Locked Room Mystery

Barry Forshaw
DEATH IN A COLD CLIMATE
A Guide to Scandinavian Crime Fiction

Barry Forshaw
BRITISH CRIME FILM
Subverting the Social Order

Emelyne Godfrey
MASCULINITY, CRIME AND SELF-DEFENCE IN VICTORIAN LITERATURE

Emelyne Godfrey
FEMININITY, CRIME AND SELF-DEFENCE IN VICTORIAN LITERATURE AND SOCIETY
From Dagger-Fans to Suffragettes

Christiana Gregoriou
DEVIANCE IN CONTEMPORARY CRIME FICTION

Lee Horsley
THE NOIR THRILLER

Merja Makinen
AGATHA CHRISTIE
Investigating Femininity

Fran Mason
AMERICAN GANGSTER CINEMA
From *Little Caesar* to *Pulp Fiction*

Fran Mason
HOLLYWOOD'S DETECTIVES
Crime Series in the 1930s and 1940s from the Whodunnit to Hard-boiled Noir

Linden Peach
MASQUERADE, CRIME AND FICTION
Criminal Deceptions

Steven Powell (*editor*)
100 AMERICAN CRIME WRITERS

Alistair Rolls and Deborah Walker
FRENCH AND AMERICAN NOIR
Dark Crossings

Susan Rowland
FROM AGATHA CHRISTIE TO RUTH RENDELL
British Women Writers in Detective and Crime Fiction

Adrian Schober
POSSESSED CHILD NARRATIVES IN LITERATURE AND FILM
Contrary States

Lucy Sussex
WOMEN WRITERS AND DETECTIVES IN NINETEENTH-CENTURY CRIME FICTION
The Mothers of the Mystery Genre

Heather Worthington
THE RISE OF THE DETECTIVE IN EARLY NINETEENTH-CENTURY POPULAR FICTION

R.A. York
AGATHA CHRISTIE
Power and Illusion

Crime Files
Series Standing Order ISBN 978–0–333–71471–3 (hardback) 978–0–333–93064–9 (paperback)
(outside North America only)

You can receive future titles in this series as they are published by placing a standing order. Please contact your bookseller or, in case of difficulty, write to us at the address below with your name and address, the title of the series and one of the ISBN quoted above.

Customer Services Department, Macmillan Distribution Ltd, Houndmills, Basingstoke, Hampshire RG21 6XS, England

---

100 American Crime Writers

Edited by

Steven Powell
University of Liverpool, UK

First published 2012 by
PALGRAVE MACMILLAN

Palgrave Macmillan in the UK is an imprint of Macmillan Publishers Limited,
registered in England, company number 785998, of Houndmills, Basingstoke,
Hampshire RG21 6XS.

Palgrave Macmillan in the US is a division of St Martin's Press LLC,
175 Fifth Avenue, New York, NY 10010.

Palgrave Macmillan is the global academic imprint of the above companies
and has companies and representatives throughout the world.

Palgrave® and Macmillan® are registered trademarks in the United States,
the United Kingdom, Europe and other countries

ISBN: 978–0–230–52537–5

This book is printed on paper suitable for recycling and made from fully
managed and sustained forest sources. Logging, pulping and manufacturing
processes are expected to conform to the environmental regulations of the
country of origin.

A catalogue record for this book is available from the British Library.

A catalog record for this book is available from the Library of Congress.

10 9 8 7 6 5 4 3 2 1
21 20 19 18 17 16 15 14 13 12

Printed and bound in the United States of America

In Memory of
Rachel Alexander,
1980–2010

Contents

Acknowledgements

Undertaking such a project as *100 American Crime Writers* would not be possible without a loving family, and I am fortunate to have family here and in the United States who have always given me unfailing support, particularly Don and Ann Lyons in Detroit. To my wife Diana, I thank you for the enormous contribution you have made towards the project and for your daily support. I would also like to thank Professor David Seed at the University of Liverpool for his advice and mentorship over the last few years. I feel privileged to be a part of the web community that contributes to crime fiction criticism and would like to express my gratitude to the writers and bloggers who generously and enthusiastically give their time to the study of a genre which for most of us is nothing short of a lifelong passion. I would like to thank the several crime writers who generously assisted the contributors by providing information for their entries, Catherine Mitchell, Felicity Plester and Christabel Scaife at Palgrave Macmillan for their advice and expertise, Clive Bloom for his reading of the manuscript and many helpful suggestions, all of the contributors for their hard work and dedication, but special gratitude is reserved for Christopher Routledge who made the book possible.

Contributors

Delphine M. Cingal is Assistant Professor at Panthéon-Assas-Paris 2. She is a specialist in Anglo-Saxon detective fiction and has published articles in France and abroad. Her PhD was on P. D. James. She is also one of the organisers of the week-end noir festival in Neuilly-Plaisance, near Paris. She is also a Chevalier des Arts et des Lettres.

Tim Foster is a Teacher of English and Film Studies at a school in Bedfordshire, and has a PhD on contemporary American fiction from the University of Nottingham. His favourite work of American crime fiction is Caleb Carr's *The Alienist* (1994).

David Hering tutors and lectures on American literature, crime writing and postmodern literature at the University of Liverpool. He is the editor of *Consider David Foster Wallace: Critical Essays* (2010).

Megan Hoffman is a PhD candidate and teaching assistant in the School of English, University of St Andrews. She has previously published and presented work on contemporary women's crime fiction as well as nineteenth- and twentieth-century British and American crime fiction. She is working on her thesis, which focuses on representations of femininity in the novels of British women 'golden age' crime writers.

Martin Lightening is a freelance documentary cameraman who has been a fan of American Detective fiction since he discovered Mickey Spillane as a young teenager, later graduating through Raymond Chandler to all the usual suspects. He always packs a paperback in his camera kit when travelling. Sometimes he gets a chance to read it.

Susan Massey obtained her PhD from the University of St Andrews in 2010. Her thesis was titled 'The Uncocked Gun? Representations of Masculinity in Contemporary Crime Fiction'. She is working in London, pursuing a non-academic career in librarianship. However, she still retains a keen interest in contemporary crime writing, particularly in the depiction of gender within the genre. Her publications include an article on male authors for the *Greenwood Encyclopedia of British Crime Writing* (2008) and an article on Henning Mankell for the collection *The Millennial Detective* (2011).

Esme Miskimmin teaches at the University of Liverpool. She has research interests in crime fiction and Renaissance drama, which she occasionally combines. Her publications include the volume *Encyclopedia of British Women's Writing 1900–1950* (2006) and chapters in *Popular Responses to the*

First World War (ed. Stacy Gillis) and the *Blackwell Companion to Crime Fiction* (ed. Charles Rzepka and Lee Horsley).

Juri Nummelin is a Finnish writer, editor and translator and an aficionado of all things hard-boiled and noir. Juri has written and edited more than 40 books and blogs in English at his *Pulpetti* blog.

Chris Pak is a final year PhD candidate specialising in science fiction at the University of Liverpool. Although he maintains an interest in other contemporary fiction, he has published reviews and a prize-winning essay in the science fiction journal *Foundation: The International Review of Science Fiction* and has articles in the collections *The Postnational Fantasy: Nationalism, Cosmopolitics and Science Fiction, Science Fiction and Computing: Essays on Interlinked Domains* and *Mathematics in Popular Culture: Essays on Appearances in Film, Fiction, Games, Television and Other Media.*

J. Kingston Pierce is a Seattle journalist and author and the editor of *The Rap Sheet* (www.therapsheet.blogspot.com), the senior editor of *January Magazine* (www.januarymagazine.com) and the lead crime-fiction blogger for *Kirkus Reviews* (www.kirkusreviews.com). His non-fiction books include *San Francisco: Yesterday & Today* (2009) and *Eccentric Seattle* (2003).

Diana Powell is a PhD candidate at the University of Liverpool. Her thesis is entitled 'The Victorian Counter-Reformation', and she has published several articles on this subject. She has research interests in American Golden Age crime fiction and contemporary female crime authors.

Steven Powell is the editor of *Conversations with James Ellroy*. He is the co-founder of the crime website *Venetian Vase* (www.venetianvase.co.uk).

Christopher Routledge is a freelance writer, editor and academic whose 1998 PhD dissertation was on Raymond Chandler. In the 1990s and early 2000s, he published several academic articles on crime fiction. He is also co-editor, with Adrienne Gavin, of *Mystery in Children's Literature* (2001).

Steve Scott is a retired commercial banker living in Murfreesboro, Tennessee. He has been reading and collecting the works of John D. MacDonald since 1974, and in 1981 he assisted MacDonald's bibliographers Walter and Jean Shine in documenting the publication history of the author's short fiction. He has written over 200 articles on MacDonald's writings, published on his blog *The Trap of Solid Gold* (www.thetrapofsolidgold.blogspot.com).

Maureen Sunderland is an independent scholar. She obtained her PhD from Newcastle University in 2009. Her thesis was titled 'The Long Goodbye: Hard-Boiled Interpretations of the City, Femininity and Masculinity after Chandler'. The work focused on Chandler's legacy within the detective fiction genre as interpreted by four American writers: Chester Himes, Ross Macdonald, James Ellroy and Walter Mosley.

Introduction

Steven Powell

Any attempt to trace the genesis of American crime fiction is hampered by the need or desire to locate a source and date, which is inevitably open to revision and dispute. The oldest author to appear in this volume is Edgar Allan Poe (b.1809) whose 'The Murders in the Rue Morgue' (1841) is widely credited as the first detective story. Poe's 'tales of ratiocination' featuring C. Auguste Dupin were a significant influence on the Golden Age of detective fiction, and his influence can still be seen in the work of contemporary crime writers. Although Poe and his successors laid much of the foundations of the crime fiction genre that a modern-day reader would identify, American crime fiction, however, can be said to have pre-dated Poe. Sara Crosby argues that some of the earliest American crime writing is to be found in the popular execution sermons of seventeenth-century New England which were written to pass judgment on condemned men. The decline in church influence and advances in publishing caused these 'sermons' to evolve into different forms, and Crosby identifies 'crime writers' amongst the first generation of American novelists, including William Hill Brown, Susanna Rowson, Hannah Webster Foster and Charles Brockden Brown, all of whom were particularly fascinated with the subject of crime and the criminal (Crosby 2010).

To understand the historical developments and trends in American crime fiction, it is necessary to examine similar trends in British crime fiction in regards to late nineteenth- and early twentieth-century writing. This was a period when trends in British and American crime writing often paralleled but sometimes moved in opposition to one another. Julian Symons argued that there were essentially two Golden Ages in the crime fiction field: the Golden Age of the Short Story and the Golden Age of Detective Fiction. Even within these two ages, opposition to the dominant trend was emerging in the form of a more realist style (Symons 1972). During the Golden Age of the Short Story, which was exemplified by the works of Poe in America and Arthur Conan Doyle's Sherlock Holmes stories in Britain, the Dime Novels, including the long-running Nick Carter series

1

beginning in 1891, were also flourishing. The successor to the first Golden Age, the Golden Age of Detective Fiction, is generally regarded as the period between the two World Wars, and is often identified as an idiosyncratically British form, if only because the settings of country houses and rigid class structures did not apply so easily to American society. However, Americans also succeeded in this form, and among the American Golden Age writers, John Dickson Carr and Jacques Futrelle achieved popularity on both continents. Just as the Dime Novels were popular during the era of the classic detective short story, so too another more radical form of crime fiction emerged during the second Golden Age. In the 1930s, the pulp magazines *Black Mask* and *Dime Detective* began to publish detective short stories by a new breed of crime writers including Carroll John Daly, Raymond Chandler and Dashiell Hammett. The magazines were dubbed 'pulps' as they took their name from a new wood-pulping procedure whereby the trademark slick covers could be produced quickly. *Black Mask* introduced tough, urban private detectives, such as Philip Marlowe and Sam Spade, who were far removed from the aloof, eccentric intellectual 'detective' developed by the Golden Age writers. Violence, sexuality and instinct were brought closer to the reader, stripping away the sanitising veil of scientific and intellectual crime solving. The prose style was shortened to reflect the immediacy of this new genre and the cynical thought processes of the world-weary protagonists, although Chandler himself was fond of using elaborate similes. Many *Black Mask* writers transitioned successfully to novel writing, often expanding the material of their short stories into novel-length narratives. The hard-boiled style continued to thrive with the rise of the paperback industry in the 1940s, which allowed the reading public greater access to crime fiction, and led to the reprinting of Chandler and Hammett's 1930s hardcovers.

Cinema contributed to the success of the hard-boiled style, with a series of films in the 1940s and 1950s, which were considered crime melodramas at the time of their release, but have been retrospectively labelled as film noir. With film noir, like many other terms in crime fiction criticism, it can be difficult to find an agreed definition as critics such as Andrew Pepper have exposed the problem of various generic labels – even the term crime fiction itself. In the essay 'Towards a Definition of Film Noir', Raymond Borde and Étienne Chaumeton were amongst the first critics to explore some of the cinematic conventions which may lead to a definition of film noir:

> The moral ambivalence, the criminality, the complex contradictions in motives and events, all conspire to make the viewer co-experience the anguish and insecurity which are the true emotions of contemporary *film noir*. All the films of this cycle create a similar emotional effect: *that state of tension instilled in the spectator when the psychological reference points*

are removed. The aim of *film noir* was to create *a specific alienation*. (Borde and Chaumenton 1955, p. 25)

It is possible to see that the themes of alienation in hard-boiled fiction have influenced film noir, with James M. Cain's *The Postman Always Rings Twice* (1934) adapted into film a total of four times in Europe and America. The bleak, cynical philosophy of the novel was an inspiration for Albert Camus' existentialist novel *L'Etranger* (*The Stranger* 1942) which itself was an important work in shaping film noir. Cinema has in turn influenced fiction, with the contemporary crime writers James Ellroy and Megan Abbott drawing upon film noir and its most iconic location, Los Angeles, in their fiction. Ellroy's Los Angeles Quartet series and Abbott's revisionism of the film noir *femme fatale* show how the cinematic portrayal of crime fiction can influence the modern literary understanding of the genre.

If crime writing has sometimes become repetitive and formulaic within the constraints of these narrative trends, it is also capable of reinvention, either through sudden radical shifts or more conservatively nostalgic re-imagination, which has produced every possible variation of the hard-boiled private detective. Raymond Chandler wrote in 'The Simple Art of Murder', a key text of the Hard-boiled School, 'Old-fashioned novels which now seem stilted and artificial to the point of burlesque did not appear that way to the people who first read them' (Chandler 1995, p. 977). It holds true that Philip Marlowe now seems like a fantasy version of a private detective as much as Ian Fleming's James Bond is a fantasy version of a spy. Hard-boiled fiction began to look dated, as crime writers – including Jim Thompson and Charles Williams in the 1950s – began to create darker, altogether more psychologically disturbing protagonists. In the 1970s, a new generation of crime writers, led by Elmore Leonard and George V. Higgins, began to disassemble the mystery narrative in favour of dialogue-driven storytelling, with characters plunged from one seemingly random violent situation to another. Despite this, the hard-boiled style has fared better with American writers in that it has progressed and adapted itself more successfully than classic detective fiction. Crime fiction's many sub-genres – such as the police procedural, the most notable practitioner of which was Ed McBain with his 87th Precinct series – often employ recognisably hard-boiled traits. However, as Lee Horsley notes, 'Debate has centred on the question of whether the hard-boiled sub-genre possesses genuinely radical potential or is, in late twentieth-century terms, inherently conservative, imposing in the end a resolution that makes the private eye the instrument of a repressive political order' (Horsley 2005, p. 9). If the hard-boiled private detective may now be considered 'conservative', one can recognise the Golden Age texts had the potential to be subversive as they were not striving for the 'realism' which has given hard-boiled its perceived conservatism.

The latest volume in Palgrave Macmillan's Crime Files series, *100 American Crime Writers*, is an anthology of short, concise critical biographies of American writers whose work falls into one of the most popular of genres, crime fiction. Selecting which authors to include, and by extension who to exclude, from this anthology was an often difficult task. Of course, the reputation of certain writers is so important that a study of American crime fiction would not be complete without them: Raymond Chandler, Dashiell Hammett, Patricia Highsmith, Mickey Spillane, Elmore Leonard and James Ellroy are among a number of writers who have achieved this distinction. For those crime writers who have not maintained such a degree of prominence, the historical record can be, as in the cases of Paul Cain and Charles Williams, disputed and obscure. The challenge for the contributor and editor has been to separate fact from fiction, myth from reality and present a clear, balanced account of the author's life and work. For even with crime writers whose biographical record appeared to be complete, new research and details are continually emerging which shed new light, as in, for example, Christopher Routledge's entry on Raymond Chandler. Several of the crime writers that are discussed had become obscure by the time of their death, as with David Goodis, Gil Brewer and even Jim Thompson, now amongst the most critically admired of crime writers. But the ever-expanding field of critical work on the genre has helped to revive interest in their work.

Also included are figures whom Rosemary Herbert has dubbed 'incidental crime writers', such as William Faulkner and Truman Capote, who are not generally associated with crime fiction but made at least one significant contribution to the field. This volume is an anthology and not a monograph. Thus it does not follow a strict or linear critical argument, as in Stephen Knight's critique and reassessment of crime fiction's genre labels or Megan Abbott's examination of white masculinity. Rather, the thematic and historical issues of the genre are explored in how they relate to each author naturally. The reader will find discussion on the decline of the Golden Age style and the rise of hard-boiled crime fiction in the entries on Raymond Chandler and Dashiell Hammett, and the entries on Sara Paretsky and Marcia Muller discuss the female private eye. The book can be read sequentially if so desired, but as the entries are arranged alphabetically this is not a necessity. Also present in the volume are two essays written by the editor, 'Out of the Venetian Vase: From Golden Age to Hard-boiled' and 'After These Mean Streets: Crime Fiction and the Chandler Inheritance', which immediately follow the Introduction and contextualise the entries which follow.

This volume does not contain extensive bibliographies of the crime writers discussed. As crime writers tend to be prolific, and some have publications running into the hundreds, merely listing works would prove redundant in a volume of this kind. Instead the writing is focused on an analysis of the author's key works, and where applicable, on the discussion of important moments in their lives which affected their fiction. With *100 American Crime Writers* we have attempted to bring an original, incisive and encompassing study of American crime writers and the genre which will be of interest to the scholar, student and general reader of crime fiction. As the title of this volume suggests there is one important rule that must be met to warrant an author's inclusion: all of the authors must either be born or naturalised US citizens.

'Out of the Venetian Vase': From Golden Age to Hard-boiled

Steven Powell

> Hammett took murder out of the Venetian vase and dropped it into the alley; it doesn't have to stay there forever, but it was a good idea to begin by getting as far as possible from Emily Post's idea of how a well-bred debutante gnaws a chicken wing.
>
> (Chandler, 1995, pp. 988–9)

In 'The Simple Art of Murder', Raymond Chandler irreverently praises the innovation of his peer and rival Dashiell Hammett. With the Continental Op, Hammett had not so much invented a new structure as destroyed the old one. Crime fiction had become too obsessed with controlled environments – and Hammett was the first to break from this metaphorical Venetian Vase and into the gritty, lower class world where crimes were committed out of desperation and depravity. The Golden Age of detective fiction that Hammett rebelled against is generally considered to be the 20-year period between the two world wars. Classic detective fiction was the reigning detective model during this period: the intellectually brilliant but aloof 'thinking machines' exemplified in the fiction of Jacques Futrelle, John Dickson Carr, Willard Huntington Wright (writing as S.S. Van Dine) and C. Daly King owed a significant debt to the British author Arthur Conan Doyle's Sherlock Holmes. And it should be noted that the variations of classic detective fiction – the locked room mystery, impossible crimes, the had-I-but-known school – were all firmly established before the end of the First World War, the date set for the commencement of the Golden Age. Indeed, Edgar Allan Poe's 'The Murders in the Rue Morgue' (1841) established the locked room, the superior detective and the puzzling clues that will ultimately lead to the near-miraculous solving of the case. As Julian Symons has argued, the rise of the short detective story was the first Golden Age, which 'began with Holmes and ended with World War I' (Symons, 1972, p. 92).

Just as the popularity of classic detective fiction preceded and overlapped the narrowly defined parameters of the Golden Age, the hard-boiled style cannot, likewise, be sharply defined. As with classical detective fiction, the hard-boiled private detective originated in the short story, with the pulp magazines – most famously *Black Mask* (1920–1951) – publishing in the 1920s. After World War II, classical detective fiction in America would find refuge in the short story through the popularity of the *Ellery Queen Magazine* (1941–), as the form was increasingly looked upon as quintessentially British. Yet the fact that Chandler was compelled to direct such opprobrium at the Golden Age school, can be partially attributed to the success of these writers and their characters, such as Van Dine's Philo Vance, whom Chandler described as 'probably the most asinine character in all of detective fiction' (Chandler, 2005 p. 985). The first Philo Vance novel, *The Benson Murder Case*, was published in 1926, with the twelfth and last, *The Winter Murder Case*, appearing in 1939; Chandler's first short story appeared in *Black Mask* in 1933 and his debut novel, *The Big Sleep*, in 1939. It was during this short period of time that the urbane and cerebral detective all but disappeared in favour of the urban and physical private dick. And while a pure hard-boiled style has also now come to pass, as Chandler prophetically foresaw in his comments on where Hammett took the genre, 'it doesn't have to stay there forever', the hard-boiled form has shown an extraordinary capacity for reinvention that classic detective fiction lacked.

For Chandler, the distinction between hard-boiled and classic detective fiction was not one of nationality but one of style: 'Fiction in any form has always intended to be realistic.' (Chandler, 2005, p. 977) But, he adds that the perception of realism changes with time. Those who continued to write in the classical style were unconvincingly aping the past and hemming in their characters with out-dated rules.

Much emphasis in Golden Age fiction was placed not only on the methodology of solving a crime, but also on the structure of the novel itself. In some cases, such as Arthur B. Reeve's Craig Kennedy, the methodology overshadows the characterisation, with the focus on scientific and psychological developments. But whereas Kennedy's mind is aided by gadgetry, Jacques Futrelle has his detective reign supreme in the story as the almost superhuman 'thinking machine' possesses all he needs to solve a case. S.S. Van Dine and John Dickson Carr sought to balance their detectives' skills against their personal flaws. But although Carr's creation Dr Fell's physical impairments (he is obese and walks with the aid of two canes) suggest vulnerability, they also cement his position as a purely cerebral presence in the process of detection.

In classic detective fiction the sleuth, who is isolated socially in exchange for oracle-like powers, takes centre stage in the novel and guides the readers, as they do the characters, to a solution. It is therefore fitting that Dr Fell solves the mystery of the murders in *The Hollow Man* (published in the US as *The Three Coffins*, 1935) by examining the rules of the fictional locked room. Dr Fell's triumphant explanation replicates the denouement of classical fiction by revealing the method of the story, which is in itself a form of deductive reasoning.

The rules of classic fiction have also been laid out most notably by S.S. Van Dine in the 'Twenty Rules of Detective Fiction'. Van Dine explains that his first rule is to enter a contract of fairplay with the reader: 'The reader must have equal opportunity with the detective for solving the mystery. All clues must be plainly stated and described' (Van Dine, 2000). Yet Van Dine argued that by necessity detective fiction had to be worth the time and effort the reader had invested in the story, a point that Carr would make through his intricate, sustained locked-room mysteries. This sentiment explains the popularity of impossible crimes, and the interest of Golden Age authors in the supernatural and Gothic fiction. C. Daly King's Travis Tarrant novels evidence elements of horror and superstition. Carr plays with the suggestion of werewolves, the undead and magic solutions in his novels. As Carr's biographer Douglas G. Green noted, 'Carr's detectives act almost like exorcists. They bid the demons be gone and reason is returned to the world' (Greene, 2009). This return is essential to classic detective fiction, as the appearance of order, which the hard-boiled authors would purposefully debunk, is the main aim of the Golden Age detective. Thus, Van Dine stipulates that no supernatural cause can be given in order to truly achieve this effect in his eighth rule: 'The problem of the crime must be solved by strictly naturalistic means' (Van Dine, 2000).

By contrast, the hard-boiled private detective is not called upon to perform such intellectual feats, nor are the stories and novels contrived so that everything will be revealed in the conclusion. Sam Spade and Philip Marlowe were by no means unintelligent, but rather than possessing a superhuman intellect their qualities were bravery, guile and a dogged commitment to detective work. As Leonard Cassuto has written of the transitions Chandler was making, 'Chandler turned away from the intricate plots of the likes of Ellery Queen and S.S. Van Dine because they're too intellectual to activate the power of sympathy' (Cassuto, 2009, p. 85). Yet this imbalance can also be found in the hard-boiled style. The ultra-violent PIs exemplified by Carroll John Daly's Race Williams and Mickey Spillane's Mike Hammer put action before thought, dispensing with their own brand of rough street justice as they see fit. Thus, their machismo detaches them from the sympathetic engagement of Chandler's Marlowe or Ross Macdonald's Lew Archer in a completely different fashion to the intellectual indifference of Philo Vance. Justice or sympathy are only achieved if the reader shares their brutal sense of righteousness.

When post-Golden Age crime writers have formally discussed their craft, such as hard-boiled pulpster Frank Gruber in his memoir *The Pulp Jungle* or nearer the present day Elmore Leonard's article 'Easy on the Adverbs,

Exclamation Points and Especially Hooptedoodle' for the *New York Times*, they have focused less on the rules of crime writing – which have diversified to the extent that there are now very few – and more on stylistic guidelines. Leonard's third rule is quite simply: 'Never use a verb other than "said" to carry dialogue' (Leonard, 2001). Gruber outlined an eleven-point formula for the mystery novel. Although he claims to have devised and revised this model between 1934 and 1936, his rules are notable for their simplicity, as if in order to amplify a theme, the hard-boiled style must out of necessity also simplify it to produce the greatest effect. The sparse, immediate prose style of hard-boiled was in part a reaction to the excesses of classic detective figures such as Van Dine's heavy use of tangential footnotes or C. Daly King's index of clues in *Obelists at Sea* (1935). However, in violence and setting, the hard-boiled style embellishes where the Golden Age, such as the locked-room mystery, is restrictive, as evidenced by Gruber's fourth rule: 'The story must be played against a colourful or unusual background. The streets of a big city are not necessarily colourful. If they're not, make them so' (Gruber, 1967, p. 181).

The classic detective, through Dr Fell, defiantly makes a case against realism through his pact with the reader: 'we're in a detective story, and we don't fool the reader by pretending were not. Let's not invent elaborate excuses to drag in a discussion of detective stories. Let's candidly glory in the noblest pursuits possible to characters in a book' (Carr, 2002, p. 152). The rules of classic detective fiction, much like the rules that govern other genres, were internal and self-serving. The Golden Age writers never attained Chandler's definition of realism, nor is there any indication, as Dr Fell makes clear, that they ever intended to. In 'The Problem of Cell 13', Jacques Futrelle's academic detective Professor Van Dusen claims that nothing is impossible to the human mind, and thus accepts a challenge to escape from a locked cell through pure logic. Van Dusen succeeds of course, and while his method breaks no natural laws, his logic is reliant upon a fair amount of luck and chance, which by no means would have been available to him if the narrative had not been structured so precisely. Yet no matter how realistic the hard-boiled private detective appeared in comparison, he was still undoubtedly a fantasy creation. If Philo Vance and Nero Wolfe made an art of pomposity, aloofness and eccentricity, then the wisecracks of Philip Marlowe were also highly stylised. Memorable lines such as, 'It was a blonde. A blonde to make a bishop kick a hole in a stained glass window' (Chandler, 2000b, p. 229), rely on a sophisticated usage of simile and metaphor far removed from daily urban conversation. A certain form of the detective novel dated, but the stories remained variations of fantasy. And while the hard-boiled style proved more durable than Golden Age detective fiction, the successors of Chandler and Hammett, whom William Marling has dubbed 'the Second Generation', instigated some radical changes, further removing the crime genre from its more fantastical elements. While there are still many writers who imitate Chandler's formula, only providing a variation on the central PI, these writers tend to be located on the more self-reverential ground of the genre, and not the cutting edge.

After These Mean Streets: Crime Fiction and the Chandler Inheritance

Steven Powell

> I think that Chandler, who I have less affection for by the day, spawned a whole number of easy imitators. His style is easy to adapt to the personal prejudices of the individual writers, which is why you now have the gay private eye, the black private eye, the woman private eye, and every other kind of private eye. But I don't think that's the realistic archetype of twentieth-century violent intrigue. (Hogan, 2012, p. 57)

James Ellroy begrudgingly acknowledges the enormous impact that Chandler's work had on shaping and directing the genre for decades to come. By the time of his death in 1959, Chandler's writing had been in decline for some years, but through his private detective Philip Marlowe, he had created the standard by which many imitators would be judged. Marlowe was by no means the first hard-boiled detective in American crime fiction: Carroll John Daly's Race Williams and Dashiell Hammett's Continental Op came before him, and they in turn were preceded by the now nearly forgotten Jim Hanvey, created by Octavus Roy Cohen, and the African American PI Sadipe Okukenu, from the pen of John E. Bruce. But Chandler's Marlowe certainly helped to popularise the hard-boiled detective and set the formula that his successors would conform to or consciously deviate from. Chandler could also lay claim to a certain originality in the PI, as Sean McCann argues, 'The detective who is brash in Daly, and icy in Hammett, is a sorrowful man in Chandler' (McCann, 2010, p. 53).

Chandler's quasi-manifesto on the role of the PI, 'Down these mean streets a man must go who is not himself mean', encapsulated the essence of Marlowe's character (Chandler, 2005, pp. 991–2). Marlowe is an honest man living in a dispiritingly amoral world. He may feign indifference to right and wrong with cynical one-liners and colourful metaphors, but this shields a personal code of honour and determination to see some form of justice achieved. Thus alienated within his setting, Marlowe seeks to help

11

his clients, when possible, even if that means sacrificing his own dwindling innocence, as when he chooses to spare his dying client General Sternwood from the shocking truth about his daughter in *The Big Sleep*: 'Me, I was part of the nastiness now. Far more a part of it than [General Sternwood] was. But the old man didn't have to be' (Chandler, 2000a, p. 164). Marlowe's often extra-judicial interventions are not the vengeful justice sought by Spillane's ultra-violent Mike Hammer: Marlowe does not operate from the same position of power nor the same conviction of rightness; his victories and defeats exist within the opaque morality of the novels. Important to Marlowe's outsider status is the repeated Arthurian imagery in the novels, which evokes the unspoken codes of honour and chastity that he singularly upholds. Chandler heightens the contrast of Marlowe's honour code and societal norms through Marlowe's backstory: Marlowe had once worked in the DA's office, but his career came to an abrupt end as he was forced out for reasons that are never fully revealed. As a consequence, it is not surprising that Marlowe holds a rather ambiguous and sceptical relationship with the police. On their side, the police are wary of Marlowe's investigative methods and view him with suspicion because his position and honour code grant him freedom from their political system. When their interests align, however, the police often respect Marlowe's tenacity and independence.

The influence of Chandler on his successors may have been fluid, subtle and even at times unconscious, but it was present even if it was sometimes manifested as a reaction against his model. Mickey Spillane's creation Mike Hammer, in his use of sadistic violence, deviates greatly from Marlowe's intelligent, street-smart detection. Ross Macdonald expands upon the intellectual model into psychology with Lew Archer. Macdonald drew on Chandler's model but moved past the duty-led detective to a less hardened shamus: Archer is a shrewd, steady detective, but he is emotionally affected by his cases as though he is a priest in a very secular parish. *The Wycherly Woman* (1961) ends with Archer coercing a killer into writing a confession, but he is aware that the confession holds only a slender redemptive power for the both of them. Other deviations or expansions on the Marlowe type were to follow: Ernest Tidyman and Walter Mosley created black PIs with John Shaft and Easy Rawlins and thus introduced a new socio-cultural perspective to the genre. Shaft and Rawlins expand on Marlowe's isolation: they are not only on the fringes of the law as PIs, they are also outside the dominant social structure. Chester Himes, who wrote eight novels set in Harlem featuring police detective duo 'Coffin' Ed Johnson and 'Grave Digger' Jones, created the sort of literary black neighbourhood, as Megan Abbott writes 'that served only as a temporary exotic interlude in Chandler, Hammett and Spillane' (Abbott, 2002, p. 161).

Fictional private eyes continued to spring up from various sorts of backgrounds: Marcia Muller debuted one of the first female shamuses, Sharon McCone, in *Edwin of the Iron Shoes* (1977), which was followed by Sara

Paretsky's V.I. Warshawski novels and Sue Grafton's Kinsey Millhone series. McCone draws on Marlowe's street-smart PI, but although McCone's sex is not made an issue (in that she does not regularly deal with sexism), she is hardly sexless like the mostly chaste Marlowe. In fact, part of the drama from the McCone series is derived from her relationships with men. In a break from the detective as a type of knightly rescuer, John Lutz presents a shambolic and downtrodden Alo Nudger, who is divorced and living above a doughnut shop. James Sallis created one of the most radical breaks in the PI tradition with the alcoholic Lew Griffin, by making the actual investigations less important to the novels than his dubious character. Cases run over, often unsolved, from one novel to the next, creating a detective novel without either of the expected tropes of the genre: the security of a strong, able character or an inevitable solution. As far as setting and context, William F. Nolan stretched the boundaries of crime fiction by locating his detective Sam Space on other planets. However, having satirised the model by emphasising its adaptability, other authors have turned back to Chandler to give new birth to his type. Robert B. Parker was amongst the most dedicated disciples of Chandler. Parker's creation Spenser was strongly modelled on Philip Marlowe and, indeed, his name is also a nod to Elizabethan literature.

James Ellroy gave his own contribution to the Chandler detective model in his first novel, *Brown's Requiem* (1981), wherein the lead protagonist Fritz Brown is a car repo-man and PI. However, after vowing never to write another Chandleresque novel, Ellroy experimented with an interesting variation on the detective protagonist. Although based within a police department, Lloyd Hopkins is the epitome of the maverick lone detective who disregards regulations and uses his own unorthodox, sometimes violent and illegal, methods to solve cases. Hopkins invariably walks a thin line between investigation and breaking the law, often resorting to vigilantism and is sometimes indistinguishable from his recidivist prey. Renegade detectives make for entertaining characters, but most people employed in police investigation do not feel as comfortable transgressing the law as the private detective.

The centrality of the PI within the crime novel was challenged most notably by Ed McBain's 87th Precinct novels. McBain wryly stated that the last time a real private eye solved a murder was 'never'. With his 87th Precinct novels, McBain sought to create a more realistic model through the development of the police procedural sub-genre. Rather than focusing on a lead detective or detective figure, McBain examined the intricacies of police investigation through many characters spread across different levels and departments of one precinct, so that the department is in itself a form of character. Joseph Wambaugh's early police novels explored the relationships and camaraderie of policemen in and outside of work, shifting from McBain's focus on method toward character. Novels such as *The Blue Knight*

(1972) and *The Choirboys* (1975) eschewed detailing the methods of police work in homicide investigation and instead focused on the daily lives of policeman: from the banality and bureaucracy of beat patrols to the disintegrating and debauched private lives of the policeman outside of work. There has been a proliferation of writers who have excelled at writing from a criminal perspective, and thus challenging the socially conservative portrayals of detective figures that emerged from police dramas. Donald Westlake and Richard Condon wrote crime novels which examined the laws and conventions of people who live as part of an illicit underworld society. George V. Higgins portrayed the thin dividing line between criminals and the police in his novels on the Boston underworld. Edward Bunker's four novels include some of the most harrowing depictions of prison life in crime fiction. An ex-convict who spent most of his early life in prisons such as Alcatraz and San Quentin, Bunker essentially turned the police procedural upside down by portraying institutions and the legal system from an unregenerate and unapologetic criminal's point of view. What follows is a vision of corruption and brutalisation in a country which demonises and dehumanises prisoners by trapping them in a life of crime. Bunker's bleakly realistic narratives leave little to no hope for the possibility of reform.

The sciences have provided alternative, less corruptible, authorities to the Law. Patricia Cornwall's forensic thrillers are amongst them. In several crime novels, one of the most important aspects of police investigation is the criminal's psychology, and the human mind becomes part of the mystery to be unfolded. Thomas Harris' ground-breaking *Red Dragon* (1981) introduced the villainous Dr Hannibal 'the Cannibal' Lecter and the FBI profiler who catches him, Will Graham. One of the most notable police psychologists is Jonathan Kellerman's Alex Delaware. Most events in the Delaware novels are conveyed through his first-person narration, thus the reader has broadly the same amount of information as Delaware to unravel the mystery and is similarly drawn into the psychologist's role. Delaware's place within the department also draws him into other crime-novel tropes, as Delaware becomes the observant, intellectual partner to the more traditional Detective Milo Sturgis, who conducts most of the police work.

Moving away from any centre of power, legal, scientific or even criminal are luckless innocents, seemingly accidentally drawn into violent intrigue. Elmore Leonard and BarbaraNeely have excelled at portraying these incidental detectives. Such characters typically work in professions external to detective work but through chance or circumstance assume the role of detective to solve mysteries or simply to comprehend bizarre and violent events. The prolific Leonard has written scores of novels featuring protagonists from a number of random backgrounds who are drawn into a web of crime and mayhem. In *Cat Chaser* (1982) George Moran is a Miami-based hotel owner drawn into a web of intrigue from his military past. BarbaraNeely's Blanche White is a black housekeeper who seems to naturally gravitate towards trouble and violent scenarios. Blanche's name literally and ironically means to whiten, and while this humorously reminds the reader she is black, it also refers to her invisibility: Blanche suffers from racial discrimination, usually at the hands of upper class Southern families who employ her and treat her as though she is invisible, thus she is able to see crimes without being seen. Although Blanche is not a private detective, she inhabits the external role where PIs investigate on the boundaries of a society to which they will never fully belong.

The destruction of one style for another is never entire, and the reaction to Chandler, as to the Golden Age authors before him, is one of movements and counter-movements, re-imaginings, inventions and expansions. Although it is legitimate to ask, along with James Ellroy, who is 'the realistic archetype of twentieth century violent intrigue?', in a genre as diverse and iconoclastic as crime fiction, Chandler's shadow arguably may still be the longest (Powell, 2012, p. 170).

Abbott, Megan (1971–)

An author of increasing stature whose novels have provided a hard-hitting but realistic female voice in crime fiction by revising and re-imagining the traditional roles of the heroine and the *femme fatale*. Abbott's monograph, *The Street was Mine* (2002), is a study of the hard-boiled white man, which examines the complex relationship between the protagonist and the society that gave birth to him and subsequently blamed him for its ills.

Born in Warren, Michigan and raised in Grosse Pointe Woods, Abbott graduated from the University of Michigan with a BA in English (1989–93) and completed her PhD in English and American Literature from New York University (1994–2000). Abbott was married to author Joshua Gaylord from 1998 to 2011. Abbott has worked for Union Settlement Association, a social service agency in East Harlem, since 2003 and taught literature at New York University, the State University of New York and the New School. She worked for a Michigan senator during his election campaign in 1994. Abbott's first five novels have garnered popular success and critical praise, and she has explored a range of other publishing media, including a short story tie-in 'The Girl' for the *L.A. Noire* (2011) graphic video game.

Novels

Abbott's powerful writing style and her iconoclastic female characters have put her at the forefront of neo-noir. *Die a Little* (2005) and the Edgar award-winning *Queenpin* (2007) conform tangentially to the familiar 1940s and 50s crime novels and films noir, yet Abbott's shift of not only the point of view but also of the action to within the distinctly female realm has brought a new perspective to the genre. In *Die a Little*, the machinations of the glamorous Hollywood seamstress Alice are unpicked by her husband's kid sister Lora, who is disturbingly drawn to the sexually deviant underworld she investigates. *Queenpin* is more consciously styled as a noir thriller; set in the Club Tee-Hee sometime in the early 1960s, an unnamed 20-something first person narrator describes how she fell under the criminal spell of

Gloria Denton, a Mob luminary loosely based on the real-life Virginia Hill, the ill-fated paramour of Bugsy Siegel. Abbott began watching film noir as a child, long before she read crime fiction, and she has stated that she pictures noir actors when she writes. Abbott was inspired to become a novelist after reading James Ellroy's *The Big Nowhere* (1988), and she considered her first two novels 'lovesongs' to the author (Godfrey, 2009). But it is her third novel, *The Song is You* (2008), that is most striking in its construction and plot similarities to Ellroy's *The Black Dahlia* (1987). The novel is a fictional account of the unsolved disappearance of actress Jean Spangler in 1949, a case which evoked memories of the 1947 torture murder of Elizabeth Short. *The Song is You* is told from the perspective of the rag magazine man, Hollywood fixer and amateur detective, Gil Hopkins, 'Hop'.

In *Bury Me Deep* (2009) the descent of the respectable housewife Marion Seeley, through a socially destroying and self-destructive passionate affair, leads her to a form of madness that ends with her institutionalisation. Marion is seduced into her destruction by both her female friends, who draw Marion into the affair, and by the man who uses Marion only to discard her.

The End of Everything (2011) is a coming-of-age novel with a 1980s midwest suburban setting similar to Abbott's own upbringing. Although it breaks from her previous historical and geographical settings, *The End of Everything* explores Abbott's familiar themes with depth and haunting insight.

Suggested reading

M.E. Abbott (2002) *The Street Was Mine* (New York: Palgrave Macmillan).
M.E. Abbott (2009) 'Megan Abbott: An Email Conversation with Rebecca Godfrey' in *Barnes and Noble Review*, http://bnreview.barnesandnoble.com/t5/Interview/Megan-Abbott/ba-p/1202, date accessed 20 July 2011.
M.E. Abbott (2011) *Megan Abbott* http://meganabbott.com/index.html.

Diana Powell

Auster, Paul (1947–)

A novelist, poet, memoirist and translator, Auster has also written screen-plays and created a card game, *Action Baseball*. Auster has occasionally worked as a director or co-director on several of his own scripts, including *Smoke* (1995) and its sequel *Blue in the Face* (1995), *Lulu on the Bridge* (1998) and *The Inner Life of Martin Frost* (2007). Auster is best known for his 'meta-physical thrillers' and meta-fictional stories.

Paul Benjamin Auster was born 3 February 1947 in Newark, New Jersey. After dropping out of Columbia University, Auster lived for a while in France, wrote poetry and began taking on translation and hack writing work. Auster's writings are marked by chance happenings, random events and arbitrariness. Even in his autobiographical memoir *Hand to Mouth* (1997), Auster appeals to chance, describing how he 'lucked out' of the draft in 1969 and then largely as 'a matter of chance' found work on an oil tanker, the *Esso Florence* (Auster, 1998, p. 47). Auster married Lydia Davis in 1971 and they had one son. His second wife is the novelist Siri Hustvedt whom he married in 1981. They have a daughter together.

Though not generally considered a crime and detective fiction writer as such, early in Auster's career he wrote a well-executed detective novel, *Squeeze Play* (1978), under the pseudonym Paul Benjamin. Having written the novel 'for the money' (Auster, 1998, p. 121), Auster has said that it is not a 'legitimate' book (Mackenzie, 1999). But in fact *Squeeze Play* illustrates the depth of Auster's understanding and affection for crime and detective fiction, in particular the work of Dashiell Hammett. It is arguably a base on which later novels exploring the limits of genre and plotting could be built. Of these *The New York Trilogy* (1986) is the first and most widely known.

The New York Trilogy established Auster as a writer of strange and compel-ling stories with an absurdist edge. It was first published as three separate short novels: *City of Glass* (1985), *Ghosts* and *The Locked Room* (both 1986). The three seemingly connected stories involve changes in identity, strange coincidences and aimless wanderings in the 'labyrinth' of New York. *City Of Glass*, for example, begins with a wrong number when Daniel Quinn receives a call from someone wishing to speak to a detective named Paul Auster.

The New York Trilogy set a playful tone that has resurfaced in all of Auster's work and is suggested through the fascination with names and their meaning, the significance of 'clues' and the ironic notion of free will. Elements of detection occur in many of his stories and books, but in *The Book of Illusions* (2003) and *Oracle Night* (2005) the connection with hard-boiled detective writing became more explicit. *The Book of Illusions* is self-consciously a tribute to Hammett, while *Oracle Night* is based in part on the 'Flitcraft parable' from Hammett's *The Maltese Falcon* (1929).

Auster has sometimes been criticised for going over the same ground in successive novels, but his reworking of many of the tropes of crime and detective fiction through a lens fashioned by Lacanian psychoanalysis, American transcendentalism, and French existentialism, has made him one of the most interesting and quirky occasional practitioners in the genre.

Suggested Reading

P. Auster (1998) *Hand to Mouth: A Chronicle of Early Failure* (London: Faber).

D. Barone (1995) *Beyond the Red Notebook: Essays on Paul Auster* (Philadelphia: University of Pennsylvania Press).

Christopher Routledge

Ballard, W(illis) T(odhunter) (1903–80)

A hard-boiled crime and western writer, whose background was firmly in the pulp magazines, W. T. Ballard was extremely prolific, writing over a thousand short stories and novelettes, almost a hundred novels and employing over 20 different pseudonyms. Many of Ballard's protagonists were private detectives or in the case of his first series character, Bill Lennox, a troubleshooter for a powerful Hollywood studio.

Life and career

Ballard was born 13 December 1903, in Cleveland, Ohio. He was educated at Westtown Preparatory School and Wilmington College. He married Phoebe Dwiggins in 1936, and they had one son.

At the age of 12, Ballard's first published piece appeared in *Hunter-Trader-Trapper* magazine. Ballard's short stories began to appear regularly in *Black Mask* magazine from 1933 onwards. Ballard was one of the leading writers in the magazine, and with Cleve F. Adams he was the manager behind a group of *Black Mask* writers called the Fictioneers. The group held meetings in a restaurant and talked about the writing business. According to Ballard, it was a good excuse to get drunk. Other members of the Fictioneers included Raymond Chandler, Horace McCoy, John K. Butler and Dwight Babcock.

Ballard's most famous series character was Bill Lennox, officially a publicist for General Consolidated Studios, Lennox is a form of showbiz detective hired to keep relatives of movie stars and moguls out of trouble. He appeared in 27 short stories, most of which were published in *Black Mask* but also within the novels *Say Yes to Murder* (1942), *Murder Can't Stop* (1946), *Dealing Out Death* (1948), and *Lights, Camera, Murder,* (1960). Ballard used his own experiences as a writer in Hollywood for material for the Lennox series. He was fired from Warner Bros abruptly, when after making a derogatory remark about Jack Warner, he turned around to find Warner was standing right next to him.

Ballard's later protagonists included the private eye duo of Tony Costaine and Bert McCall, who appeared in a series of novels published under the pseudonym Neil MacNeil by Gold Medal Books between 1958 and 1966. An interesting stand-alone novel is *Murder Las Vegas Style* (1967), a melancholy look into the world of casinos and the personal life of LA private detective Mark Foran, who travels to Vegas to act as a bodyguard for a retired Army Colonel. Ballard is different from many hard-boiled writers in that he wrote plausible and sympathetic portrayals of private detectives and their relationships with women. Bill Lennox, for example, does not chase women because he is devoted to his girlfriend Nancy Hobbs. In *Walk in Fear* (1952), private eye Hal Boyd falls in love with a young lady he is hired to protect.

With the decline of the hard-boiled pulps, Ballard shifted almost entirely to westerns in the 60s and 70s, even though he still wrote an occasional crime novel or an entry to a series (Ballard wrote *The Kremlin File* (1973) as part of the Nick Carter Killmaster spy series.). His westerns were published under his middle and last name Todhunter Ballard, or using pseudonyms such as John Hunter and Jack Slade. Ballard's western novels are as fast-paced and well-written as his crime novels. Amongst his best westerns are *Duke* (1965), an epic tale of cattle driving, and Ballard's personal favourite, *Gold in California*, which won the Western Writers of America's Spur Award for Best Historical Novel of 1965. Willis Todhunter Ballard died on 27 December 1980.

Suggested reading

S. Mertz (1979) 'W. T. Ballard: An Interview' http://www.blackmaskmagazine.com/ballard.html, date accessed 5 May 2011.

B. F. Murphy (1999) *The Encyclopedia of Murder and Mystery*, (New York: St Martin's Minotaur).

J. L. Traylor (1985) *Hollywood Troubleshooter: W. T. Ballard's Bill Lennox stories* (Bowling Green, Ohio: University Popular Press).

Christopher Routledge

Bannon, Ann (1932–)

Ann Bannon is the pseudonym of Ann Weldy whose series of novels, the Beebo Brinker Chronicles, has led some critics to retrospectively crown her 'the Queen of Lesbian Pulp Fiction'. The Beebo Brinker Series alternates between the titular character and her friends Laura, Beth and Jack. Despite belonging in the pulp genre and featuring the strikingly colourful and luridly suggestive jacket design artwork noted of the genre, Bannon's narratives contain little to no actual crimes. Instead, the novels explore young women coming to terms with their emerging sexuality in a variety of locales, from the conservative setting of 1950s American campus life to the socially liberal Greenwich Village, New York. Bannon explored the emotional violence that ensues from issues such as misogyny and sexual jealously. Eschewing the sensationalism common throughout the pulps, Bannon's novels combine homo-erotica with a realistic depiction of characters who suffer tremendous personal loss but achieve a measure of hope and optimism.

Early life

Bannon was born Ann Weldy in Joliet, Indiana, on 15 September 1932. Bannon was raised in nearby Hinsdale, Illinois. She was educated at the University of Illinois at Urbana-Champaign where she was a member of the Kappa Kappa Gamma Sorority and witnessed lesbian relationships between sorority girls. During this time, she began to examine and realise her own lesbianism. Majoring in French, Bannon graduated in 1954 and subsequently married an engineer. Bannon has said very little publicly about her marriage other than to acknowledge it as emotionally hurtful and difficult. Her husband's career led them to adopting a nomadic lifestyle for several years. They had two children. Although her husband was aware of Bannon's sexuality, he never read any of her novels and forbid her to use her married name, Thayer, as he did not want the family to be associated with her books. Bannon and her husband were separated for much of their marriage and finally divorced after 27 years.

The Beebo Brinker Chronicles

Bannon began writing her first novel at the age of 22, whilst living as a housewife in the suburbs of Philadelphia. She was influenced by the only two lesbian novels she had read at that time, Radclyffe Hall's *The Well of Loneliness* (1928) and *Spring Fire* (1952) by Vin Packer (the latter concerned two sorority sisters who have a passionate affair). Bannon wrote to Packer asking for writing advice, and Packer responded positively. Bannon's first novel, *Odd Girl Out* (1957), is heavily indebted to *Spring Fire*. The story revolves around the lives of friends Laura, Beth and Emmy at a fictional Midwestern university. Laura and Beth both date men, but find their relationships with the opposite sex unfulfilling. Most of the time they date with the purpose of conforming to the social expectations of the legalistic and hypocritical Student Union. The two women begin a secretive lesbian affair, but it is the strait-laced heterosexual Emmy whose life is destroyed by scandal when she is caught sleeping with her boyfriend. The novel ends with Laura and Beth making life-changing decisions after having explored their sexuality, but it is ambiguous as to whether or not their decisions are based on any sense of their true identity. The second novel, *I Am a Woman* (1959), introduces Beebo Brinker (real name Betty Jean), a stereotypically butch, wisecracking, but sexually alluring lesbian. The exploration of lesbian sexuality is paralleled by the depiction of the male characters, who are often baffled by lesbianism and uncertain how to act. However, *I Am a Woman* ends on a far more outwardly optimistic note than Bannon's previous novel or indeed any comparable lesbian pulp novel of the era. This was reflected by the social changes occurring in the United States and the overwhelmingly positive reader response to her work. Although largely ignored by critics at the time of publication, Bannon's work provoked an emotional response from readers and Bannon received thousands of letters from women identifying themselves with the lesbian characters. All of her novels were written pseudonymously and anonymously, with Bannon only admitting authorship upon their republication in 1983. After *I am a Woman*, *Women in the Shadows* (1959) returned to a darker theme, examining the self-hatred in Laura and Beebo's relationship. Male-on-female physical violence, a subtle undercurrent throughout the series, is brutally actualised in the novel when one character is raped. The final novel of the series to appear as part of a linear chronology, *Journey to a Woman* (1960), reintroduces the character of Beth who was expelled from college several years earlier after a sex scandal. Now married to a successful businessman, Beth feels bored and constrained in her loveless relationship. Bannon's fifth novel, *The Marriage* (1960), is often not regarded as part of the Brinker series as it tells the story of Page and Sunny, whose seemingly happy marriage is rocked by a revelation of incest. Brinker series regulars Laura and Jack appear in the novel in supporting roles. The final novel in the series, and Bannon's latest novel to date, *Beebo*

Brinker (1962) is a prequel to the series, detailing Beebo's arrival in New York, her first meeting with the homosexual Jack Mann who begins to tease out her lesbianism, and her journey to Hollywood as the lover of film star Venus Bogardus. Similar to the first novel, the denouement sees the protagonists returning to earlier relationships, somewhat tainted by their other lustful pursuits but with the hope of resuming their past love.

Later life and critical recognition

After the publication of *Beebo Brinker*, Bannon studied for a master's degree at Sacramento State University and a doctorate in Linguistics at Stanford University. She began a successful career in academe, but the impact of her novels and the importance of lesbian pulp fiction was rapidly fading from the literary scene. In 1983, Barbara Grier of the lesbian Naiad Press contacted Bannon with an offer to republish all of her novels. Around this time, Bannon had just been through a stressful divorce and developed chronic fatigue syndrome. Her novels have had several republications since, and a significant body of critical studies has been published on her work. Her novels have become required reading on LGBT studies at colleges throughout the US. In 2007, the off-Broadway theatre company, the Hourglass Group, staged *The Beebo Brinker Chronicles*, adapted by Kate Moira Ryan and Linda S. Chapman. It was a critically and commercially successful play based on the first three novels of the series. Ann Bannon has received several major awards for her contribution to lesbian literature including most recently in 2008, the Alice B Award and the Pioneer Award from the LAMBDA Literary Foundation.

Suggested reading

C. Nealon (2001). *Foundlings: Lesbian and Gay Historical Emotion Before Stonewall* (Durham, NC: Duke University Press).

M. Sky (2007) *Twilight Tales: Ann Bannon's Lesbian Pulp Series 'The Beebo Brinker Chronicles'* Ph.D. (Ottowa: Library and Archives Canada).

S. Stryker (2001) *Queer Pulp: Perverted Passions from the Golden Age of the Paperback* (San Francisco: Chronicle Books).

Steven Powell

Bloch, Robert (1917–94)

Prolific American writer of crime, horror and science fiction, best known for his 1959 novel *Psycho*, which was adapted into the classic horror film of the same name directed by Alfred Hitchcock.

Early life and influences

Robert Albert Bloch was born on 15 April 1917 in Chicago, Illinois, to American parents of German-Jewish heritage; his father was a bank cashier and his mother a schoolteacher and social worker. Living in and around Chicago for the first decade of his life, Bloch was a voracious reader of books either owned by his parents or borrowed from the public library. He read classic American authors such as Washington Irving, Nathaniel Hawthorne and Mark Twain as well as adventure novels by Walter Scott and Edgar Rice Burroughs. Two events were to have a significant effect on his subsequent choice of career – a viewing of Lon Chaney in the silent film of *The Phantom Of The Opera*, which terrified the young Bloch, and the discovery of the horror and fantasy periodical *Weird Tales*. Both of these events occurred around 1927, the period when the family moved from Chicago to Milwaukee, Wisconsin.

Although he cited Edgar Allan Poe, Raymond Chandler, James Joyce and John Dos Passos as influential to his literature, the primary influence on the young Bloch's nascent writing career was inarguably the legendary American horror writer H.P. Lovecraft, whose work appeared frequently in *Weird Tales*. A fan of Lovecraft's stories, which often mix Gothic horror tropes with elements of science fiction and demonic mythology, Bloch corresponded with the writer from 1932, when he was aged just 15, until Lovecraft's death in 1937. Lovecraft suggested that Bloch write short stories and offered his encouragement and advice. Bloch sold his first story to *Weird Tales* in 1934, aged 17. Bloch has the distinction of appearing, albeit disguised as 'Robert Blake', in Lovecraft's story 'The Haunter Of The Dark', after Bloch had written Lovecraft into his own 1935 story 'The Shambler

From The Stairs'. Bloch killed Lovecraft off in the story after gaining the writer's permission to do so. At 18, Bloch received an invitation to join The Milwaukee Fictioneers, a group of writers including Laurence A. Keating and Stanley Weinbaum, and began to pursue his writing career in earnest.

Beginning of career

In 1940 Bloch married Marion Ruth Holcombe and shortly thereafter they had a daughter, Sally Ann. He supported his family by advertising agency copywriting as well as continuing to write short fiction. In 1943 he penned perhaps the most significant story of his career thus far, 'Yours Truly, Jack The Ripper'. After reading Marie Belloc Lowndes' *The Lodger* (1913) Bloch claims that 'all I did was say to myself: "What if Jack the Ripper was still alive today?"' (Walker, 1974). Until the publication of *Psycho*, this was the story most strongly associated with Bloch, and it found its way to a wider audience after being adapted for radio following its publication in *Weird Tales*. The story was subsequently, in Bloch's words, 'anthologized to death' (Penzler, 1976). The infamous Victorian serial killer would prove a creative touchstone for Bloch for the rest of his career, most notably in the 1967 Bloch-penned *Star Trek* episode 'Wolf in the Fold'. Much of Bloch's short horror fiction is written in the tradition of American Gothic horror as practiced by Hawthorne, Irving and Poe, though is notable for a sense of understated and morbid humour absent from the work of many of his contemporaries.

In the early 1950s, with his wife's health deteriorating (she was finally diagnosed with TB of the bone, after years of misdiagnosis) Bloch, Marion and Sally Ann moved to Weyauwega, Wisconsin, to be near his wife's family. During this time, Bloch wrote prolifically, producing several novels, including *Spiderweb*, *The Kidnapper*, *The Will To Kill* (all 1954), and *Shooting Star* (1958), and making appearances on the TV panel show *It's A Draw*. He also produced a collection of short fiction, *Terror in the Night*, which was published with *Shooting Star* in 1958. In his autobiography *Once Around the Bloch* (1993) he revealed his frustrations in this mid-1950s period regarding the difficulty of supporting his family with his chosen career and also his fear of writer's block or the drying-up of the market. However, within the next half-decade, Bloch would gain sudden international fame and a life-long reputation as a master of crime and horror fiction. His story 'The Hell-Bound Train' won a prestigious Hugo award in 1959, but it was his next novel that was to prove the catalyst for major recognition.

Psycho

Despite a long and diverse writing career, Bloch remains best known for his 1959 novel *Psycho* and the subsequent 1960 Hitchcock film. *Psycho* was inspired by one of the most notorious true crime stories in modern American history, the 1957 case of Ed Gein. Gein, a farmer from Wisconsin, confessed to the murder and flaying of two women as well as exhuming corpses. Gein manufactured furniture and even clothes from his victims' skin before being brought to justice (the Gein case has proved influential in American crime and horror culture – it also inspired Tobe Hooper's seminal 1974 horror film *The Texas Chainsaw Massacre* and Thomas Harris' *The Silence of the Lambs* (1988)). The murder site was located only a relatively short distance from where Bloch was living at the time. Bloch, in his own words, 'came up with the mother-fixation, and the rest followed' (Walker, 1974).

Psycho is significant in both Bloch's career and the pantheon of American crime and horror fiction for its approach to psychological horror. The broader, more fantastical elements of Bloch's previous work are here rejected in favour of a Gothic psychodrama involving strong Freudian elements – the character Norman Bates dresses up as his deceased mother, with whom he had an intense and submissive relationship. In the novel's naturalistic narrative monsters exist psychologically within the mind rather than manifesting themselves in the flesh. The release of the novel and the massive success of Hitchcock's film adaptation the following year ensured that Norman Bates became a household name and a cultural byword for manic or psychotic behaviour. Hitchcock's film toned down some of the violence of Bloch's novel. Mary Crane is beheaded in the novel, rather than stabbed. However, a significant amount of transgressive material remained, and Bloch is indirectly responsible, through Hitchcock's adaptation, for breaking a number of American filmmaking taboos as shots of flushing toilets and unmarried couples in bed were uncommon or unheard of before the film's release.

Most notably, the issue of Bates's transvestism remained unscathed in the transition from page to screen, and the novel has endured as a key psychoanalytic cultural touchstone, with countless studies and criticisms made of Bates's relationship with his mother. The cultural impact made by both novel and film became central to Bloch's reputation, and subsequent publications of his work strongly flagged up his authorship of *Psycho* on their covers. Bloch returned to Norman Bates with the publication of *Psycho II* (1982) and *Psycho House* (1990), though he had no writing involvement with the three Hollywood sequels, and the filmmakers did not use his sequels as a basis for the screenplays. Both of Bloch's sequel novels make wry references to Bates's popularity as a horror icon and the success of the original film – *Psycho II* is set in Hollywood, while *Psycho House* has the Bates Motel becoming a tourist attraction.

Screenwriting and later career

Bloch moved to California during the shooting of *Psycho* in response to an invitation to write for syndicated television. During the 1960s, he wrote episodes for such shows as *Lock Up, The Man from U.N.C.L.E, Thriller, Alfred Hitchcock Presents* (his episode 'The Sorcerer's Apprentice' was censored by the network for being too disturbing) and *Star Trek*. Bloch's marriage to Marion ended in divorce, and in 1964 he married Eleanor Alexander.

During the 1960s Bloch also worked as a screenwriter, collaborating with infamous horror movie maker William Castle on the 1964 films *Strait-Jacket* and *The Night Walker*. His most sustained and prolific screenwriting relationship, however, was with the British horror film company Amicus. His first two films for Amicus as a screenwriter were *The Psychopath* (1966) and *The Deadly Bees* (1967) but his most fruitful collaborations with the company employed the 'portmanteau' device, whereby a film contains a series of separate tales with a linking narrative. Portmanteau horror films were popular in the 1970s, proving the perfect medium for adapting Bloch's short stories for the screen. The Amicus films *Torture Garden* (1967), *The House That Dripped Blood* (1971) and *Asylum* (1972) all employed this formula, each containing four of Bloch's stories.

During the 1960s, 1970s and 1980s Bloch continued to produce novels, working in the territories of science fiction, *Ladies' Day* and *This Crowded Earth* (both 1968) and *Sneak Preview* (1971); psychopathic thrillers, *Night-World* (1972) and *American Gothic* (1974); and straight dramatic fiction *The Star Stalker* (1968). He also released several story collections, and his short fiction was later anthologised in three volumes in *The Complete Stories of Robert Bloch* (1990). Important later works include *Strange Eons* (1978), which rekindles Bloch's relationship with H.P. Lovecraft, casting the late writer's tales of demonic gods as a harbinger of coming doom for the earth. In *Night Of The Ripper* (1984), Bloch returned to the mystery of the unidentified Victorian serial killer that had proved a creative muse throughout his career.

Bloch died of cancer on 23 September 1994. In a 1935 interview with a local Milwaukee journal the 17-year-old Bloch said of death with characteristic dry humour, 'The more I read of it, the more I fear it. I guess it is my imagination, but right now there doesn't seem to be much I can do about it.'

Suggested reading

R. Bloch (1993) *Once Around the Bloch: An Unauthorized Autobiography* (New York: TOR).

David Hering

Block, Lawrence (1938–)

Winner of multiple awards, including the Gumshoe Lifetime Achievement Award in 2005, Block has over 50 books to his credit. His best-known series detective character, Matt Scudder, divides his energy between battling his alcohol addiction and investigating cases. Other series characters include Evan Tanner and Bernie Rhodenbarr, protagonist of the innovative 'Burglar Who ... ' series of novels.

Lawrence Block, who also writes under the pseudonym Paul Kavanagh, was born 24 June 1938 in Buffalo, New York. He published his first story aged 19 in 1958. A college dropout (he briefly attended Antioch College in Ohio) Block's apprenticeship as a writer included writing pornographic and erotic novels under pseudonyms such as 'Sheldon Lord' (with Donald Westlake) and 'Jill Emerson'. The high productivity required of a pulp paperback writer suited Block. He has maintained an output of over a book a year for 50 years, with works ranging from crime and detective fiction, anthologies, books about the craft of writing and a memoir entitled *Step By Step* (2009). Block has been married twice; firstly to Loretta Ann Kallett in 1960, a marriage which produced three children. From 1983 he has been married to Lynne Wood.

The 1960s

Block's career as a writer of bestselling crime and mystery fiction began in 1958, when he published a short story, 'You Can't Lose' in *Manhunt* magazine. Unusually, he has continued to write short stories alongside his novels, and by 2010 he had published well over 100 in magazines as diverse as *Off Beat Detective Stories*, *Cosmopolitan*, and *Playboy*.

From the early 1960s, Block made a living writing soft-porn novels and stories under a variety of pseudonyms. Block ghost-wrote at least part of the William Ard novel, after Ard's death, *Babe in the Woods* (1960), featuring New York private detective Lou Largo. Block's first 'Tanner' novel, *The Thief Who Couldn't Sleep*, appeared in 1966. Featuring spy Evan Tanner, the Tanner novels are an adventure-mystery series that follow its protagonist around the world, recovering lost gold and smuggling dissidents out of the Soviet Union. The central conceit of the eight Tanner books (the eighth, *Tanner on Ice*, appeared in 1998 after a break of almost 30 years) is that, following an injury in the Korean War, Tanner never sleeps.

Scudder and Rhodenbarr

Block continued to write pulp soft-porn novels into the 1970s, but by then his more mainstream mystery stories were beginning to receive some attention. The success of the Tanner novels led to his best-known series characters, PI Matt Scudder and burglar Bernie Rhodenbarr.

Scudder is the more conventional of the two. A former New York cop turned unlicensed private eye, Scudder first appeared in the 1976 novel *The Sins of the Fathers*. In the early novels Scudder is an alcoholic haunted by his experiences as a cop. Scudder's tortured psyche places him in a tradition of traumatized detectives, though in his case the trauma comes from accidentally causing the death of a child in an off-duty shootout.

Highlights of the 16-novel series include the Shamus Award-winning *Eight Million Ways to Die* (1982), the nominated *A Ticket to the Boneyard* (1990), *The Devil Knows You're Dead* (1994) and the Edgar–nominated *A Dance at the Slaughterhouse* (1991). Part of the appeal of the Scudder books is the development of Scudder as a character as he recovers from his addiction. In later books, Scudder is a committed member of Alcoholics Anonymous and is married to Elaine, an ex-hooker. *Eight Million Ways to Die* was filmed by Hal Ashby in 1986 with Jeff Bridges in the Scudder role. It received largely negative reviews, and no further Scudder novels have been adapted into film.

The Scudder books are diverse in themselves, but Block's 'burglar' series, which began with *Burglars Can't Be Choosers* (1977), takes the genre in an entirely different direction. The Bernie Rhodenbarr series, characterised by their 'burglar' titles, concerns a professional thief, who usually finds himself wrongly accused of some greater crime than burglary, and must find the perpetrator.

Unlike Matt Scudder, Rhodenbarr does not age as the series progresses, and his basic thief-by-night circumstances barely change. The second book in the series, *The Burglar in the Closet* (1978), which forms the basis for the 1987 Whoopi Goldberg film *Burglar!*, is a good example of the plot format for the series. Rhodenbarr is interrupted while burgling an apartment and hides from the owner and her companion, emerging from the closet only to find the woman dead and the jewels he planned to steal gone.

The Rhodenbarr novels are light-hearted humorous capers, written in a knowing, literate style, with many of the jokes aimed at cultural obsessives and collectors. (One of Block's minor series characters, John Keller, appears in the series as a hitman who collects stamps.) The third book in the series,

The Burglar Who Liked to Quote Kipling (1979), won the Nero Wolfe Award. The first in the series in which Rhodenbarr has become a bookshop owner by day, but falls foul of the law when he tries to steal a rare volume of Rudyard Kipling.

Block took almost a ten-year break from the Rhodenbarr series between the publications of *The Burglar Who Painted Like Mondrian* (1983) and *The Burglar Who Traded Ted Williams* (1994). Later books, including *The Burglar in the Library* (1997) and *The Burglar in the Rye* (1999), are satires of, respectively, Agatha Christie and J.D. Salinger. The Rhodenbarr novels are in many ways an irreverent balance to the darker, and occasionally moralising, Scudder series.

Another series character, Chip Harrison, began in two of Block's erotic novels before the author developed the series into a self-reverential spoof of detective fiction. *No Score* (1970) and *Chip Harrison Scores Again* (1971) are coming-of-age novels written under the pseudonym of the leading character Chip Harrison and focusing on the sex-crazed teenager's attempts to lose his virginity and gain sexual experiences. In two further novels, *Make Out With Murder* (1974) and *The Topless Tulip Caper* (1975), the series undergoes a change of style as Chip becomes an assistant to Leo Haig, a fat private detective who emulates Nero Wolfe in the hope he will one day meet his idol. The series contains many crime fiction in-jokes as Chip plays Archie Goodwin to Haig's Nero Wolfe.

Block is also a non-fiction writer, with four fiction-writing handbooks to his name, as well as *Gangsters, Swindlers, Killers, And Thieves: The Lives and Crimes of Fifty American Villains* (2004), and *Step By Step* (2009), an autobiography in which he explains his life-long fascination with walking, running, and in particular race walking.

Suggested reading

L. Block (1990) 'Lawrence Block', *Contemporary Authors Autobiography Series*, 11 (Detroit: Gale).

L. Block (2009) *Step By Step: a Pedestrian Memoir* (New York: William Morrow).

L. Block and E. Bulow (1995) *After Hours: Conversations with Lawrence Block* (Albuquerque, University of New Mexico).

K. B. Smith (2011) 'Lawrence Block' *Thrilling Detective* http://www.thrillingdetective.com/trivia/block.html, date accessed 22 September 2010.

Christopher Routledge

Brackett, Leigh (1915–78)

Predominantly a science fiction and fantasy writer, Leigh Douglass Brackett's comparatively smaller output of hard-boiled detective and crime novels, short stories and screenplays have nevertheless been significant. Born in Los Angeles, California, Brackett married science fiction writer Edmond Hamilton in 1946 and moved to Kinsman, Ohio. Brackett died in 1978 from cancer in Lancaster, California, while working on the screenplay for *The Empire Strikes Back* (1981).

Brackett's early writing career

Brackett began her writing career in 1940 with a science fiction short story, 'Martian Quest', published in *Astounding Science Fiction*. Her first novel was *No Good From a Corpse* (1944), a hard-boiled detective story influenced by Raymond Chandler and Dashiell Hammett. It was this novel that prompted Hollywood director Howard Hawks to hire Brackett to write the screenplay with William Faulkner and Jules Furthman for the highly regarded film adaptation of *The Big Sleep* (1946), a collaboration that initiated a long working relationship between Hawks and Brackett. She also wrote the scripts for *The Long Goodbye* (1973) and *Crime Doctor's Man Hunt* (1946, from a story by Eric Taylor), and two teleplays for the series *The Alfred Hitchcock Hour* (1963), among other contributions to television and film.

As a member of the Los Angeles Science Fantasy Society (LASFS) fan club, Brackett met and developed relationships with other science fiction, fantasy and crime writers of the California pulp scene, including Fredric Brown and William F. Nolan. Brackett also met Ray Bradbury at LASFS in the 1940s and became a mentor figure to him in a mutually beneficial professional relationship. The two writers regularly traded manuscripts for review between the years 1941 and 1944. Bradbury completed her novella, 'Lorelei of the Red Mist' (published in *Planet Stories*, 1946), when Brackett went to Hollywood to work on the film adaptation of *The Big Sleep*, beginning an almost 20-year hiatus in which she did not publish in the pulps, her first fiction market. Brackett and Edmond Hamilton also influenced each other's writing and co-wrote several science fiction stories together. Some critics attribute an increase in the quality of Hamilton's writing to Brackett's influence, while Hamilton himself mentioned Brackett's lack of plotting in her early writing, which gradually improved in her later career.

Brackett's crime fiction

Brackett wrote five crime novels and about nine short stories (excluding edited and re-titled reprints). In *No Good From a Corpse,* detective Edmond Clive returns to Los Angeles after successfully concluding a high-profile case in San Francisco. On his return, he reunites with Laurel Dane, for whom he has long suppressed his romantic feelings. She soon reveals that her true identity is Sue Tanner, and that her safety has been threatened. Dane attempts to reconcile Clive with his childhood friend Mick Hammond, who has been sheltering her, but Dane is murdered and Hammond framed for the crime. The narrative follows Clive's investigation as he tries to clear Hammond of suspicion and find Dane's murderer.

Other novels include *Stranger at Home* (1946), which was ghost-written for the British film actor George Sanders. It tells the story of Michael Vickers, who disappeared in Mexico four years prior to the beginning of events in the novel and is presumed dead. The novel focuses on his return to his family and his attempt to discover the identity of those who engineered his disappearance. *An Eye for an Eye* (1957), adapted for television as *Markham* (1957), is a missing persons novel in which divorce lawyer Ben Forbes' wife is kidnapped by Al Guthrie, the ex-husband of one of Forbes' clients (Lorene). Guthrie offers to release Forbes' wife on the condition that he act on his behalf to persuade Lorene to return to him.

The Tiger Among Us (1957, subtitled 'A Novel of Unrelenting Suspense' for its 2001 publication) was adapted for film as *13 West Street* (1962). It is a story of aggression and vigilantism that reflects the growing alarm over teenage delinquency and violent crime in the context of an increasing awareness of social inequality among 1950s suburban Americans. Walter Sherris, a respectable family man, is set upon by a gang of five teenagers whose brutal attack leads to Sherris' hospitalisation. His determination to see his attackers arrested makes him a target of further aggression. The metaphor of the tiger refers to a postulated, deep-rooted violence in human nature that emerges as a consequence of repression amongst socially respectable suburbanites. *The Tiger Among Us* offers a critique of social stereotyping as much in its examination of moral panic in response to casual violence and urban crime. *Silent Partner* (1969), some of which was set in Iran, was Brackett's last crime novel.

Brackett and women

Brackett's crime fiction often features tough women in roles departing from typically sexist stereotypes, but it also enforces such stereotypes by representing their behaviour as typically masculine. In *No Good From a Corpse*, Dane is praised for her ability to drive like a man, while in *The Tiger Among Us*, Sherris' wife Tracey is criticised at the beginning of the novel for abandoning her husband out of fear that he may never recover from the coma caused by his beating. Tracey's position as a mother who is financially dependent on her husband, and the emotional difficulties that this raises, is ignored. Howard Hawks originally thought Brackett was a man before he hired her to write *The Big Sleep*, and went so far as to praise her in the following terms: 'She wrote like a man – she writes good' (McBride, 1982, p. 138). Hawks' comment is indicative of the widespread perception that crime fiction, as a market for gritty realism, is 'masculine' writing. This is a perception Brackett herself endorsed, and she often claimed that she was always a masculine writer. This may be a consequence of her writing within the conventions and audience expectations of crime fiction whereas, in comparison to her writing outside of the genre, her identity as a female writer was widely known and publicised by the editors of the science fiction pulps that her short stories appeared in.

Much criticism and commentary on Brackett focuses on her contributions to science fiction and her adaptations of Chandler's *The Big Sleep* and *The Long Goodbye*. The latter film, directed by Robert Altman, divided critics and Chandler fans alike in its portrayal of Philip Marlowe as the archetypal 1970s layabout. Elliott Gould appeared deliberately unshaven and unkempt in the role of the detective.

Edmond Hamilton edited an anthology of Brackett's work *The Best of Leigh Brackett* (1977). Hamilton died the year of its release from complications following kidney surgery. Leigh Brackett died the following year and they are buried together in Kinsman, Ohio.

Suggested reading

L. Brackett (2001) 'From *The Big Sleep* to *The Long Goodbye*' *The Big Book of Noir*. E. Gorman, L. Server and M. H. Greenberg, eds. (New York: Carroll and Graf) pp. 137– 42.

J. L. Carr (1986) *Leigh Brackett: American Writer* (Polk City, Iowa: C. Drumm).

B. Falk (2007) 'Leigh Brackett: Much More than the Queen of Space Opera!' http://www.bewilderingstories.com/issue250/brackett1.html, date accessed 21 June 2011.

S. Swires (1991) 'Leigh Brackett: Journeyman Plumber' *Backstory 2: Interviews with Screenwriters of the 1940s and 1950s*, P. McGilligan ed. (Berkeley: University of California Press) pp. 15–26.

Chris Pak

Brewer, Gil (1922–83)

Gil Brewer is one of the unacknowledged giants of the noir paperback writers from the 50s and 60s, whose best novels have a feverish quality to match the works of Jim Thompson and David Goodis. Brewer was at times on the verge of a breakthrough to mainstream success, but it never came. Due to numerous reprints and archive findings, Brewer's reputation has been rising in recent years.

Gilbert John Brewer was born on 20 November 1922, in Canandaigua, New York. He dropped out of school but remained an omnivorous reader with a thirst for knowledge. Brewer served in the US Army during World War II, seeing combat in France and Belgium and earning a Veteran's Disability pension after being wounded in action. He tried serious literary writing, but his agent Joseph Shaw – the former legendary editor of *Black Mask* – convinced Brewer to try his hand at crime writing. Brewer sold a significant number of stories to crime pulps, such as *Detective Tales*. When he eventually started writing suspense novels, he drafted *So Rich, So Dead* in five days. *Satan Is a Woman* quickly followed and became his first published novel, although both were published in 1951. *13 French Street*, also written in 1951, was his greatest success. This story of a love and death triangle sold over one million copies and was reprinted eight times.

Gil Brewer wrote convincingly about ordinary people, and the influence of Ernest Hemingway is evident in his novels' lean prose style. Yet his greatest writing combines surrealism with existentialism. One of his recurring themes is how a venal man is destroyed by a wicked and scheming woman.

Bill Pronzini has cited *A Killer Is Loose* (1954) as one of Brewer's best works. In the novel a down-on-his-luck ex-cop saves the life of a man who turns out to be a deranged psychopath. *The Red Scarf* (1958) concerns a cash-strapped motel owner who comes across blood money, and *Three-Way Split* (1960) tells the story of a doomed diving expedition to retrieve Spanish gold. *Flight to Darkness* (1952) is a dark novel about a Korean War veteran who is discharged from a psychiatric hospital and accused of murder. He has no recollection of the crime and does not know whether he is insane or the victim of a set-up. Brewer also created several notable private detectives, including Lee Baron in *Wild* (1958) who is hired by a former lover to find her missing husband, and Sam and Tate Morgan of the Morgan Private Investigations Agency in *The Bitch* (1958).

Nearly all of Brewer's novels from the 50s were paperback originals, *The Red Scarf* and *The Angry Dream* (1957) were his only hardcovers, and many of them were published by Fawcett. In the 1960s Brewer's career went into decline: he spent money recklessly and would often write a book in three to five days when he was broke. This gruelling process would leave him in a state of nervous exhaustion, and he was reliant on pills and alcohol to fall asleep. He suffered a mental breakdown and was committed to a state hospital for a period. In 1970, he was involved in a serious car crash and the doctors were unable to give him medication to relieve the pain because of his high blood-alcohol level. The last works to appear under his name were three novelisations of the *It Takes a Thief* television series, featuring series character Al Mundy, a cat burglar hired by US Intelligence. By the end of his career, Brewer was reduced to ghostwriting, including five novels for Israeli soldier Harry Arvay's Max Roth series.

In the last decade of his life, living in a state of near-destitution, Brewer worked on several projects that would never see publication: a literary novel partly based on his addictions, 'Anarcosis', written in a stream-of-consciousness style, and a suspense novel about homosexuals, called 'The Skeleton'. Despite joining Alcoholics Anonymous and attempting to reform, Brewer's dependence on drugs and alcohol was worsening; his wife found him dead 2 January 1983.

Suggested reading

E. Gorman (1998) 'Forgotten Writers: Gil Brewer' *The Big Book of Noir*, L. Server, E. Gorman and M.H. Greenberg eds. (New York: Carroll and Graf), p. 191.
V. M. L. Brewer (2010) 'Notes on Gil Brewer' *Gil Brewer, noir fiction writer* http://www.gilbrewer.com/notesverlaine.htm, date accessed 28 September 2009.

Juri Nummelin

Brown, Fredric (1906–72)

Detective, mystery and science fiction writer best known for *The Fabulous Clipjoint* (1947), which won the Edgar Award for best first mystery novel and launched the characters Ed and Ambrose Hunter. Also highly regarded are *The Screaming Mimi* (novel 1949, film 1958), *The Far Cry* (1951) and *The Lenient Beast* (1956).

Born in Cincinnati, Ohio, Brown spent a semester at Hanover College, Indiana, then at the University of Cincinnati (1927), although he did not gain a degree. He published hundreds of short stories, over 30 novels and a teleplay for Alfred Hitchcock throughout his 30-year career. Brown married Helen Ruth in 1929 and had two sons; by 1930 they had moved to Milwaukee, and in 1937 he began working as a proof-reader for the *Milwaukee Journal*, during which time he wrote his first detective short story, 'Monday's an Off Night'. Brown was a member of the Milwaukee Fictioneers Club, where he met Robert Bloch, and the Los Angeles Science Fantasy Society (LASFS), where, among other science fiction, fantasy and crime writers, he met Ray Bradbury, Leigh Brackett and William F. Nolan. In 1947 he divorced his first wife, became a full-time writer and, in 1948, married Elizabeth Charlier. Brown travelled extensively in America but lived for several years in Taos, New Mexico, from 1949 before moving to California in 1952. Apart from the two years he spent scriptwriting in Van Nuys, California (1961–62), he lived in Tucson, Arizona from 1954 due to his deteriorating ill health.

Brown is best known for his sense of humour, his mastery of the 'short-short' (short stories of two or three pages which he wrote predominantly for the science fiction market) and his strongly plotted stories which often involved some form of plot twist. *The Fabulous Clipjoint* is a story of emotional self-investigation, which parallels its mystery narrative: Ed Hunter, assisted by his uncle, a one-time private eye turned carnival barker, investigates his father's murder and in the process learns more about himself, developing a new respect for the father he had not previously admired. The novel was followed by six sequels in the Ed and Ambrose Hunter series. Brown's later mysteries include *The Screaming Mimi*: a powerful re-working of the beauty and the beast story in which an alcoholic newspaper reporter investigates a series of 'ripper' murders. The novel is set from the perspective of an omniscient narrator who periodically addresses the reader. There is also an appearance of a homeless man named Godfrey which is shortened to 'God'. The novel is set in Chicago and constructs a critique of the grittiness and decay of the city. In contrast, the narrative of *Night of the Jabberwock* (1950) is driven by the encroachment of fantastic elements inspired by *Alice in Wonderland* and their rationalisation through the detective formula.

Suggested reading

F. M. Nevins and M. H. Greenberg eds. (1985) *Carnival of Crime: The Best Mystery Stories of Fredric Brown* (Carbondale: Southern Illinois University Press).

J. Seabrook (1993) *Martians and Misplaced Cues: The Life and Work of Fredric Brown* (Bowling Green, OH: Bowling Green State University Popular Press).

C. P. Stephens (1992) *A Checklist of Fredric Brown* (New York: Ultramarine Publishing Company).

Chris Pak

Browne, Howard (1908–99)

Mystery writer born in Omaha, Nebraska, who wrote under an array of pseudonyms, including John Evans, William Brengle, Alexander Blade, Jack Lait, Lee Mortimer, John Pollard, John X. Pollard, Lawrence Chandler, Lee Francis, Roy Huggins, Ivar Jorgensen, H. B. Carleton and Peter Phillips. Browne worked as managing editor of science fiction and fantasy pulps at Ziff-Davis publications from 1941–56. He married Esther Levy in 1931, but they divorced in 1959, and he married Doris Kaye the same year. He had a son and two daughters from his second marriage. He assumed editorship of several magazines, succeeding renowned editor Raymond A. Palmer in 1950, and established the pulp magazine *Mammoth Detective Stories*. Browne attempted to restore a measure of realism into the predominantly fantastic science fiction style that was being published in *Amazing Stories* during the period. In 1956 he left Ziff-Davis for Hollywood, where he wrote radio plays and scripts for television and film, including *The St. Valentine's Day Massacre* (1967), four episodes of *Mission: Impossible* (1971–73) and *Capone* (1975).

Browne began his writing career by publishing in a range of genre magazines in the 1940s, but he is best known for his private detective stories featuring Paul Pine, who first appeared in *Halo in Blood* (1946) followed by other Halo books, *Halo for Satan* (1948) and *Halo in Brass* (1949). These hardboiled mysteries were significantly influenced, Browne admitted, by James M. Cain and Raymond Chandler. Browne claimed to have told Chandler that he had made his living by copying Chandler's style. Widely regarded as his best Paul Pine novel, *The Taste of Ashes* (1957), continues the series: Pine refuses a contract offered by the prosperous Serena Delastone only to accept another offer by the wife of an acquaintance, Linda Jellco, which turns out to be essentially the same case. His investigation takes him to the affluent area of Olympic Heights. The Delastones are prominent citizens, and Colonel Delastone, like his wife Serena, is an influential member of City Hall. Much of this novel uncovers the corruption beneath the veneer of respectability cultivated by the police and by the Delastones. *The Paper*

Gun (limited publication in 1985) was Browne's last, albeit unfinished, Paul Pine mystery.

A major theme of Browne's mystery writing is the failure of legal systems. Browne's highly regarded *Thin Air* (1954) is a stand-alone missing persons novel in which the protagonist, Ames Coryell, attempts to solve the mystery surrounding the disappearance of his wife when the police, unable themselves to solve the case, turn their suspicion on him. A late novel, *Pork City* (1988), further demonstrates the range of Browne's writing talent. Adapted from his rejected screenplay, 'The Violent World of Jake Lingle', *Pork City* is a portrait of a prohibition era gangland slaying based around the 1930 murder of *Chicago Tribune* journalist Alfred J. Lingle and the subsequent events surrounding the investigation led by detective Patrick Roche. *Pork City* is a wittily cynical exploration of 1930s crime in Chicago and the political machinations that both impede and make farcical the processes of law enforcement.

Suggested reading

Anon (1956) 'Browne Leaves Ziff-Davis for Hollywood' *Fantasy Times*, 247 (3), May 1956.

J. Adrian (1999) 'Obituary: Howard Browne' *The Independent*, 15 November 1999, http://www.independent.co.uk/arts-entertainment/obituary-howard-browne-1126255.html, date accessed 4 June 2010.

W.F.Nolan (2002) 'Collecting Howard Browne' *Firsts: The Book Collectors Magazine*, 12 (8), October 2002.

Chris Pak

Bunker, Edward (1933–2005)

One of the toughest authors in the history of American crime writing, Bunker spent 18 years of his early life behind bars and used his criminal life and intricate knowledge of the penal and parole system as inspiration for his acclaimed crime novels *No Beast So Fierce* (1973) and *Dog Eat Dog* (1995). In his work Bunker portrayed a brutally violent world of crime, invariably seen from the perspective of hardened and unapologetic criminals, but Bunker was also scathing and passionate in exposing the cruelty of a justice system dependent on harsh punishments and unforgiving treatment of ex-convicts.

Early life and incarceration

Edward Bunker was born 31 December 1933, to Edward N. and Sarah Bunker, a stage-hand/set designer and chorus girl in Busby Berkeley Musicals respectively. His parents divorced when he was five and part of the divorce settlement was that Edward should attend boarding school. During his childhood, Bunker was ferried between a succession of foster homes, military cadet schools and boarding schools. Frequently in trouble and often running away from wherever he was housed, Bunker was eventually picked up by the police and placed in juvenile hall at the age of 11 after attacking his father. This was almost certainly the genesis for Bunker's distrust or hatred for authority and institutions. Bunker was shifted between juvenile halls and state hospitals, where he was put under observation when he feigned insanity. Bunker was severely beaten by attendants at a state hospital known as Pacific Colony, but it was during his time there that he began to develop a knowledge of the unwritten rules of survival that inmates must adhere to if they are to live through incarceration, a knowledge which he would later render so vividly in his crime narratives. Bunker was moved to the Preston School of Industry, a reform school where he quickly developed his love of reading novels through studying books found in the institution's library. Bunker was incarcerated at Lancaster prison at the age of 15 after a parole violation. In one incident he was tear-gassed in the face after assaulting a guard. At the age of 19, Bunker was stopped by the police whilst carrying marijuana; he tried to escape, and in the ensuing car chase, he crashed into three other cars and a mail truck. Bunker was given an indeterminate sentence at San Quentin prison. The youngest ever inmate to serve time at the notoriously brutal prison, he would be there for the next five years of his life. Bunker had first met the convicted robber and rapist Caryl Chessman during a stint at the Los Angeles County Jail, but they had adjoining cells in San Quentin as Chessman awaited execution on Death Row. A fellow convict surreptitiously brought Bunker a copy of *Argosy* magazine hidden in a towel. The lead piece was an extract from Chessman's book *Cell 2455, Death Row*. The revelation that a fellow convict had written a published book convinced Bunker that he too would be able to become a writer: 'Suddenly, with the force of revelation, I said aloud: "Why *not* me?"' (Bunker, 1999, p. 171). Bunker sold some of his blood to pay for a correspondence course from the University of California and began his first attempts at writing.

Relationship with Louise Wallis and fugitive years

In 1950, through the influence of his lawyer Al Matthews, Bunker was sent to work for the former silent movie star Louise Wallis née Fazenda, wife of the legendary Hollywood producer Hal B. Wallis. Louise Wallis was a noted philanthropist and would become Bunker's benefactress and friend. In letters he wrote to her from prison, he would address her as 'Mom', and when Bunker decided to become a writer in prison, Wallis sent him a portable typewriter. Wallis introduced Bunker to such esteemed intellectual figures as Ayn Rand and Aldous Huxley. On one notable occasion, Wallis introduced Bunker to Marion Davies and a very frail William Randolph Hearst at Davies's house. Later that day, they visited Hearst's San Simeon estate (the inspiration for Xanadu in Orson Welles' *Citizen Kane* (1941)). Bunker was relaxing in the swimming pool when word reached them that Hearst had died, and they had to leave the estate immediately. Bunker was sentenced to 90 days in county jail for parole violations which he would later claim were trumped up by the police, who suspected him of being the serial killer the 'Hollywood Prowler'. He escaped from the minimum security facility and would spend the next few years travelling across the US as a fugitive on the FBI's most wanted list. Bunker was captured in Los Angeles and resorted to feigning insanity, which led to him being adjudged criminally insane and committed to Atascadero State Hospital. Finding the conditions to be more inhuman than any prison he had been in, Bunker was finally transferred out of Atascadero as his girlfriend at the time knew the California Supreme Court Justice. Bunker spent the late 1960s in Folsom prison and, although the atmosphere was charged due to the racial tensions of the time, he tried to focus on his writing. Bunker's first published work were now lost journalistic pieces for the prison papers *San Quentin News* and *Folsom Prison Observer*. His attempts at writing novels and short stories met with little success at first. His first six novel manuscripts were all rejected for publication. Bunker's agents Armitage Watkins and Gloria Loomis showed interest in his sixth attempt. Towards the end of his prison sentence, Bunker received a phone call in prison from Watkins who informed him that his novel was to be published by W.W. Norton publishers. The novel was titled *No Beast So Fierce*, a quote taken from Shakespeare's *Richard III*, and when Bunker was released from Folsom, pre-production had already begun on the film adaptation, *Straight Time* (1978), starring Dustin Hoffman in the lead role. After his release, Bunker was at first restricted to a halfway house. His counsellor was a young woman named Jennifer Steele, and although she was then married to someone else, the two were to form a friendship and marry in 1979. In 1994, when Bunker was 60 years old, he became a father for the first time. Bunker and Steele would later divorce.

Novels and Hollywood years

Bunker's debut novel sets the tone for the theme of his literary output. The plot concerns an ex-con, Max Dembo, recently released from prison and trying to go straight but feeling suffocated by the harsh restrictions on parolees brutally enforced by his sadistic parole officer. Max feels drawn back to a life of crime as his only viable option. The novel combines an unapologetic first-person account of criminal life, right down to the unforgettably coarse final line, with a scathing attack on the injustices of the US prison and parole system. Bunker's follow-up novel, *The Animal Factory* (1977), concerns a middle class American who has his comfortable existence turned upside down when he is sentenced to San Quentin prison on a drugs charge. The sub-culture of imprisoned youth would form the basis of his novel *Little Boy Blue* (1981), told from the perspective of an eleven-year-old boy, Alex Hammond, who is constantly rebelling against the system which imprisons him in foster homes and care institutions. The novel is a thinly veiled autobiography. Although set during the Second World War, the conflict is barely referenced in the novel as it has no relevance to the characters' lives. Despite critical acclaim, *Little Boy Blue* was a commercial disappointment, with the first edition selling less than 4,000 copies in the US. It would be another 15 years before the appearance of Bunker's next published novel. During this interim, Bunker worked extensively in Hollywood. He wrote an adaptation of James Ellroy's novel *Suicide Hill* (1985), which was never produced, and received an Academy Award nomination for his screenplay to the prison-escape film *Runaway Train* (1986). Bunker also served as technical advisor to the crime films *American Heart* (1992) and *Heat* (1995), the latter of which stars ex-convict turned actor Danny Trejo in a minor role. Trejo had been Bunker's friend and fellow inmate at Folsom prison. Bunker had many minor acting roles in films, most notably as Mr Blue in Quentin Tarantino's heist film *Reservoir Dogs* (1992). The film and role became culturally symbolic of the meta-fictional aspects of crime fiction and films. Tarantino had studied Bunker's *No Beast So Fierce* and has described it as 'The greatest first-person crime novel I have ever read.' Although he had no involvement in the screenplay, and even expressed scepticism at its inaccurate portrayal of criminals, *Reservoir Dogs* led to an increase in sales of Bunker's novels. What is more, Bunker developed a certain Mr Blue-inspired celebrity persona, even using the sobriquet in the title of his memoirs: *Mr Blue: Memoirs of a Renegade* (1999), which was published in the US as *Education of a Felon* (2001). In the early 90s, Bunker changed agent and publisher, moving to the crime fiction/ true crime specialty No Exit Press. There was a resurgence of interest in his work which resulted in significantly high sales in France and the United Kingdom. The last novel published in his lifetime was *Dog Eat Dog* (1995). Bunker's most action-packed book follows three friends in the criminal underworld: Troy, Mad Dog McCain and Diesel. Bunker explores the changing face of urban violence with a professional criminal being indebted to a crazed heroin addict for past deeds. Criminal codes have disappeared in an orgy of drug-fuelled violence. Bunker's life-long atheism is evident throughout the story by the apparent lack of meaning and motivation in much of the narrative; situations which seem stable and controlled descend rapidly into violence with the slightest provocation, and the characters find themselves in one violent encounter after another with little or no connectivity. In the last decade of his life, Bunker would be plagued with ill-health. He underwent surgery for cancer of the bladder and an angioplasty for a minor heart attack. He suffered from hepatitis C and finally died of diabetes in 2005 at the age of 71. Two books by Bunker have been published posthumously, the first of which was written prior to the publication of his first novel and may have been his first novel manuscript, *Stark* (2006). *Stark* is a period crime novel set in Oceanview, California, 1962. It is believed to have been written by Bunker in either the early 1960s or during a prison sentence in the late 1960s and early 1970s. *Stark* was followed by the short story collection *Death-Row Breakout* (2010).

Suggested reading

E. Bunker, (1999) *Mr Blue: Memoirs of a Renegade* (Harpenden: No Exit Press).
C. Waring (2011) 'Born Under a Bad Sign: the Life of Edward Bunker' http://www.crimetime.co.uk/features/edwardbunker.php, date accessed 5 November 2011.

Steven Powell

Burke, James Lee (1936–)

James Lee Burke is best known for the Dave Robicheaux series, two of which have been made into films (*Heaven's Prisoners* starring Alec Baldwin, 1996, and *In The Electric Mist* with Tommy Lee Jones as Robicheaux, 2009). Burke has also written four novels featuring Texas attorney Billy Bob Holland as the investigator and a further three focusing on his cousin Sheriff Hackberry Holland, as well as several stand-alone novels and two collections of short stories.

Early life and beginnings of literary career

Burke was born 5 December 1936, in Houston, Texas, and grew up on the Louisiana–Texas coast. He now lives in New Iberia, Lousiana (although he has a second home in Missoula, Montana), and he draws upon these various settings in vivid detail in his novels. He studied at the Southwestern Louisiana Institute and went on to graduate with a BA in English (1958) and MA (1960) from the University of Missouri. His work experiences after graduation were varied, including working as a landman for an oil company, a pipeliner, a reporter, a social worker and a university professor – all experiences which arguably inform his novels in terms of their detailed and varied characterisation and milieu. Burke wrote continuously during this period, mainly short stories, and his first of several literary novels, *Half of Paradise*, was published in 1965. This was followed by *To the Bright and Shining Sun* (1970) and *Lay Down My Sword and Shield* (1971), both of which went out of print relatively quickly. There was then a 13-year hiatus in his career as a published author, a gap partly attributed to Burke's struggle with alcoholism, before his short story collection *The Convict* (1985) was published. This was followed by the novel *The Lost Get-Back Boogie*, which according to Burke was rejected by publishers 111 times over a period of nine years, before its publication in 1986 by Louisiana State University and its subsequent nomination for a Pulitzer Prize.

Dave Robicheaux series

It was not until the publication of his first crime novel, *The Neon Rain* (1987), also the first Dave Robicheaux novel, however, that his writing career really took off. Robicheaux begins *The Neon Rain* as a New Orleans homicide detective, a Vietnam veteran, and a tough yet poetic man with an alcohol problem. Like many fictional detectives, Robicheaux has a strong yet flexible sense of justice and morality, and a dislike of officialdom: 'Like many others, I learned a great lesson in Vietnam: Never trust authority' (Burke, 2002, p. 143). His investigation into the death of a young black prostitute leads him into confrontation with the New Orleans underworld, but also reveals the corruption of the force that he serves on. At the end of the novel he resigns, requesting early retirement, and moves to New Iberia. He buys a boat rental and bait business and in the later novels he also takes on the job of sheriff's deputy for the city.

The two worlds that Robicheaux inhabits – his home and business on the Bayou Teche, and his life as a detective – emphasise the many contrasts in the novels, including those between the urban and natural worlds, perhaps suggested by the titles of several of the novels, such as *The Neon Rain* and *In the Electric Mist with the Confederate Dead* (1993). The latter novel even alludes to a supernatural world, with Robicheaux having a series of dream-like encounters with Confederate soldiers serving under General John Bell Hood. Tensions also exist between innocence (epitomised in the character of Robicheaux's adopted daughter Alafair) and corruption (seen in the many gangsters, pimps and prostitutes that he encounters during his investigations) and also within individuals and society in general. The often brutal nature of society in the novels is tempered with a sense of humanity's potential for compassion and tenderness, frequently shown through the female characters, such as his wife, Annie, who he meets in *The Neon Rain* and who is violently slaughtered in *Heaven's Prisoner's* (1988) shortly after they rescue and 'adopt' Alafair.

This violence, both of content and language, is a notable feature of Burke's writing, but it is often presented through contrastingly poetic language that involves or evokes the natural world, such as the description of the dead girl in *The Neon Rain*: 'Her young face looked like a flower unexpectedly cut from its stem' (Burke, 2002, p. 10). Conversely, there is often an element of the man-made in the evocative descriptions of nature, such as the sky above the Bayou at the end of *The Neon Rain*: 'The fall sky was such a hard blue you could have struck a match against it, the yellow light so soft it might have been aged inside oak' (Burke, 2002, p. 275). In several books, Robicheaux addresses events from the past, which often return to haunt the present, a key theme in the series: both the detective's own past and a broader American history are addressed. Sometimes these are the events of the immediate past: he returns briefly to New Orleans in *Last Car to*

Elysian Fields (2003), for example, or he goes much further back, investigating events from his own youth, as in *Pegasus Descending* (2006) or *Purple Cane Road* (2000), in which he addresses the killing of his mother when he was a child.

The character of Robicheaux continues to age and develop throughout the series, forming new relationships and re-marrying, acquiring a partner in the form of Cletus Purcell, and moving away from the Bayou into town. By the time of *The Glass Rainbow*, the now-adult Alafair is a student at Stanford and Robicheaux and Louisiana itself are very different from what they were in the first novel, the setting forever altered in the wake of Hurricane Katrina, the aftermath of which is the setting for *The Tin Roof Blowdown* (2007). The next book in the Robicheaux series, *Creole Belle*, is due for publication in 2012.

Other writing

In *Cimarron Rose* (1997), Burke introduced an alternative detective figure in Billy Bob Holland, a Texas attorney and ex-cop. Like Robicheaux, Holland is troubled by events in the past, both the violent acts of his ancestors and his own accidental killing of his best friend, L. Q. Navarro, who appears to Holland as a ghost and converses with him. As in his previous work, family, secrecy and corruption are themes in these novels, and they have the same descriptive poeticism as the Robicheaux books. There have been no Billy Bob Holland novels since *In the Moon of Red Ponies* (2004), but in *Rain Gods* (2009) he resurrected the character of Hackberry Holland, Billy Bob's cousin who featured as the detective in the 1971 novel *Lay Down My Sword and Shield*. Hackberry is a Texas Sherriff with a past that includes time as a POW during the Korean War.

James Lee Burke has been married to Pearl Pai Chu since 1960, and they have four children. Their daughter, Alafair Burke, is also a crime writer. Burke has received a number of awards for his crime writing, including the 2002 Louisiana Writer Award. He also won the Mystery Writers of America Edgar Award for *Black Cherry Blues* (1989) and again in 1998 for *Cimarron Rose*. In 2009 he was named Grand Master by the Mystery Writers of America.

Suggested reading

B. Bogue (2006) *James Lee Burke and the Soul of Dave Robicheaux: A Critical Study of the Crime Fiction Series* (Jefferson, NC: McFarland).
J.L. Burke (2004) *James Lee Burke.com* http://jamesleeburke.com.

Esme Miskimmin

Burnett, W(illiam) R(ipley) (1899–1982)

Novelist and screenwriter W. R. Burnett had a career spanning more than 30 years, during which he wrote the stories for several of twentieth-century Hollywood's most successful movies, including *Little Caesar* (1931), *High Sierra* (1941), and the film noir classic, *The Asphalt Jungle* (1950). His numerous books and stories develop the typically corrupt hard-boiled sensibility into a critical one, in which characters try to live well, but are crushed, by circumstance and economic necessity, into crime, moral collapse, and personal failure.

Early life and career

W.R. Burnett was born in Springfield, Ohio, on 25 November 1899. He was educated at the now defunct Miami Military Institute in Germantown, Ohio, and latterly attended Ohio State University. He worked as a statistician for the State of Ohio from 1921–27, after which he left his civil service job and moved to Chicago, then at the height of its notoriety for political corruption and the influence of gangsters, particularly Al Capone and the 'Chicago Outfit'. Burnett already had several unpublished novels, and stories behind him, but it was his experiences working in the down-at-heel Chicago Northmere Hotel, which gave him the material for which he became famous. The petty criminals, small-time gangsters, hit men, prize fighters, and drunks he encountered as a night clerk fed directly into his first published novel, *Little Caesar* (1929).

Little Caesar was a sensation when it first appeared, and Burnett was soon working as a screenwriter in Hollywood. A film adaptation of the novel, which debuted in 1931, made a star of its then unknown male lead, Edward G. Robinson. While writing screenplays, including the 1932 hit *Scarface*, Burnett continued turning out novels. *The Silver Eagle*, which appeared in 1932, told the story of a man who is drawn into dealings with the mob. It did not enjoy the success of his first novel, but nevertheless cemented his reputation as a writer of hard-boiled gangster novels. However, Burnett was also a prolific and highly accomplished writer of short stories, and in 1930 he won the prestigious O. Henry Award for his story 'Dressing Up', which had appeared in *Harper's Magazine* in November 1929.

Like many publications of this genre and time period, Burnett's novels achieved great success when they were first published but are now most remembered in the twenty-first century for the movie adaptations they spawned. His tough, cynical tales of people for whom moral certainties do not apply, made them ideal material for the troubled period between the 1920s and the Cold War, a period in which social change, economic difficulty, and the shadow of war, undermined the moral framework of the past. In Burnett's work, good deeds can be done by bad people, while those who appear trustworthy are often corrupted and amoral. In *The Asphalt Jungle* (1949), for example, criminals and a crooked lawyer double-cross one another to their mutual disadvantage, while in *High Sierra* (1940) a gangster's tough exterior belies his kindness and sensitivity. In the latter novel, Roy Earle, played in the movie adaptation by Humphrey Bogart, tries to evade capture in the hope of establishing a new life with the girl he loves. Burnett cleverly and carefully portrayed his criminal characters as sympathetic but not worthy of admiration. *The Asphalt Jungle* is in some regards a caper narrative following the planning and execution of a robbery, although the emphasis on realism is at odds with the comedic style with which the caper subgenre is often associated. Inevitably, the criminal plan does not succeed as events do not go according to plan and human frailties become increasingly apparent as the robbers desperately try to maintain control of events.

As Lee Horsley explains in *Twentieth-Century Crime Fiction* (2005), *High Sierra* and novels like it are 'studies in exhaustion and defeat, of unremitting struggle and poverty' (Horsley, 2005, p. 167). For Horsley, Burnett's novels fit into a hard-boiled tradition of social criticism, in particular of an economic system in which people have no control over their lives. In an interview published after his death in 1986, Burnett himself said of *Little Caesar*, 'if you have this type of society, it will produce such men. That's what I was looking for, a type. Rico was doomed from the first. If he had a tragic flaw, it was over-impulsive action. But he is the picture of overriding ambition' (Mate and Mulligan, 1986, p. 57). In Burnett's work this loss of autonomy is often played out in a tension between the harsh urban reality of crime and decay, and the pastoral dreams of his protagonists. William Marling argues that Burnett 'was able to break down the usual antipathy toward the gangster through the latter's nostalgia for a lost green paradise' (Marling, 2009).

Burnett continued writing movie scripts until 1972, two of which, *Wake Island* (1942), and *The Great Escape* (1963), were Oscar nominated. Marling estimates he wrote the scripts or novels behind at least 56 movies, and worked with directors John Huston, John Ford, Howard Hawks, and Nicholas Ray, and actors such as Bogart, Alan Ladd, and Frank Sinatra. In later life, despite his contribution to Hollywood film, Burnett was more popular in Europe than in the United States. Burnett, who also wrote under the pseudonyms John Monahan and James Updike, married Whitney Forbes Johnston in 1943 and they had two children together. He died on 25 April 1982 in Santa Monica, California, and is buried at the Forest Lawn Memorial Park Cemetery in Glendale. His obituary in *Time* magazine sums up his sensibility in one of his own observations: 'You're going to have trouble and you die – that much you know. And there's not much else you do know' (Anon, 1982).

Suggested reading

L. Horsley (2005) *Twentieth-Century Crime Fiction* (Oxford: Oxford University Press).

W. Marling (2009) 'W.R. (William Ripley) Burnett' *DetNovel.com* http://www.detnovel.com/Burnett.html, date accessed 11 May 2011.

K. Mate and P. Mulligan. *Backstory 1: Interviews with Screenwriters of Hollywood's Golden Age* (contains an interview with Burnett), University of California Press, 1986.

M. Spellman 'W.R. Burnett: American Realist' *Shots: Crime and Thriller Ezine* http://www.shotsmag.co.uk/feature_view.aspx?FEATURE_ID=118, date accessed 11 May 2011.

Christopher Routledge

Cain, James M(allahan) (1892–1977)

One of the pioneers of American hard-boiled crime fiction, Cain ranked alongside writers such as Raymond Chandler and Dashiell Hammett in his contribution to crime writing. His profound influence is based on his most acclaimed novels, *The Postman Always Rings Twice* (1934), *Serenade* (1937), *Double Indemnity* (serialised in 1936, published as a novel in 1943) and *Mildred Pierce* (1941). The clipped prose style and fatalistic outlook of these works have come to define the genre. Cain himself detested genre labels and desired to break free of crime writing and become a renowned literary figure. Joyce Carol Oates wrote of Cain, 'Though he deals constantly with the artistic, Cain, it will be said, never manages to become an artist' (Oates, 1968, p. 110). His failed attempt at more serious and respectable projects led to his gradual disappearance from the literary scene until the late 1960s and 1970s when scholarly crime fiction studies created a renewed interest in his work.

A distinguished east-coast family

Cain was born in Annapolis, Maryland, 1 July 1892, to James W. and Rose Cain. Cain's father was first a professor at St John's College and then, from 1903, President of Washington College. James M. Cain, who graduated from Washington College in 1910, would drift between a series of jobs in Maryland over the next four years. During this time he studied voice in Washington D.C., fostering a life-long love of music that would be a recurring theme in several of his novels. Cain claimed the idea of becoming a writer came to him 'out of the blue' in 1914 while sitting on a bench in Lafayette Park and looking at the White House. His first attempts to become a writer met with little success: he tried unsuccessfully to sell stories to magazines while teaching English and Mathematics at Washington College, where he gained a master's degree in Drama. Cain then moved into journalism, working as a reporter for the *Baltimore American* and then the *Baltimore Sun*. In 1918, following the United States' entry into the First World War, Cain enlisted as a private in the Army. He served in France with the 79th Division, seeing action in the Meuse-Argonne campaign, which he later fictionalised in the short story 'The Taking of Montfaucon' (1929). Cain continued to gain experience in journalism throughout his military service as the editor of his company newspaper *The Lorraine Cross*. Cain was discharged in 1919. His brother Edward, who had served in the military as an aviator, was killed in a plane accident the same year. Upon returning to the US, Cain resumed work for the *Baltimore Sun*, and in 1920 he married the first of his four wives, Mary Rebekah Clough, his college sweetheart. Their marriage was a troubled one which ended in divorce. In 1927, Cain married the Finnish-born Elina Sjosted Tyszecka, becoming step-father to her two children Leo and Henrietta. In 1922, Cain was sent by the *Sun* to cover the treason trial of William Blizzard, the union leader of a group of coal miners in Charleston, West Virginia. He also wrote articles on the case for the *Atlantic Monthly* and *The Nation*. Through the assignment he met H.L. Mencken who would become a life-long friend and mentor. He tried to use his experiences in West Virginia as the basis for a novel, exhaustively researching Virginian culture and dialect in the process and even working as a coal miner for a short while, but as was so often the case in Cain's career, the project came to nothing. In 1924, Cain was forced to resign from St John's College after a dispute with the college President. He moved to New York where, with the help of Mencken, he secured a job writing editorials for Walter Lippmann at the *New York World*. Cain held this job for seven years until the *World* was bought by Roy Howard in 1931 and discontinued, but it was during this period that Cain's literary career began to develop. *Crashing the Gates* was Cain's first play. Staged in Connecticut and Massachusetts in 1926, it closed before it reached Broadway. Cain's first short story 'Pastorale' was published in the *American Mercury* in 1928, and in 1930, Cain saw the release of *Our Government,* a collection of his satirical dialogues published by Alfred A. Knopf that were previously published in the *Mercury*. Cain would continue to write stories for the *Mercury*, including the notable 'The Baby in the Icebox' which was the basis of the 1934 film *She Made Her Bed*. Perhaps it was his association with the *Mercury*, and not with the *Black Mask* magazine where so many other crime writers made their name, that gave Cain his high literary ambitions. But Cain's first novel was definitely in the emerging hard-boiled crime fiction genre, and it was here that Cain would cement his reputation.

The early novels

The Postman Always Rings Twice was published by Alfred A. Knopf in 1934 and was an immediate commercial success as well as a source of much controversy, being banned for a period of time in Boston. The story is narrated in the first person by Frank Chambers, a drifter who finds himself at a diner in rural California and ends up working there. Chambers introduces the story with the words, 'They threw me off the hay truck about noon' (Cain, 1982, p. 3). And this casual, aimless opening perfectly conveys the small depression-era world that the characters operate in, seemingly governed entirely by chance and nonetheless leading the protagonists to their doom. Chambers begins a somewhat sadomasochistic love affair with the sultry, much younger wife of the owner of the diner. She persuades Chambers to help her murder her husband, but although they are not prosecuted for committing the crime, Chambers eventually gets his comeuppance when he is sentenced to death for a murder he did not commit. Chambers ends the narration moments before his execution asking the reader to pray for him. *The Postman Always Rings Twice* was an influence on Albert Camus' existentialist novel *The Stranger* (1942), and its dark melancholic tone has led it to being retrospectively labelled a *roman noir*, literally translated a black novel. Other crime writers who would fall into this category include Dashiell Hammett and David Goodis. Cain's novel *Double Indemnity* was first published as a serial in *Liberty* magazine in 1936. The series was so popular that it reportedly added eight million readers to *Liberty's* circulation. It would not appear as a published novel until its inclusion in the 1943 Cain anthology *Three of a Kind*. As with the previous novel, Cain was partly inspired by the case of Ruth Snyder who was executed in Sing Sing prison in 1928 after being convicted with her lover, Judd Gray, of the murder of her husband Albert Snyder. Evidence against Snyder and Gray had included a forged signature on Albert Snyder's $48,000 life insurance policy, which had a double indemnity clause. Once again, Cain has the lead character tell the story through first-person narration, leaving the full consequence of events in the balance until the protagonist reveals everything in the very last line. As with *The Postman Always Rings Twice,* the characters are so passionately involved with each other that they are blind to or wilfully ignore their inevitable self-destruction. With his next novel, *Serenade*, Cain explored the theme of a male-female destructive relationship outside of a planned murder, but a murder does occur abruptly late in the narrative. The lead protagonist, John Howard Sharp, is a failed singer travelling through Mexico who meets Juana, a beautiful woman of Mexican-Indian ethnicity. The relationship is compromised by Sharp's closeted homosexuality which psychologically prohibits him from singing. Cain was sceptical of homosexuality and researched the link between voice and sexuality. He surmised that if singing was a natural expression of talent, a singer who could not sing might evidence non-normative behaviour such as homosexuality. Thus, Sharp's failure as a singer is a result of his attraction to his former mentor Winston: 'Every man has got five per cent of that in him, if he meets the one person that'll bring it out, and I did, that's all.' *Serenade* was followed by *Love's Lovely Counterfeit* (1942), which although intended for magazine serialisation, was only published in a novel format. The last of Cain's novels to achieve a high critical distinction was the melodrama *Mildred Pierce*. Cain adopts a third-person narrative for the story of the titular character. Mildred Pierce is a remarkably strong-willed woman who overcomes physical hardships and the failure of her marriage. She rises from poverty to own and manage a restaurant and provide everything she can to advance the musical career of her daughter Veda. Once again, love and desire become indistinguishable and all consuming. As a mother, Mildred wants to control her daughter as though she were a lover, and her love for her child becomes perversely stronger by the fact it is never reciprocated. Indeed, Veda holds her in contempt. The novel also marked a change in direction for Cain, as the narrative does not contain a murder, and the obsession is contingent on the drama of domesticity.

Hollywood years and film adaptations

In the same year that Cain lost his job with the *World*, he began work as a scriptwriter for Paramount studios. For the next 17 years, Cain would continue to write scripts for a number of studios. Although this would prove to be the most financially lucrative period of Cain's career, as he worked as a screenwriter on dozens of completed projects, he only received three film credits: *Algiers* (1938), *Stand Up and Fight* (1939) and *Gypsy Wildcat* (1944). Ironically, Cain had no formal involvement with any of the film adaptations of his work, but several acclaimed films would be based on his novels and consequently make him a major influence on the classic film noir period of the 1940s and 1950s. *Double Indemnity*, directed by Billy Wilder and adapted by Raymond Chandler (who disliked the novel), was released as a film in 1944. A considerable success for everyone involved, including Fred MacMurray who was cast against type as the murderous Walter Huff character (renamed Walter Neff in the film). Cain's original ending was forbidden by the Hays Production Code, so an alternative ending was shot with Neff being executed in a gas chamber for his crimes. However, this ending was scrapped at the eleventh hour as Wilder considered Neff's fate was better implied through the thrilling final confrontation with insurance investigator Barton Keyes. Once again, controversy surrounded the story: singer Kate Smith started a campaign imploring the public not to see the film on moral grounds, which only added to its success. The following year saw another triumphant Cain adaptation with the release of *Mildred Pierce* with Joan Crawford in the title role. The film won Crawford an Oscar for Best Actress, and she cited it as her favourite role. It is a reasonably faithful adaptation of Cain's novel of obsession and self-deceit, but a murder is added to the plot to make the narrative more recognisable as a mystery thriller. In 1946, *The Postman Always Rings Twice* was released starring John Garfield and Lana Turner. It would prove to be another influential film noir, although it lacked the power of previous adaptations including the earlier

French film, *Le Dernier Tournant* (1939) and Luchino Visconti's *Ossessione* (1943). *Ossessione* was filmed in Fascist Italy during the Second World War and was banned by the Mussolini government shortly after its release. Due to copyright issues, it would not receive an international release until 1976, but it is now recognised as a classic of Italian cinema. More than his work as a screenwriter or the film adaptations of his works, Cain's contribution to cinema can be recognised in the film noir themes of existential despair and the moral desperation of the male individual following his lustful desire to self-destruction.

Cain's years working in Hollywood often found him at his most politically active. Cain was a registered Democrat for most of his life, but it was on the murky issue of copyright laws that would lead him into a controversial campaign for reform. Cain wrote four articles for *Screen Writer* magazine in which he proposed the creation of an American Author's Authority to hold author's copyrights and represent them legally. This plan was vigorously opposed by several writers including James T. Farrell who helped set up the American Writer's Association as an alternative to Cain's plan. Ultimately, after a protracted campaign, Cain lost support for the AAA, but he remained proud of a meeting he arranged that attracted over 600 writers to gather AAA support at the Henry Hudson Hotel in New York, later claiming it was the largest number of writers ever gathered in one place in the history of literature. Many of the writers who opposed Cain's plan supported communist politics, and Cain would remain distrustful of all communists working in Hollywood, although he opposed the House Committee on Un-American Activities on moral grounds.

Return to Maryland

When Cain left Hollywood and returned to Hyattsville, Maryland, in 1948, he was at the height of his commercial success. The Civil War novel *Past All Dishonour* (1946) and the incest-themed *The Butterfly* (1947) sold very well. Although they were not as critically successful as previous novels, Cain regarded both novels as his best work. But the tide of reviews had turned against Cain and against the hard-boiled style in general. In his review of *The Moth* (1948) James Baldwin said of Cain:

> At the top of his amazingly overrated form, as in *The Postman Always Rings Twice*, in *Double Indemnity* and *Serenade*, he was, when not downright revolting, obscurely and insistently embarrassing. (Baldwin, 2010, p. 259)

Cain found himself cut off in Hyattsville – his life in Los Angeles had been exciting and he counted many movie stars amongst his friends. Cain divorced Elina Tyszecka in 1942. He had a brief marriage to former silent movie star Aileen Pringle from 1944 to 1946. In 1947, Cain married the former opera singer Florence Macbeth. He had followed her career for several years, and although their marriage was not without its problems, they would stay together until her death in 1966. Florence was ill for much of the latter part of her life, and Cain would spend more and more of his time at home caring for her. At the same time his novels were facing increasing criticism: *The Root of His Evil* (1951), *Galatea* (1953), *Mignon* (1963) and *The Magician's Wife* (1965) all received largely scathing reviews. Cain became entrenched in historical research for projects that came to nothing or even more embarrassingly were rejected for publication. Help came from an unlikely source in 1965. When reviewing Norman Mailer's novel *American Dream*, the distinguished novelist and founder of the New Journalism movement Tom Wolfe compared Mailer's writing style unfavourably to Cain's. Wolfe elaborated on his admiration for Cain in the introduction to the omnibus *Cain x3* (1969):

> Cain was one of those writers who first amazed me and delighted me when I was old enough to start looking around and seeing what was being done in American literature (Cain, 1969, p. v).

This sparked renewed interest in Cain's early work, although it did little to improve the consensus on his later novels. Cain suffered a major heart attack in 1969, and he began to spend more and more time indoors and was sometimes looked after by his neighbours. Two new novels by Cain were published in the last decade of his life, *Rainbow's End* (1975) and *The Institute* (1976) but both met with largely indifferent and negative reviews. James M. Cain died in 1977 at the age of 85. In 2012, Hard Case Crime will publish Cain's novel *The Cocktail Waitress*, which the author was working on at the time of his death. Although opinion is divided on Cain's contribution to American literature, he is well-regarded by crime fiction scholars and, as Roy Hoopes put it, 'He was undeniably one of the most provocative and popular novelists America ever produced' (Hoopes, 1982, p. xiii).

Suggested reading

J.M. Cain (1969) *Cain x3: The Postman Always Rings Twice, Mildred Pierce, and Double Indemnity,* Wolfe, T., intro (New York, Knopf, 1969).

R. Hoopes (1982) *Cain* (New York; Holt, Rinehart and Winston).

D. Madden (1970) *James M. Cain* (Boston: Twayne Publishers).

J.C. Oates (1968) 'Man Under Sentence of Death: The Novels of James M. Cain,' D. Madden, ed., *Tough Guy Writers of the 30s* (Carbondale, Illinois: Southern Illinois University Press) pp. 110–28.

Steven Powell

Cain, Paul (1902–66)

Although relatively little is known of his life, and his publications were limited to one novel and a handful of short stories, Cain has developed a critical following from the impact of his novel *Fast One* (1936), a significant work in the hard-boiled genre.

Life and career

Born George Carrol Sims on 30 May 1902, in Des Moines, Iowa, few objective facts can be established of his early biography, which is comprised mostly of speculation. He grew up in a working-class neighbourhood of Chicago, and he claimed to have spent his early life travelling the Americas, Africa, Asia and Europe working alternately as 'a bosun's-mate, a Dada painter, a gambler' (Cain, 2004, p. 233). By 1925 he had moved to Los Angeles and was working in Hollywood. His first credited work was under the name George Ruric as production assistant on Josef von Sternberg's silent film *The Salvation Hunters*. He also worked as assistant director on von Sternberg's *A Woman of the Sea* (1926). He next appears as the author Paul Cain, the pseudonym for which he is best known in the crime fiction world, with his short story 'Fast One' appearing in the March 1932 issue of *Black Mask*. Between 1932 and 1936 Cain contributed regularly to *Black Mask,* publishing 17 stories. Cain's only published novel, *Fast One,* is drawn from five of his stories: 'Fast One', 'Lead Party', 'Velvet', 'The Heat' and 'The Dark'. The lead protagonist in *Fast One* is Gerry Kells, a gunman-gambler who becomes embroiled in the Mob rivalry and political corruption of 1930s Los Angeles. The narrative is complex and difficult to summarise due to its episodic nature. It features multiple plot twists, black humour, cynical philosophy, surreal and even incoherent moments: 'mostly', according to critic Max Décharné, 'it seems propelled more by the logic of dreams or nightmares' (Décharné, 2004, p. 12). The novel is dedicated to the Hollywood actress Gertrude Michael whom Cain dated and who was the inspiration for the character S. Granquist, Kell's moll who is with him at the violent, enigmatic and moving denouement. Six years before the publication of his own classic work *The Big Sleep* (1939), *Fast One* was printed with a recommendation from Raymond Chandler, who described the novel as 'some kind of high point in the ultra hard-boiled manner' (Décharné, 2004, p. 9). *Fast One* was adapted into film as the rather tepid *Gambling Ship* (1933) featuring Cary Grant as an unlikely Kells, here renamed Ace Corbin, in a film practically unrecognisable from its literary source.

Later years

Cain left the *Black Mask* in 1936, possibly because of the firing of editor Joseph T. Shaw, or it may have simply been to pursue his more financially lucrative screenwriting career. Cain wrote screenplays under the pseudonym 'Peter Ruric'. The films he was credited with cover a diverse set of subjects: the two most associated with the crime genre are an adaptation of Ayn Rand's play *The Night of January 16th* (1941) and *Grand Central Murder* (1942). Cain's final film credit as Ruric came in 1948. The critic William Marling attributes his disappearance to sickness, but in the author's biography in *Fast One* Cain describes himself as 'a "no" man in Hollywood', regularly turning down job offers (Cain, 2004, p. 223). Cain resurfaced in the late 1950s writing articles on food for *Gourmet* magazine and working as a television writer. He died in Los Angeles, 23 June 1966. Cain's work has been reprinted in recent years as his critical reputation has grown. The only other book that he wrote which was published in his lifetime was *Seven Slayers* (1946), a collection of seven stories from his *Black Mask* years. Fast One was reissued by No Exit Press in 1987.

Suggested reading

M. Décharné, 'Introduction' *Fast One* by Cain, P. (Harpenden: No Exit Press) pp. 7–12.

W. Marling (2009) 'Paul Cain' *Detnovel.com* http://www.detnovel.com/CainPaul. html, date accessed 23 May 2010.

W. Nolan (1985) *The Black Mask Boys* (New York: William Morrow).

Steven Powell

Capote, Truman (1924–84)

Although not generally considered a crime writer, Truman Capote's one venture into the field was the groundbreaking *In Cold Blood* (1966) for which he coined the term the 'non-fiction novel'. *In Cold Blood* depicts the murders of Kansas farming family the Clutters, the subsequent investigation into the crime and the arrest and execution of the two killers, Richard 'Dick' Hickock and Perry Smith. *In Cold Blood* is regarded as one of the key early works of the true crime genre.

Capote was born Truman Streckfus Persons in New Orleans to Arch Persons and Lillie Mae Persons (nee Faulk). When his parents divorced four years after his birth, Capote's mother moved to New York, leaving her son in the care of cousins in Monroeville, Alabama, until her remarriage to Joseph Capote. These formative years in the South would shape Truman Capote's future writing, much of which is considered to be influenced by the Southern Gothic tradition. From 1941 until 1944, Capote worked as a copy boy at *The New Yorker*. After leaving the magazine, Capote devoted his time to writing; his first novel, *Other Voices, Other Rooms*, was published in 1948. Capote found continued success with *The Grass Harp* (1951) and the novella *Breakfast at Tiffany's* (1958), which was adapted into a 1961 film starring Audrey Hepburn and George Peppard.

A short article in the *New York Times* covering the 1959 murders of Herbert Clutter, his wife and their two children in Holcomb, Kansas, caught Capote's attention, and he travelled to Kansas with his friend, fellow writer Harper Lee, in order to conduct his own investigation into the crime. Capote's interest in the murders turned into six years of research and writing. The resulting novel, *In Cold Blood*, examines the psychology of the killers as well as the actual murders and the effect of the crime on the community of Holcomb. *In Cold Blood* became a landmark in New Journalism, a term coined by Tom Wolfe in 1973 to describe the application of literary techniques to works of nonfiction. However, Capote's behaviour towards Hickock and Smith has come under scrutiny in recent years. Capote felt he could not finish the book until the two killers were executed and, according to some sources, when he received the news they would finally be put to death he was overjoyed. Capote's behaviour was a precursor to the ethical issues which would later plague the true crime genre he helped to popularise. A 1967 film version of the novel was shot on location at the Clutter family's house in Holcomb and was nominated for four Academy Awards. Two more recent films have examined Capote's involvement in the case, *Capote* (2005) starring Philip Seymour Hoffman in the title role, and *Infamous* (2006) which featured Toby Jones as the author.

Capote's flamboyant persona and courtship of famous friends made him a fixture in New York City society, but barbed portrayals of several well-known acquaintances in chapters from an unfinished novel called *Answered Prayers* alienated many of Capote's influential supporters when they were published in 1975 and 1976. Capote's social rejection was a factor in his increased alcohol and drug abuse, and he died in Los Angeles, California, on 25 August 1984.

Suggested reading

G. Clarke (1988) *Capote: A Biography* (New York: Simon and Schuster).

R. Keeble and S. Wheeler (2007) *The Journalistic Imagination: Literary Journalists from Defoe to Capote and Carter* (London and New York: Routledge).

Krebs, Albin 'Truman Capote Is Dead at 59; Novelist of Style and Clarity: Truman Capote, Writer of Style and Clarity, Dies' *The New York Times*, 26 August 1984, p. 1, p. 42.

J.J. Waldmeier and J. C. Waldmeier, eds. (1999) *The Critical Response to Truman Capote* (Westport, CT: Greenwood Press).

Megan Hoffman

Carr, John Dickson (1906–77)

A giant of the Golden Age of detective fiction, Carr achieved popularity on both sides of the Atlantic with his locked-room mysteries and impossible crime novels. Carr's stories were heavily influenced by the concept of the supernatural, which was most often rationally debunked as a staged illusion by the end of the novel. Carr's biographer, Douglas G. Green noted, 'Carr's detectives act almost like exorcists. They bid the demons be gone and reason is returned to the world' (Greene, 2009). Later in his writing career, Carr would channel his interest in the Romantic into historical mysteries: his tale *The Devil in Velvet* (1951), in which a character's pact with the devil sends him back in time to the seventeenth century, was his bestselling novel. A prolific writer, Carr published up to four novels a year in addition to radio plays and short stories.

Born in Uniontown, Pennsylvania on 30 November 1906, Carr began writing mystery stories in high school. He graduated from Haverford College in 1928, after which he went to Paris to study at the Sorbonne where he wrote a historical romance that he later destroyed without publishing. He wrote his first novel *It Walks by Night* (1830) either in Paris or after his return. He met Clarice Cleaves, a British national from Bristol, England, on board an ocean liner. They married in America in 1931 and returned to England in 1832. They would have three children. The Carrs remained in England throughout World War II, only returning to America in 1941 for Carr to offer his services to the US government. Carr worked on US propaganda radio show *Suspense* while awaiting orders, then, when ordered back to England to write propaganda for the BBC, Carr created the radio show *Appointment with Fear* based on *Suspense*. During his time in England, Carr was invited to join the London Detection Club, as one of only two Americans ever admitted. Anthony Berkeley, Margery Allingham, G.K. Chesterton, E.C. Bentley, Dorothy L. Sayers, John Rhode, and Agatha Christie were also members. A staunch conservative, Carr remained in post-war Britain under the Labour government only long enough to finish his authorised biography *The Life of Sir Arthur Conan Doyle* (1949) and his collaboration with Doyle's youngest son Adrian on new Sherlock Holmes mysteries, *The Exploits of Sherlock Holmes*, published in 1954. He 'escaped Socialism' for New York, returning in 1951 when Churchill regained power and staying until 1958, after which he eventually settled in Greenville, South Carolina, where he remained until his death in 1977. Carr worked as a reviewer for *Ellery Queen's Mystery Magazine* (1969–77). Over the course of his career, Carr won many accolades: *Ellery Queen's Mystery Magazine* Contest Award (1950), Mystery Writers of America Edgar Allan Poe Award (1949, 1969) and Grand Master Award (1962). He also served as President of Mystery Writers of America (1949).

Novels

Carr's most famous creations are his series characters the police magistrate Henri Bencolin, Dr Gideon Fell and Sir Henry Merrivale.

Of the three men, Henri Bencolin, created during Carr's turn as a literary editor of his college paper the *Haverfordian*, is the darkest. The novels in which he appears contain none of the humour of Carr's later sleuths and are steeped in gothic turns. In *It Walks by Night* (1930), a man is beheaded on his wedding night by what may have been a werewolf, until Bencolin reveals the true culprit. Bencolin shares with his literary predecessor Sherlock Holmes, a singular fascination with unsolvable crimes and a drug habit. But although Sherlock Holmes's ambivalence to the world outside of crime might be over-looked, Bencolin is both manipulative and misanthropic in *The Lost Gallows* (1931). Thinking him too sinister, Carr abandoned Bencolin and created the corpulent, muttering Dr Gideon Fell and the grumbling and temperamental Sir Henry Merrivale.

Modelled on G. K. Chesterton and possibly Dr Johnson, Dr Gideon Fell, retired historian and journalist, serves as a consultant to Scotland Yard. Fell first appears in the novel *Hag's Nook* (1933). Instead of making Fell the lead protagonist, Carr keeps him on the periphery, preventing or correcting wrong conclusions, but not necessarily actively gathering evidence. His relevance to police operations is reinforced as purely cerebral as his phys-ical condition, Fell must use two canes to walk, prevents most other roles. In what critics perceive to be Carr's best novel, the locked-room mystery *The Three Coffins* (1935) published in the UK as *The Hollow Man*, Fell assists on a case wherein one man is murdered in a locked room and another is murdered on a city street a few blocks away. The murders occur without the murderer leaving any marks in the snow outside, a seemingly supernat-ural feat which leads into an incredible backstory of men buried alive. Fell assures other characters he has identified the killer, only to revise it several times. Fell's analysis leads him into meta-discourse, wherein he outlines the history of locked-room fiction in his famous and lengthy 'Locked Room Lecture'. His knowledge is different from the police's practical and experiential understanding of human nature or forensics, and it is this creative thinking, which is not based in the sciences but rather the humanities, that eventually solves the case. Fell, who appeared in 23 of Carr's novels, is noted for his respect for the past, his sense of chivalry and fair play. He is an author himself of books on seventeenth-century romance and ancient drinking culture, and he has a wife that remains unnamed.

Sir Henry Merrivale (H.M.) was created because Carr's output overwhelmed his publisher Harper & Brothers. Carr would publish 22 Merrivale novels with Marrow publishers, first under the pseudonym of Carr Dickson and then as Carter Dickson. Marrow had selected these two pseudonyms, ignoring Carr's choice and infuriating Harper & Brothers in their closeness to his real name. Although for some, the true identity of Carter Dickson was an open secret, in regards to the Merrivale novels, P.G. Wodehouse was also suspected as author. Merrivale and Fell were so authentic in their British mannerisms that British readers believed Carr a UK national. Merrivale is Carr's most accomplished protagonist, as a medical doctor, barrister, former chief of military intelligence and a member of the gentry (inheriting a baronetcy title that is among the most ancient). However, as a counterbalance to these qualities, Carr involves the comparatively fit H.M. in physical comedy. He hums words to songs of questionable taste whilst walking through offices filled with female secretaries, his suitcase escapes his grasp and is chased downhill by a pack of dogs, he launches a ship by smacking the mayor instead of the hull with a champagne bottle and he has a Chinese ambassador thrown down four flights of stairs in a case of mistaken identity. Carr's most acclaimed Merrivale novel is *The Judas Window* (1938), reprinted as *The Crossbow Murder* (1964), wherein Merrivale defends in court a man accused of murdering his father-in-law in a locked room.

Historical mysteries

Carr tried his hand at true crime in 1936, producing *The Murder of Sir Edmond Godfrey*, an examination of the unsolved murder of Godfrey in 1678. In 1950, however, Carr's writing took a new direction. As the locked room mystery had been firmly in decline for some years, and Carr was unsuited to hard-boiled fiction, Carr latterly focused on historical mysteries and fantasy beginning with the Georgian tale *The Bride of Newgate* (1950). In novels such as *The Devil in Velvet* (1951) and *Fire, Burn!* (1957), the protagonist travels back in time to Restoration and pre-Victorian settings. In a throw-back to Dr Fell's solving of *The Hollow Man* using fictional plots, Carr also employed writers of fiction as detectives: Wilkie Collins solves a murder in *The Hungry Goblin: A Victorian Detective Novel* (1972) and Carr creates a fictitious Wilkie Collins locked-room mystery to help solve a 1948 murder in *The Deadman's Knock* (1958). Edgar Allan Poe quietly solves the crime in the short story 'The Gentleman from Paris' (1950) a few months before his death, and Jacques

Futrelle, creator of 'the Thinking Machine' is mentioned aboard the Titanic in *The Crooked Hinge* (1938).

Radio plays and film

Of Carr's radio plays, *Cabin B-13* is one of the most notable. *Cabin B-13* is the harrowing tale of a new bride who boards an ocean liner for her honeymoon only to find out the groom has disappeared and that the ship's crew doubt his existence and her sanity. Her fear over her groom's whereabouts is heightened by a threat to her inherited wealth and the stress of not being believed. The story first appeared as part of the American radio show *Suspense* and was later made into the movie *Dangerous Crossing* (1953). Such was the popularity of the radio play, that 'B-13' was expanded into a radio series of its own, with the ship's doctor telling tales from B-13 of impossible crimes in far-flung places. Other film adaptations of Carr's work include, *City after Midnight* (1957) a retelling of *The Emperor's Snuff Box* (1942), and 'The Gentleman from Paris' was adapted for the MGM film *The Man with a Cloak* (1951).

Suggested reading

D.G. Green (2009) 'John Dickson Carr: Explaining the Inexplicable' *Mysterynet.com* http://www.mysterynet.com/books/testimony/carr/, date accessed 4 August 2011.

D. G. Greene (1995) *John Dickson Carr: The Man Who Explained Miracles* (New York: Otto Penzler Books).

S.T. Joshi (1990) *John Dickson Carr: A Critical Study.* (Bowling Green, Ohio: Bowling Green University Popular Press).

Diana Powell

Caspary, Vera (1899–1987)

Vera Caspary is best known for writing the classic crime novel *Laura* (1942), which was also adapted into an acclaimed 1944 film of the same name directed by Otto Preminger. Caspary's works also include crime novels such as *Bedelia* (1945) and *Evvie* (1960) as well as various plays and screenplays. Caspary's work is notable for its depictions of active, independent women characters and its questioning of traditional gender roles.

Caspary was born in Chicago to Paul and Julia Caspary (nee Cohen). The youngest of four siblings, Caspary spent her childhood in Chicago. She attended a business college to train as a secretary upon graduating from high school, and after holding several office jobs, Caspary was hired to write copy at an advertising agency. Following her father's death in 1924, Caspary moved to New York and supported herself and her mother by taking writing jobs, including a stint as editor of *Dance Lovers Magazine*. Caspary's first novel, *Ladies and Gents*, was published in 1929. She continued to earn enough money to live on by writing magazine articles while producing novels such as *The White Girl* (1929) and *Thicker Than Water* (1932), a semi-autobiographical study of Jewish immigrants living in Chicago. In 1933, Caspary moved to Hollywood and managed to sell several stories to film studios, but she soon returned to New York. In New York, Caspary joined the Communist Party under an assumed name, though she quickly became disillusioned with the party and moved back to Hollywood where she again turned her hand to writing screenplays.

While in Hollywood, Caspary began to write a crime novel that became *Laura*, her best-known work. The novel's plot involves the investigation into the murder of attractive advertising executive Laura Hunt. The novel is narrated as multiple-viewpoint first person which establishes each character's relationship with Laura whilst she was alive and also posthumously as the detective assigned to the case becomes obsessed with Laura. *Laura* ran in the magazine *Colliers* as a serial in 1942 before its publication in novel form the following year. Caspary sold the film rights, and *Laura* was made into a popular film starring Gene Tierney and Dana Andrews. Caspary never again achieved the same level of success as she did with *Laura*, but she continued to write crime novels. *Bedelia* depicts a seemingly ideal wife who is discovered to be a serial killer who has murdered several husbands. In *The Man Who Loved His Wife* (1966) a jealous husband plans for his suicide to look like murder.

In 1948, Caspary married her long-time partner Isidor 'Igee' Goldsmith. In the early 1950s, Caspary was questioned about her involvement in the Communist Party by the House Un-American Activities Committee and was subsequently greylisted, making it difficult for her to obtain work as a screenwriter for several years. Caspary moved back to New York after Goldsmith's death in 1964, where she continued to write novels and a memoir, *The Secrets of Grown-Ups* (1979). Caspary died of a stroke in New York City on 13 June 1987.

Suggested reading

Anon. (1987) 'Vera Caspary, Screenwriter and Novelist' *The New York Times*, June 17, 1987   http://www.nytimes.com/1987/06/17/obituaries/vera-caspary-screenwriter-and-novelist.html, date accessed 8 September 2011.

Emrys, A.B. *Wilkie Collins, Vera Caspary and the Evolution of the Casebook Novel* (Jefferson, NC: McFarland, 2011).

McNamara, Eugene. *'Laura' as Novel, Film and Myth* (Lewiston, NY: Edwin Mellen Press, 1992).

Megan Hoffman

Chandler, Raymond (1888–1959)

Among the most admired and influential of all American crime and detective fiction writers, Chandler is best known for the seven novels he completed between 1939 and 1958, which were set in Los Angeles and featured the private detective Philip Marlowe. The novels are celebrated for their sharp dialogue, humour, evocative, descriptive passages and style. Chandler championed the idea that readers of crime and detective fiction might be interested in qualities besides plot and action; his style is so distinctive that similar writing is described as 'Chandleresque'. Chandler's novels helped establish Los Angeles as the archetypal nightmare city of the twentieth century; they have been widely adapted for radio, television and film.

Born in Chicago on 23 July 1888, Raymond Thornton Chandler was the only child of Florence (Thornton) Chandler and Maurice Chandler. His mother was born in Waterford, Ireland, around 1863; his father was born in 1859 in Pennsylvania and is believed to have been an engineer on the Union Pacific railroad. They married in 1887, but by 1895 they were separated. The Chandlers moved frequently between Chicago and Plattsmouth, Nebraska, where young Raymond attended the East Fourth Ward School in 1895 and 1896. In June of 1900, Chandler and his mother sailed out of Montreal for Liverpool and made their way to London, where they set up home in Upper Norwood with his grandmother and an unmarried aunt, Ethel. Chandler's mother was not especially welcome in London, and the boy became protective of her.

In the autumn, Chandler began as a day pupil at Dulwich College, a private school in South London, where he followed both P.G. Wodehouse and C.S. Forrester as a pupil. He was a talented scholar, but lacking the funds to go to university, on leaving school he prepared to enter the civil service and travelled in France and Germany studying languages. In 1907 he became naturalised as a British subject and took his civil service examinations, placing third out of six hundred applicants. He began work at the Admiralty soon afterwards.

Biographer Frank MacShane suggests that Chandler did not have the temperament for the civil service. He began writing poetry, most of which had no literary merit, then left the Admiralty to work as a reporter on the *Daily Express*, before moving to the *Westminster Gazette*. He also wrote reviews for *The Academy*, but none of this was enough for him to earn a living. In 1912 he borrowed £500 from his uncle Ernest and left for the United States. According to immigration records, he sponsored his mother's arrival in the United States in December that year. He later claimed to have paid off his 'irate' uncle in full at six per cent interest.

Los Angeles, war, and the oil business

Chandler made his way to San Francisco, and by 1912 he was taking a night school course in bookkeeping. With the help of Warren Lloyd, a lawyer he had met and befriended during his voyage to the United States, he found a job at the Los Angeles Creamery. The Lloyd family became an important part of Chandler's life, and it was at one of their cultural evenings that he met Cissy Pascal, who was then married to the pianist Julian Pascal.

By 1917 Chandler and his mother were living together in Santa Barbara, where Chandler was employed at the local branch of the creamery. He signed his United States draft registration card on June 17th, claiming exemption from the draft 'on account mother' – he told friends he had poor eyesight – and in August he joined the Canadian army. MacShane surmises that this was because, unlike the United States Army, the Canadians paid his mother a severance allowance. Chandler served in France and was later the sole survivor of an artillery attack on his trench, an episode he later wrote up in a sketch called 'Trench Raid' and more indirectly in his 1953 novel *The Long Goodbye*.

In 1919, after a brief period in the newly formed Royal Air Force, Chandler returned to Los Angeles to resume his friendship with the Lloyds and to begin a love affair with Cissy Pascal. She divorced, but she did not marry Chandler until 6 February 1924, four months after the death of his mother. Cissy gave her age as 43, but she was in fact ten years older.

With the help of the Lloyds, Chandler took a job at the Dabney Oil Syndicate and became part of the California oil boom of the 1920s. He was a talented auditor and a brilliant office manager, but his personal life was a mess. He drank heavily, had many affairs, and his relationship with Cissy, as she approached the age of 60, became difficult. In February 1930, they separated. It is unclear how long they remained apart, but by 1932, when he was fired from his job, Cissy's health was deteriorating. Perhaps because of that, she and Chandler were together again.

The pulps

Out of work in the Great Depression, aged 44, and with very little money, Chandler taught himself to write fiction by imitating others, rewriting stories by writers such as Ernest Hemingway and Erle Stanley Gardner in order to understand how they worked. Chandler had been earning around $1000 a month as far back the early 1920s, and he must have felt very insecure foraging a new career in writing, but he persevered, supported by Paul Lloyd, who paid him $100 a month in these difficult years. His first published story, 'Blackmailers Don't Shoot,' appeared in *Black Mask* magazine in December 1933. It took five months to write and earned him $180.

Working with *Black Mask* editor Joseph 'Cap' Shaw, Chandler was published alongside writers such as Gardner, Horace McCoy, W.T. Ballard, and Norbert Davis, and at *Black Mask* he was among Shaw's most regular contributors. He introduced description and style to a genre that favoured plot and sensation, and succeeded in changing Shaw's expectations of what *Black Mask* readers enjoyed. In a period of around ten years, he published 22 stories in magazines including *Black Mask* and *Dime Detective Magazine*. By 1938, however, Chandler was outgrowing the possibilities offered by the pulp magazines and had begun writing his first novel, *The Big Sleep*.

Philip Marlowe

In 'The Simple Art of Murder,' which first appeared in *Atlantic Monthly* (December 1944), Chandler published his manifesto for the tough fictional private eye, arguing, famously that 'down these mean streets a man must go who is not himself mean, who is neither tarnished nor afraid. The detective in this kind of story must be such a man. He is the hero, he is everything' (Chandler, 1995, pp. 991–2). Chandler's own detective hero, Philip Marlowe, features in all seven of his completed novels, and the one he did not finish, *Poodle Springs*.

Marlowe's origins are in the heroes of Chandler's early stories, such as Ted Malvern, a private eye named Mallory, and a narcotics-squad undercover agent called Pete Anglich. One of the opening paragraphs of *The Big Sleep*, published when Chandler was 51 years old, establishes Marlowe's worldview and attitude:

> The main hallway of the Sternwood place was two stories high. Over the entrance doors, which would have let in a troop of Indian elephants, there was a broad stained-glass panel showing a knight in dark armor rescuing a lady who was tied to a tree and didn't have any clothes on but some very long and convenient hair. The knight had pushed the vizor of the helmet back to be sociable, and he was fiddling with the ropes that tied the lady to the tree and not getting anywhere. I stood there and thought that if I lived in the house, I would sooner or later have to climb up there and help him. He didn't seem to be really trying. (Chandler, 2000a, p. 3)

Many hard-boiled detectives were a cynical, urbanised version of the western hero, but Marlowe owes his best qualities to the knights of English Romance literature. He is honest, and honourable, even when it does him no good; his attitude to women is courtly and protective. Marlowe's characterisation as a knight-detective extends from his name to the plots of the novels themselves. Even the titles of the novels have a ring of Romance about them, though only one, *The Lady in the Lake* (1943), makes direct reference to a specific tale.

Marlowe's moral sense is what sets him apart from most of the other characters he encounters. There are others whom he trusts in some limited way, including Bernie Ohls, the police detective in *The Big Sleep*, but on the whole Marlowe is alone and resistant to companionship or aid. In *The Long Goodbye* (1953), the novel in which, arguably, Marlowe's position is most marginalised and threatened, he spends 56 hours in jail because he refuses to betray the confidence of a client, partly because to do so would be bad for business, but also because of the way he is treated by the police. He tells them 'I was balanced on a knife edge and you could have swung me either way. But you had to abuse me, throw coffee in my face, and use your fists on me [...] From now on I wouldn't tell you the time from the clock on your own wall' (Chandler, 2000a, pp. 403–4).

The novels

The Big Sleep (1939) is probably Chandler's best known novel and is the one that established his reputation as a hard-boiled novelist. Chandler drew on his experience as a writer of pulp short stories, blending together several early works, in particular 'Killer in the Rain' (1935) and 'The Curtain' (1936), to create the longer narrative. The novel's plot is notoriously complex, but this is only part of what makes it worth reading. The character and voice of Marlowe, and the depiction of Los Angeles as a city of bright modernity and dark underlying corruption, are now familiar, but Chandler's analysis extends to environmental destruction and the increasingly pervasive influence of drugs and pornography. In later novels, in particular *The Long Goodbye* (1953), Chandler unpicks the effects of consumerism and moral relativism.

Chandler followed *The Big Sleep* with *Farewell, My Lovely* (1940), and then *The High Window* (1942) and *The Lady in the Lake* (1943). Chandler was not a fast writer, and these early novels drew extensively on previously published stories and notes. He kept records of the material he had used in each novel, making lists of similes, which he then ticked off as he used them. The distinctiveness of Chandler's prose, in particular his dialogue, and his use of simile and metaphor, took him beyond the general run of crime writing and into a more literary arena where he was admired by writers as diverse as W.H. Auden and Ian Fleming. Examples such as 'Dead men are heavier than broken hearts,' and, describing 'Moose' Malloy in *Farewell, My Lovely*: 'he looked about as inconspicuous as a tarantula on a slice of Angel food,' have become known as 'Chandlerisms'.

The Little Sister (1949) marks a shift in Chandler's ambition as a novelist. Chandler was often criticised for writing crime fiction when he could be doing something more literary, and by implication, more important. But it was not until *The Long Goodbye*, winner of the Edgar Award for Best Novel in 1955, that Chandler broke free of his roots in the pulps, creating a detective novel that is among the most ambitious of its time.

The Long Goodbye was written under difficult circumstances. Chandler was struggling with alcohol, and Cissy was elderly and unwell. Nevertheless, the story of the disappearance of Terry Lennox, and Marlowe's dealings with the drunken writer, Roger Wade, takes place alongside Marlowe's own personal fragmentation and increasing weariness. Marlowe's realisation that he has become an anachronism in a culture where identity, and morality, have become relativistic and contingent, leads to his own 'sell out' at the end of the seventh novel *Playback* (1958) and his return in the unfinished *Poodle Springs*, driving a Cadillac belonging to his rich wife. Robert Altman's 1973 film adaptation of *The Long Goodbye* emphasises Marlowe's otherworldliness by setting the story in contemporary LA but making Marlowe a throw-back to the 1940s.

Hollywood

All of Chandler's novels except *Playback* (1958) have been adapted for film, most notably *The Big Sleep* (1946), directed by Howard Hawks, starring Humphrey Bogart and Lauren Bacall. *The Big Sleep* is a landmark of the film noir era and is one of the highlights of Bogart's career. Later adaptations had mixed success, though Robert Mitchum was a convincing Marlowe in *Farewell, My Lovely* (1975) and in a less accomplished remake of *The Big Sleep* (1978).

Chandler also worked as a screenwriter in Hollywood, though his experience was not a happy one. His introduction to screenwriting came with *Double Indemnity* (1944), an adaptation of the James M. Cain novel of the same name. Chandler, who described the experience as 'agonising', did not like the book and did not like Billy Wilder the director. *The Blue Dahlia* (1946), based on an original screenplay by Chandler, was nominated for an Oscar and was a huge success, but it too had a difficult gestation. Chandler finished the film running on a combination of booze and coffee, supported by a relay team of secretaries who typed up his dictation. Chandler fell out with Alfred Hitchcock while working on *Strangers on a Train* (1951), and as a result very little of his original work remains, but 'Raymond Chandler' was a bankable name, and it remains on the credits.

Final years

After Cissy's death on 12 December 1954 Chandler spent a considerable amount of time in London. In 1956 he reasserted his American citizenship when the British authorities demanded that he should pay British taxes, but he was increasingly erratic, depressed and drunk much of the time, including during an interview with Ian Fleming recorded by the BBC. He had plans for a play, a cookbook, and other writing projects, but he returned to La Jolla embroiled in personal and financial troubles. In 1959, by then an alcoholic wreck, Chandler proposed marriage to Helga Greene. Though she accepted, they never married, and Chandler died from pneumonia at the Scripps Clinic in La Jolla on 26 March 1959. He was buried four days later at Mount Hope State Cemetery, San Diego.

Suggested reading

R. Chandler (1950) *The Simple Art of Murder* (London: Hamish Hamilton).

I. Hamilton (1990) *Writers in Hollywood* (London: Heinemann).

T. Hiney (1997) *Raymond Chandler: A Biography* (London: Random House).

T. Hiney and F. MacShane, eds. (2000) *The Raymond Chandler Papers: Selected Letters and Non-fiction, 1909–1959* (London: Hamish Hamilton).

L. Latker (2010) *Shamus Town.* http://homepage.mac.com/llatker/, date accessed 2 November 2010.

F. McShane (1976) *The Life of Raymond Chandler* (London: Jonathan Cape)

J.K. Van Dover, ed.(1995) *The Critical Response to Raymond Chandler* (Westport, Conn.: Greenwood Press).

Acknowledgement is due to Loren Latker, for his work uncovering school records, the 'memorandum of agreement' between Chandler and Cissy, and other details of Chandler's early life which do not appear in the two existing biographies.

Christopher Routledge

Coben, Harlan (1962–)

Bestselling writer of mystery thrillers and creator of the Myron Bolitar series, Coben was born in Newark, New Jersey. Coben studied political science at Amherst College. One classmate and friend was Chris Christie, the future Governor of New Jersey. Coben was a member of the Psi Upsilon fraternity alongside *The DaVinci Code* (2003) author Dan Brown. Coben has received many awards for his novels including the 1997 Edgar Allan Poe Award, bestowed by the Mystery Writers of America, the 1997 Shamus Award from the Private Eye Writers of America for his novel *Fade Away* (1996). He has also received a 1998 Shamus Award for his novel *Back Spin* (1997), and the 1996 Anthony Award for his novel *Deal Breaker* (1995). Among the many nominations that his stand-alone novel *Tell No One* (2001) garnered, it won the Audie Award for Best Audio Mystery / Suspense Book (read by Steven Weber). Coben lives in Ridgewood, New Jersey, with his wife Anne Armstrong-Coben MD and their four children.

Writing

Coben began his career with two stand-alone novels, *Play Dead* (1990), in which celebrity Laura Ayars' husband mysteriously disappears during a swim on their honeymoon, and *Miracle Cure* (1991), which limns the plotlines of a hunt for a serial killer who targets the recipients of a cure for AIDS and the examination into the mystery of the cure itself. Coben achieved critical success with his first Myron Bolitar novel *Deal Breaker*, thus beginning a series that he would continue for over two decades. Bolitar is a former basketball player whose promising career was cut short after an accidental sports injury permanently damaged his knee. As a sports agent, Myron's rich celebrity clients often fall victim to blackmail, kidnappings and murders. Along with his friend and financial agent Windsor 'Win' Horne Lockwood III, Bolitar was recruited out of Duke University to work as an undercover FBI agent before establishing his company, MB SportsRep.

Coben's use of sports as a way of connecting masculinity to notions of self-worth and power is evident throughout the series.

In *Deal Breaker* Kathy Culver, fiancé to one of Bolitar's top clients Christian Steele, reappears after having been missing and presumed dead. Culver's sister Jessica, a former lover of Bolitar's, re-enters his life in connection with his investigation, establishing a romantic motif of return and rejection that appears intermittently throughout the series. Kathy Culver's return triggers the threat of blackmail to Steele and sets Bolitar on an investigation that leads him to exhume his client's past.

The theme of memory and a buried past recurs frequently in Coben's writing. In the stand-alone 2007 novel *The Woods*, a teenager who was believed to have been murdered at a summer camp is found decades later, only recently deceased. Paul Copeland delves into the circumstances surrounding these brutal and traumatic murders, one victim of which was Copeland's own sister. Running parallel to this narrative thread is that of his mother's disappearance at about the same time. In light of information supplied by Copeland's ex-KGB uncle, Copeland's investigation seems to suggest that these two disappearances are connected.

Several of Coben's novels have been adapted for film, including his 2001 novel *Tell No One*, starring Francois Cluzet, Kristin Scott Thomas, and Coben himself in an uncredited cameo appearance. This successful adaptation won the Lumiere for best picture and four out of the nine Cesar awards it was nominated for. The translated novel also won the *Le Grand Prix des Lectrices de Elle* for fiction. The story concerns Dr David Beck, who is still in mourning for his late wife who died eight years ago, when other bodies are discovered near the place where his wife had died and the authorities and other interested parties begin to suspect Beck himself. Disturbed by email messages containing information that only his wife was privy to, and a live feed that appears to show his wife alive and well, his investigation to clear his name leads him to unearth the mystery behind the murders and raises the troubling question of whether his wife is still alive. The theme of a 'return from the dead' and of privileged information appears frequently throughout his oeuvre.

Columns

Many of Coben's stories are set in New Jersey, and some of his characters, like Coben, are Amherst College graduates. Some characters, such as Copeland in *The Woods*, have friendships with politicians that were nurtured during their time at college, much like Coben's relationship with Chris Christie. Further tributes to Coben's friends and family can be found in many of his works. Coben began writing articles and stories for newspapers and magazines after 2000, with a regular 'Backpage' column in *Parade* and a commissioned short story, 'The Key to my Father', in *The New York Times* (June 2003).

This short story reflects Coben's longstanding interest in sport, family and memory, all of which are evident in his mysteries. In his article 'Corky: A Tribute to my Mom', first published in the *Newark Star Ledger* (2006), he describes his mother in terms reminiscent of his description of Will Klein's mother in *Gone for Good* (2002). Coben's signature motifs, such as the disappearance and reappearance of family members long thought dead, can be linked to Coben's elegiac approach to the transience of familial relationships and the permanence of such bonds in memory. In March 2008, Coben wrote an article for *The New York Times* in which he uses the classic crime trope of the undercover agent. In the 'The Undercover Parent' Coben argues strongly for the use of surveillance software to monitor and protect the use of the internet by minors, once again bringing together his interest in ideas of the family and crime.

The release of Coben's first Mickey Bolitar novel *Shelter* in 2011 begins a new series character. Introduced in *Livewire* (2011), Mickey is the nephew of Myron Bolitar. The death of Mickey's father and his mother's internment in a rehabilitation centre leads him to begin a new life with his uncle, Myron, and he is soon drawn into the investigation of a conspiracy involving his father and girlfriend. This series character is targeted toward a younger readership and aims to expand upon Coben's already extensive readership.

Suggested reading

J.W. Bertens and T. D'haen (2001) 'On the Ball' *Contemporary American Crime Fiction*, (Hampshire: Palgrave). pp. 122–24.

H. Coben (2011) *The Official Harlan Coben Website.* http://www.harlancoben.com /index.html, date accessed 15 March 2011.

E. Konigsburg (2007) 'Paperback Writer', *The Atlantic* (July / August 2007) http://www. theatlantic.com/magazine/archive/2007/07/paperback-writer/5988/, date accessed 12 March 2011.

Chris Pak

Collins, Max Allan (1948–)

Enthusiastic and prolific, Collins works not only across a wide range of crime and suspense fiction sub-genres but in a variety of media as well. He has written dozens of original novels and short stories, audio dramas, graphic novels, comic strips and created comic-book series, co-edited short-story collections, and completed unfinished works left in his care by the late Mickey Spillane. Collins has scripted and directed films and put together non-fiction books about the history of mystery stories, men's adventure magazines and vintage pin-up-girl art. With ample reason, Kevin Burton Smith calls him 'a baby-boomer renaissance man' in the genre (Smith, n.d.)

An only child and life-long Midwesterner, Collins was born in the small east Iowa town of Muscatine on 3 March 1948. His early goal was to be a cartoonist. But watching television shows such as *Peter Gunn* and *77 Sunset Strip* led to his discovery of Spillane, Dashiell Hammett and Raymond Chandler and inspired Collins to try his hand at crime fiction. 'I sent my first novel out in the mail in the summer between ninth and tenth grades,' he once told an interviewer, 'I wrote something like four or five Spillane novels (plus an Ian Fleming pastiche) with titles like *Kiss and Kill*, *The Gray Flannel Thugs*, and *Die Slow, Savage*. My detective was Matt Savage, who made Mike Hammer look tame' (Pierce, 1999).

Collins studied English for two years at Muscatine Community College, where he also reignited a relationship with Barbara Jane Mull, his girlfriend from fifth grade. They were married on 1 June 1968. In that same year, he enrolled at the University of Iowa, in Iowa City, and attended the undergraduate writing workshop taught by novelist Richard Yates of *Revolutionary Road* fame. Despite some institutional resistance to his goal of creating tough, 'commercial' crime fiction, Collins achieved an undergraduate degree in English from the University of Iowa in 1970 and secured a placement in the school's Graduate Writers Workshop. In 1972 he received a Master of Fine Arts degree in creative writing. Collins' graduate thesis was a trilogy of novels, eventually published as *Bait Money* (1973), *The Broker* (aka *Quarry*, 1976), and *No Cure for Death* (1983).

Early novels and transition to historical fiction

Collins worked for his local newspaper, *The Muscatine Journal*, during the summers of his undergraduate years. After earning his master's degree, Collins began teaching English and Journalism at Muscatine Community College (1972–77). His first novel – published when he was only 25 years old – was *Bait Money*, which introduced Nolan, a professional thief and hitman longing for retirement. The character bore some similarities to the more famous Parker, created by Richard Stark – the pseudonym for Donald E. Westlake. Nolan returned in *Blood Money* (1973), as well as in six subsequent books, the last being *Mourn the Living* (1999).

Following *Blood Money*, Collins alternated his novels between three different protagonists – none of them originally designed to lead a series. In addition to Nolan, there was the equally criminal Quarry (not his real name), who had killed 'probably thirty men' in Vietnam before returning to the States, divorcing his unfaithful wife and re-creating himself as a hit man. Quarry remorselessly kills people he regards as deserving of death, such as murderers more morally depraved than even he is. Collins concocted five Quarry novels, starting with *The Broker* and ending with *Primary Target* (1987; aka *Quarry's Vote*), but then dropped the character until 2006, when he resurrected him in *The Last Quarry* (the basis for the 2008 movie *The Last Lullaby*). Collins has since continued the series with *The First Quarry* (2008), *Quarry in the Middle* (2009) and *Quarry's Ex* (2011). Lighter in tone and more traditional in style, but with some hard-boiled action, were Collins' books about Mallory, a mystery writer and amateur sleuth. Mallory was strongly based on Collins himself; he even lived in 'Port City, Iowa', a thinly veiled Muscatine. The five Mallory adventures, beginning with *The Baby Blue Rip-Off* (1983), let Collins explore his love of crime fiction and its purveyors. *Kill Your Darlings* (1984) was set at a Bouchercon mystery fan convention.

With the release of *True Detective* in 1983 Collins claimed he found the character 'I wanted to spend a good portion of my life writing about': Chicago private eye Nathan Heller (Kingston Pierce, 1999). Six feet tall, half-German Jew and half-Irish Catholic, Heller was born in 1905. His father, Mahlon, was a union organiser and the owner of a leftist bookshop, who, after failing to dissuade his only son from joining the 'graft-happy' Chicago Police Department, and then despairing at Heller's willingness to perjure himself in order to advance in the department, took his own life with Heller's Browning automatic. Heller still carries the gun, describing it as 'the closest thing to a conscience I've got' (Pierce, 1999). In over a dozen cases Nate Heller has been drawn into one controversial historical mystery after another, from the 'alleged' 1934 murder of bank robber John Dillinger, *True Crime* (1984), and the kidnapping of Charles Lindbergh Jr, *Stolen Away* (1991), to the assassination of Las Vegas mobster Benjamin 'Bugsy' Siegel, *Neon Mirage* (1988), the disappearance of American aviatrix Amelia Earhart,

Flying Blind (1998), and big-screen sex-symbol Marilyn Monroe's 1962 'suicide' in *Bye Bye Baby*, (2011). In each instance, Heller finds the historical record to be false, and the 'truth' stranger than anyone knew.

The well-researched Heller novels are brimming with period atmosphere; whether Collins is describing Heller's entrance into a swank 'speakeasy', conversing with FBI Director J. Edgar Hoover, singer Frank Sinatra and star attorney Clarence Darrow, or allowing him the carnal perks of working for future film star Jayne Mansfield. Heller faces challenges as he ages: he is discharged from the army during the Second World War for mental instability, becomes a father in middle-age and grows his A-1 Detective Agency into a nationwide business. However, he remains a classic of his breed – someone not averse to taking a dishonest buck, who has no faith in 'the system' being anything but corrupt. He is capable of rough justice, yet remains a romantic, ever susceptible to falling in love.

Memorable characters and novels

Expanding his portfolio of period crime fiction, Collins composed four novels, beginning with *The Dark City* (1987) that found Eliot Ness of *The Untouchables* fame moving to Cleveland, Ohio in the mid-1930s to take command of the city's police and fire departments. He wrote several novels that placed eminent mystery writers tackling crimes in the midst of man-made and wartime disasters, including Jacques Futrelle in *The Titanic Murders* (1999), Leslie Charteris in *The Hindenburg Murders* (2000), and Agatha Christie in *The London Blitz Murders* (2004). Collins also produced the graphic novel *Road to Perdition* (1998), a Depression-era gangster tale that was adapted into an Academy Award-winning film in 2002 and spawned the sequel novels *Road to Purgatory* (2004) and *Road to Paradise* (2005). Under the alias Patrick Culhane, he recast Old West Marshal Wyatt Earp as a 1920s private detective rescuing Doc Holliday's wayward son in *Black Hats* (2007) and created Peter Maxwell, a young naval ensign who unmasks a killer aboard a wartime ammunitions ship in *Red Sky in Morning* (2008). Collins wrote a pair of tongue-in-cheek mysteries – *A Killing in Comics* (2007) and *Strip for Murder* (2008) – set in New York's post-World War II comics-publishing world. Collins brought his knowledge and experience of the comics industry to the narratives. From 1977 to 1993 he scripted the syndicated strip *Dick Tracy*, and he and artist Terry Beatty were behind the comic-book series *Mike Mist* and *Ms. Tree*. The latter being the longest-running PI comic book to date.

Collins' drive has led him to experiment in multiple artistic fields. He novelised movies such as *Maverick* (1994), *Saving Private Ryan* (1998) and *American Gangster* (2007), and he has written books expanding on the television series *CSI*, *NYPD Blue* and *Bones*. Collins has also developed independent films, including the Lifetime Television film *Mommy* (1996), and drafted songs for his rock band, Crusin'. Collins is also a frequent literary collaborator. He and his wife, fellow author Barbara Collins – using the joint byline 'Barbara Allan' – have co-written the 'Trash 'n' Treasures' series of antiques mysteries which began with *Antiques Roadkill* (2006). In addition, he and his fellow native Iowan Matthew Clemens have co-written thrillers such as *You Can't Stop Me* (2010), starring a host of a crime-based reality television series. Collins' most notable literary collaborator was his friend and mentor Mickey Spillane. Collins had enjoyed Spillane's Mike Hammer adventures and regaled him with fan mail for years before befriending the author in 1981. When Collins' son Nathan, who was named after Heller, was born in 1982, Collins chose Spillane as the boy's godfather, and the two novelists went on to co-edit short-story collections. Since Spillane's death in 2006, Collins has completed several of his unpublished works, including three Hammer novels, *The Goliath Bone* (2008), *The Big Bang* (2010) and *Kiss Her Goodbye* (2011) and the stand-alone novel *The Consummata* (2011). Collins adapted briefer fragments of Spillane's fiction into short stories and audio dramas.

For his efforts, Collins has twice won the Private Eye Writers of America's Shamus Award for Best Hardcover Novel for *True Detective* and *Stolen Away*, and in 2006 the organisation gave him its lifetime achievement award, The Eye. The Historical Mystery Appreciation Society presented him with its own 'Herodotus' Lifetime Achievement Award in 2002. A collection of pulp fiction artwork, *Men's Adventure Magazines*, by Collins, George Hagenauer, Steven Heller and Rich Oberg was awarded the Anthony Award for Best Nonfiction in 2005.

Suggested reading

Pierce, J.K. (2010) 'A High Point for Hammer,' *The Rap Sheet*, 17 May 2010, http://therapsheet.blogspot.com/2010/05/high-point-for-hammer.html, date accessed 19 May 2011.
Kingston Pierce, J. (1999) 'Killers, Cover-ups and Max Allan Collins' *January Magazine*, September 1999, http://januarymagazine.com/profiles/collins.html, date accessed 18 May 2011.
Smith, K.B. (nd) 'Authors and Creators: Max Allan Collins' *The Thrilling Detective* http://www.thrillingdetective.com/trivia/mac.html, date accessed 6 December 2011.

J. Kingston Pierce

Condon, Richard (1915–96)

A prolific crime writer of satirical political thrillers, Condon developed a dense, signature prose style throughout his 25 novels. Born in New York City, Condon graduated from De Witt Clinton High School before serving in the United States Merchant Navy and working several jobs, including a brief stint in advertising. Condon joined Walt Disney Productions in 1936, where he publicised such movies as *Fantasia* (1940) and *Dumbo* (1941). He worked in publicity in Hollywood for two decades before the publication of his first novel, *The Oldest Confession* in 1958. He married Evelyn Hunt in 1938 and had two daughters. Condon's autobiographical *And then we Moved to Rossenara: or, The Art of Emigrating* (1973) recounts his departure from America for Paris in 1950 before he moved to Spain, Mexico, Switzerland, and then finally Ireland in 1971. He returned to America in 1980 to settle in Dallas, Texas.

Early writing, spies and political thrillers

During his time as a Hollywood publicist and agent, Condon worked at several companies including the Hal Horne Organisation, Twentieth-Century Fox, and his own, Richard Condon Inc. Although moderately successful in this capacity, Condon often complained that his work at Hollywood prevented him from writing. In 1951–52 Condon worked as a theatrical producer in New York, during which time he wrote the play *Men of Distinction* (1953). While Condon was working at United Artists, Max E. Youngstein, Condon's boss, began withholding money from Condon's paycheck, depositing small amounts into a Mexican bank account. In 1957 Youngstein fired Condon, presenting him with the keys to a Mexican bungalow overlooking the sea, as well as the savings pilfered from his paycheck, and encouraged him to begin work on his first novel. Condon's second novel, *The Manchurian Candidate* (1959), was dedicated to Youngstein.

The Manchurian Candidate is Condon's most well-known novel and was adapted for film in 1962 and 2004. The 1962 film was directed by John

Frankenheimer and starred Frank Sinatra, Laurence Harvey and Janet Leigh, while the 2004 film was directed by Jonathan Demme and starred Denzel Washington, Liev Schreiber and Meryl Streep. The novel is a fiercely satiric political thriller in which Raymond Shaw, a sergeant stationed in Korea during the Korean War, is captured with his platoon by the joint Russian-Chinese communist alliance and brainwashed before being sent back to America to receive a Medal of Honour. *The Manchurian Candidate* combines reflections on war with a science fiction treatment of Pavlovian mind control, a spy narrative, assassinations and a critique of McCarthyism. The film was withdrawn from cinemas in 1964, the year following President Kennedy's assassination. There are many stories regarding the film's haphazard circulation; it has been reported that Frank Sinatra bought the rights to the film in 1972, removing it from circulation in 1975. The film remake updates the action so that Operation Desert Storm is the military conflict of the backstory.

Presidential assassination is the theme of Condon's 1974 novel *Winter Kills*, which was also adapted for film in 1979. This novel describes the CIA-influenced assassination of the fictitious US President Tim Keegan, a thinly disguised portrait of President John F. Kennedy. Keegan's half-brother, Nick Thirkield, is reluctantly drawn into an investigation 14 years after the murder when one of the shooters in the conspiracy confesses to the assassination on his deathbed. Condon's satirical narrative style is a prevalent feature of much of his works, and he extends this outlook to the American film industry in his 1967 novel *The Ecstasy Business*, which recounts the murder attempts on the fictional Welsh movie star and Hollywood actor Tynan Bryson during the filming of a new movie. Condon drew on his experiences working in Hollywood to provide material for the parody. *An Infinity of Mirrors* (1964) continued his examination of the theme of politics and war: the novel tells the story of a Prussian colonel who falls in love with a Parisian Jewish woman. They marry before the onset of the Second World War, and the novel traces their diverging paths during the rise of the Third Reich and the events of the War.

Gangsters and crime writing

Mile High (1969) is a secret history of the fictional gangster Edward West during the Prohibition era. In this novel, as in his political thrillers, Condon's major themes, the abuse of power, greed, the connection between politics and crime, and the legacy of American history come under scrutiny and attack. Condon's Prizzi saga, consisting of *Prizzi's Honor* (1982), *Prizzi's Family* (1986), *Prizzi's Glory* (1988) and *Prizzi's Money* (1994), centre on the mobsters of the New York-based Prizzi Mafia family. Condon adapted the first novel of the sequence with Janet Roach for the Academy Award-nominated film, which was released in 1985, directed by John Huston and starred Jack Nicholson, Kathleen Turner and Robert Loggia. *Prizzi's Honor* is a black comedy that recounts the double dealings between Prizzi hitman Charley Partanna and his lover Irene Walker, a freelance assassin and wife of a crook whom Partanna had assassinated for stealing from the Prizzi family. The Prizzis order Partanna to assassinate Walker, and the hitman finds himself dangerously compromised between love and duty. *Prizzi's Family* is a prequel to *Prizzi's Honor* and focuses on Partanna's formative years. *Prizzi's Glory* focuses on Partanna's wife, Maerose Prizzi, and her attempt to restore honour to the Prizzi family during a period of decline. *Prizzi's Money* in many ways inverts *Prizzi's Honor*: Charley Partanna is hired to assassinate Julia Asbury, the daughter of a Prizzi hitman, with whom he falls in love.

Other films adapted from Condon's works include *The Happy Thieves* (1962, from *The Oldest Confession*) and *A Talent for Loving* (1969). Richard Condon died on 9 April 1996.

Suggested reading

S.L. Carruthers (1998) '"The Manchurian Candidate" (1962) and the Cold War Brainwashing Scare' *Historical Journal of Film, Radio and Television* 18 (1) 75–94.

M. Gussow (1996) 'Richard Condon, Political Novelist, Dies at 81' *The New York Times* April 1996, http://www.nytimes.com/1996/04/10/nyregion/richard-condon- political-novelist-dies-at-81.html, accessed 30 April 2011.

M.F. Jacobson and G. González (2006) *What Have They Built You to Do? The Manchurian Candidate and Cold War America* (Minneapolis: University of Minnesota Press).

Chris Pak

Connelly, Michael (1956–)

As a writer Connelly had his first major success with the still ongoing series of novels featuring LAPD detective Hieronymus 'Harry' Bosch, the first of which, *The Black Echo*, was published in 1992 and won the Edgar Award for Best First Novel from the Mystery Writers of America. The Bosch series now consists of 17 novels. Connelly has also written various other novels featuring the recurring characters Rachel Walling, an FBI agent; Jack McEvoy, a reporter; Mickey Haller, a lawyer; and retired FBI agent Terry McCaleb. Through his novels, Connelly has created an extensive and complex fictional universe: a number of his series characters interact in crossover novels, for example, in *The Narrows* (2004) – a sequel to *The Poet* (1996) – Bosch, Walling, McCaleb, and Black all feature. It is characteristic of Connelly's work that whilst the depth of research and the ingenuity of the plotting mark the novels as typical police procedurals, his development of key protagonists such as Bosch means that the narratives are often constructed around the maverick interventions of an individual, making them more akin to private investigator stories, which is what Bosch eventually becomes. Connelly's books have won, amongst other accolades, the Anthony Award, the Macavity Award, the Los Angeles Times Best Mystery/Thriller Award and the Ridley Award. His novel *Blood Work* (1998) won the *Grand Prix*, the highest honour for a mystery novel in France.

Early life and journalistic career

Connelly was born on 21 July 1956 in Philadelphia, Pennsylvania, and lived there until the age of 12, when his family moved to Fort Lauderdale, Florida. At the age of 16 Connelly inadvertently became involved in a police investigation after seeing a suspicious-looking man throw an object into a hedge. Connelly retrieved the item and found it to be a gun wrapped in a towel. After putting the gun back in the hedge, Connelly followed the man to a bar and later that night informed the police. It was to be his first contact with the police, and it began his fascination with the lives and work of police officers which he would explore in his fiction. After graduating from the University of Florida in 1980 with a major in journalism and a minor in creative writing, Connelly went to work as a crime reporter on papers in Fort Lauderdale and Daytona Beach. Connelly and two other reporters wrote a magazine feature on the aftermath of the Delta Flight 191 crash in 1985. The project took almost a year of research, and Connelly spent a lot of time with the survivors. Connelly was nominated for a Pulitzer Prize for the feature. After the acclaim he received for this piece, he was hired by the *Los Angeles Times*, a career progression which saw him move to the city of Raymond Chandler's private detective, Philip Marlowe. Connelly began studying Chandler's work after viewing Robert Altman's 1973 adaptation of *The Long Goodbye*. Whilst working the crime beat for the *Los Angeles Times*, Connelly wrote three novel manuscripts, the first two he did not attempt to get published and the third was published whilst he was still a reporter. In the mid-90s, Connelly devoted himself to writing fiction full-time.

Hieronymus Bosch and other series characters

His first novel *The Black Echo* is a complex tale of murder and bank robbery which was partly based on an unsolved bank robbery that occurred in Los Angeles the day before Connelly arrived to start work for the *LA Times*. The novel introduces the character of Harry Bosch as an iconoclastic outsider in the LAPD 'family' and a brilliant and fearless detective whose refusal to play institutional politics has made him loathed by his often corrupt superiors. Bosch's name is taken from the fifteenth-century Dutch painter whose paintings Connelly had studied at college. Connelly felt that Bosch's paintings, which addressed themes of debauchery and human defilement, would serve as a useful metaphorical connection to the urban tensions in contemporary LA. Bosch's back-story as a Vietnam War veteran and son of a prostitute accounts for the remarkable empathy he has with the victims of an egotistical criminal. *The Last Coyote* (1995) is a story that sees Bosch investigating the 30-year-old unsolved murder of his mother. *Lost Light* (2003) was the first novel in the series to be narrated in the first-person by Bosch so as to accentuate his personal involvement with the case, a theme which Connelly has explored in greater depth as the series has progressed. It was also the first novel of the series in which Bosch has become a licensed private investigator after leaving the LAPD. One of Connelly's most acclaimed novels outside of the Bosch series is *Blood Work*, which examines the concept of survivor's guilt and draws on the experiences of one of Connelly's friends who underwent a heart transplant and on the testimony of the survivors of the Delta airline crash. The main protagonist from *Blood Work*, Terry McCaleb, comes into conflict with Harry Bosch in *A Darkness More Than Night* (2001), as their two separate murder investigations converge in disturbing ways. In 2005, Connelly published his first ever legal thriller *The Lincoln Lawyer* and introduced the eponymous hero, Mickey Haller; Maxim Jakubowski, writing in *The Guardian*, stated that Connelly had 'reinvigorated the legal thriller' in what was 'probably his best work since *The Poet*' (Jakubowski, 2005). Two of Connelly's books were released in 2009: *The Scarecrow* reunites Rachel Walling and Jack McEvoy for the first time since the events described in *The Poet*, whilst *Nine Dragons* sees Bosch transported from his usual Los Angeles environment to Hong Kong as he tracks his missing daughter. Connelly has also published the stand-alone Cassie Black novel, *Void Moon* (2000), and Black reappears under an alias in *The Narrows* (2004).

Like his contemporary Dennis Lehane, Michael Connelly's crime fiction has garnered critical and popular acclaim. Throughout his career, Connelly has stuck to a schedule of producing at least one novel a year; some of his other projects include a CD compilation of the jazz music mentioned in the Bosch novels, *Dark Sacred Night, The Music Of Harry Bosch* (2003), and a limited edition DVD guide to some of the locations featured in his novels, *Blue Neon Night: Michael Connelly's Los Angeles* (2004). Both were given away free to fans and those purchasing his novels. Connelly also presented an episode of *Murder by the Book* in 2006, which examined the US killing spree of Australian-born serial killer Christopher Wilder. The esteem in which Connelly's work is held by critics seems in no small measure due to both his intricate knowledge of Los Angeles as a city, and his willingness to develop characters, particularly Bosch, over a series of works. Connelly has been equally committed to faithfully depicting Los Angeles life in the wake of the Rodney King scandal, the ensuing race riots and the 1994 Northridge earthquake. In most of his work, the accurate descriptions of the canyons, hills, freeways and landmarks of Los Angeles help to map a recognisable terrain. Whilst Connelly rarely allows the pace of his narratives to be slowed by incidental detail, he does utilise symbolism in tandem with his long-range plotting skills. In the early Bosch novels, there are repeated references to just how unstable the detective's home in the hills above Studio City is; by the time of the fourth Bosch outing, *The Last Coyote*, his house has been condemned due to earthquake damage just at the same time that his girlfriend leaves him and he is dismissed from the LAPD following his assault of a senior officer. Connelly has also experimented stylistically with his prose style as *The Poet* contains free indirect discourse from the point of view of the criminal. The Bosch novels have yet to be adapted into films, but an adaptation of *Bloodwork* was directed by and starred Clint Eastwood as Terry McCaleb in 2002. *The Lincoln Lawyer* was directed by Brad Furman in 2011 and starred Matthew McConaughey as Mickey Haller. Michael Connelly married Linda McCaleb in 1984, and they currently live in Florida.

Suggested reading

M. Connelly (2011) *Michael Connelly* http://www.michaelconnelly.com

C. Gregoriou (2007) *Deviance in Contemporary Crime Fiction* (Houndmills, Basingstoke: Palgrave Macmillan).

K. Levendorf and D. Stoyer 'Harry Bosch' *Thrilling Detective* http://www.thrilling-detective.com/eyes/bosch.html, date accessed 27 June 2011.

Tim Foster

Cornwell, Patricia (1956–)

A descendant of Harriet Beecher Stowe, with a literary career that began in journalism and biography, Patricia Cornwell found almost instant success in the crime fiction field with her debut novel *Postmortem* (1990), which introduced medical examiner Dr Kay Scarpetta and focused on forensic science methods involved in modern police investigations.

Early life

Born Patricia Carroll Daniels on 9 June 1956, in Miami, Florida, Cornwell was raised in Montreat, North Carolina. Her father, Sam Daniels, was an appellate lawyer who served as a law clerk to Supreme Court Justice Hugo Black. After Sam Daniels walked out on the family on Christmas Day 1961, her parents divorced and Cornwell suffered a particularly unhappy childhood. When her mother was hospitalised for severe depression, Cornwell was placed in the foster care system but received emotional and financial support for several years from the evangelist Billy Graham and his wife Ruth Bell Graham. The Graham family encouraged Cornwell to write, and she credits them for their unfailing support. Cornwell's first book was a biography of Ruth Bell Graham, *A Time for Remembering* (1983), reissued in 1997 as *Ruth, A Portrait*.

She attended King College in Bristol, Tennessee, followed by Davidson College where she married one of her English professors, Charles Cornwell, who was 17 years her senior. Charles later became a pastor, and their separation in 1989 led to divorce. Cornwell married Staci Ann Gruber in 2005 in a civil ceremony in Massachusetts, then the only US State where homosexual marriage was legal. After graduating from Davidson in 1979, she worked as an investigative crime reporter for the *Charlotte Observer*, covering crime and prostitution cases. From 1984 to 1990 she worked as a technical writer and computer analyst at the Office of the Chief Medical Examiner of Virginia, Dr Marcella Fierro. Dr Fierro, and the experience Cornwell gained of forensic work during these years, proved an inspiration for the Kay Scarpetta series.

The Kay Scarpetta novels

Cornwell started writing fiction in the 1980s, but her first three novels which featured a male detective were all rejected for publication. *Postmortem* was rejected by seven major publishers before it was accepted by Scribner's. In *Postmortem*, Scarpetta assists in the investigation of a series of brutal murders of women. Scarpetta flushes out the killer using the high-risk strategy of provoking him through news reports which subsequently make her a target. Most of the Scarpetta series is focused on the tensions between her emotional and professional life. In the second novel, *Body of Evidence* (1991), a reclusive author of romantic fiction is stabbed to death after being stalked for months, as the investigation unfolds Scarpetta finds herself living the same nightmare life the victim suffered in the months leading up to her murder.

The Scarpetta novels were amongst the first police procedurals based on forensic science, before the form was popularised through the television series *CSI: Crime Scene Investigation, Bones* and *Crossing Jordan*. Cornwell is meticulous in researching the novels, checking investigative details with sources at the coroner's office and with the police. The novels also reflect the technological improvements in forensic science and the evolution of forensic methods: later novels such as *Port Mortuary* (2008) feature virtual autopsies with 3-D CT scanning and robotics.

Kay Scarpetta acts as the first-person narrator of several of the early novels, and focuses her narration on her research, on forensic details and on her relationships with her family and her colleagues; her best friend is detective Pete Marino, and she has a precocious but difficult niece, Lucy, who later becomes an FBI agent. However, the climax of each novel is usually a violent confrontation with the criminal whom Scarpetta has been hunting. Several villains, including Temple Gault and Carrie Grethen, have escaped justice to be confronted again in following novels. Scarpetta has a passion for cooking, and Cornwell has authored two spin-off cookbooks influenced by the character's favourite recipes: *Scarpetta's Winter Table* (1998) and *Food to Die For: Secrets from Kay Scarpetta's Kitchen* (2002).

The tumultuous and well-publicised events in Cornwell's personal life – her divorce, her emerging lesbian sexuality, and her fight against alcoholism – have influenced the development of her literary characters: Scarpetta's niece, Lucy Farinelli, is a lesbian and has a drinking problem; Pete Marino drinks too much and harbours secret romantic feelings for Scarpetta. Scarpetta's love for Kay and Pete forms the emotional centre of her life, which by necessity is often coldly objective and scientific by nature, although Scarpetta always treats the victims of crime and their grieving families with respect. Scarpetta's own romantic relationships with Mark James, then Benton Wesley, have also been complex and traumatic, adding to the suspense of the series. Lucy's relationships are equally problematic as she falls in love with her programming partner at Quantico, Carrie Grethen, who is in fact the accomplice of the serial killer her aunt is chasing, Temple Gault. Grethen appears in *The Body Farm* (1994), *From Potter's Field* (1995) and *Point of Origin* (1998). The series is renowned for its strong female characters and Grethen continues this trend but from the perspective of pure evil. Eschewing traditional conceptions of femininity and maternity, Grethen's strengths are her cunning and icy intelligence which mask a psychotic bloodlust. Grethen, and several other villains of the series, all embody the concept of the self-regarding celebrity serial killer with seemingly supernatural powers of evading capture. With *The Last Precinct* (2000), Cornwell changed the narration of the novels from past to present tense. *Blow Fly* (2003) was the first novel of the series to be narrated in the third-person, a change in style which allowed for a greater range of character perspectives, including a closer look at the mind and motives of the killers. *Port Mortuary* reverts back to Scarpetta's point of view.

A life in the public eye

Although *Postmortem* received immediate commercial and critical success, Cornwell has met with difficulties in her personal life that have exposed her to often unfavourable media scrutiny. In 1993, she was involved in a serious car crash when her Mercedes hit a van and flipped over three times. Cornwell was drinking heavily at the time and received treatment for alcoholism at a clinic in Newport, Rhode Island, where she was diagnosed as bipolar. This event followed her affair with Margo Bennett, a married FBI agent whom she had met while doing research for her novels. Bennett's estranged husband and former FBI agent Eugene Bennett attempted to murder his wife by kidnapping a church minister in an effort to trap her. Eugene Bennett was sentenced to 23 years in prison in 1997, and Cornwell denied the affair had been responsible for his crime spree.

The publication of *The Last Precinct* began a new round of personal trials for Cornwell. The author Leslie Sachs claimed Cornwell had plagiarised his 1998 novel *The Virginia Ghost Murders*. He sent letters to her publisher, wrote about it on his webpage and even put stickers on his novel accusing Cornwell of plagiarism. Cornwell was granted a preliminary injunction against him by the US District Court of Eastern Virginia which also shut down his website and required all the stickers to be removed from his novel. Sachs fled to Belgium to escape the injunction. The libel suit was heard in Virginia in 2007, and Cornwell testified of her fear of being attacked after Sachs wrote that she was a neo-Nazi who was trying to have him murdered. As a result, she hired bodyguards and asked for a broader injunction. The judge demanded the defamatory posts be removed.

Cornwell was awarded $37,780 to cover the expenses of the trial. Sachs did not attend the proceedings or present any form of defence.

Jack the Ripper research and other projects

In 2002, Cornwell was once again at the centre of controversy with the publication of her true crime book, *Portrait of a Killer: Jack the Ripper – Case Closed.* The book was the culmination of a self-financed investigation in which she named the German-born British painter Walter Sickert of being the infamous Victorian serial killer. Cornwell made no reference to the work of writers Stephen Knight and Jean Overton Fuller who had already made similar claims implicating Sickert. Cornwell's book was scathingly received by both book reviewers and art critics who admire Sickert's work. In an attempt to prove her accusations, she purchased several Sickert paintings, and it is alleged that she destroyed one of them in the hopes of finding clues to the Ripper murders. Cornwell later donated her collection of Walter Sickert paintings to Harvard Art Museum.

Outside of the Kay Scarpetta novels, Cornwell has created two more series in the crime fiction field: the Andy Brazil/Judy Hammer novels and the Win Garano series. The Brazil/Hammer series are made of three novels: *Hornet's Nest* (1997), *Southern Cross* (1999) and *Isle of Dogs* (2001). Superintendent Judy Hammer works for the Virginia State police. Her right-hand man is a journalist Andy Brazil, who is assigned to follow the police on duty. Hammer also relies on the help of Deputy Chief Virginia West. The novels were a moderate success, although none achieved the status of the Kay Scarpetta series. *Hornet's Nest* features some of the core themes of Cornwell's writing, such as a graphic and grisly series of sexual mutilation murders, but the plot unravels in a more freewheeling style with an emphasis on comedy and romance.

The two novels in the Winston 'Win' Garano series proved more successful, and both were adapted into films. Win Garano is a dapper, sage and highly competent Massachusetts State Investigator who is of mixed-race parentage. Garano works for Monique Lamont, an ambitious and calculating District Attorney. *At Risk* (2006) was directed by Tom Loughlin and released in 2010. Andie MacDowell and Daniel Sunjata starred as Lamont and Garano respectively. The same year, Loughlin directed an adaptation of the second novel *The Front* (2008), with MacDowell and Sunjata reprising their roles. In *At Risk*, which began as a serialisation in the *New York Times,* Cornwell returns to the familiar territory of the Scarpetta novels with a forensic investigation, albeit here it is initiated for cynical reasons as Garano is forced to investigate a cold case of an elderly woman beaten to death 20 years ago in what seems to be a ploy to advance Lamont's political career.

Cornwell has received numerous awards and honours throughout her literary career. She was granted the ECPA Gold Medallion Book Award in the

Biography/Autobiography category for *A Time for Remembering*. *Postmortem* was awarded the Edgar Award, the John Creasey Memorial Award, the Anthony Award and the Macavity Award in 1991, which makes Cornwell the only author to have received these awards in a single year. The novel also won the *Prix du Roman d'Adventures* in 1992. Patricia Cornwell received the Gold Dagger for *Cruel and Unusual* in 1993, the Sherlock Award for Best Detective for the character Kay Scarpetta in 1999 and the British Book Awards' Crime Thriller of the Year for *Book of the Dead* in 2008. Cornwell is the first American author to receive this award.

The film rights to the Scarpetta novels have been acquired by Twentieth Century Fox studios. Angelina Jolie has been slated to play Scarpetta, although as of the time of writing pre-production on any Scarpetta film has yet to begin. Several studios have spent millions of dollars in movie development plans for the series which never came to fruition. At one point Cornwell courted Hollywood actresses Jodie Foster and Demi Moore to play Scarpetta, but Foster showed no interest and Cornwell and Demi Moore had serious disagreements about the potential project.

Patricia Cornwell currently lives in Massachusetts with her wife Staci Gruber, an Assistant Professor of Psychiatry at Harvard University. Cornwell has been a strong supporter of the Republican Party and is a close friend of former President George H.W. Bush, whom she refers to as 'Big George'. Recently, Cornwell has supported Democratic candidates including Hilary Clinton. She has also begun campaigning for gay rights. A one-time supporter of capital punishment, Cornwell reversed her position while researching for her novel *Predator* (2005) after she witnessed an execution by lethal injection.

Cornwell is a philanthropist, and her donations helped to found the Virginia Institute for Forensic Science and Medicine and created scholarships to the University of Tennessee's National Forensics Academy and Davidson College's Creative Writing Program. As a member of the McLean Hospital's National Council, she is an advocate for psychiatric research. She has also made donations to the John Jay College of Criminal Justice for the Crime Scene Academy.

Suggested reading

L. Mizejewski (2004) *Hardboiled & High Heeled: The Woman Detective in Popular Culture* (New York: Routledge).
P. Cornwell (2011) *Patricia Cornwell* http://www.patriciacornwell.com/.

Delphine Cingal

Crais, Robert (1953–)

Crais was born 20 June 1953, in Independence, Louisiana, to a family of oil refinery workers. He was brought up on the banks of the Mississippi River. At the age of 15, Crais read a copy of Raymond Chandler's *The Little Sister* (1949), which began his life-long fascination with crime fiction. Crais moved to Hollywood in 1976 and began his writing career as a scriptwriter for police procedural television series such as *Miami Vice, Cagney and Lacey* and *Hill Street Blues,* winning an Emmy Award for *Hill Street Blues.* In the mid-1980s Crais resigned his position as a contract writer and television producer to pursue a career as a novelist. His initial efforts were rejected for publication, but Crais began to formulate a character, Elvis Cole, loosely based on his father who died in 1985. With his debut novel *The Monkey's Raincoat* (1987), Crais introduced his series characters Elvis Cole and Joe Pike who have to this date appeared in 14 of his 17 novels.

Cole and Pike

Elvis Cole is a private investigator who has a variety of colourful eccentricities. Despite his outwardly glib manner, Cole is a tough Vietnam veteran trained in martial arts. Joe Pike is an ex-marine and occasional mercenary who assists Cole in his investigations. Crais had originally intended Pike to be killed at the end of the first novel but decided both characters had the potential to form a series. His decision was vindicated: *The Monkey's Raincoat* won the Anthony Award for Best First Novel in 1988. Crais continued with the series and achieved critical distinction with the eighth novel, *L.A. Requiem* (1999). In *L.A. Requiem,* Crais combined literary devices often absent from his previous novels, such as multiple points of view and intersecting storylines. Several of Crais's novels have examined the social history of Los Angeles and the Los Angeles Police Department. The depiction of South Central gangs and corrupt cops in *Free Fall* (1993) was inspired by the Rodney King riots, and *Sunset Express* (1996) featured a character and narrative that strongly resembled O.J. Simpson and his criminal trial. *The*

Watchman (2007) was the first novel in the series to feature Pike in the dominant role, and Crais has since alternated the series between Cole and Pike as the lead character. The other novels in the Cole/Pike series are *Stalking the Angel* (1989), *Lullaby Town* (1992), *Voodoo River* (1995), *Indigo Slam* (1997), *The Last Detective* (2003), *The Forgotten Man* (2003) and *Chasing Darkness* (2008). Crais's first non-series novel *Demolition Angel* (2000) introduced former LAPD bomb technician Carol Starkey, who later became a major character in the Cole/Pike series. Crais's second stand-alone novel *Hostage* (2001) was adapted into the 2005 film of the same title directed by Florent Emilio Siri with Bruce Willis in the leading role.

Steven Powell

Crumley, James (1939–2008)

American author of hyper-violent hard-boiled crime novels, Crumley never achieved mainstream commercial success in the crime writing market in the US during his lifetime, but his critical reputation has flourished in the years since his death. His novel *The Last Good Kiss* (1978) has been cited by crime writers such as Michael Connelly, George Pelecanos and Dennis Lehane as one of the finest novels in the genre.

Life and career

Born in Three Rivers, Texas, on 12 October 1939, Crumley attended the Georgia Institute of Technology on a Navy scholarship but left early to enlist in the U.S. Army, in which he served from 1958 to 1961. After leaving the Army, Crumley enrolled in the Texas A&I on a football scholarship, graduating with a BA in History in 1964. He received an MFA in Creative Writing from the University of Iowa in 1966. He then joined the English faculty at the University of Montana at Missoula, the city that would become his home and setting for much of his fiction. Crumley's first novel, *One to Count Cadence* (1969), was a Vietnam War-themed narrative which the author adapted from his master's thesis. Whilst he was struggling to write a follow-up novel, Crumley's close friend the poet Richard Hugo introduced him to the novels of Raymond Chandler. After deciding to write crime fiction, Crumley's second novel was the Chandler-inspired *The Wrong Case* (1975), which introduced readers to his first series character, the private detective Milo Milodragovitch. With his third novel, *The Last Good Kiss*, Crumley created his second series character C.W. Sughrue. Sughrue is significantly more violent and impulsive than Milodragovitch, as he is cynically embittered by a constant feeling of betrayal. The violent scenes are hyperbolically lurid, but for Sughrue the sheer thought of violence can lead to extended revenge fantasies reminiscent of Mickey Spillane's Mike Hammer novels. Like Hammer, Sughrue sees himself as a moral man forced to use amoral methods to enforce his code. Hired to track down a derelict author on a drinking binge, Sughrue's opening first-person narration to the novel have become iconic of Crumley's prose style, which merges poetic Romanticism with a cynical hard-boiled philosophy:

> When I finally caught up with Abraham Trahearne, he was drinking beer with an alcoholic bulldog named Fireball Roberts in a ramshackle joint just outside of Sonoma, California, drinking the heart right out of a fine spring afternoon. (Crumley, 1988, p. 1)

Crumley based Trahearne on his friend Richard Hugo, and the influence of Hugo's poetry would be an ongoing motif throughout his later novels. Crumley continued the Milodragovitch series in the novels *Dancing Bear* (1983) and *The Final Country* (2001), and the Sughrue series in *The Mexican Tree Duck* (1993) and *The Right Madness* (2005). He brought the two private detectives together in *Bordersnakes* (1996), in which both characters alternate first-person narration as they embark on seemingly separate vendettas which gradually converge. Crumley was married five times and fathered five children. He suffered from ill-health throughout much of his life and his final novel, *The Right Madness*, is dedicated to friends and family who cared for him during his illness. The narrative of *The Right Madness* often reads like an elegy to his career with the story climaxing in the Isle of Skye, Scotland, to which Crumley had travelled on several occasions and was the inspiration for one of Richard Hugo's volumes of poetry. James Crumley died on 17 September 2008.

Suggested reading

M. Fox (2008) 'James Crumley, Crime Novelist, Is Dead at 68' *The New York Times*, 19 September 2008 http://www.nytimes.com/2008/09/20/books/20crumley.html, date accessed 5 June 2011.

C. McDonald (2009) 'James Crumley: The Right Madness' *Rogue Males: Conversations and Confrontations about the Writing Life* (Madison, WI: Bleak House) pp. 7–20.

Steven Powell

Daly, Carroll John (1889–1958)

One of the most important figures in the history of the genre, Carroll John Daly was instrumental in the development of the hard-boiled school of crime writing. Although his popularity waned in the latter half of his career, and his work has not aged well, he is credited with writing one of the first hard-boiled crime stories with 'The False Burton Combs' which appeared in *Black Mask* magazine, December 1922. Daly wrote 17 novels and hundreds of short stories, occasionally using the pseudonym John D. Carroll.

Life and career

Carroll John Daly was born in Yonkers, New York, on 14 September 1889. He was educated at Yonkers High School and the Catholic De La Salle Institute. His early ambition was focused on becoming an actor, and he attended and graduated from the American Academy of Dramatic Arts before abandoning the career. Daly's love of theatre led him to work as an usher and projectionist and eventually the owner and manager of a chain of theatres in New York and New Jersey, including the first film theatre on the Atlantic City boardwalk. Daly married Margaret G. Blakley in 1913, and they had one son together. Daly's writing career began in 1922. Although he was to write for a variety of pulp magazines such as *Dime Detective*, *Detective Fiction Weekly* and *Clues,* it would be at *Black Mask* where he would find his greatest fame. Daly's first notable story at *Black Mask* was 'The False Burton Combs', in which the first-person narrator is unnamed and is not actually a detective but an adventurer who is paid to impersonate the Burton Combs of the title. Lee Horsley notes that the narrator 'occupies, at different stages of the story, the three roles kept carefully separate in most classic detective fiction, that is, victim, murderer and detective' (Horsley, 2009, p. 28).Thus, in the story's cynicism and toughness, Daly contributed to the genesis of many classic elements of the hard-boiled style.

Race Williams and other detectives

Daly's contribution would extend to creating some of the very first hard-boiled detectives. Kevin Burton Smith has identified Octavus Roy Cohen's Jim Hanvey and John E. Bruce's Sadipe Okukenu as literary PIs with hard-boiled traits that predated Daly's characters by at least a year, but Daly's detectives evidence more characteristics of what critics and readers would recognise as hard-boiled. And it was Daly's PIs that helped to form and popularise the genre. His first detective was the simply and aptly named 'Three Gun Terry' in a story of the same name for *Black Mask* in 1923. In the short story 'Knights of the Open Palm', Daly introduced his most popular character, Race Williams. As 'Knights of the Palm' was published in June 1923, the introduction of Williams predates the first appearance of Dashiell Hammett's Continental Op by several months. Williams works in a variety of jobs in several big-city locations, but he is always essentially an investigator whose favoured method of solving cases is violence not detection. He charges $25 an hour, plus extra if he has to kill someone, which is often. Williams has a strong moral code, which, in his own view, transcends the conventions of the law and justifies his use of violence. Similarly, he regards criminals as worse than just people who break the law, but evil foreigners and communists who hate America. Williams has a sidekick manservant, Jerry, an ally in the police department, Sergeant O'Rourke, and an opponent in Inspector Nelson. The Race Williams stories set the formula for future PIs and was a particular influence on Mickey Spillane's Mike Hammer. Daly's first novel *The White Circle* (1926) features a hero named Stacey Lee who dons a white mask and goes to battle against an evil organisation called the Black Circle. His second novel *The Snarl of the Beast* (1927) features Williams and is often regarded as the first private detective novel. Daly wrote seven more Race Williams novels including *The Third Murderer* (1931) in which Williams is pitted against three brothers – two of whom are gangsters and one is a genius. The story was notable for the gangsters' moll Florence Drummond aka 'The Flame' or 'The Girl with the Criminal Mind'. The novel was originally serialised as ' "The Flame" and Race Williams'. Another notable Williams' novel was *Murder from the East* (1935) set in the fictional country of Astran. *Death's Juggler* (1935) featured Satan Hall, a police detective every bit as violent, even murderous, as Race Williams. After Williams, Daly's most popular detective was Vee Brown. Frail-looking and less brutal than Williams, Brown is still quicker on the draw than the gangsters he is up against. In his spare time he writes popular songs under his real name Vivian. Brown was the leading character in two novels, *Murder Won't Wait* (1933) and *Emperor of Evil* (1936). In the latter, Brown meets his most interesting nemesis, the outwardly respectable, debonair Vincent Van Houton who is the secret head of the Black Death organisation and is also the Devil.

He is so skilled at hiding his identity, the police refuse to believe his guilt. Daly's sole screen credit is providing the story to *Ticket to a Crime* (1934) which featured another of his detective creations, Clay Holt. At the height of his popularity, Daly led a reclusive and modest existence in White Plains, New York. It has been claimed by William L. DeAndrea in *Encyclopedia Mysteriosa* and by other critics that Daly's name on a magazine cover could increase sales by up to 15 per cent. In a *Black Mask* readers' poll, Daly was named the fans favourite author, beating Erle Stanley Gardner and Dashiell Hammett into second and third place.

Decline in popularity and later years

Despite being one of the first hard-boiled crime writers, Daly's prose often descended into overblown melodrama, undermining any sense of gritty realism associated with the emerging genre. His narratives lacked the precision of style and plotting of some of his contemporaries and the undercurrent of social commentary found in Hammett's work. Daly was not well regarded by legendary *Black Mask* editor Joseph T. 'Cap' Shaw and stopped writing for the magazine in 1934 only to return with occasional pieces after Shaw left in 1936. By the late 1930s Daly was beginning to lose his popularity, and his work became more sporadic as he was unable to sell his fiction. His final novels were *Murder at Our House* (1950) and *Ready to Burn* (1951), the latter featuring Satan Hall. Daly moved to California where he ended his career writing dialogue for comic books. In his last years, Daly received a letter of tribute from Mickey Spillane: 'Yours was the first and only style of writing that ever influenced me in any way. Race was the model for Mike' (Spillane, 2011). Carroll John Daly died on 16 January 1958.

Suggested reading

L. Horsley (2009) *The Noir Thriller* (Basingstoke: Palgrave Macmillan).
W. F. Nolan (1985) *The Black Mask Boys: Masters in the Hard-boiled School of Detective Fiction* (New York: W. Marrow).

Steven Powell

Davis, Norbert (1909–49)

A prolific writer of hard-boiled fiction, Davis was born in Morrison, Illinois. His parents broke with family tradition by choosing not to name him after his distant relation, the Scottish poet Robert Burns, a connection long prized by the family. He began writing in the late 1920s and early 1930s while studying for a law degree at Stanford, California. He never completed the law exam, but his first published story, 'Reform Racket', appeared in *Black Mask* in 1932. Due in part to his idiosyncratic blend of humour with a hard-boiled style gleaned from the pages of *Black Mask*, Davis found success difficult to achieve and sometimes struggled to find a wider audience for his many stories and later novels. He was a member of the Fictioneers and collaborated with its founder W.T. Ballard to write *Murder Picks the Jury* (1947, credited as Harrison Hunt). Davis was respected by another member of the Fictioneers and a onetime neighbour, Raymond Chandler. The Austrian philosopher Ludwig Wittgenstein was another admirer of his work. Davis's second wife was the writer Frances Crane, with whom he moved to Connecticut in 1949. Later in that year he committed suicide in Massachusetts.

Davis is best known for his characters William 'Bail Bond' Dodd and Max Latin, both of whom appeared in his *Dime Detective* short stories. Latin was the perfect vehicle for Davis's eccentric humour. Latin's 'office' is the back booth of a restaurant where he spends most his days drinking. When he is hired on a case so many madcap laughs ensue that Ed Lin has argued that Latin is a more intelligent precursor to detective Frank Drebin in the *Naked Gun* film series. The five Latin stories were released in the much-admired volume *The Adventures of Max Latin* (1988) with an introduction by John D. MacDonald. Davis was also well-known for the screwball pair Doan and Carstairs, a detective and a massive Great Dane, the latter being argu-ably the main character of many of the Doan and Carstairs stories. Norbert published several novels featuring this pair, including *Holocaust House* (1940), *The Mouse in the Mountain* (1943), *Sally's in the Alley* (1943) and *Oh, Murderer Mine* (1946). All of these stories, including his short story 'Something for the Sweeper' (1937), are now widely available on the internet. The Doan and Carstairs stories typify Davis's first person narrative style, which looks askance and with something of a lightly ironic tone at many of the unusual situations that the pair encounter, yet it is ultimately leavened with a whimsical humour and faith that the crises the pair fall into will be resolved.

Suggested reading

J.L. Apostolou (2001) 'Norbert Davis: Profile of a Pulp Writer' *Black Mask Magazine. com* http://www.blackmaskmagazine.com/bm_03.html, date accessed 29 October 2010.

D. Geherin (1986) 'Max Latin: Norbert Davis' *The American Private Eye: The Image in Fiction* (New York: Frederick Ungar) pp. 50–5.

L. Server (2002) 'Davis, Norbert' *Encyclopedia of Pulp Fiction Writers: The Essential Guide to More Than 200 Pulp Pioneers and Mass-market Masters* (New York: Facts on File, Inc.) pp. 77–9.

Chris Pak

Eberhart, Mignon G(ood) (1899–1996)

Mystery writer best known for her unusual detective characters Nurse Sarah Keate and sidekick Lance O'Leary and detective writer Susan Dare, she also contributed stories to popular series such as *Rex Stout Mystery* and *The Saint*.

Born Mignonette Good in Lincoln, Nebraska, on 6 July 1899, Eberhart attended Nebraska Wesleyan University (1917–20) and became a journalist before publishing her first novel in 1929. Her writing career spanned almost 70 years and included 59 novels, several plays, and many short stories, but she had her greatest successes with novels concerning detective heroines Sarah Keate and Susan Dare, which were originally published from the 1930s to the 1950s. She was an early champion of the female sleuth and an award-winning writer of suspense and mystery stories. Eberhart was awarded a D.Litt. by Nebraska Wesleyan University in 1935. Eberhart was married three times: firstly to Alanson C. Eberhart in 1923. They were later divorced, and she married John P. Hazen Perry in 1946 whom she divorced in 1948. She remarried Alanson Eberhart the same year.

Sarah Keate first appeared in *The Patient in Room 18* in 1929. In this, as in later novels, the nurse-detective with her private eye sidekick Lance O'Leary must catch a killer to clear Keate of suspicion; the device of having the narrator as prime suspect is an Eberhart specialty. Most of Eberhart's work sold well, but more successful from a literary point of view are the stories featuring Susan Dare, a mystery writer who uses her analytical skills to solve real mysteries. Because of her female detectives and predictable plotlines, Eberhart is often described as 'the American Agatha Christie', but in fact Sarah Keate predates Christie's own female detective, Miss Marple, who first appeared in 1930. Though Eberhart wrote clue-puzzle mystery stories, the gothic elements of her work are very much in the spirit of her time; similar features appear in the much darker and tougher work of Cornell Woolrich. Many of Eberhart's tales feature a mixture of romance, exotic locations and plotting reminiscent of the 'had-I-but-known' school pioneered by Mary Roberts Rinehart. Another memorable series character was James Wickwire, a senior banker and amateur sleuth who has to save his bank and clients against various criminal scams. Eberhart managed to achieve a remarkable consistency over her long career. She served a term as president of the Mystery Writers of America (1977) and won several awards, including the Scotland Yard Prize (1930) for *While the Patient Slept*, the Mystery Writers of America Grand Master award (1970) and the Malice Domestic Lifetime Achievement Award (1994). Ten of Eberhart's novels and stories were adapted into films, including *The Patient in Room 18* (1929) filmed in 1938 and *The White Cockatoo* (1933) filmed in 1935. Eberhart died aged 97 on 8 October 1996, in Greenwich, Connecticut.

Suggested reading

R. Cypert *America's Agatha Christie: Mignon Good Eberhart, Her Life and Works* (Selinsgrove, PA: Susquehanna University Press, 2005).
M. Gussow (1996) 'Mignon Eberhart, Novelist, 97; Blended Mystery and Romance' *New York Times*, October 9. p. D19.

Christopher Routledge

Ellroy, James (1948–)

One of the most innovative and controversial American crime writers to emerge in the past 30 years, James Ellroy has achieved originality and distinction in his historical crime novels written in a radically sparse hard-boiled prose style.

Life

Born Lee Earle Ellroy on 4 March 1948 in Los Angeles to Geneva Odelia Ellroy (née Hilliker), a registered nurse, and Armand Lee Ellroy, a freelance accountant, Ellroy's childhood would prove volatile: his parents' fractious, troubled marriage ended in divorce in 1954. Geneva Hilliker retained primary custody of her son, and in early 1958, they moved to the small town of El Monte near Los Angeles, which Ellroy's father described as 'Shitsville USA'. Ellroy himself did not take to El Monte and his relationship with his mother became strained. She drank excessively and once struck him when he told her he would prefer to live with his father. On 22 June 1958, Ellroy returned home after a weekend with his father to find the police there. They informed him that his mother had been murdered. Her strangled body was found in an ivy strip outside the local Arroyo High School. An investigation ensued, but the case was never solved. Ellroy's immediate reaction to the news of his mother's murder was ambiguous, as he would later recall in his memoir *My Dark Places*, 'I hated her. I hated El Monte. Some unknown killer just bought me a brand-new beautiful life' (Ellroy, 1997, p. 83).

If the ten-year-old Ellroy was repressing grief over the death of his mother, he was nevertheless more outwardly relieved that he could now live with his carefree, workshy father. For his eleventh birthday, Ellroy was given two books by his father: *The Complete Sherlock Holmes* by Arthur Conan Doyle, and *The Badge* (1958), a non-fiction literary accompaniment to the television series *Dragnet*, written by the creator and star of *Dragnet*, Jack Webb. It would be the latter book which spurned Ellroy's life-long fascination with both true crime and crime fiction. Webb had influential connections within the Los Angeles Police Department, up to and including Chief William H. Parker. *The Badge* was written as pro-LAPD propaganda and detailed police procedure and included some of the more violent cases, which the censorship laws of the time prohibited from being portrayed on television. One case in particular was to haunt Ellroy for the rest of his life. *The Badge* featured a ten-page summary of the unsolved murder of Elizabeth Short, aka 'The Black Dahlia'. The tortured body of Miss Short had been discovered on a vacant lot on 15 January 1947. Elizabeth Short's murder led to one of the biggest homicide investigations in Los Angeles' history. For Ellroy, who was born one year after the murder occurred, the Black Dahlia case would provide the necessary symbiotic link to the unsolved murder of his mother, and Elizabeth Short provided the means for him to love and grieve for his mother by proxy. Ellroy began to have nightmares about the murder, but he would also fantasise about rescuing Elizabeth Short and catching her killer. Ellroy would acknowledge the connections between Geneva Hilliker and Elizabeth Short in his fictionalisation of the Dahlia case, his breakthrough novel *The Black Dahlia* (1987). He claimed to have wept after finishing the last page. The dedication to the novel reads:

> *Mother:*
> *Twenty-nine Years Later,*
> *This Valediction in Blood.*
> (Ellroy, 2006)

In the short term, reading *The Badge* did little to encourage Ellroy's compliance with societal norms. Soon after his mother's death, Ellroy began to truant from school and to shoplift. Armand Ellroy was usually unemployed and working on get-rich-quick schemes which invariably went wrong. His father's health began to rapidly decline after a series of strokes and heart attacks, and he had little control over his son. Ellroy's reading habits quickly moved from Sherlock Holmes and Hardy Boys stories to Nero Wolfe and Mickey Spillane. From 1962 to 1965, Ellroy was enrolled at the predominantly Jewish Fairfax High School. As one of the few Gentile students in attendance, Ellroy sought attention by making anti-Semitic comments and joining the American Nazi Party. After being expelled from school for fighting and truancy, Ellroy briefly joined the United States Army, and was stationed at Fort Polk, Louisiana. Finding military life repressive compared to the lack of accountability at home, Ellroy faked a nervous breakdown in order to be discharged. That same year Armand Ellroy died in hospital after one final stroke: his last words to Ellroy were 'Try to pick up every waitress who serves you.' Ellroy cashed his father's last three social security cheques and used the money to get drunk. Aside from his alcoholism, between 1966 and 1969 Ellroy was a serious substance abuser of amphetamines and Benzedrex nasal inhalers. He would go through periods of homelessness, often sleeping in the parks of Los Angeles carrying around with him a bust of Beethoven: Ellroy is an admirer of German Romanticism in Classical music. Ellroy was also feeding an addiction to his sexual voyeurism, often breaking into the upper-middle class houses of Hancock Park in LA, making himself sandwiches from other people's food and sniffing women's underwear. His drug addiction could fuel night-long masturbation sessions. Ellroy received his first arrest for burglary in 1968, and due to the increased security presence in LA following the paranoia created by the Charles Manson family murders, he stopped breaking into houses the following year. But his troubles with the law would continue; between 1968 and 1975, Ellroy was arrested multiple times for offences such as petty theft and driving under the influence. Although Ellroy was never sentenced to prison, he did serve several short terms in the Los Angeles County Jail. In the mid-70s Ellroy nearly died from a lung abscess, pneumonia and post-alcoholic brain syndrome. He achieved sobriety through Alcoholics Anonymous and began caddying at the Hillcrest Country Club until he was fired for punching a fellow caddy who owed him money. He subsequently worked at the Bel-Air Country Club and began to outline and draft his first novel in 1979. For his debut work, *Brown's Requiem* (1981), Ellroy drew heavily on his experiences as a caddy and his love for Classical music – his original title for the novel was 'Concerto for Orchestra'. The story is told from the first-person perspective of Fritz Brown, a car repossesor and low-rent private eye who is hired by the psychopathic racist golf caddy Freddy 'Fat Dog' Baker to spy on his sister Jane, who Fat Dog has grown to hate due to her close relationship with an elderly Jewish man. There are elements of Ellroy in both the Brown and Fat Dog characters. It transpires that both Jane and Fat Dog are unaware of their Jewish heritage. Ellroy made the characters Jewish to atone for his past anti-Semitism. Well read in hard-boiled crime fiction, Ellroy was heavily influenced by Raymond Chandler in his debut novel, and he included several overt references to the author, such as when Brown is walking into the Hotel Westwood:

> The flat finished white stucco walls, ratty Persian carpets in the hallway and mahogany doors almost had me convinced it was 1938 and that my fictional predecessor Philip Marlowe was about to confront me with a wisecrack. (Ellroy, 2001, p. 193)

Ellroy was able to find an agent and subsequently publisher (Avon) for the novel relatively quickly. Upon the publication of *Brown's Requiem,* Ellroy changed his name from Lee Earle Ellroy to James Ellroy, taking his new first name from a pseudonym his father had used, 'James Brady'. Ellroy moved to Eastchester NY, just outside New York City and worked as a caddy at the Wykagl Country Club. Although *Brown's Requiem* was greatly indebted to Chandler, Ellroy abruptly decided to never write another private eye novel and, furthermore, would argue that Chandler's contribution to crime fiction is overstated and minor in comparison to Dashiell Hammett. Ellroy's second novel, *Clandestine* (1982), is a heavily fictionalised, chronologically altered account of his mother's murder with name changes. The case is solved in the novel, with the culprit being a character modelled on Ellroy's father. Ellroy claimed to have written the novel as a means of ridding himself of the influence of his mother's murder in his fiction. His next few projects would be very different, but his inability to find a publisher for his work would mark a low point in his career. Ellroy wrote half of an historical fiction novel, 'The Confessions of Bugsy Siegel', which he eventually abandoned. He also wrote a graphically violent novel 'L.A. Death Trip' about a psychological duel between a detective and a serial killer, which Avon refused to publish and was subsequently turned down by 17 other publishers. Shortly thereafter, his agent dropped him as a client. Ellroy's luck changed when he visited the Mysterious Bookstore in New York and abruptly walked into the office of renowned crime fiction editor and publisher Otto Penzler and introduced himself as the 'Demon Dog of American crime fiction'. Penzler had no idea who Ellroy was at the time, but after reading his two published novels he became convinced Ellroy was a major talent. The 'Demon Dog' persona was skilfully developed by Ellroy and went a long way to making him one of the most recognisable and famous American crime writers of his time. Ellroy, Penzler, and agent Nat Sobel began to radically rework 'L.A. Death Trip', which was eventually published by the Mysterious Press as *Blood on the Moon* (1984). Ellroy had originally ended 'L.A. Death Trip' with the detective and serial killer killing each other, but Ellroy was persuaded by Penzler to turn Detective Lloyd Hopkins into a series character. Hopkins would return in two more novels, *Because the Night* (1984) and *Suicide Hill* (1985). Hopkins was an ambiguous character – intellectually brilliant but racist and sexually obsessive – and he would signal Ellroy's emerging morally ambivalent, sometimes abhorrent but complex, sympathetic characters.

In 1986, Ellroy wrote one final book for Avon. He was paid a forward which finally enabled him to quit caddying and start writing full-time. Avon insisted on the title *Silent Terror*, but Ellroy's first choice of title was *Killer on the Road*. A bizarre first-person narrative of a serial killer on a murderous rampage through the US, *Silent Terror* was republished in 1990 by Avon with Ellroy's preferred title.

Los Angeles quartet

Ellroy was paid a substantial sum for the film rights of *The Black Dahlia* shortly before the novel was published. Ellroy seized the opportunity to raise his profile by donating the bulk of the money to the publicity budget for the novel. *The Black Dahlia* was a critical and commercial success, which Ellroy built upon by writing three follow-up novels set in the Los Angeles of the 1940s and 1950s: *The Big Nowhere* (1988), *L.A. Confidential* (1990) and *White Jazz* (1992), which would be known collectively as the L.A. Quartet. *The Big Nowhere* was set amidst the violent paranoia of the Red Scare. *L.A. Confidential*, an epic narrative set from 1950 to 1958 which included fictionalised accounts of LA lore such as the Bloody Christmas police scandal and the killing of Johnny Stompanato, would mark the beginning of Ellroy's clipped and sparse prose style. Ellroy claimed to have arrived at the style almost by accident: after the publishers decided the original 800-page manuscript needed to be reduced for the sake of publishing costs, Ellroy decided that not a single scene could be excised without compromising the narrative. Instead, he revised the manuscript by removing any unnecessary words: verbs, adverbs, conjunctions. Thus, Ellroy was able to dramatically reduce the length of the manuscript without losing a single scene. *White Jazz* ended the Quartet with Ellroy adapting the prose style which merges surreal and disorientating jazz with the first-person narrative fever dream of racist, insomniac detective Dave 'the Enforcer' Klein.

Underworld U.S.A. trilogy

Ellroy's next project would surpass the Quartet in ambition and achievement, and it had its origins in his reading of Don DeLillo's fictional biography of Lee Harvey Oswald, *Libra* (1988). DeLillo's novel fascinated Ellroy and inspired him to write about the Kennedy assassination. He strived to make his novel *American Tabloid* considerably different from DeLillo's. Thus, Lee Harvey Oswald, the main protagonist in DeLillo's novel, does not appear in *American Tabloid* (1995). Ellroy's novel is set between 1958 and 22 November 1963 and is taken from the perspective of the intelligence community and the underworld figures conspiring to assassinate President Kennedy. Ellroy's intention was to demythologise the Kennedy era and the notion of Kennedy as a Liberal martyr. In the prologue to the novel, Ellroy was uncompromising about his fictional version of events: *'America was never innocent. We popped our cherry on the boat over and looked back with no regrets'* (Ellroy, 1995).

American Tabloid won *Time* magazine's Novel of the Year. Ellroy's next book was his memoir *My Dark Places* (1996) which detailed his unsuccessful reinvestigation into his mother's murder. The book was emotionally powerful as Ellroy comes to a loving, respectful relationship with his mother that he never achieved when she was alive. Ellroy followed *American Tabloid* with two sequels which form the Underworld U.S.A. trilogy, *The Cold Six Thousand* (2001) and *Blood's A Rover* (2009). *The Cold Six Thousand* begins on the day of the Kennedy assassination and includes the FBI's infiltration of the Civil Rights Movement and the escalation of the Vietnam War before ending with the assassinations of Martin Luther King and Robert F. Kennedy. Ellroy's prose style came under criticism for the first time with *The Cold Six Thousand* as critics complained the novel was alienating and difficult to read. During the exhaustive publicity tour for the novel, Ellroy suffered from panic attacks and became paranoid that he was suffering from melanoma. The tour was cancelled early with Ellroy citing ill health and exhaustion. The tour preceded the break-up of his second marriage. Ellroy was married to publishing executive Mary Doherty from 1988 to 1991. He then married feminist writer Helen Knode. This union was dissolved in 2006, after the stresses of *The Cold Six Thousand* tour led to Ellroy's addiction to painkillers: Ellroy overdosed three times before beating the addiction in a rehabilitation clinic. Ellroy's personal problems led to the delay in writing the concluding volume of the trilogy, *Blood's A Rover*. However, during this time, he revised the novel's content on the advice of his ex-wife Helen Knode. Ellroy also added elements of his most recent circumstances, namely fictionalising two recent love affairs in the novel. The character of the ultra left-wing activist 'Comrade' Joan Rosen Klein is based on a woman he has publicly identified simply as Joan with whom he had an affair towards the end of his second marriage. The novel is dedicated 'To J.M Comrade; For Everything You Gave Me' (Ellroy, 2009). The following year saw the release of Ellroy's second memoir, *The Hilliker Curse*, which expanded on Ellroy's often destructive relationships with women throughout his life, including the two relationships which inspired much of the narrative of *Blood's A Rover*. In 2010, Ellroy announced that he was writing a second LA Quartet: four novels that would precede the original Quartet chronologically and feature many of his iconic characters.

Suggested reading

A. M. Flügge (2010) *James Ellroy and the Novel of Obsession* (Trier: Wissenschaftlicher Verlag Trier).

S. Powell (2012) *Conversations with James Ellroy* (Jackson: University Press of Mississippi).

P. Wolfe (2005) *Like Hot Knives to the Brain: James Ellroy's Search for Himself* (Lanham: Lexington Books).

Steven Powell

Evanovich, Janet (1943–)

Janet Evanovich is best known for her popular series of crime novels featuring bounty hunter Stephanie Plum. To date, the series consists of 18 books, all set in Trenton, New Jersey. Evanovich has also written two NASCAR-themed crime novels and a graphic novel (co-written with her daughter) featuring auto mechanic and amateur sleuth, Alexandra Barnaby. Before she turned her attention to crime fiction, Evanovich produced three romance novels under the name Steffie Hall and nine under her own name. She has also co-written with Charlotte Hughes a series of humorous romantic suspense novels set in South Carolina. Evanovich has won numerous awards for her writing, including the Crime Writers Association's John Creasy Memorial Award, Last Laugh Award and Silver Dagger Award; Left Coast Crime's Lefty Award; the Independent Mystery Booksellers' Dilys Award; and the Quill Award for Mystery/Suspense/Thriller.

Early years

Evanovich was born Janet Schneider on 22 April 1943, in South River, New Jersey. She recalls that her family, particularly a supportive aunt, was tolerant of her 'loony imagination' as a child (Evanovich, 2011). Evanovich graduated from South River High School and then studied painting at Douglass College, a women's college that is part of Rutgers University in New Jersey. While at Douglass, Evanovich earned money by working various jobs including office temp, waitress, insurance claims adjuster and used car saleswoman. She married Peter Evanovich, a doctoral student in mathematics at Rutgers University in 1964 and graduated from Douglass with a BA in 1965. After the births of her two children, Alexandra and Peter, Evanovich decided to become a homemaker. She relates that far from stifling her creativity, activities she engaged in while staying at home with her children, such as cooking, colouring and playing with toys, in fact stimulated her imagination.

When she reached her 30s, Evanovich began to write in her free time, but she did not immediately find success. At first she attempted to write the 'Great American Novel' and completed three manuscripts in the course of ten years. All were rejected by publishers. Evanovich then tried her hand at genre fiction and wrote two romance novels. When these met with more rejections, Evanovich took a hiatus from writing and joined a temp agency, working as a secretary. Four months later, the second of the romance novels she had submitted, *Hero at Large*, was accepted by Berkley/ Jove Publications.

Professional success

Evanovich's *Hero at Large* was published in 1987 in Berkley/Jove's Second Chance at Love category romance line under the pseudonym Steffie Hall. Delighted with the 'staggering' two thousand dollars she had been advanced for her first published novel, Evanovich left her secretarial job and began to write full time. For the next few years, Evanovich produced romances for Bantam Loveswept. She then found that she was getting bored with romance and wanted to move toward writing novels that included more action.

Evanovich claims that her protagonist Stephanie Plum's career was inspired by the Robert De Niro action comedy film *Midnight Run* (1988), in which De Niro plays a bounty hunter. Once she had an idea of who she wanted her main character to be and what that character would do, Evanovich spent time researching the life of a bond enforcement agent before beginning to write. She shadowed bond enforcement agents and members of the Trenton police department, learned how to shoot a gun and even took improvisational acting classes in order to help her create the quick, witty dialogue that characterises the Plum series. Evanovich admits that there are elements of her own life in the Plum novels, particularly in some of Stephanie Plum's experiences and habits and in the close-knit community of 'the Burg' where the stories take place; she comments, 'I wouldn't go so far as to say Stephanie is an autobiographical character, but I will admit to knowing where she lives' (Evanovich, 2011). The first novel in the series, *One for the Money*, was published in 1994. It received good reviews and the film rights were sold to Columbia Tristar. It was finally adapted for the big screen and released in 2012 starring Katherine Heigl in the Plum role and directed by Julie Anne Robinson. Plum had previously been portrayed by Lynn Collins in an unsuccessful television film in 2002. Evanovich recognised early the value of keeping readers engaged with her work. After the third Stephanie Plum book – *Three to Get Deadly* (1997) – was published, Evanovich began to hold a naming contest for each book in the Plum series: fans submit ideas, and the winning name becomes the title of the next novel. The sixth book in the series, *Hot Six* (2000), was the first of Evanovich's novels to reach the number one spot on the New York Times Best Seller list. The rest of the novels in the series to date have all debuted at number one. All of the novels in the series are numerically titled in sequence; thus, *Seven Up* (2001), *Hard Eight* (2002), *To the Nines* (2003).

Evanovich has stated that she aims to achieve the feel of a character-driven television comedy like *Seinfeld* with her novels in the Plum series. Consequently, the strongest attributes of the series are its idiosyncratic, appealing characters and slapstick action sequences. The series is also notable for its feminist slant, which is evident in quirky but strong and diverse female characters such as Plum, former prostitute Lula who becomes Plum's co-worker and sidekick, and Plum's eccentric but canny Grandma Mazur. Plum is a divorcee who grows to enjoy honing her ever-improving skills in a non-traditional career and balks at the idea of a conventional 'Burg' marriage to attractive police officer Joe Morelli. Plum vacillates between sexual relationships with Morelli and the mysterious Ranger, thereby providing a source of constant romantic conflict and effectively allowing Plum to remain independent.

After the Plum series proved to be a popular success, Evanovich created a business called 'Evanovich Inc.', started with the money from the film option on her first Plum novel, in order to better market her name and her work. Evanovich's husband, son, daughter and son-in-law are employed full-time by Evanovich Inc. Through strategic marketing and shrewd business decisions, including purchasing back the rights to Evanovich's original romance novels before the books could be reissued and selling them to a different publisher, Evanovich Inc. has become a multi-million dollar company. Evanovich also co-wrote with Ina Yalof a how-to guide for aspiring writers, *How I Write: Secrets of a Bestselling Author* (2006), after she found herself constantly answering questions from fans ambitious to begin their own writing careers. Evanovich currently lives in Hanover, New Hampshire, and continues to write the Stephanie Plum series and other fiction.

Suggested reading

T. D'haen (2009) 'Plum's the Girl! Janet Evanovich and the Empowerment of Ms Common America' *Investigating Identities: Questions of Identity in Contemporary International Crime Fiction*. M. Krajenbrink and K.M. Quinn eds. (Amsterdam: Rodophi).

W.J. Heising (1999) *Detecting Women 2: Reader's Guide and Checklist for Mystery Series Written by Women* (Dearborn, MI: Purple Moon Press).

E.B. Lindsay (2007) 'Janet Evanovich (1943-)' *Great Women Mystery Writers*. (Westport, Conn: Greenwood Press).

Megan Hoffman

Faulkner, William (1897–1962)

Winner of two Pulitzer prizes and recipient of the Nobel Prize in Literature (1949), Faulkner wrote one out-and-out crime thriller, *Sanctuary* (1931), but crime and detection feature in several of his other stories and the themes of morbidity, perversion and obsession are present throughout his work. Faulkner was also a screenwriter, sharing a credit with Leigh Brackett and Jules Furthman for the screenplay of Howard Hawks's 1946 adaptation of Chandler's *The Big Sleep*.

William Faulkner (originally 'Falkner') was born 25 September 1897 in New Albany, Mississippi, and grew up in nearby Oxford, Mississippi, the town where he lived for most of his life. His earliest published works include poetry, plays and short stories, but he is best known for his experimental 'regionalist' novels about the inhabitants of Yoknapatawpha County, including *Sartoris, The Sound and the Fury* (both 1929), *As I Lay Dying* (1930), *Light in August* (1932) and, arguably his greatest achievement, *Absalom, Absalom!* (1936). Faulkner married Estelle Franklin in 1929 and the union produced two daughters: in 1931 Estelle gave birth to a girl they named Alabama. The birth was premature, and Alabama lived only a few days. In 1933, their second daughter Jill was born.

Sanctuary was written deliberately as a commercial thriller and was described by Andre Malraux as 'the intrusion of Greek tragedy into the detective story' (Malraux, 1952, p. 94). It tells the story of Temple Drake, a Mississippi debutante who is kidnapped by a vicious killer named Popeye. *Sanctuary* is a violent book with scenes of murder and rape. It was, Faulkner said, 'the most horrific tale I could imagine' (Blotner, 1991, p. 233). Unsurprisingly, it was initially rejected by editor Harrison Smith on the grounds of taste. Besides charting Temple Drake's decline, the novel explores mob justice, the inconsistent morality of small town officials and the limitations and arbitrariness of the legal system.

Sanctuary is significant not only for its boundary-testing subject matter, but also because it is an early and successful example of a crime novel with aspirations beyond the genre. Faulkner later wrote a series of mystery stories featuring the detective character Uncle Gavin, who also appears in *Intruder in the Dust* (1948). Faulkner claimed to have learned plotting from Melville Davisson Post, whose best-known detective is Uncle Abner.

Faulkner's contribution to crime fiction also extends to film. He contributed scripts to many B movies in the 1940s, but also worked on movies such as *To Have and Have Not* (1944) (with Jules Furthman), and he made an uncredited contribution to the 1945 adaptation of James M. Cain's novel *Mildred Pierce*. He was working as a screenwriter in 1949 when he was awarded the Nobel Prize in Literature. Faulkner was a heavy drinker, often planning his drinking binges between writing projects. He died of a heart attack on 6 July 1962.

Suggested reading

J. Blotner (1991) *Faulkner: A Biography* (New York: Vintage Books).
D. Minter (1980) *William Faulkner: His Life and Work* (Baltimore: MD, Johns Hopkins University Press).

Christopher Routledge

Fearing, Kenneth (1902–61)

Poet and novelist notable for his innovative, experimental detective and mystery narratives, as well as his left-wing political views which were occasionally channelled through his writing.

Fearing was born in Oak Park, Illinois, a location famous as the birthplace of Ernest Hemingway. Fearing attended the same school, Oak Park and River Forest High School, as Hemingway and, like the author, edited the school newspaper. He attended the University of Illinois and the University of Wisconsin before moving to New York in the mid-1920s, ostensibly to become a journalist but also to write poetry.

During the 1920s and 1930s, Fearing began to make his name as a poet with the collections *Angel Arms* (1929), *Poems* (1935) (which won him the first of two Guggenheim Fellowships, the second being awarded in 1939), and *Dead Reckoning* (1938), with a *Collected Poems* following in 1940. His work was published in *The New Yorker*, and he was also one of the founding editors of the left-wing publication *The Partisan Review*. However, to support himself Fearing also wrote lurid pulp fiction and soft-core pornography, for which he adopted the pseudonym Kirk Wolff.

Fearing's most notable novels are *The Hospital* (1939), *Dagger Of The Mind* (1941), *Clark Gifford's Body* (1942) and his most celebrated work *The Big Clock* (1946). *The Big Clock* is a detective story with an unusual approach to narrative and genre themes. Like *The Hospital*, it is compiled as a series of chapters written from the first-person perspectives of different characters. The novel largely ignores the police force, locating itself instead within a vast magazine publishing empire which also acts as an allegory for the tiers of American society. The never-ending social and financial machinery of the titular 'Big Clock' is a novelistic development of the themes of encroaching mechanisation explored in Fearing's poetry. By not making a mystery of the central murder itself, and instead creating a premise whereby the protagonist, George Stroud, must investigate himself as a suspect, Fearing turns the motifs of the detective novel into a voyage of unpleasant self-discovery. Stroud learns from his associates that that the man he is tracking is a vain, snobbish and philandering drunk. There is also an atypical, for the genre, focus on contemporary art. A key plot point features a painter named Louise Patterson, based on a real life expressionist painter and friend of Fearing, Alice Neel. The novel was later adapted into two films: John Farrow's faithful 1948 adaptation starring Ray Milland and Charles Laughton, and the 1987 film *No Way Out*, which updated the plot to incorporate the politics of the Cold War.

Although he continued to publish, the final decade of Fearing's life was characterised by heavy drinking, poverty and general bad health. He died in New York on 26 June 1961 of a malignant melanoma.

Suggested reading

C. Nelson (n.d) 'Kenneth Fearing' *Modern American Poetry* http://www.english. illinois.edu/maps/poets/a_f/fearing/fearing.htm, date accessed 22 February 2011.
R. M. Ryley (1994) 'Introduction' *Kenneth Fearing: Complete Poems*. R. M. Ryley, ed. (Orono, ME: The National Poetry Foundation) pp. xlix–lxi.

David Hering

Fisher, Rudolph (1897–1934)

African-American novelist and short story writer, best known for his pioneering work in black detective fiction, as well as balancing careers in both writing and medicine.

Born Rudolph John Chauncey Fisher on 9 May 1897 in Washington DC, and raised by his parents in Rhode Island, Fisher graduated from public school before attending Brown University between 1915 and 1919. He received an MA in Biology in 1920, the same year that he entered Howard Medical School where he studied roentgenology (the science and uses of X-Rays in medicine). In the years after graduation, he began practising as a roentgenologist while also writing and contributing short stories to periodicals. His first published short story 'City Of Refuge' appeared in *The Atlantic Monthly* in February 1925. During the 1920s, he began to associate with the key figures of the Harlem Renaissance (Langston Hughes called him 'the wittiest of these New Negroes of Harlem' (Hughes, 1976, p. 301)). Paul Robeson was also a friend, and Fisher's essay 'The Caucasian Storms Harlem' (1927) satirically discussed the prevailing trends of black entertainers playing to white audiences.

Fisher's story 'High Yaller' (1925) explored the various prejudices between black Americans of different skin tone, and his first novel, *The Walls Of Jericho* (1928) presented an often satirical picture of Harlem divided along the lines of class, discussing the relationships between characters of different social strata alongside an evocation of the biblical tale of Joshua.

The Conjure Man Dies

Fisher's second and final novel *The Conjure Man Dies* (1932) plays upon a number of established detective and mystery conceits in its tale of the murder and apparent resurrection of a Harlem mystic named N'Gana Frimbo. The central crime is a variation on the locked room mystery, while the gathered cast of potential suspects and deductive reasoning of the detectives recalls the work of Sir Arthur Conan Doyle and Agatha Christie. However *The*

Conjure Man Dies is principally remarkable for being the first novel to feature an African-American detective. All characters, including the protagonists – Dr John Archer and detective Perry Dart – are black, and Fisher incorporates within an ostensibly plot-driven murder mystery a meditation on race and a portrait of Harlem's underworld that is both informative and satirical. There is a dry reference to Harlem's murder 'epidemic', and a comic sub-plot wherein a private investigator, the bumbling Bubber Brown, attempts to save his friend Jinx Jenkins from the central murder charge.

With the character of Frimbo, Fisher creates a complex, articulate enigma whose conversations with Archer create a forum for discussion of the inter-section between race, mysticism, philosophy, psychology and medicine, as well as the question of the African-American's relationship to Africa. Frimbo's belief in escaping the philosophy of determinism through out-of-body experiences, as well as his alleged royal heritage allegorises the individual's role in questions of crime, destiny and race. In the novel, the invented Kingdom of Buwongo is crucially adjacent to Liberia, a country founded by freed American slaves. John Archer would appear once more in a posthumously published story, 'John Archer's Nose', in 1935.

In the early 1930s, Fisher began to suffer from intestinal and stomach complaints. He died, aged 37, on 26 December 1934, following several operations. It has been speculated that Fisher's extensive use of X-Ray equipment may have led to his early death.

Suggested reading

R. Fisher (1987) *The Short Fiction of Rudolph Fisher*, ed. Margaret Perry (New York: Greenwood Press).

O.L. Henry (1996) 'Rudolph Fisher: An Evaluation' *The Harlem Renaissance, 1920–1940*, 6, C. D. Wintz ed. (New York: Garland Publishing). pp. 447–53.

David Hering

Friedman, Kinky (1944–)

A flamboyant and often controversial figure, the self-professed 'Texan Jewboy' Kinky Freidman came to prominence first as a country musician, before turning his hand to crime fiction. Recently, Friedman has expanded his interests to include politics, running, unsuccessfully, for Governor of Texas in 2006.

Background

Richard S. 'Kinky' Friedman was born on 1 November 1944 in Chicago, Illinois, the son of a Jewish doctor, S. Thomas Friedman, and his wife, Minnie. Thomas and Minnie had two more children, Roger and Marcie. They relocated to a ranch called Echo Hill, near Kerrville in central Texas while the family was still young. This combination of Texan upbringing paired with strong Jewish roots is what lends Friedman's lyrics and fiction its distinctive voice.

From a young age, Friedman proved precocious, writing and performing musical skits and excelling at chess. When he was only seven years old, Friedman was chosen to compete against the American chess grandmaster, Samuel Reshevsky, in one of 50 matches Reshevsky played simultaneously in the city of Houston. Although he lost, Friedman gained the distinction of being the youngest competitor by a considerable margin. Friedman attended high school in Austin and later attended the University of Texas. He graduated in 1966, having obtained both a Bachelor of Arts degree, majoring in Psychology, and also an enduring nickname, after he was dubbed 'Kinky' by a classmate in honour of his curly hair.

Although he formed his first band – the short-lived King Arthur & the Carrots – while still a student, Friedman put his musical career on hold to serve with the United States Peace Corps immediately after graduation. He spent two years teaching on the island of Borneo before returning to Texas, where he formed his second band, Kinky Friedman and The Texas Jewboys. As their name suggests, the Jewboys were not overly concerned with political correctness. Instead, they favoured a provocative and satirical style that was most clearly reflected in Friedman's lyrics. Selected titles from Friedman's oeuvre include 'Ride 'em Jewboy', a tribute to the victims of the Holocaust; 'They Ain't Makin' Jews like Jesus Anymore', in which Friedman addresses the topic of anti-Semitism, and the ballad, 'Get Your Biscuits in the Oven and Your Buns in Bed.' Friedman also recorded a popular cover of Chinga Chavin's 'Asshole from El Paso'. The Jewboys' cavalier attitude to conventional taste and decency may have earned them the disapproval of both Friedman's father and many Jewish-owned record stores, which refused to stock their music, but it also ensured they built up a sizable cult following. Although never to trouble the mainstream, Friedman and his band toured widely during the '70s, playing with a range of influential musicians, including Bob Dylan, Willie Nelson and Waylon Jennings. They released three albums before disbanding in 1979, when Friedman moved to New York. Over the next four years he made regular solo appearances at the Lone Star Café and also released two further albums.

In recent years, much of Friedman's music has been reissued, introducing his irreverent material to a whole new audience. A tribute album, featuring other artists performing the songs of the Texas Jewboys, was released in 2006. Entitled *Why the Hell Not*, contributors included Lyle Lovett, Willie Nelson and Dwight Yoakam. Friedman himself has moved on to non-musical projects. In addition to his writing, he has entered into politics, running for Governor of Texas in 2006 as an independent candidate on a unique platform of 'Dewussification'. Friedman came fourth out of six, polling 12.6% of the vote and losing to the incumbent Rick Perry, whom he later endorsed as the best candidate for the Republican nomination for the 2012 presidential election. While socially liberal in some respects – he supports gay marriage and is against the death penalty – Friedman is also in favour of strengthening immigration controls and of repealing anti-smoking legislation. He published his political manifesto in *You Can Lead a Politician to Water, But You Can't Make Him Think: Ten Commandments for Texas Politics* (2007). At present, he has not ruled out a further attempt to gain office but is currently focusing his attention on his online cigar emporium. Friedman is also a passionate animal lover and, together with his sister, runs the Utopia Animal Rescue Ranch.

Crime writing

In the mid-1980s, Friedman began to tire of the peripatetic lifestyle of the professional musician and decided to relocate permanently to his family's compound in Texas. Encouraged by his sister, Marcie, herself a fan of the genre, Friedman began to write crime fiction. His first novel, *Greenwich Killing Time*, was published in 1986 and since then he has authored a further 17 books, all featuring an unlikely private detective by the name of Kinky

Friedman. The textual Friedman is a largely autobiographical protagonist who shares many of his creator's character traits and eccentricities; key amongst which are a love of country music, cigars and cats, referred to in *When the Cat's Away* (1988) as 'the three spiritual linchpins of my life' (Friedman, 2000, p. 6).

The series is principally set in Greenwich Village, New York City, and follows the picaresque adventures of Friedman as he balances his stalling musical career, drinking commitments and womanising with a side venture as an amateur PI, a line of work he stumbled into after saving a victim from attack by a would-be mugger. Operating out of his converted loft at 199B Vardam Street, Friedman tends to spend more time considering the activities of Winnie Katz's lesbian dance class in the apartment above his, than in actually detecting. But when he does turn to work, he is assisted by his band of 'Village Irregulars' – the journalist McGovern, a professional PI called Rambam and his Dr Watson-styled sidekick, Ratso. As one might expect given Friedman's background, many of his investigations are linked to the world of country music. In *A Case of Lone Star* (1987), Kinky and his Irregulars hunt a serial killer who preys on country musicians and leaves Hank Williams's lyrics as clues at the crime scene. Willie Nelson requires Friedman's professional services when his life is threatened in *Roadkill* (1997) and members of Friedman's old band, the Texas Jewboys, are targeted in *Musical Chairs* (1991).

The perpetration, and resolution, of crime in Friedman's narratives often seems tangential to the novels, which are principally vehicles for Friedman's own self-portraiture. Friedman's writing is not renowned for its intricate plotting or taut, compelling narratives. His style can best be described as meandering and anecdotal, which can make his storylines difficult to follow. The appeal of the series rests upon the forceful personality of the fictionalised Friedman. Friedman's first-person narrator adopts a cynical and world-weary tone, at times striking a pitch similar to that of Raymond Chandler's Philip Marlowe. However, by paralleling one of the most iconic private detectives in crime fiction with a man whose leisure outfit of choice is a sarong, Friedman manages to create humour at the expense of his protagonist, and by extension himself, while also undermining the conventional narrative of the mystery genre. Like Marlowe, Friedman displays a flair for one-liners, although his sense of humour is much more tongue-in-cheek. Some of his more notable witticisms include the observation that Jesus asked for separate checks at the end of the Last Supper and, in response to Rambam's 'Everyone loves a cowboy', Kinky opines, 'Except Crazy Horse' (Friedman, 1994, p. 98). While Friedman possesses the potential to offend, he also has a more sensitive side, the best evidence of which comes in the close relationship he shares with his feline companion and in the dedication made by the real Friedman of one of his novels to the memory of his cat, Cuddles. The Kinky Friedman series came to a surprising conclusion, at least for the foreseeable future, in *Ten Little New Yorkers* (2005).

Friedman has written two non-series works of fiction, *Kill Two Birds and Get Stoned* (2003) and *The Christmas Pig* (2006). Since embracing politics, his writing has been focused on non-fiction. His publications include the sagacious *What Would Kinky Do? How to Unscrew a Screwed Up World* (2008), *Kinky Friedman's Guide to Texas Etiquette* (2003) and *Cowboy Logic* (2007), a collection of folk wisdom.

Suggested reading

K. Friedman (2011) *Kinky Friedman* www.kinkyfriedman.com

M. McGovern and K. Friedman (1999) *Eat, Drink, and Be Kinky: A Feast of Wit and Fabulous Recipes for Fans of Kinky Friedman* (New York: Simon & Schuster).

Susan Massey

Futrelle, Jacques (1875–1912)

Most sources state Jacques Futrelle was born on 9 April 1875, in Pike County, Georgia, and died on 15 April 1912 onboard the R.M.S. Titanic. However, new research by Victor Berch for *Crime Fiction IV: A Comprehensive Bibliography* suggests Futrelle may have been born in 1873 and his birthname was John Heath Futrell. In the 1900 census, when Futrelle was living in Manhattan with his family, his birth date is given as 1873. His father was Wiley Harmon Heath, a teacher in Atlanta, and his mother was Linnie Bevill Futrell. He attended public schools in Pike County but was also schooled at home by his father who taught him French. The family was apparently of French Huguenot descent.

Career as journalist

Futrelle worked first for the *Atlanta Journal* at the age of 18 and then for the *Boston Post*. He later returned to the *Atlanta Journal*, where he established the paper's first sports department. In 1895 he married Lily May Peel, a writer. The marriage would produce two children: Virginia and John Jr, who later called himself Jacques. The family first stayed in Scitutate, Massachusetts, where Futrelle had a house built he named Stepping Stones and which overlooked the harbour. They later moved to New York, but Futrelle maintained Stepping Stones as a second home. Futrelle was working as telegraph editor for the *New York Herald* when the Spanish-American War broke out in 1898. The long and arduous hours he spent covering the conflict took its toll, and an exhausted Futrelle resigned from the *Herald* and retreated to Stepping Stones to recover. In 1902, he became the manager of a small theatre in Richmond, Virginia. He wrote several plays and even acted in a few of them. At the same time, he started writing detective short stories.

The thinking machine

After moving to Boston, Futrelle worked for the *Boston American* owned by William Randolph Hearst. Futrelle first came to prominence as a crime writer with his invention of detective Professor S.F.X. Van Dusen, 'Ph. D., LL. D., F. R. S., M. D., etc., etc., etc.', best known as 'The Thinking Machine' for his indomitable use of logic. The Thinking Machine is a towering intellectual whose genius, like Sherlock Holmes's, is completely devoid of emotion and often gives him the appearance of being supremely arrogant. He has a sidekick in newspaper reporter Hutchinson Hatch. Van Dusen's and Hatch's working relationship is similarly styled to Holmes's and Watson's, with Van Dusen being the intellectual superior but Hatch more practical by nature. Augustus S.F.X. Van Dusen first appeared in 1905 in the *Boston American* in Futrelle's short story 'The Problem of Cell 13', a forerunner of the locked room mystery genre. No crime actually takes place; rather, Van Dusen manages to escape from the titular cell 13 through his use of logic in a solution that strictly adheres to the laws of physics but stems from the idea that nothing is impossible for the human mind. The story was featured in H.R.F. Keating's *Crime & Mystery: The 100 Best Books* (1987), and it was also selected by science fiction writer Harlan Ellison for Lawrence Block's *Master's Choice* (1999).

'The Problem of Cell 13' was adapted for television several times, among which a 1962 adaptation by Arthur A. Ross for the US series *Kraft Mystery Theater* with Claude Dauphin as The Thinking Machine was awarded the 1963 Edgar Award for Best Episode in a TV series. 'Cell 13' was also adapted as an episode of *The Rivals of Sherlock Holmes* in 1973, with Douglas Wilmer as Van Dusen. The same series also featured an adaptation of Futrelle's 'The Superfluous Finger' (1906), again with Wilmer in the role. Between 1978 and 1999, a German radio station (RIAS) produced and broadcasted 79 radio plays using the character of Professor Van Dusen.

In 1906, Jacques Futrelle decided to give up journalism altogether to concentrate on writing novels full-time. His works include *The Chase of the Golden Plate* (1906), in which Van Dusen has a relatively minor role, and several non-series novels such as *The Simple Case of Susan* (1908), *Elusive Isabel* (1909) and *The High Hand* (1911). *The Diamond Master* (1909) is often regarded as his finest work; the plot concerns an attempt to ruin the world economy with artificial diamonds. The story was adapted into the now lost silent film serials *The Diamond Master* (1921) and *The Diamond Queen* (1929).

The Thinking Machine stories often concentrate on the technological advancements of the time. In 'The Problem of the Lost Radium'(1906) which takes place in a laboratory at 'Yarvard,' a combination of Yale and Harvard, Professor S.F.X. Van Dusen even crosses paths with famous French scientist Marie Curie and helps her solve the mystery of the disappearance of one ounce of radium. In 'The Problem of Dressing Room A' (1906) the genesis of Van Dusen's sobriquet is revealed. After winning a game of chess against a Russian champion, the loser retorts, 'You are not a man; you are a brain – a machine – a thinking machine' (Futrelle, 2004, p. 4). An unusual example of Van Dusen's detective methods can be found in the short story 'The Grinning God' (1907) which Futrelle co-authored with his wife Lily May. The first part, 'Wraiths of the Storm' was written by Lily May as an impossible problem, which the Thinking Machine then solved in part two, 'The House That Was', which was written by Futrelle.

Death and legacy

After celebrating with friends in London what was to be his last birthday, Futrelle boarded the Titanic on 10 April 1912. The party ended late, but Jacques Futrelle and Lily May managed to reach Southampton on time to board the ship. His wife later regretted the fact that Futrelle never drank much, as otherwise they would never been able to board Titanic for its ill-fated voyage.

Francis Browne, who later became a Jesuit priest, took a photograph of Futrelle on the decks of *Titanic* before he disembarked at Queenstown (now Cobh), Ireland. This is the last picture of the author, standing in front of the *Titanic*'s sports room. Futrelle and his wife spent their last days together in a first-class cabin, cabin C-123. During the chaotic evacuation, Futrelle refused to board a lifeboat, but he made sure Lily May was safely boarded on lifeboat 9 and promised he would somehow catch up with her. The last time she saw her husband, he was smoking a cigarette with John Jacob Astor. Lily May was then rescued when her lifeboat was picked up by the RMS *Carpathia*. As with most victims of the disaster, Futrelle's body was not recovered. Futrelle's mother was shocked by her son's death and died three months after him. They share a headstone at Poplar Springs Methodist Church cemetery in Adrian County, Georgia.

Futrelle's last novels, *My Lady's Garter* (in which his wife inscribed 'To the heroes of the Titanic, I dedicate my husband's book') and *Blind Man's Bluff* were published posthumously (in 1912 and 1914). Lily May expanded *The Simple Case of Susan* (1908) into *Lieutenant What's-His-Name* (1915) and the *Ellery Queen's Mystery Magazine* published some uncollected stories in 1949 and 1950.

Lily May Futrelle died in 1967, aged 91, and was buried in Sciutate. Their daughter Virginia died in 1981 and their son Jacques died in 1979 after a career as an editorialist for the *Washington Post*.

Futrelle's contribution to the Golden Age of detective fiction is still highly regarded, and several crime writers have paid tribute to him in their works. Futrelle is referenced in John Dickson Carr's *The Crooked Hinge* (1938), and in Max Allan Collins *The Titanic Murders* (1999), where Futrelle investigates a series of murders taking place aboard the doomed ship.

Suggested reading

R. W. Kauffmann, 'Jacques Futrelle: A Tribute from Reginald Wright Kauffmann' *New York Times*, 12 May 1912 p. BR290.

P. Liukkonen (2008) 'Jacques Futrelle (1875–1912)' *Books and Writers* http://kirjasto. sci.fi/futrell.htm, date accessed 9 July 2011.

Delphine Cingal

Gardner, Erle Stanley (1889–1970)

One of the bestselling authors of all time, Gardner practiced law before becoming a prolific contributor to early twentieth-century pulp fiction magazines and penning more than 140 novels. During his five-decades-long career, he created upwards of three dozen protagonists. Certainly the most celebrated was Los Angeles defence attorney Perry Mason, whose escapades were dramatised in print as well as in films and on television. However, Gardner also developed novels around three other memorable series leads: small-town District Attorney Doug Selby and mismatched gumshoes Bertha Cool and Donald Lam (which Gardner wrote of under the pseudonym 'A.A. Fair'). In his later years, Gardner devoted energy and capital to an organisation charged with investigating dubious criminal convictions, and he was an ardent conservationist. But most of his time was spent concocting stories. When asked why he wrote, Gardner said he did it 'to make money' and 'to give the reader sheer fun' (Krebs, 1975, p. 34). He succeeded greatly at both tasks.

Descended from Colonial New Englanders, Gardner was born in Malden, Massachusetts, on 17 July 1889. Gardner's father was a civil engineer who had helped to construct a breakwater in Portland, Maine, and was recruited to a similar project in Portland, Oregon, moving the family, including the ten-year-old Erle, to the West Coast. In 1902, the Gardners and their three sons (Erle being the middle child) relocated again, this time to Oroville, a town in northern California that had supplied prospectors during the California Gold Rush (1848–1852) and remained an active centre of gold dredging. Gardner's father, Charles, represented a company with a stake in the area's mining activities, which also evidently interested the future author: a number of Gardner's later crime novels would incorporate mining ventures and scams (particularly the 'salting' of mines to make them appear falsely prosperous).

Young Erle boasted prodigious energy and was hard to keep quiet or even confined within four walls. In Oroville, he took to sleeping outside, usually on his family's rooftop. 'That Erle! That Erle!' his mother, Grace, would exclaim in grudging acquiescence of his maverick ways. 'That Erle' could also be rowdy and a troublemaker. He was suspended more than once from high school, and he had only recently commenced studies in law school at Indiana's Valparaiso University before he had to leave following a confrontation with a professor who objected to Gardner holding boxing matches in his dorm room.

Establishing a legal career

Since a college degree was not then required of an aspiring lawyer, Gardner chose instead to 'read' the law with California attorneys he thought 'had something on the ball'. He was finally admitted to the bar in 1911 at the age of 21. Armed with what he said was 'a fund of practical legal knowledge, all the brash impetuosity of youth, and virtually no inferiority complex' (Hughes, 1978, p. 57), Gardner opened an independent office in the San Joaquin Valley town of Merced, only to have it fail. He moved from there to more roisterous Oxnard, in the southern part of the state, where he signed on with I.W. Stewart, a corporate litigator who wanted Gardner to take over his smaller cases, often involving members of the Chinese community. Again, the work was far from lucrative, but Gardner's outmanoeuvering of both police and more seasoned advocates earned him a valuable reputation for smarts, deviousness, and devotion to his clients.

It also won him the attention of a woman who worked in Stewart's office, Natalie Frances Talbert, who had moved from Mississippi to California in 1900. 'Nat,' as friends knew her, was four years and one day older than Gardner, but she possessed a sweet disposition and an inquisitive mind he found enchanting. The pair eloped to San Diego on 9 April 1912. Nine months later, on 25 January 1913, their only child, a daughter they named Natalie Grace (after both her mother and her paternal grandmother), was born.

In 1915, Gardner entered a new business partnership, this time with Harold Frank 'H.F.' Orr, an attorney in Ventura, northwest of Los Angeles. Orr was interested mainly in corporation law, leaving Gardner to perform, much to his liking, any courtroom dramatics. Gardner was enticed away from the practice two years later by Joe Templeton, the son of one of his former school principals, who worked as a manufacturer's agent in San Francisco and thought Gardner had all the makings of a gifted salesman. After transferring his wife and daughter to Oakland, Gardner took up a 'hectic career' dashing about the western United States, consulting with the heads of plants that fabricated tires and other products, and arranging to promote their goods. But the enterprise collapsed after three years, and Gardner returned to Ventura with his family and rejoined Orr's law office.

Representing clients in legal jeopardy, though, no longer satisfied Gardner. He craved fresh challenges, and also thought it prudent to establish a second source of income. With no prior experience of writing fiction, Gardner set his sights on the then burgeoning pulp fiction market.

Finding the right protagonist

As an author, Gardner was no overnight wonder. Even he knew his initial efforts were 'pretty lousy.' To protect his reputation, he mailed his stories to magazine editors under a pseudonym, Charles M. Green. However, as a self-trained lawyer Gardner surmised he could also teach himself to be a writer. So he kept submitting new fiction and collecting occasional payments, plus many more rejection slips, until finally in 1923, the fast-rising star among crime-fiction pulp magazines, *Black Mask*, accepted a novelette from Gardner called 'The Shrieking Skeleton'. His literary career was launched.

Gardner spent the next decade churning out millions of words of fiction during his off-work hours, becoming *Black Mask*'s most productive contributor. Gardner also had stories published in *Argosy*, *Detective Fiction Weekly*, *Dime Detective*, *Clues*, and western pulps. At the beginning of his career, he speed-typed his work with only two fingers, continuing far into the night, but he eventually switched to dictating his stories into a machine for transcription by secretaries. His protagonists constituted a flamboyant bunch from both sides of the law, including 'phantom crook' Ed Jenkins, 'human fly' detective Speed Dash, gentleman thief Lester Leith, millionaire adventurer Sidney Zoom and his police dog, con-man Paul Pry, and of course, crusading defence attorney Ken Corning. It was another fictional counsellor-at-law, however – one who never appeared in the pulps – who scored Gardner his greatest renown.

Perry Mason debuted in Gardner's first published novel, *The Case of the Velvet Claws* (1933), which found him assisting a blackmailed political candidate – and being implicated in murder. It was a fairly hard-boiled adventure, like other early instalments in this series, with Mason showing himself as handy with his fists as he is with his juridical intelligence. It was a winning combination that led Raymond Chandler to label Mason 'the perfect detective'. Comparisons were easily made between Mason and his creator: they were of similar age, they were also both fiercely loyal, appreciative of good food, avid outdoorsmen and familiar enough with the law to use it to their clients' advantage. Additionally, readers learned from the books that Mason was tall and powerfully built, with 'wavy hair' and 'rugged features' that might have been 'carved from granite'. He drove cars recklessly, 'like Hell on wet roads' (Brunsdale, 2010, p. 557). He would not flinch from breaking rules if it was necessary – and he thought he could get away with it.

Fortunately, he had two allies to help keep him out of the slammer. The first was Della Street, his faithful Girl Friday. 'Slim of figure, steady of eye', (Gardner, 1978, p. 4) with curly hair and 'perfect' legs, she was about 15 years younger than her boss and came from a wealthy family that had 'lost their money'. Although their relationship was mainly professional, the pair shared sporadic kisses, and it was obvious that Della loved Mason. Nevertheless, she rebuffed his marriage proposals, saying at one point, 'I don't think you need a wife, but I know damn well you need a secretary who's willing to go to jail occasionally to back your play' (Gardner, 1937, p. 186). Della Street was modeled primarily on Agnes Jean Walter Bethell (1902–2002), one of three Walter sisters who did secretarial work in Gardner's law office, and whom he came to know well.

Also vital to Mason's success was private eye Paul Drake. Tall like the attorney, but stoop-shouldered and susceptible to stomach troubles from eating poorly during long hours, Drake was a former small-town boy and was far less disposed than Mason was to circumvent the law in pursuit of information. He ran a 24-hour investigative agency out of the same building where Mason was headquartered. A convenient arrangement, since the defender provided Drake and his operatives with nearly all of their business.

Big plans for the small screen

Gardner was already scaling back his legal practice by the time *The Case of the Velvet Claws* hit bookshops, and not long afterward he became a full-time author, taking the Walter sisters with him as typists. He went on to compose 82 Perry Mason novels, two of which were published posthumously: their titles beginning with 'The Case of...,' followed by a verb and a noun, frequently alliterative (e.g., *The Case of the Lucky Legs*). The series quickly gained followers drawn to its pell-mell storytelling pace, dialogue-heavy construction, and intricate plots. Mason stories followed a simple, engaging formula: the lawyer would be hired by an innocent party, perhaps someone who did not fully comprehend the events leading to his or her troubles; Mason and Drake would find evidence to prove their client did not commit the crime, that somebody else was responsible instead; and then the attorney would endeavour to wring a confession from the guilty party. Since the outcome of Mason's cases was almost never in doubt, the stories' appeal was in seeing what quasi-legal manoeuvres he would employ to exonerate the defendant. Amongst the most well-regarded entries in the series are *The Case of the Perjured Parrot* (1939), *The Case of the Dubious Bridegroom* (1949), *The Case of the Fiery Fingers* (1951) and *The Case of the Terrified Typist* (1956), which ends with a very rare courtroom defeat for Mason that is subsequently reversed on appeal.

Bookstores made Perry Mason popular, but it was the medium of film and television that turned him into a household name. A half-dozen Mason films, most starring Warren William, were shot in the 1930s, beginning with *The Case of the Howling Dog* (1934). From 1943 to 1955, CBS Radio broadcast a 15-minute daily Mason program that was heavy on action, light on courtroom drama – and displeased Gardner greatly. So greatly, in fact, that in the 1950s he decided to take charge himself of introducing Mason to the growing medium of television. He formed a production company, Paisano Productions (named after a ranch Gardner owned in Temecula, California), hired a retired actress to run things day to day, helped to choose the show's cast – in particular, star Raymond Burr (who won the Mason role over star actor Fred MacMurray) – reviewed the scripts, and split the profits with the CBS-TV network. *Perry Mason* first aired on 21 September 1957. Many episodes were adapted from Gardner's books, but simplified for the small screen and regularly concluded with the killer confessing in court – an awkward device unseen in the Mason novels prior to the debut of the new television production.

Perry Mason finally went off the air in May 1966. In the fall of 1973, though, CBS sought to reawaken the magic with *The New Perry Mason*, starring Monte Markham; the show lasted only 15 episodes. It was left to Burr to resurrect LA's most illustrious defence attorney in 26 TV films shown between 1985 and 1993.

Other projects

Aside from his prolific work in writing the Mason novels and contributing to the television franchise, Gardner also wrote two concurrent series. The first, beginning with *The D.A. Calls It Murder* (1937), featured Doug Selby, a young lawyer elected as the district attorney for fictitious Madison County, California. Reform-minded in an oft-corrupt agricultural community, Selby faced formidable and ample opponents, among them the county seat's chief of police and a rascally attorney named Alphonse Baker Carr ('old A.B.C.'). He was aided, however, by county sheriff Rex Brandon and Sylvia Martin, a reporter for the local newspaper and his unofficial investigator. Over the course of the nine Selby novels, its protagonist left the DA's office to work for military counterintelligence during World War II, but was re-elected after his return to the county. These books, which conclude with 1949's *The D.A. Breaks an Egg*, cast light on the failings of the American justice system and make clear Gardner's affection for California's dry, rural reaches. *The D.A. Draws a Circle* (1939) was the basis for a 1971 TV film and unsuccessful series pilot, *They Call It Murder*, starring Jim Hutton.

More boisterous, humorous, and filled with fast-flowing banter – as well as more head-spinning in their plotting – were Gardner's 29 Bertha Cool and Donald Lam novels. Almost all are told from the first-person viewpoint of Lam – a pseudonym which implies Lam is running from his murky past, but his real name is not revealed. By his own description, Lam is a brave and 'brainy little runt' who lost his license to practice law after advising a gangster that 'it would be possible to commit a murder so there was nothing anyone could do about it' (Gardner, 1939, p. 70). His inaugural appearance, in *The Bigger They Come* (1939), found Lam, in his mid-20s, being hired as an operative by Bertha, a blustery, fractious woman in her 60s, who was notable for her outlandish exclamations such as 'Kipper me for a herring!' and 'Peel me for a grape!'; her weight (well in excess of 200 pounds), and her management of a confidential investigations agency in Los Angeles that she inherited from her deceased, adulterous husband. Unlike the Mason series, the characters changed over time. The ultra-frugal Bertha constantly chided Lam for wasting money. However, his legal acumen and willingness to take on high-risk cases boosted the agency's business sufficiently that she accepted him as a partner (in *Double or Quits*, 1941). At the end of *Owls Don't Blink* (1942), one of the finest novels of the series, Lam enlisted in the navy as the United States entered World War II, leaving Bertha (who, by this point, had dropped to a comparatively sylphlike 165 pounds) to solve crimes on her own. After he returned, the Cool and Lam agency moved to new offices and took on a socially higher breed of clientele. The final Cool-Lam book, *All Grass Isn't Green*, was released in 1970, but it was long before then – and much to the surprise of many readers and reviewers – that authors Gardner and 'A.A. Fair' were revealed as one and the same.

Gardner stressed 'speed, situation, and suspense' in his storytelling, but his books benefited too from research sources among professionals in forensic, legal, and investigative fields (Steinbrunner and Penzler, 1976, p. 165). Some of these authorities befriended the author, and in the late 1940s helped him found an organisation, the Court of Last Resort, that sought to reopen cases which might have resulted in wrongful convictions. Gardner's 1952 book about the Court won him an Edgar Allan Poe Award from the Mystery Writers of America. In 1962, the MWA presented him as well with its Grand Master Award.

On 26 February 1968, Gardner's long-estranged wife, Natalie, died of a heart attack. Six months later, on August 7, the author wed Jean Bethell, the secretary with whom he had enjoyed an office relationship even more extensive than Perry and Della's. But their happiness was short-lived: cancer cost Erle Stanley Gardner his life on 11 March 1970.

Suggested reading

D.B. Hughes (1978) *Erle Stanley Gardner: The Case of the Real Perry Mason* (New York: William Morrow).
K.B. Smith (n.d.)'Authors and Creators: Erle Stanley Gardner', by Kevin Burton Smith, *The Thrilling Detective*, http://www.thrillingdetective.com/trivia/gardner.html

J. Kingston Pierce

Gault, William Campbell (1910–95)

Although best remembered for writing two private detective series – one about Italian-descended Joe Puma, the other starring former football great Brock 'The Rock' Callahan – Gault also contributed extensively to pulp magazines and wrote young-adult sports fiction. Critic Anthony Boucher called him 'a fresh voice – a writer who sounds like nobody else', while author Bill Pronzini applauded Gault's 'vivid evocation of both upper class and bottom feeder lifestyles' (Pronzini, 2008).

Born on 9 March 1910, in Milwaukee, Wisconsin, Gault studied at the University of Wisconsin before becoming the manager of downtown Milwaukee's Blatz Hotel (1932–39). In the mid-1930s, however, after winning a newspaper-sponsored short-story contest, he began devoting much of his energy to fiction-writing. Gault married Virginia Kaprelian in 1942 and they had two children together. During World War II he served with the 166th Infantry (1943–45), then returned to the US and produced stories for crime, romance, and science-fiction periodicals, as well as *The Saturday Evening Post* and *McClure's*. By the late 1940s his works – often featuring a Duesenberg-driving dick named Mortimer Jones – were cover-promoted in *Black Mask*.

Gault joined the postwar migration to Los Angeles and switched to novel-writing. The first of his 30-plus books for juvenile readers, *Thunder Road*, was published in 1952, as was his initial plunge into the mystery genre, *Don't Cry for Me*, a stand-alone novel with a particularly intimate narrative voice, which won the Edgar Award for Best First Novel. During the 1950s, he produced more than half a dozen other one-off narratives, including *The Bloody Bokhara* (1952), his only Milwaukee-set novel; a much-lauded boxing mystery, *The Canvas Coffin* (1953); and 1954's *Run, Killer, Run* (aka *The Sweet Blonde Trap*), which Jon L. Breen noted was 'a rare third-person Gault novel' that 'illuminates his political stance: Republican, socially concerned, anti-McCarthyite, a consistent voice for non-simplistic morality' (Pierce, 2010).

LA gumshoe Joseph 'Joe' Puma debuted in *Shakedown*, a paperback released in 1953 under one of several Gault pseudonyms, 'Roney Scott'. Brawny and appealing to female clients, but also arrogant and ruthless at times, Puma headlined seven novels, notably *Sweet Wild Wench* (1959) and *The Hundred Dollar Girl* (1961). That latter book explored a theme Gault used often in his stories: the corruption of professional sports. Gault further examined the subject in his other PI series, featuring Brock Callahan, the son of a hoodlum-slain San Diego cop. Callahan was a Stanford University football standout who spent nine years with the Los Angeles Rams until age and injuries forced a career change. Early Callahan tales, such as *Day of the Ram* (1956) and *The Convertible Hearse* (1957), showed him as a Beverly Hills-based sleuth, tackling crimes for the affluent. Along with Thomas B. Dewey's Mac and Lew Archer, the creation of Ross Macdonald (a friend of Gault's, who dedicated his last novel to the author), Callahan helped to popularise the 'compassionate' shamus. Somewhat unusually compared to other carefree PIs, the character even had a steady girlfriend: dainty but quarrelsome interior decorator Jan Bonnet. In the early 1960s, though, Gault abandoned detective fiction to make more money composing young adult sports novels. Not until 1982 did Callahan make a comeback in the last seven of his 14 book-length adventures. Now married to Jan, Callahan is comfortably semi-retired, thanks to his significant inheritance from an ill-fated uncle, and living in 'San Valdesto', a thinly camouflaged Santa Barbara.

The Private Eye Writers of America gave Gault's 1982 novel, *The CANA Diversion*, in which Callahan investigates the murder of Joe Puma, the Shamus Award for Best Paperback Original, and in 1984 he received that same organisation's lifetime achievement award, The Eye. Gault died on 27 December 1995.

Suggested reading

W.L. DeAndrea (1994) *Encyclopedia Mysteriosa* (New York: Macmillan).
B. Pronzini, Bill (1992) 'Some Words About William Campbell Gault' *Dead Pigeon* by W. C. Gault. (New York: Carroll & Graf Publishers).

J. Kingston Pierce

Goodis, David (1917–67)

A writer of novels, short stories and screenplays, Goodis made a memorable contribution to crime fiction through his idiosyncratically bleak and quirky take on noir fiction, which has led to him being posthumously dubbed 'Philadelphia's noir prince'.

Early life

David Loeb Goodis was born in Philadelphia on 2 March 1917. Goodis was the eldest of three boys in a middle class Jewish family. Goodis was educated at Simon Gratz High School and attended Indiana University, later graduating from Temple University, Philadelphia, in 1938 with a degree in journalism. After a short stint working for an advertising agency, Goodis moved to New York where he lived from 1939 to 1946. Now a freelance writer, Goodis contributed a prodigious output of short stories under pseudonyms such as Logan C. Claybourne, David Crewe, and Lance Kermit for the publications *Horror Stories, Terror Tales, Western Tales, Dime Mystery, Fighting Aces, Manhunt* and other magazines. His first novel, *Retreat from Oblivion*, was published by Dutton in 1939 and is unusually sprawling and ambitious for a debut work. Its narrative is also uniquely political when compared to his later crime novels.

Hollywood career and novels

In the mid-1940s Goodis moved to Los Angeles to begin a screenwriting career. Although he earned around $1,000 a week, Goodis' time in Hollywood was not a productive one. Most of the scripts he worked on, including an adaptation of Raymond Chandler's *The Lady in the Lake*, were never produced, and he became distrusted for his erratic behaviour. Goodis did find some success with films; he scripted the film noir *The Unfaithful* (1947), and his second novel *Dark Passage* (1946) was adapted into a memorable thriller. *Dark Passage* was the final film to feature Humphrey Bogart and Lauren Bacall starring together. He also wrote two more novels during his time in Los Angeles: *Nightfall* and *Behold this Woman* (both 1947). The former was filmed by Jacques Tourneur in 1957. Goodis returned to Philadelphia in 1950 where he lived with his parents and helped to look after his schizophrenic brother Herbert who was confined to Norristown State Hospital from 1963. Goodis divided his time between the house, the city's bars and nightclubs and Superior Billiards club. Goodis' writing skills peaked during this time: he produced works which had a renewed pessimistic vision and colourful ill-fated characters. Goodis excelled at creating reclusive protagonists who once lived lives of fame and success but are reduced to existentialist despair and urban cynicism. In *Cassidy's Girl* (1950) the lead character, Jim Cassidy, is a former ace fighter pilot whose career with the airlines falls apart when he is blamed for a plane crash. Ostracised and drifting in and out of prison, Cassidy lands a job as a bus driver in Philadelphia where he marries a beautiful but heartless woman. The novel charts their passionate but violently destructive relationship. *The Moon in the Gutter* (1953) concerns one man's unsuccessful private investigation into the death of his sister. Although he has the opportunity to marry into a wealthy family and leave the deprived areas of Philadelphia, he cannot leave the streets that have a grim hold on his identity after the death of his sibling. Whitey in *Street of No Return* (1954) is a former singer turned alcoholic who at the beginning of the novel finds the body of a policeman, killed, it seems, during a race riot. Whitey becomes a suspect in his murder and is then plunged lucklessly, and for a Goodis novel typically, into a series of bizarre events.

Goodis had an affinity for the man on the street at the end of his luck with seemingly nothing to lose. The novels poetically examine the perpetual misfortunes of people who are either self-destructive or who have no further options. *Black Friday* (1954) begins with the leading character John Hart walking the streets of Philadelphia in bitterly cold weather contemplating suicide in an effort to cheer himself up. *The Blonde on the Street Corner* (1954) explores a familiar theme of Goodis' novels, a man caught between two women. One of Goodis' most acclaimed novels is *Down There* (1956), adapted for film by Francois Truffaut as *Shoot the Piano Player* (1960). The plot concerns a gifted piano player, Eddie Lynn, who once drew huge crowds for his concerts at Carnegie Hall but is reduced to playing in a seedy bar in Philadelphia after his lover's suicide. The plot is secondary in importance to character and atmosphere; Eddie seems to lurch from one random violent episode to another. The title alludes to the depths of despair and gloom the characters fall into and naturally inhabit. The deliberately inconclusive but mournful resolution accentuates Eddie's depression and failure to comprehend his role in events. The miserable loner trapped in Philadelphia after once living a life of success closely paralleled Goodis' own life and formed character-driven narratives Goodis could write with ease. *Night Squad* (1961) was the final novel published in his lifetime. The plot concerns a disgraced ex-police officer, Corey Bradford, whose life turns upside down after he saves the life of a city gangster from two gunmen. The gangster hires him to find out who sent the gunmen, but then the police want Bradford to help them put the gangster behind bars. As is often the case in Goodis' fictional universe, fate has conspired against the lead character and there is no possibility of a happy way out. In 1965 Goodis sued the television networks United Artists-TV and ABC on the grounds that the hugely successful television series *The Fugitive* was based on *Dark Passage*. The case dragged on and was still not resolved at the time of Goodis' premature death. In 1972, the Goodis estate accepted a settlement of $12,000.

The enigma of David Goodis

Goodis died at the age of 49 on 7 January 1967 at the Albert Einstein Medical Centre after suffering from a stroke. According to his cousin, Paul Halpern, Goodis had been mugged and beaten a few days earlier, suggesting the possibility that his injuries may have precipitated the stroke. Goodis had been suffering from heart disease in his final years, and after his mother's death in 1966, he was admitted to a mental hospital for a short time. Goodis' final novel, *Somebody's Done For*, was published later that year. His reputation had declined by the time of his death, and his work soon went out of print, but recent years have seen a revival of interest in his life and work. Goodis is one of a handful of American noir writers who was, at least for a period of time, more highly regarded by French critics than in his own country. The only full-length biography on the writer is *David Goodis: A Life in Black and White* (1984) by the French writer Phillipe Garnier. On the fortieth anniversary of his death, Goodis fans and scholars gathered in Philadelphia for the first GoodisCon, a convention dedicated to studying his life and work. Goodis is attributed with 18 novels, although research undertaken by writers for the website Goodis.com indicates Goodis may have written over a dozen unpublished and so far untraced manuscripts which are referenced on his tax records. For many years Goodis was thought to have never married, and the obituaries printed at the time of his death made no mention of any marriage. However, research by Larry Withers and Louis Boxer reveal Goodis was married to Elaine Astor for three years. They married in 1943 at Ohev Shalom Congregation in Los Angeles and divorced in 1946. Goodis is rumoured to have engaged in sexual relationships with obese black women. Some critics, such as Bill Sherman, have dismissed the suggestion as a 'myth' invented to try and explain the themes of violent, sadomasochistic sex in his novels. Goodis was in a secretive relationship with the black sculptor Selma Burke during the 1950s.

Suggested reading

D. Goodis, *Shooting Pool with David Goodis* http://www.davidgoodis.com.

P. Garnier (1984) *Goodis, la vie en noir et blanc: biographie* (Paris: Editions du Seuil).

J. Sallis (1993) *Difficult Lives: Jim Thompson, David Goodis, Chester Himes* (Brooklyn, NY: Gryphon).

Steven Powell

Grafton, Sue (1940–)

The daughter of lawyer and crime fiction writer Cornelius Warren Grafton, Sue Grafton has arguably surpassed her father's legacy with her long-running Alphabet series of novels featuring female private investigator Kinsey Millhone.

Early life

Born on 24 April 1940, in Louisville, Kentucky, Sue Taylor Grafton attended the University of Louisville for one year before transferring to Western Kentucky State Teachers College for two years. In 1961 she received her BA in English Literature with minors in humanities and fine arts.

Grafton started writing at the age of 18 and initially wrote seven novellength manuscripts, two of which were published: *Keziah Dane* (1967) and *The Lolly-Madonna War* (1969). The latter was adapted into the film *Lolly-Madonna XXX* in 1973. Faced with the relative lack of success of her early attempts at novel writing, she turned to writing teleplays, and adapted two novels by Agatha Christie with her third husband, Steven Humphrey, whom she married in 1978. Grafton's first two marriages, to James L. Flood in 1959 and Al Schmidt in 1962, both ended in divorce.

Grafton started writing detective fiction in response to an emotionally painful period of her life. The process of divorcing her second husband lasted for six years, the marriage had produced two children and the custody battle was fierce. Grafton started imagining ways of murdering her husband and, instead of actually acting on these fantasies, she adapted them into a narrative. Grafton was relieved to channel her anger into something creative which ultimately proved to be financially lucrative. Detective fiction also became a way out of screenwriting, which she had grown disillusioned with, but it was not until 1990, after *'G' is for Gumshoe*, that Grafton was able to stop working as a screenwriter, as her novels were not an immediate commercial success with her first novel, *'A' is for Alibi* (1982), selling only around 6,000 copies.

The alphabet series

In creating her own series, Grafton was influenced by writers who used serial titles, as her father had with his two Gil Henry novels *The Rat Began to Gnaw the Rope* (1943) and *The Rat Began to Hang the Butcher* (1944), which were both taken from the first two lines of a nursery rhyme. She was reading Edward Gorey's alphabetical macabre story *The Gashlycrumb Tinies* (1963) when she decided to start a series of novels. After checking that there was at least one crime-related or appropriate word starting with each of the twenty-six letters of the alphabet, 'The Alphabet novels' were born.

The stories are generally set near Santa Teresa, California, a fictionalised version of Santa Barbara invented by Ross MacDonald for the Lew Archer novels. The narrator of the stories is Kinsey Millhone, a private investigator, and the stories are her reports to her clients. In 1982, Grafton published *'A' is for Alibi,* an investigation of a cold case murder in which the victim's wife, Nikki Fife, had been found guilty and convicted. After serving her sentence, Fife asks Millhone to find the real murderer. Fife, the second wife of the murder victim, a prominent divorce lawyer and a womaniser Laurence Fife, was convicted for poisoning her husband's medication in order to kill him before he could divorce her. His first divorce had been particularly difficult, and the police believed Fife had killed her husband in order to avoid the ordeal that the first wife, Gwen, had been through.

All of Grafton's novels have followed a sequential alphabetical title system: *'B' is for Burglar* (1985), *'C' is for Corpse* (1986) and *'D' is for Deadbeat* (1987) and so on. The timeline of the novels is not strictly chronological, partly to allow Millhone to stay young enough to be a viable private investigator. *'U' is for Undertow* takes place in April 1988: Millhone is then 38, but the novel was published in 2009. According to Sue Grafton in a 2009 *Los Angeles Times* interview, the last book in the series will be entitled *'Z' is for Zero* and Millhone will be around the age of 40. As of the time of writing, the latest novel in the series is *'V'* is for *Vengeance.*

Kinsey Millhone

Kinsey Millhone was born in Santa Teresa, California, in 1950. Her mother, Rita, was estranged from her wealthy family when she married Randall Millhone, a postal worker. When she was five, Kinsey Millhone and her parents were in a tragic car accident and both of her parents died. She never fully recovered from the trauma. She was brought up by her Aunt Gin, an independent-minded woman who had also become estranged from the family. Millhone is influenced by Gin's independence and approach to education. During her teenage years, Millhone was rebellious and smoked marijuana. Millhone is once again left to fend for herself when Aunt Gin dies; however, in *'U' is for Undertow,* she finds out that her grandmother had tried to adopt her after her parents' death, and even hired a private investigator to locate her, but Aunt Gin had an affair with the investigator and prevented Millhone from meeting the rest of her family. Grafton has suffered similar family hardship: C.W. Grafton died in 1982, the year the first novel in the series was published, and her mother Vivian died on Grafton's twentieth birthday. Consequently, Grafton has imbued Millhone with the same qualities she has always strived for: perseverance, independence, and courage.

After graduating from high school, Millhone first worked as a police officer in Santa Teresa, and quickly grew to hate the bureaucracy and her male-chauvinist colleagues, resigning her position after only two years. She then trained to become a private investigator. After a couple of years in a detective agency, she decided to work on her own and, in exchange for doing a few investigations for them, got an office in the building occupied by California Fidelity Insurance.

Kinsey is twice divorced and has several unsatisfactory relationships with men during her investigations, sometimes with recurring series characters such as detective Cheney Phillips.

In *'O' is for Outlaw* (1999), she investigates an assault on a Vietnam veteran for which her ex-husband Michael Macgruder is a suspect. At the time of the assault, they were still married and Macgruder had asked Millhone for a false alibi. Millhone had refused and walked out on him. However, she discovers he might have been innocent, as his real alibi was that he was with his mistress at the time of the attack.

Millhone lives in a small studio apartment that she rents from her close friend Henry Pitts. The apartment is a modest, remodelled garage. In *'E' is for Evidence* (1988), the apartment is destroyed by explosives in an attempt to murder her and, in *'G' is for Gumshoe* (1990), Pitts has the place beautifully restored and redecorated. Millhone drives a small 1968 Volkswagen that she loves and in which she keeps her clothes and other things she might need should she have to suddenly leave to work on a case. Her car is destroyed, however, in *'I' is for Innocent* (1992).

Millhone has gained a reputation outside of the series and is mentioned in semi-crossover novels by Sara Paretsky, Bill Pronzini and Marcia Muller. Grafton has been awarded three Anthony Awards, with *'B' is for Burglar* and *'C' is for Corpse* winning the first two ever awarded. She was also the recipient of three Shamus Awards for Best PI Hardcover Novel for *'B' Is for Burglar, 'G' Is for Gumshoe* and *'K' Is for Killer* (1994). In 2000, Grafton was granted the 2000 YWCA of Lexington Smith-Breckinridge Distinguished Woman of Achievement Award. In 2004, she received the Ross Macdonald Literary Award. In 2008 Sue Grafton was awarded the Cartier Dagger by the British Crime Writers' Association, honouring a lifetime's achievement in the field. In 2009 Grafton received the Grand Master Award from the Mystery Writers of America. Unlike most of her contemporaries, Grafton has consistently refused to have her novels adapted into films and has made her children swear never to sell the rights to her novels to the film industry after her death.

Suggested reading

N. H. Kaufman and C. M. Kay (1997) *G is for Grafton: the World of Kinsey Millhone.* (New York: Henry Holt).

S. Weinman (2009) 'Closing in on the Letter Z' *L.A. Times,* 17 December http://www.latimes.com/entertainment/news/la-et-sue-grafton17–2009dec17,0,3603461. story, date accessed 7 July 2011.

Delphine Cingal

Grubb, Davis (1919–80)

Short story writer and novelist, whose bestselling depression-era Southern Gothic novel *The Night of the Hunter* (1953) was adapted into one of the most celebrated movies of the film noir period. Grubb wrote ten novels and many crime and horror stories; his stories appeared in magazines as diverse as *Colliers* and *Good Housekeeping*. But it is his first published novel, *The Night of the Hunter,* for which he is best known and for which he received most praise.

Davis Grubb was born and grew up in Moundsville, West Virginia, where his father was an architect and his mother worked for the Department of Public Assistance. He went to school in Moundsville and Clarksburg, and then spent some time working for a local radio station. Grubb was colour blind, but nevertheless attended the Carnegie Institute of Technology, in Pittsburgh, Pennsylvania, where he studied painting and drawing. He left in 1939 after only one year.

According to the West Virginia Wesleyan College author guide, Grubb began his writing career in 1940 in New York, where at first he worked for NBC and later became a copywriter in radio. Grubb wrote short stories in his spare time and made his first sale in 1944 to *Good Housekeeping*. It was another six years before Grubb began writing novels and a further three before the publication of *The Night of the Hunter*, his debut.

The Night of the Hunter is based on the real-life story of Harry Powers, known as the Bluebeard of Quiet Dell, a serial killer who was executed in Grubb's home town on 18 March 1932. Powers lured women by taking out lonely hearts ads in newspapers and charming them with letters and promising them happiness; he was convicted of the murders of two women and three children.

Grubb's take on the story recasts Powers as Harry Powell, who pursues the wife of his executed cellmate in an effort to recover the proceeds of her former husband's last robbery. Calling himself Reverend Powell, he befriends and eventually marries the widow before killing her. The children, who do not trust him, run away. Realising that the children know where the money is, 'Preacher' Harry Powell, who is one of the most compelling villains in the genre, goes after them.

The Night of the Hunter is in the tradition of nineteenth-century Southern Gothic, but its themes of broken families and itinerant criminals are more contemporary. The story is set in the Depression era, but in the widow's vulnerability the novel also reflects post-war concerns about family life, the absence of men, and the promise of the next generation.

The grotesque amorality of Harry Powell, contrasted with the trustworthiness of his assumed role, has parallels in the paranoia of 1950s culture and made the novel ideal for adaptation in the film noir style. The directorial debut of English-American actor Charles Laughton, with Robert Mitchum in the role of Powell and Shelley Winters as the widow, with a script by Laughton and James Agee, makes for a strange, sinister, and otherworldly film. However, the film was not a success upon its initial release, and Laughton never directed again. The film's reputation has risen since its release, and it is now widely regarded as being among the best to have come out of the film noir period in Hollywood.

Later works

Grubb's other novels and stories have not attracted as much attention as *Night of the Hunter*, which was a bestseller and was widely praised by critics: it was a National Book Award finalist in 1955. Grubb went on to write in a number of different genres, including horror, and in his last novel, *Ancient Lights* (1982), science fiction; in 1955, he published *A Dream of Kings*, a Civil War-era romance marred by its tendency to melodrama. More successful was *The Watchman* (1961), a murder plot set in West Virginia, while *Fool's Parade* (1969) became a successful movie thriller, starring James Stewart. Grubb never repeated the success of his first novel, either in literary quality or sales. In a review of *Shadow of My Brother* in 1966, *Time Magazine* summed up the problem with much of Grubb's later work: 'uncontrolled bombast, near-hysterical characters, and [a] determination to leave no grit unhominized' (Anon, 1966).

As a short story writer, Grubb was a favourite of Alfred Hitchcock, who adapted several of his stories for television. Grubb wrote many short stories and published several collections, including *The Siege of 318: 13 Mystical Stories* (1978). In 1989, a collection of stories was published entitled *You Never Believe Me*, while in 2005 a further attempt was made to rehabilitate Grubb with the release of the anthology *12 Tales of Suspense and the Supernatural*. Grubb died in New York City on 24 July 1980, the day after his 61st birthday.

Suggested reading

'Davis Grubb' *West Virginia Wesleyan College, Annie Merner Pfeiffer Library* http://www.wvwc.edu/library/wv_authors/authors/a_grubb.htm, date accessed 19 October 2010.

J. Welch (1980) *Davis Grubb: A Vision of Appalachia*, PhD, Carnegie-Mellon University.

Christopher Routledge

Gruber, Frank (1904–69)

A prolific writer of private eye novels, westerns, television and film screenplays and hundreds of pulp short stories (often under pseudonyms such as Stephen Acre, Charles K. Boston and John K. Vedder), Gruber's output included over 300 short stories, 70 screenplays and 150 teleplays. Frank Gruber never received the recognition of many of his contemporaries, but his work remains notable for its volume and diversity. Born 2 February 1904, in Elmer, Minnesota, Gruber worked a number of jobs including a period in the US Army (1920–21) before he began his career as a self-employed writer in 1934, a career inspired by reading the works of his literary hero Horatio Alger. Gruber married Lois Mahood in 1931 and worked as a trade journal editor and correspondence school teacher to provide regular income. In 1920s and 1930s he produced countless short stories of which only a relatively low number were finally sold to magazines. He did eventually become a regular contributor to pulp magazines, including the most prestigious, *Black Mask*. Gruber wrote a series of short stories featuring Oliver Quade, a crime-solving encyclopaedia salesman. Gruber himself possessed an impressively encyclopaedic knowledge of American history, and his work is full of factual asides and short informative digressions. Gruber's private detective Simon Lash featured in three novels. Lash is an amateur historian more interested in studying and collecting items of historical Americana than he is in detective work. The first novel, *Simon Lash, Private Detective* (1941), ends with Lash saving his failing investigation agency from financial ruin when he discovers a rare and priceless Mormon book at the hideaway of a killer. As his name suggests, Lash is capable of mean displays of temper and often verbally undermines his less quick-witted partner Eddie Slocum. Adept at quirky characterisations, Gruber also created the two-man private eye team of Johnny Fletcher and Sam Cragg. Although they were ostensibly private eyes, Fletcher and Cragg were actually travelling con artists. They appeared in 14 novels together, beginning with *The French Key* (1940) and ending with *Swing Low Swing Dead* (1969). Gruber was an expert at writing westerns and was more prolific in that genre than any other. He wrote a well-received biography of one of the foremost practitioners of the western genre, *Zane Grey: A Biography* (1970). In novels such as *The Silver Jackass* (1941), Gruber combined the crime and western genres in his tale of two Los Angeles PIs, Otis Beagle and Joe Peel, whose search for a cache of silver bullion leads them to the Nevada desert. The pair also appeared in the novels *Beagle Scented Murder* (1946) and *The Lonesome Badger* (1954). With the decline in the popularity of the pulps, Gruber increasingly turned to writing film and television screenplays. Some of his more notable credits include the television series *Shotgun Slade* (1959–61) with actor Scott Brady in the title role of Slade, a cowboy and private detective. Several of Gruber's novels were adapted into films, including *The French Key* in 1946 and *Simon Lash, Private Detective* was adapted as *Accomplice* (1946) with Richard Arlen in the role as Lash. Gruber's memoir, *The Pulp Jungle* (1967), detailed much of the hardship and struggles in his early writing career and included an eleven-point plot formula for a successful story. He died 9 December 1969.

Suggested reading

F. Gruber (1967) *The Pulp Jungle* (Los Angeles: Sherbourne Press).
J. Reilly ed. (1985) *Twentieth-Century Crime and Mystery Writers* (New York: St Martin's Press).

Steven Powell

Hammett, Dashiell (1894–1961)

Although he wrote only five novels, Dashiell Hammett is a seminal figure in twentieth-century crime fiction. In his work, Hammett shaped and defined the hard-boiled school of crime writing, paving the way for authors such as Raymond Chandler, Ross Macdonald and Mickey Spillane. With his spare prose and unsentimental style, Hammett became central to the emergence of a specifically American form of crime fiction, one that offered a genuine alternative to the British clue-puzzle model.

Background

Samuel Dashiell Hammett was born on the 27 May 1894 on a farm called Hopewell and Aim in St Mary's County, Maryland. He was the second child of Richard Hammett, a farmer, and his wife, Anne Bond Dashiell, a trained nurse. While Sam, as Hammett was known, was still a child, the family moved to Philadelphia before returning to Maryland and settling in Baltimore. Here, Hammett attended the Baltimore Polytechnic Institute until the age of 13, when he dropped out to get a job to help support his family financially after his father became incapacitated by ill health. Over the next few years, Hammett worked as a newsboy, a freight clerk, a railroad labourer, a messenger, a stevedore and an advertising manager, before joining the Pinkerton National Detective Agency in 1915.

Founded by Allan Pinkerton in 1850, the Pinkerton Agency first came to prominence when it foiled a plot to assassinate President-elect Lincoln in 1861. Pinkertons continued to provide security for the President during the Civil War and, by the time Hammett joined their ranks at the age of 21, the agency had become one of the largest private law enforcement organisations in the world. Hammett spent eight years as a Pinkerton operative, during which time he travelled across America and worked on cases including those of the notorious gambler Nicky Arnstein and Roscoe 'Fatty' Arbuckle, a silent film actor and comedian accused of the rape and manslaughter of Virginia Rappe in 1921. Hammett would later draw on his career as a detective to provide the inspiration for his short stories and novels.

Hammett's career with the Pinkerton Agency was interrupted by World War I, as he temporarily left the organisation to enlist in the United States Army. He joined the Motor Ambulance Corps as a sergeant but quickly fell ill with influenza, which developed into tuberculosis. Hammett spent the rest of the war in the Cushman Hospital in Washington State, and his health never fully recovered. It was while in hospital, suffering from a relapse in 1920, that he met and fell in love with a nurse, Josephine Dolan. The couple were married in 1921 and moved to San Francisco, where they had two daughters, Mary Jane and Josephine. Unfortunately, due to the contagious nature of Hammett's illness, he was regularly forced to live apart from his wife and daughters, staying in a local hotel rather than the family home.

Hammett briefly returned to work with the Pinkerton Agency but left, for good, in 1922. His poor health is usually cited as the reason, but Hammett, whose personal politics tended towards the radical, also found himself disillusioned with the often violent involvement of the Pinkertons in strike-breaking. During his career, Hammett was employed by the Anaconda Copper Company to end a strike in Butte, Montana. Once there, he was allegedly also offered $5000 to kill one of the union organisers. Hammett declined: the role of hired muscle was not one he relished.

Writing career

After leaving the Pinkertons, Hammett enrolled in Munson's Business College where he took classes in journalism. He also found regular employment as a copywriter for a chain of jewellery stores, and, in his spare time, began to write his own fiction. In 1922, Hammett's work was published for the first time, when the short story 'The Parthian Shot' appeared in the journal *The Smart Set*. A second, more significant publication came in December of the same year when 'The Road Home' was included in the popular pulp magazine *Black Mask*. Between 1922 and 1930, over three dozen of Hammett's stories, many of which featured a detective known only as 'the Continental Op', were printed by *Black Mask*, and Hammett became one of the magazine's most popular writers. While Hammett did not invent the figure of the hard-boiled detective hero, his writing helped to popularise both the character and hard-boiled style, and, thanks to his own personal experiences as a Pinkerton agent, invested it with a degree of realism. The Op – professional, tough and independent – was such a successful character that Hammett's work was soon being imitated by the other writers at *Black Mask*.

In 1929, Hammett's first novel, *Red Harvest*, was published. It had already been serialised in *Black Mask* and, like Hammett's stories, featured the Continental Op as its protagonist. Drawn from his experiences in Butte,

Hammett sets the novel in the fictional Personville, or Poisonville as it is known to its inhabitants, a mining town riven with corruption, political intrigue and insidious violence, which the Op is given the impossible task of cleaning up. The pervasive urban decay found in *Red Harvest* is a hallmark of all Hammett's fiction, in which metropolitan settings are typically depicted as hostile environments, threatening not only the physical safety of the detective but also his personal integrity. This negative representation of the urban world was only one of the ways in which Hammett brought innovation to the crime writing genre. He was also responsible for the development of a distinctive hard-boiled tone, one that was rooted in the American vernacular. In *Red Harvest*, Hammett uses the Op as a first-person narrator, and the reader is thus forced to witness events from his dispassionate, disillusioned perspective. Hammett's style would later be embellished by Chandler and his protagonist Philip Marlowe, the master of the wise-crack; but Hammett gave hard-boiled crime fiction the sparse language and detached narrative that would become emblematic of the genre. *Red Harvest* was included in *Time* magazine's 100 Best English-language Novels from 1923 to 2005.

Hammett followed *Red Harvest* later the same year with *The Dain Curse*. Set in San Francisco and again featuring the Continental Op, the novel is almost gothic in tone, dealing as it does with ghosts and family curses, as well as the more mundane matter of a jewel theft. In 1930, Hammett published his third novel, *The Maltese Falcon*. The text introduces a new detective hero, Sam Spade. The cynical, straight-talking and street-wise Spade became the model on which many of Hammett's successors would base their protagonists. In the novel, Spade and a Dickensian cast of supporting characters, including the *femme fatale* Brigid O'Shaughnessy, search for the mysterious and priceless falcon statue of the title. Along the way, Spade's partner is killed and Spade himself falls in love with Brigid, only to realise that she, along with everyone else in the novel, is motivated by greed and cannot be trusted. Again, Hammett's depiction of American society is bleak and pessimistic. The novel was filmed in 1931, and again in 1936, before John Huston's celebrated version, starring Humphrey Bogart, was released in 1941. The film cemented the iconic reputation of the novel and Bogart's role as Spade entered the public consciousness as the definitive image of the private detective.

Hammett's next novel, *The Glass Key*, was published in 1931 and holds the distinction of being Hammett's favourite among his works. The protagonist this time is Ned Beaumont, a gambler who is drawn into a murder investigation when the son of a local senator is killed. Very much a tough guy, Beaumont displays the masochistic willingness to take a beating that would become synonymous with male figures in the hard-boiled genre. Hammett followed this with his final novel, *The Thin Man*, in 1932, which features Nick Charles, a former private detective who has retired from his career following his marriage to the wealthy heiress, Nora. However, the two become embroiled in a murder investigation, which they manage to solve together, in between bouts of heavy drinking. Although noticeably softer in form and content than Hammett's earlier work, the novel sold well. In 1934, a film version of *The Thin Man* appeared, starring William Powell and Myrna Loy as Nick and Nora Charles. Such was its success that five sequels, based upon Hammett's characters, were made. In 1937, Hammett made $40,000 when he sold the rights to *The Thin Man* characters to MGM. The second and third of MGM's five Nick and Nora films were based on stories authored by Hammett, but, as the series evolved and the characters became less and less like Hammett's originals, other writers were drafted in to script the films.

Raymond Chandler cited Hammett as a major inspiration for his own writing, and Chandler played an important part in consolidating Hammett's reputation when he published the essay 'The Simple Art of Murder' in 1944. In his essay, Chandler chastises the clue-puzzle crime fiction of British authors such as Agatha Christie as fundamentally unrealistic and holds Hammett up as an example of a writer committed to a more verisimilitudinous approach in his work. According to Chandler, 'Hammett gave murder back to the kind of people that commit it for reasons, not just to provide a corpse; and with the means at hand, not with handwrought duelling pistols, curare, and tropical fish' (Chandler, 1995, p. 989). Of course, Hammett's work, while based on his own experience, is just as stylised and contrived as anything produced by Christie or her contemporaries, but it struck a chord as being more authentically American than any earlier form of crime writing. Hammett's individualistic heroes, motivated by their own moral code and set apart, by choice, from the world in which they inhabit, hark back to an earlier era, drawing on the legacy of America's mythic past, when men in the Wild West celebrated the virtues of independent agency, and a man's integrity was all he had.

Later career

While Hammett's writing career was taking off, his marriage to Josephine was disintegrating, thanks to his heavy drinking and womanising. The couple separated in 1929 and were divorced in 1937, although Hammett continued to do what he could to support Josephine and their daughters. In 1929, Hammett became involved with Nell Martin, a fellow writer to whom he dedicated *The Glass Key*. After breaking up with Martin, Hammett moved to Hollywood, where he met the aspiring playwright Lillian Hellman. Although both Hammett and Hellman were married to other people, they quickly began a relationship that would endure, off and on, for the rest of Hammett's life.

When Hammett first met Hellman his writing career was in the ascendant. He had just finished writing *The Glass Key* and began *The Thin*

Man using Hellman as the model for the character of Nora. However, *The Thin Man* was to be Hammett's last novel. In her introduction to *The Big Knockover*, a volume of Hammett's stories published in 1966, Hellman claims that Hammett was attempting to escape the confines of genre fiction and write a 'serious' novel, provisionally titled 'Tulip'. He was, however, too weakened by his long-term illness, further exacerbated by his drinking and unhealthy lifestyle, to see the project through. Regardless of the explanation, Hammett stopped writing crime fiction in 1932 and instead eked out a precarious living trying to write for Hollywood, composing radio plays and even working on a comic strip called *Secret Agent X-9*.

In the 1930s, as Hammett's writing career waned, he increasingly invested his time and energy in political activity. Hammett was a staunch antifascist and, in 1937, he joined the American Communist Party. He became involved in work to help American citizens who had fought against Franco in the Spanish Civil War and, in 1940, he campaigned to have Communist Party candidates included on the ballot in state elections. These activities succeeded in bringing him to the attention of the FBI. However, the United States entry into the Second World War deferred any action being taken against Hammett. Although he was forty-eight years old and in poor physical condition, Hammett was keen to enlist in the military. Hammett was eventually admitted into the Army Signal Corps as a sergeant and spent the duration of the war on the Aleutian Islands in Alaska, where he conducted training exercises and edited a military newspaper, *The Adakian*. He also helped compose a military booklet, *The Battle of the Aleutians: A Graphic History, 1942–1943* for which he and his collaborators received a commendation.

After his discharge from the Army, Hammett began working at the Jefferson School of Social Science in New York, where he taught creative writing classes. In 1946, Hammett joined the Civil Rights Congress, an organisation considered subversive by the American government, and was elected president of the New York chapter. The CRC maintained a bail fund used to aid those arrested for political reasons. When four men helped by the bail fund absconded in 1951, Hammett refused to provide a court of law with information that might assist in their capture. According to Hellman, Hammett simply did not know anything that might have been useful to the investigation. He refused, however, to admit this and was held in contempt of court and sentenced to six months in prison, which he served at the Federal Correctional Institute at Ashland, Kentucky. Hammett's time in jail further undermined his health, but it did not diminish the intensity of his political convictions, which were further tested by an IRS investigation that claimed he owed several thousand dollars in back taxes. Hammett was penniless by this stage of his life and had no hope of being able to pay back the amount he allegedly owed. Another blow came on the 26 March 1953, when Hammett was called to testify in front of Senator Joseph McCarthy's House of Un-American Activities Committee, which, at the time, was targeting Communist sympathisers across America. Hammett refused to co-operate with the HUAC and was, therefore, blacklisted. The State Department even went so far as to prohibit his books from American libraries overseas.

After living alone in the small town of Katonah, New York, for a period, Hammett spent the final years of his life with Hellman, staying at her apartment in Manhattan, while she took care of him. He died from complications related to lung cancer on the 10 January 1961. He is buried in Arlington National Cemetery.

Suggested reading

J. Hammett (2001) *Dashiell Hammett: a daughter remembers,* R. Layman and J. M. Rivett eds. (New York: Carroll & Graf).

D. Johnson (1984) *The Life of Dashiell Hammett* (London: Chatto and Windus); also published as (1983) *Dashiell Hammett: A Life* (New York: Random House).

R. Layman (1981) *Shadow Man: The Life of Dashiell Hammett* (New York: Harcourt Brace Jovanovich).

W. F. Nolan (1969) *Dashiell Hammett: A Casebook* (Santa Barbara: McNally and Loftin).

Susan Massey

Harris, Thomas (1940–)

Although he publishes infrequently and maintains a low profile, the thriller writer Thomas Harris is among American's most famous living novelists – regardless of genre – thanks to his creation of Hannibal Lecter, one of the most gruesomely compelling characters in modern fiction.

Background

Considering how well his name is known, there is comparatively little information available about Harris' life and background. He closely guards his privacy and has not consented to give an interview since 1984, when an American journalist unwisely suggested to Harris that some level of personal psychopathology might be necessary in order for an author to write convincingly about serial killers. Only the barest biographical sketch is, therefore, possible.

Harris was born on 11 April 1940 in Jackson, Tennessee, to William Thomas Harris Jr, an electrical engineer, and his wife Polly, a high-school science teacher. When his father retired from his job and decided to go into farming, the family relocated to the town of Rich, Mississippi. It was here that Harris spent what was, according to several sources, an unhappy childhood, developing a reputation as a loner. He did, however, find solace in books and went on to study English at Baylor University in Texas, graduating with a bachelor's degree in 1964. While still attending Baylor, Harris began working as a reporter for the local newspaper, the *Waco Tribune-Herald*. Here, he covered crime stories and was once sent to Mexico to investigate a child-prostitution ring. After his graduation, Harris travelled for a time in Europe before returning to America and settling in New York, where, in 1968, he began working as a reporter and an editor for the Associated Press. Again, his beat was the crime desk, which, in conjunction with his earlier experiences at the *Waco Tribune-Herald*, may have provided inspiration for his later fictional work.

While still at Baylor, Harris met and married a fellow student named Ann. They had a daughter, but soon divorced. Harris currently lives with his long-term partner, Pace Barnes, a publishing editor, in south Florida. The couple also have a summer home at Sag Harbor on Long Island and frequently travel to Europe. Amongst friends and acquaintances, Harris enjoys a reputation as a quiet, gentle man, whose hobbies include painting and gourmet cuisine.

The Lecter novels

Harris' first novel, *Black Sunday*, was published in 1975. Taking as its subject a Middle-Eastern terrorist conspiracy to bomb the Super Bowl by means of airship, the book now seems eerily prescient in light of the 9/11 World Trade Centre attacks and the resultant anxiety surrounding the threat of terrorist attacks on densely populated urban areas. The novel did not, however, sell well but was quickly optioned by Hollywood and made into a film, released in 1977, and directed by John Frankenheimer. With the money made from the sale of the novel's rights, Harris was able to retire from journalism to focus on his career as a writer.

In 1981, Harris followed *Black Sunday* with *Red Dragon*. Although a fine thriller in its own right, the book's merits have, to a large extent, been superseded by a character whose appearances are only fleeting but memorable: Hannibal Lecter. The main protagonist in *Red Dragon* is Will Graham, an FBI profiler, who is forced to come out of retirement and to confront his nemesis, the cannibalistic psychiatrist, Dr Lecter, in order to gain potential insight into a serial killer known as 'the Tooth Fairy'. Having put Lecter behind bars and almost losing his life in the process, Graham is loath to re-engage with Lecter, a cunning and intellectually formidable mass-murderer. A film adaptation, re-titled *Manhunter* and directed by Michael Mann, was released in 1986, and was remade as *Red Dragon* in 2002.

It is a similar, but more intensive, proximal relationship between investigator and criminal that forms the basis of Harris' third novel, *The Silence of the Lambs* (1989), in which a trainee special agent, Clarice Starling, is sent by her mentor, FBI bureau chief Jack Crawford, to encourage the incarcerated Lecter to participate in a psychological questionnaire. By tantalising Starling with information pertaining to the active serial killer Buffalo Bill, Lecter is able to establish a bond with her, exchanging details about her childhood and personal life for clues to Bill's identity. By the end of the novel, Starling has killed Buffalo Bill, whereas Lecter, having bartered his way into less restrictive custody, has managed to escape. *The Silence of the Lambs* was an immediate success and has now sold in excess of 12 million copies. In 1991, Jonathan Demme adapted the novel into a critically acclaimed film, starring Anthony Hopkins and Jodie Foster, both of whom won Academy Awards for their roles. The film shared the distinction of winning the top five Oscars,

Best Actor, Actress, Director, Screenplay and Film with *It Happened One Night* (1934) and *One Flew over the Cuckoo's Nest* (1975).

In *Hannibal* (1999), the long-awaited sequel to *The Silence of the Lambs*, the relationship between Lecter and Starling intensifies as the serial killer moves centre stage in narrative events. When Starling's career is ruined, and she is left feeling abandoned by her superiors at the FBI, Lecter reappears in her life and avenges her in predictably grim circumstances. Lecter has been living in Florence under an assumed identity, hiding from both the FBI and the sadistic disfigured paedophile Mason Verger – the only surviving victim of Lecter's original killing spree who is determined to exact revenge on the cannibal. Harris had attended the trial of Pietro Pacciani, the suspect in the 'Monster of Florence' serial murders, and the case and Italian setting proved an inspiration for the novel. At the end of the novel, Starling, having been drugged and kidnapped by Lecter, seems to enter into a romantic relationship with him of her own volition. Many fans of Starling – including, it is rumoured, Jodie Foster, who refused to reprise her earlier role in the film version of the novel – saw this as a betrayal of the character. In Ridley Scott's *Hannibal* (2001), Julianne Moore replaced Foster, while Hopkins returned in the titular role and the Lecter/Starling denouement was changed. The novel and adaptation received mixed reviews, but the commercial success of this film, coupled with the perception of Hopkins as the definitive Lecter, prompted a second cinematic version of *Red Dragon*. Directed by Brett Ratner, *Red Dragon* (2002) saw Hopkins reclaim the role that had originally been played by Brian Cox in Mann's version.

Perhaps the most surprising thing about Lecter's character, other than his regard for Starling, is that he is strangely attractive for a psychopathic cannibal. While there are obvious monstrous elements in his characterisation, he is as much antihero as villain. Cultured, impeccably mannered and blessed with unerring good taste (no pun intended), Lecter usually wields his savage gifts as an unlikely arbiter of taste and decency, striking down those he deems rude or incompetent. He kills with the pride of an artisan in his work, selecting appropriate deaths for his victims, murdering the Italian policeman Rinaldo Pazzi, for example, in a grisly manner that echoes the death of one of his fifteenth century ancestors.

In his early novels, Harris is careful to maintain an air of mystery around Lecter, refusing to offer up any kind of explanation for his murderous predilections. Although more information about Lecter's past is disclosed in *Hannibal*, it is not until *Hannibal Rising* (2006) that Harris provides a full aetiology for his character's pathological behaviour. Intended as a prequel to the Lecter series, the novel explores Hannibal's childhood and adolescence in Lithuania and finds the genesis of his cannibalism in the trauma endured by the loss of his sister, Mischa, who was herself eaten by pro-Nazi Lithuanian militiamen during the Second World War. Throughout the course of the novel, Lecter exacts retribution by tracking down and killing those responsible for his sister's death, before leaving Europe to begin his medical residency at Johns Hopkins Hospital in America.

Despite robust sales, *Hannibal Rising* was critically derided. Harris originally wrote the story as a screenplay, the film version of which appeared, to equally lukewarm reviews, in 2007. While moving Lecter to the centre of the narrative does not seem to have harmed Harris' popularity, it has had a negative impact on the quality of his writing. Harris' first two Lecter novels were based upon his extensive research into criminal psychology and the science of profiling. As examples of forensic procedurals, they are among the best in the genre. Without such a firm procedural footing, both *Hannibal* and *Hannibal Rising* become bogged down in unsatisfying gothic excess, lacking the pace and tension of both *Red Dragon* and *The Silence of the Lambs*.

Suggested reading

J.Cowley (2006) 'Creator of a Monstrous Hit' *Observer*, 19 November 2006 http://www.guardian.co.uk/books/2006/nov/19/fiction.thomasharris, date accessed 5 November 2010.

D. Sexton (2001) *The Strange World of Thomas Harris* (London: Short Books).

Susan Massey

Hiaasen, Carl (1953–)

A writer of satirical crime novels and a journalist known principally for his comically grotesque tales of widespread corruption and sleaze in South Florida, Carl Andrew Hiaasen was born 12 March 1953 in Fort Lauderdale, Florida, the grandson of Norwegian settlers. His father was an attorney and his mother worked as a teacher. Both professions (local law and literature) would strongly influence his subsequent career.

As a child living on the edge of the Florida Everglades, the young Hiaasen was witness to an encroaching wave of corporate development that threatened to eradicate many wild, natural areas of Florida altogether, replacing them with condominiums, malls and highways. The destruction of natural habitats, and the corporate corruption often involved in certain planning decisions, would go on to underpin the majority of his fiction and journalism.

Education and journalism

Hiaasen attended Emory University in 1970 and transferred to the University of Florida in 1972. At both institutions he contributed pieces, often satirical in nature, to the student newspapers (*The Emory Wheel* and *The Independent Florida Alligator* respectively). Upon graduating with a journalism degree in 1974, he started work as a reporter at Florida newspaper *Cocoa Today*. In 1976, at the age of 23, he began a new job as a reporter at the *Miami Herald*, where he still works to this day. Within a few years of his arrival, Hiaasen was working as an investigative reporter. Many of these investigations dealt with subjects that would later become prevalent in his fiction – corruption, drug smuggling, corporate sleaze, and the despoiling of local wildlife by real estate development. In 1985 he began a regular column at the paper. As his novels became increasingly successful, his contributions to the *Herald* became less frequent, cutting back from three columns a week to one in recent years.

Before embarking on a solo writing career, Hiaasen co-wrote three novels with friend and fellow journalist Bill Montalbano, *Powder Burn* (1981), *Trap*

Line (1982) and *Death in China* (1984). The former two titles in particular, set in Key West and Miami, began to tackle the themes of crime and corruption that Hiaasen would embrace in his later work. Montalbano, a distinguished foreign correspondent and latterly Bureau Chief for the London *Times*, died in 1998.

Solo writing career

In 1986 Hiaasen released his first solo novel, *Tourist Season*. The novel, about a terrorist cell intent on killing off Florida's tourist economy in order to save the natural environment, displayed the themes, not to mention the darkly comic style, that would characterise his body of work.

Hiaasen's prose has a lean, reportage-style quality, which was written exclusively in the third-person narrative voice until *Basket Case* (2002). His writing makes extensive use of situational irony and free indirect speech to create an idiosyncratic, ribald and comic vision of Florida as a state swarming with corrupt developers and politicians, violent thugs, conspiracy theorists and environmentalist rebels. As well as being bitingly satirical, Hiaasen's novels also frequently make use of the farcical and the downright ridiculous in their comedy. The pivotal incident in 1993's *Strip Tease* is a slapstick-style brawl in a strip club, and a number of Hiaasen's novels make use of comic coincidences as plot devices.

Hiaasen's work also has its roots at least partially in the tradition of the Southern Gothic or the Grotesque. While his overall body of work would not specifically be classified as such, it does contain many of the motifs of the aforementioned genres. There are often appearances by physically grotesque individuals; the novel *Skin Tight* (1989) features a killer named Chemo who fixes a gardening implement to the stump of his severed arm, as well as describing the machinations of an incompetent plastic surgeon who has botched numerous procedures. There are also a plethora of comically gruesome deaths in Hiaasen's fiction that bear relation to some of the more innovative methods of dispatching characters in the Gothic tradition. Characters are often fed to the alligators that reside in the Florida swamps. In *Tourist Season* there is a particularly inventive sequence wherein the passengers of a cruise ship are showered with shopping bags containing live snakes, and in *Basket Case* a character is attacked with the frozen corpse of a monitor lizard.

Hiaasen acknowledges a literary debt to the Florida crime writer John D. MacDonald, and provided an introduction to the reissue of MacDonald's 1964 novel *The Deep Blue Good-By*. Hiaasen has said of MacDonald, 'his bittersweet view of South Florida was the same as my own' (Hiaasen, 1995, p. viii).

Despite the high body count and atmosphere of sleaze, Hiaasen's fiction generally follows a fairly strong moral code. Characters like *Strip Tease's* protagonist Erin Grant are motivated by a desire to financially support friends and family, and by and large the villains meet nasty or comically appropriate ends. Sympathies in the narratives lie with those who oppose corruption and corporate interference and fight the destruction of wildlife and ecosystems. Some of Hiaasen's novels end with an epilogue which updates the biographies of the leading characters since the end of the main narrative.

The most striking and pervasive embodiment of the militant environmentalist in Hiaasen's fiction is the character of Clinton 'Skink' Tyree, a former governor of Florida and Vietnam veteran turned roadkill-eating hermit. Tyree has so far appeared in six of Hiaasen's novels, the first being 1987's *Double Whammy* and the most recent 2010's *Star Island*. Opposed to the sprawl of development during his incumbency as governor, Tyree was defeated by a powerful cabal of corrupt politicians and developers and subsequently lives alone in the Florida swamps. A character strongly associated with 1960s hippy and rock 'n' roll values, Tyree also represents a desire prevalent throughout at least two centuries of American literature, the motivation to move away from human development and return to living alongside nature. In some respects Tyree is similar to John D. MacDonald's salvage consultant cum private detective Travis McGee in his environmental views and individualism. However there are enough distinctions between the two characters to stop Hiaasen's Clinton Tyree novels descending into a pastiche of the McGee series.

Hiaasen has a guarded attitude about being labelled specifically as a crime fiction writer. 'None of my novels, I don't think, are really whodunits', he has said. 'By page 90, everybody knows whodunit [...] The idea of using suspense or a suspense novel as a framework for satire is just useful to me and it's natural to me from doing newspaper work' (Richards, 2002).

Non fiction, children's fiction and other media

Hiaasen has also published several books of non-fiction. As well as two collections of his newspaper columns (1999's *Kick Ass* and 2001's *Paradise Screwed*), he also wrote the 1998 book *Team Rodent: How Disney Devours the World*, an excoriating attack on the Disney corporation's influence on American culture. Most recently, *The Downhill Lie: A Hacker's Return to a Ruinous Sport* (2008) is a lighter volume about his relationship with the game of golf. In 2004, Hiaasen won the Denver Press Club's Damon Runyon Award for contributions in the field of journalism.

In 2002 Hiaasen published his first book for children, *Hoot*. A critical and commercial success, it was awarded both the Newberry Honor and Rebecca Caudill Young Reader's Book Award. The plot of the book – a fight against developers building on an owl's natural habitat – has much in common with Hiaasen's adult fiction, but with the sex and violence naturally underplayed or not present. Hiaasen would subsequently write two more books for children, *Flush* (2005) and *Scat* (2009).

Additionally, Hiaasen has collaborated on song lyrics with the late musician Warren Zevon, with Zevon also writing an entire song about Hiaasen's novel *Basket Case*. The sentiments of the two writers are a natural fit, with Zevon's strange and often gruesome songs of deviants and corruption – 'Excitable Boy', 'Lawyers, Guns and Money', 'Roland The Headless Thompson Gunner' – often covering similarly satirical ground to Hiaasen.

Hiaasen's fiction – surprisingly given its tight plotting and vivid characters – has rarely been adapted for the screen, and indeed only two film adaptations of Hiaasen novels have ever been released in cinemas. The most high-profile of these was Andrew Bergman's 1996 *Striptease* starring Demi Moore and Burt Reynolds, a critically panned adaptation of the novel of the same name. A film version of *Hoot* was also released in 2006. More recently, Hiaasen has also made media appearances on satirical TV shows in the US, most notably in 2008 on *The Colbert Report*.

Suggested reading

C. Hiaasen (n.d) *Carl Hiaasen* http://www.carlhiaasen.com
L.L. Richards (2002) '*January* Interview with Carl Hiaasen' http://januarymagazine.com/profiles/hiaasen.html, date accessed 15 October 2011.

David Hering

Higgins, George V(incent) (1939–99)

George Vincent Higgins had a distinguished career in the law as a prosecutor, attorney in private practice and academic. He was also a professor and teacher of writing and an industrious journalist who wrote hundreds of articles for three major newspapers. But it would be his career as a novelist for which Higgins will be most well remembered. Although he despised the label 'crime writer', Higgins wrote 26 novels in his lifetime and came to be well regarded in the crime genre despite his dialogue-driven plots coming under criticism for being too repetitive, a consequence perhaps of his prolific output. Higgins achieved his greatest critical recognition not in his own country but in Britain, with the critics Julian Symons and Lord 'Grey' Gowrie in particular singling him out for praise, the latter commenting, 'Higgins is the great classical novelist of the late twentieth century in America' (Bruccoli and Makala, 2006, p. 3).

Early life to debut novel

Higgins was born in Brockton, Massachusetts on 13 November 1939, to Irish-American parents. Massachusetts, and in particular Boston, would become the principal setting of his novels, which often explored the Irish and Italian ethnic identities of the city. Higgins attended Boston College from 1957–61 and received his MA from Stanford University in 1965 and his law degree from Boston College Law School in 1967. During his years as a student, Higgins had already established a career in journalism, working variously as a correspondent, reporter and editor for such publications as *Journal* and *Evening Bulletin* and Associated Press in Springfield and Boston. While working as a reporter and editor, Higgins covered several stories of the New England underworld, thus gaining first-hand knowledge of the subject he would explore in his novels. Higgins's legal career began when he worked as a legal assistant in the Department of the Attorney General for Massachusetts in 1967. He latterly worked as Deputy Assistant Attorney General, Assistant Attorney General, Assistant U.S. Attorney and Special

Assistant United States Attorney. During this time, Higgins's work brought him into close contact with organised crime as he prosecuted several Mob figures in murder cases. From 1973 to 1983, Higgins worked as a criminal attorney in private practice representing such clients as Watergate conspirator G. Gordon Liddy and Black Panther member Eldridge Cleaver.

Higgins's first novel, *The Friends of Eddie Coyle* (1972), was an immediate critical and commercial success, although his writing attempts up until that point had been largely unsuccessful – he had produced up to ten manuscripts that were all rejected for publication. Higgins's intimate knowledge of the law and of journalism is evident in the unique style of his first novel, which alternates between endless reams of dialogue and a cold, impartial third-person narrative as shown through its famous opening line: 'Jackie Brown at 26, with no expression on his face, said that he could get some guns' (Higgins, 1972, p. 1). Records at Higgins's archive at the University of South Carolina show that Higgins considered using the first part of the opening sentence, 'Jackie Brown at 26', as the original title of the novel. The challenge to the reader is how to discern between dialogue which is driving the plot and dialogue given by characters as a verbose distraction. The novel concludes with only a partial sense of resolution: the ramifications of the crimes seem endless and mirror the characters' continual movement through the complex and unwieldy legal system. Thus, the novel begins and ends somewhere in the middle of events. Of *The Friends of Eddie Coyle*, Norman Mailer remarked, 'What I can't get over is that so good a first novel was written by the fuzz.' *The Friends of Eddie Coyle* was adapted into a critically acclaimed film directed by Peter Yates and starring Robert Mitchum in the title role of the aging small-time criminal forced to choose between informing on his associates and upholding his life-long criminal code. This is the only film adaptation of Higgins's work, but at the time of writing, Higgins's third novel *Cogan's Trade* (1974) is being directed for film by Andrew Dominik.

Literary career

With his second novel *The Digger's Game* (1973), Higgins further developed his conversational prose style and sparse plotting in the story of a barman Jerry 'Digger' Doherty who concocts a criminal scheme to cover his gambling debts. As much of the story is conveyed through the dialogue of the loquacious and amoral titular character, Higgins challenges the authority of the traditional, omniscient, third-person narrator. Higgins claimed he wanted to present the story not dissimilarly to how evidence is presented in a trial: the reader has to discern moral judgments and narrative resolution through everything that is seen and heard by the characters. In his third novel *Cogan's Trade*, which completes his loose trilogy of novels on the Boston underworld, Higgins displays his skill at portraying the criminal underworld's hierarchy in a narrative of the violent consequences that unravels when a Mob-protected card game is heisted. But Higgins is at his best in portraying the grifters, thieves and loan sharks. Through these characters, Higgins infuses the plot with a comedy of working-class manners. Higgins's self-knowledge of his innovative experimentation made him protest genre labels and the term 'crime writer'. Higgins focus on dialogue and character over plot paralleled the novels of Elmore Leonard who was a strong admirer of Higgins's work. The two men would later meet at the Harbourfront Reading Series in Toronto and both authors agreed that they did not have to adhere to the hard-boiled school of Dashiell Hammett and Raymond Chandler. Higgins's twenty-fifth and penultimate novel *The Agent* (1999) is often considered to be more overtly in the crime genre than previous efforts, with the first half of the narrative focusing on a homosexual sports agent whose career is in decline and the second half on the investigation into the agent's murder. Higgins also created a series character in the hard-drinking defence lawyer Jerry Kennedy, who defends clients he knows to be guilty and appears in four novels: *Kennedy for the Defence* (1980), *Penance for Jerry Kennedy* (1985), *Defending Billy Ryan* (1992) and *Sandra Nichols Found Dead* (1996). Novels such as *Outlaws* (1987), *Trust* (1989) and *Bomber's Law* (1993) feature narrative interconnectedness through subtle references to minor recurring characters. Higgins's final novel, *At End of Day* (2000), was published posthumously and is a thinly veiled fictionalised account of Boston gangster and informant James 'Whitey' Bulger and his FBI handler John J. Connolly Jr.

Higgins did not achieve the same critical recognition as his contemporaries in the crime fiction genre. This is apparent in Bruce DeSilva's review of Higgins's final novel: 'He wrote strong, sometimes brilliant dialogue. But that's about all he did. Dialogue was a substitute for action. Dialogue was a substitute for narrative. Sometimes it was a substitute for a coherent plot' (DeSilva, 2000, p. BR 15). After the success of Higgins's first three novels, his later attempts failed to reach as broad a readership, as his conversational prose style began to look less innovative and more repetitive with each successive and longer novel. However, in 1985 *The Friends of Eddie Coyle* was selected as one of the best American novels since the Second World War by the British Bookseller's Association, cementing Higgins's reputation in Britain as an important influence on American crime writing but also satisfying Higgins's higher literary ambitions of being considered more than a crime writer. Higgins's non-fiction works include a book on his love of baseball, *The Progress of the Seasons* (1989); a study of Boston Mayor Kevin White's relationship with the press, *Style Versus Substance* (1984); an inside account of the Watergate trials, *The Friends of Richard Nixon* (1975) and *On Writing* (1990). In the 1970s and 80s Higgins was a prolific columnist, writing for such publications as the *Chicago Tribune*, the *New York Times*, the *Wall Street Journal* and the *Atlantic Monthly*. Higgins was twice married: first to Elizabeth Mulkerin in 1965 (this union was dissolved in 1979) and latterly to Loretta Lucas Cubberley in 1979. George V. Higgins died of a heart attack at his home in Milton, Massachusetts, on 6 November 1999, one week before his sixtieth birthday. In 2003, with the assistance of his widow, the Thomas Cooper Library, University of South Carolina, acquired the George V. Higgins archive.

Suggested reading

J. Kifner (1999) 'George V. Higgins, 59, Author of Dialogue-Rich Crime Novels' *New York Times* 09 Nov 1999, p. C29.
P. Liukkonen (2008) 'George V(incent) Higgins (1939–1999)' *Books and Writers* http://kirjasto.sci.fi/higg.htm, date accessed 5 October 2011.
J. Adrian (1999) 'Obituary: George V. Higgins' *Independent,* 10 November 1999 http://www.independent.co.uk/arts-entertainment/obituary-george-v-higgins-1124755.html

Steven Powell

Highsmith, Patricia (1921–95)

Patricia Highsmith was the author of 22 novels and eight collections of short stories. She is best known as the creator of Tom Ripley, the criminal sometimes murderous antihero who featured in five of her books. Widely praised for her sinister and suspenseful psychological thrillers, Highsmith's work was initially more popular in Europe than in the United States. However, multiple film adaptations of her works and critical studies have raised her profile and her reputation in crime fiction has continued to ascend.

Background

Born Mary Patricia Plangman on 19 January 1921 in Fort Worth, Texas, Highsmith's parents, Jay Bernard Plangman and Mary Coates Plangman, who both made their living as commercial artists, separated five months before the birth of their daughter and were divorced soon after. Three years later, Mary married Stanley Highsmith, who formally adopted Patricia. Up until the age of ten, Highsmith believed Stanley to be her biological father, and she did not meet her real father, Plangman, until she was 12. By all accounts, Highsmith's childhood was not a happy one. The marriage between her mother and step-father was tumultuous, and Highsmith was regularly caught up in their disagreements. She did not have a good relationship with her step-father or her mother. As an adult, Highsmith professed dislike for her mother, and the two were completely estranged during the last 20 years of her mother's life. Mary is alleged to have told Patricia that she tried to abort her by drinking turpentine. According to her biographer, Andrew Wilson, who gained access to Highsmith's diaries, Patricia endured life-long psychological trauma as a result of the dysfunctional relationship with her mother, and it left an indelible mark on her fiction. Highsmith was, however, close to one member of her family: her maternal grandmother, with whom she lived for a while as a child. Her grandmother taught her to read and encouraged her love of literature. The young Highsmith was a voracious reader and counted Tolstoy and Dostoevsky among her favourite authors.

In 1927, Highsmith moved to New York with her mother and step-father. Here, she was educated at the Julia Richmond High School and at Barnard College, an all-female establishment affiliated with Columbia University, where she studied English, Latin and Greek, before graduating with a BA in 1942. At Barnard, Highsmith edited the college's literary magazine, while also working on her own short stories. One such story, 'The Heroine', was published in *Harper's Bazaar* in 1941 and was later included in the anthology *O. Henry's Best Short Stories of 1946*. After her graduation, Highsmith worked for a time at Bloomingdale's department store before finding a job supplying plot-lines for comic books. She was one of few women involved in the comic-book industry and worked on many of the major titles of her era. As the job was freelance, Highsmith was able to indulge her love of travel, dividing her time between New York and Mexico.

Early fiction

In 1948, Highsmith quit the comic book business in order to focus on writing her own fiction. She had already had six rejections of her first novel, *Strangers on a Train*, when the author Truman Capote arranged for her to stay at the Saratoga Springs writer's colony at Yaddo. Here, she rewrote the novel extensively, and it was finally published by Harper & Brothers in 1950. In the novel, a chance meeting on a train leads Guy Haines and Charles Anthony Bruno to agree to exchange murders: one will kill for the other and vice versa, thereby ridding themselves of unwanted family members without the police being able to trace a motive back to them. Chance meetings and poor decisions made by desperate people would become hallmarks of Highsmith's fiction, which tend to feature protagonists acting out of a lack of choice, rather than any compulsion towards evil. The naïve Guy Haines is easily manipulated by the malevolent but unstable Bruno. Highsmith had been impressed by Albert Camus' *The Stranger* (1942) and some critics have argued that bleak existentialist philosophy was an influence on her work. Though *Strangers on a Train* is arguably Highsmith's most famous stand-alone work, its fame is largely due to Alfred Hitchcock's celebrated film version, which was released in 1951 and starred Farley Granger and Robert Walker as Guy and Bruno respectively. Several further adaptations have been made – Robert Starr's *Once You Kiss a Stranger* (1969) and Danny DeVito's spoof *Throw Momma from the Train* (1987) – but Hitchcock's is considered the definitive version.

Highsmith's second book, *The Price of Salt*, was published under the pseudonym Claire Morgan in 1952. *The Price of Salt* is not a crime novel; rather, it is the story of an affair between a married woman and a shop girl. Based upon a customer named Kathleen Senn, with whom Highsmith developed an obsession while working at Bloomingdale's, the book sold well despite, or because of, its slightly scandalous content. The novel is considered by many to be groundbreaking, thanks to its depiction of a happy and healthy lesbian sexual identity at a time when many representations of homosexuality tended to be negative. Highsmith was herself a lesbian and, while she never tried to hide her sexuality, she was guarded about her private life. It was not until 1990 that she was persuaded to publish the novel, re-titled *Carol*, under her own name. Throughout her life, Highsmith had several serious affairs with women, including the artist Allela Cornell and the writer Marijane Meaker. She also had occasional relationships with men, including Marc Brandel, a fellow author she met at Yaddo. However, Highsmith never managed to find a long-term partner, which her biographer, Andrew Wilson, attributed to a tendency to fixate on unavailable, heterosexual women and an inclination towards self-destructive behaviour, a legacy of the pathological relationship with her mother.

In 1954, Highsmith published *The Blunderer*, which, like *Strangers on a Train*, hinges upon an intense and unlikely relationship between two men. Walter Stackhouse, the titular blunderer, comes under suspicion of murder when his wife, whom he wished dead, commits suicide. Stackhouse's obsessive interest in Melchior Kimmel, a man who really did kill his wife, only serves to compound his guilty conscience and draws the attention of the police. In *Plotting and Writing Suspense Fiction* (1966), the author's guide to crime writing, Highsmith states, '[t]he theme I have used over and over again in my novels is the relationship between two men, usually quite different in make-up, sometimes an obvious contrast in good and evil, sometimes merely ill-matched friends' (Highsmith, 2001, p. 138). While true of both *The Blunderer* and *Strangers on a Train*, it was in her series of novels featuring Tom Ripley that the themes of identity and friendship would come to the fore.

The Ripley novels

Tom Ripley makes his first appearance in *The Talented Mr. Ripley* (1955), which Highsmith wrote in six months while on an extended trip to Mexico. The book was critically acclaimed and was nominated for an Edgar Award for best crime novel in 1956. When the reader is introduced to Ripley, he is living in New York and is struggling to make a living. However, circumstances intervene when an accidental meeting with the shipping magnate Herbert Greenleaf sees Ripley dispatched to Europe to bring Greenleaf's prodigal son, Dickie, back to America. Naturally, all does not go according to plan. From the outset, Ripley displays an obsessive fascination with Dickie, which is unreciprocated: Dickie views Ripley as an irritant, while Greenleaf's girlfriend, Marge, believes Ripley is homosexual with designs on her man. Frustrated by Dickie and Marge's lack of acceptance, Ripley eventually murders Dickie. Demonstrating a remarkable talent for imitation and forgery, combined with a ruthless pursuit of upward mobility, Ripley assumes Dickie's identity and begins to live the life to which he believes he is entitled whilst living in constant fear of exposure. The rest of the series sees Ripley using any means possible to sustain the fiction he has created. In *Ripley Under Ground* (1970), Highsmith's protagonist is married, settled in France and funding his lifestyle by profits accrued through an art forgery scheme. When threatened with exposure, Ripley is, once again, driven to kill. A run-in with the Mafia forms the basis of the third novel in the series, *Ripley's Game* (1974), while the fourth, *The Boy Who Followed Ripley* (1980), again picks up on the theme of unlikely pairings as Ripley finds a kindred spirit in a teenage murderer. A fifth Ripley novel, *Ripley Under Water*, appeared in 1991. In this, Ripley is once again concerned with aggressive self-protection when questions begin to be asked about his past.

The Ripley series has provided fertile territory for cinematic adaptations. René Clément, Wim Wenders, Anthony Minghella and Liliana Cavani have all filmed versions of the novels, with Alain Delon, Dennis Hopper, Matt Damon and John Malkovich playing Ripley. BBC Radio 4 also broadcast adaptations of all five texts in 2009. These adaptations are a testament not only to the popularity of Ripley's character, but also to Highsmith's skill in creating him. Highsmith claimed that there was much of her own personality in Ripley's representation and she referred to him fondly as her favourite character. Although he perpetrates horrific deeds seemingly without compunction, Ripley is depicted as charming, engaging and even likable. Highsmith neatly avoids the constraints of conventional morality in her fictional world – while her protagonist's crimes are odious, the reader cannot help being on his side, wanting him to evade detection. Highsmith achieves this by restricting the reader to Ripley's point of view and, from his unscrupulous perspective, crime does seem to pay. Ripley is not presented as evil; rather he is amoral and is motivated by what he justifies as necessity. While criminal acts occur in the Ripley narratives, they are, like most of Highsmith's fiction, not straightforward mysteries. There is never any doubt about who the guilty party is. Instead, suspense is generated by the question of whether or not Ripley will get away with his crimes.

Later works

Between the first and second Ripley novels, Highsmith published prolifically. *Deep Water* (1957) takes extreme marital strife as its subject matter, telling of a husband who kills his unfaithful wife. Highsmith followed this in 1958 with *A Game for Living*, a rare whodunit. Set in Mexico, the novel is about two men who become suspects when a woman they were both involved with is murdered. Even this venture into more generic territory is thrillingly done, with an emphasis on compelling characterisation and psychological depth. Next, came *This Sweet Sickness* (1960), about a mentally unstable man who becomes obsessed with his ex-girlfriend, and *The Two Faces of January* (1961), which deals with the accidental murder of a policeman in Greece and the resulting attempt to cover up the crime. *The Cry of the Owl* (1962) deals with an act of voyeurism that escalates into murder and mob justice, and it was filmed by the celebrated French director Claude Chabrol in 1987.

Highsmith always felt much more appreciated in Europe than in her homeland of the US. In 1957 she won France's *Grand Prix de Littérature Policière* for *The Talented Mr Ripley* and, in 1963, she decided to leave America permanently, living in Italy, England and France before settling in Locarno, Switzerland. While in Switzerland, Highsmith became increasingly reclusive. A combination of depression and alcoholism exacerbated her tendency towards misanthropy, and Highsmith developed a reputation as a difficult person to deal with. She continued to write, however. In 1964 she published *The Glass Cell*, a bleak investigation into the consequences of wrongful imprisonment upon one man's psyche. Both *A Suspension of Mercy* (1965) and *Those Who Walk Away* (1967) tread territory similar to some of Highsmith's earlier work. The former deals with unhappy matrimony and fantasies of violent escape that then backfire, while the latter again tells of the suicide of a wife casting suspicion upon her husband. *The Tremor of Forgery* (1969) escapes the pattern of domestic discord, focusing instead on an accidental killing committed by a writer living in Tunisia.

After living for a period as an expatriate in Europe, the tone of Highsmith's work became more noticeably anti-American, which may have had some bearing on her lack of popularity there. *A Dog's Ransom* (1972) paints a grim picture of urban life in New York, a city that seems to be exclusively populated by criminals and reprobates. *People Who Knock on the Door* (1983) expands this critique to wider American society, while *Found in the Street* (1986) repeats Highsmith's negative depiction of New York as an epicentre of violent crime. Between these novels, Highsmith published *Edith's Diary* (1977), an equally unsettling portrayal of the descent of one woman into madness. To compensate for the disintegration of her everyday life, Edith, Highsmith's first female protagonist since *A Taste of Salt*, invents an alternate reality in her diary, and, gradually, she succumbs to this illusory world. The novel was a success and Highsmith's depiction of Edith was hailed as particularly convincing. *Edith's Diary* also did much to rescue Highsmith from accusations of woman-hating, levelled by critics taking the title of her short-story collection *Little Tales of Misogyny* (1974) as evidence.

In 1979, Highsmith was named as a Grand Master by the Swedish Academy of Detection. She was further honoured in 1990, when she was awarded the prestigious title of the Order of Arts and Letters by the French Ministry of Culture. After the publication of the final Ripley novel in 1991, Highsmith began working on what would be her final novel, *Small g: a Summer Idyll*. Set in a gay bar in Zurich, the novel seems somewhat insubstantial when compared with her earlier work. It was initially rejected by her usual publisher, Knopf, and, when finally released, received lukewarm reviews from critics. However, Highsmith did not live to see this; she died of leukemia in Locarno on the 4 February 1995, several days before *Small g* was published. At the time of her death, Highsmith was living alone, with only her cat, Charlotte, for company. The last person to see her alive was her accountant, whom she sent away. Highsmith left the bulk of her estate, worth some three million dollars, to the Saratoga Springs writer's colony, in gratitude for the time she spent there. Her archives remain in the Swiss capital, Berne.

Suggested reading

N. Mawer (2004) *A Critical Study of the Fiction of Patricia Highsmith: From the Psychological to the Political* (Lewiston, New York: Edwin Mellen Press).

J. Schenkar (2009) *The Talented Miss Highsmith: The Secret Life and Serious Art of Patricia Highsmith* (London: St Martin's Press).

A. Wilson (2003) *Beautiful Shadow: A Life of Patricia Highsmith* (London: Bloomsbury).

Susan Massey

Hillerman, Tony (1925–2008)

Author of the acclaimed 'Navajo' detective fiction series, set in the American South West, and featuring Joe Leaphorn and Jim Chee, officers in the Navajo tribal police. Hillerman's 18 'Navajo' novels are efficient police procedurals with engaging central characters, but they are most praised for their detailed exploration of Navajo life, culture, and religion. Although he was a white American, in 1987 Hillerman was given a Special Friend of the Dineh award by the Navajo Tribal Council. His novels have won many awards, including an Edgar for *Dance Hall of the Dead* (1973).

Anthony Grove Hillerman was born 27 May 1925 on a farm in Sacred Heart, Oklahoma. He was educated at a local mission school for Indian children for eight years. Sacred Heart had formally been an Indian territory and was at that time one of Oklahoma's dust-bowl villages. Hillerman grew up in a household without electricity and running water and was raised amongst the Potawatomie and Seminole Indians whom he would find it easier to identify with than the community's white ethnic groups. Hillerman later attended Oklahoma A&M College, and, from 1942, the University of Oklahoma. The advent of the Second World War interrupted Hillerman's studies. In 1943 he joined the US Army and he would see fierce combat in Europe, taking part in the D-Day Landings with the 103rd Infantry Division. He was severely wounded by a mine, returning home with silver and bronze stars for valour and a Purple Heart. Hillerman's literary career had its genesis when a journalist, who was reporting on Hillerman's wartime experiences, recommended he should try for a career in writing after reading the letters Hillerman had written home from the front. Hillerman graduated in 1948, and married Marie Unzner the same year. They had six children, five of them adopted.

After graduation Hillerman became a journalist, working for newspapers in Oklahoma and Texas, and later as the United Press International bureau chief in Santa Fe, where he also edited the city's newspaper, the *New Mexican*. He began studying for an MA in English at the University of New Mexico, before joining the faculty in 1966; he taught journalism there for 20 years.

Leaphorn and Chee series

Hillerman's first novel, *The Blessing Way* (1970) introduces Joe Leaphorn of the Navajo Tribal Police in a plot that involves a missing man, a discovery of a corpse and an anthropologist doing research into Navajo witches, known as 'Skinwalkers'. Hillerman did not originally intend Leaphorn to be a central character in the novel, but he frequently stated that the idea for a Native American detective came from the novels of Australian writer Arthur W. Upfield, who in the late 1920s and 1930s published a series of novels featuring a half-European, half-Aboriginal detective, Napoleon Bonaparte. Bonaparte's detection depends on his understanding of Aboriginal tradition. In his second Leaphorn novel, the 1974 Edgar-winning *Dancehall of the Dead* (1973), Hillerman developed this idea, bringing Leaphorn more to the fore and making the search for a missing boy the pretext for an exploration of Zuni religion. Leaphorn featured on his own in one further novel, *Listening Woman* (1978).

In *People of Darkness* (1980), Hillerman introduced a second series character, Sgt. Jim Chee. In contrast to Leaphorn, who is not a religious man, Chee is training to be a yataalii (a shaman, or medicine man). Leaphorn's rejection of superstitions like witchcraft allows him to take a more practical view of reservation life and a pragmatic view of the problems faced by the Navajo: unemployment, poverty, and alcoholism. Chee, on the other hand, is more interested in mystery, and spirituality, as motivational and inspirational forces. Leaphorn and Chee police a 25,000-square-mile area of the Four Corners of the American Southwest, the intersecting borders of New Mexico, Arizona, Utah and Colorado.

Chee appears in three novels without Leaphorn, but Hillerman brought the two together in *Skinwalkers* (1986), perhaps realising that their contrasting approaches would bring tension to the stories. Leaphorn's sceptical, modern view of detection grates against Chee's interpretive, intuitive method, but the combination allows them to investigate a series of murders, and the malign influence of criminals from beyond the reservation.

Many of the novels explore current issues affecting traditional Navajo ways of living, and the preservation of important artefacts and landscapes in an anachronistic culture which clashes with contemporary American society. In *A Thief of Time* (1988), Leaphorn and Chee investigate the plundering of archaeological sites by 'pot hunters', while *Coyote Waits* (1990), which won the Nero Wolfe Award for Mystery in 1991, begins with vandalism of a rock formation and develops, by way of the murder of a policeman, and the trial of a shaman, to an exploration of the idea of the 'trickster'.

Hillerman's detective novels are for the most part cleverly plotted and well-paced. But Hillerman's fascination with and respect for the Navajo, Hopi, and Zuni peoples, and his attention to detail in describing their lives, has resulted in his books appearing on reading lists for cultural anthropology courses. Hillerman's analysis of issues affecting the people living on the reservations is at least as important as the stories themselves. His last of the 18 Leaphorn/Chee novels was *The Shape Shifter* (2006), but he was also the author of several other books, including the novel *The Fly on the Wall* (1970), and the children's book *Buster Mesquite's Cowboy Band* (2007).

Hillerman's anthologies include (with Rosemary Herbert) *The Oxford Book of American Detective Stories* (1996), and *A New Omnibus of Crime* (2009). Among his non-fiction books, most of which are about New Mexico and Arizona, are *Indian Country: America's Sacred Land* (1987), and his autobiography *Seldom Disappointed: A Memoir* (2001). Three of Hillerman's Leaphorn and Chee novels were adapted into television films for PBS American Mystery! Specials, and *The Dark Wind* was adapted for the big screen in 1991 with Fred Ward and Lou Diamond Phillips in the roles of Leaphorn and Chee.

Hillerman was President of the Mystery Writers of America and won an Owen Wister Award for lifetime achievement from the Western Writers of America in 2008. He received a Malice Domestic Lifetime Achievement Award in 2002. In 1991 he received the French *Grand Prix de Litterature Policiers* and was made an MWA Grand Master. Tony Hillerman died of pulmonary failure in 2008. He had been in declining health for some time having endured two heart attacks, operations for prostate and bladder cancer and the long term effects of his war wounds. Hillerman's books are sometimes criticised for being too moralising, but they are entertaining mysteries brimming with fascinating detail about the Navajo, and the American South West, its landscape and people.

Suggested reading

T.Hillerman (2002) *Seldom Disappointed* (New York: Harper).

J. Holley (2008) 'Tony Hillerman, 83; Penned Navajo Series' *The Washington Post*, 28 October 2008 http://www.washingtonpost.com/wp-dyn/content/story/2008/10/28/ST2008102801372.html, date accessed 1 October 2010.

J.M. Reilly (1996) *Tony Hillerman: A Critical Companion* (Critical Companions to Popular Writers) (Westport, CT: Greenwood Press).

Christopher Routledge

Himes, Chester (1909–84)

Best known for his 'Harlem domestic' novels, a series of hard-boiled detective stories featuring the black police partnership of 'Grave Digger' Jones and 'Coffin' Ed Johnson, Chester Himes began writing with the intention of producing radical and serious works of fiction which addressed issues of racial oppression and discrimination in the United States. He desired a writing career which would see his critical reputation rival that of Richard Wright or James Baldwin and, for many years, remained embittered and disappointed that financial necessity drove him to writing in a genre which he considered inferior to his high literary ambitions. Yet, although Himes was not the first black crime writer, or even the first to feature a black detective, the 'Harlem domestic' series *A Rage in Harlem* (1957), *The Crazy Kill* (1959), *The Real Cool Killers* (1959), *All Shot Up* (1960), *The Big Gold Dream* (1960), *Cotton Comes to Harlem* (1965), *The Heat's On* (1966), *Blind Man with a Pistol* (1969) and the unfinished *Plan B*, all written from exile in France, contain a number of distinctive features which ensure their status as iconic works which are both original and challenging to the genre.

Early life

Born Chester Bomar Himes in Jefferson City, Missouri, 19 July 1909, Himes's family life, although reasonably stable both socially and financially, was unhappy due to a combination of racial tension and family tragedies. Both parents were well-educated – Estelle Bomar Himes worked as a teacher before her marriage and Himes's father Joseph was a lecturer – and ambitious for their children. However, the lighter-skinned Estelle, according to her son, despised and repeatedly humiliated her husband because of his blackness. After the family moved to Cleveland in 1925, they lived in a white Jewish neighbourhood where the problems intensified. The family unhappiness was compounded when Himes's brother was blinded in a school chemistry laboratory and Himes was badly injured in a fall down a lift shaft – the family ascribing both accidents at least partially to racial discrimination. The acid attack, in *A Rage in Harlem*, which leaves Coffin Ed Johnson both physically and emotionally scarred may be a reference to Himes's brother's accident: it seems clear that the repeated negative presentations of 'high-yellow' women and engagement with inter-racial sexual problems in the novels is a product of his parents' marriage problems.

Prison

Himes became a student at Ohio State University in 1926 but was expelled after an incident where he was held responsible for taking a group of other students to a brothel. After his return, in disgrace, to Cleveland, he met his future wife, Jean, and began drifting into petty crime which eventually escalated into the armed robbery of an elderly couple, resulting in him being sentenced, at the age of 19, to 25 years in prison. During his time in prison, he had a passionate homosexual relationship, narrowly escaped death, and became enthralled by the anecdotes of his fellow prisoners and the stories in the pulp magazines he enthusiastically devoured. Those anecdotes, and the hard-boiled stories he read, inspired the Harlem environment and the detective partnership which he presented in the Harlem Domestic series. In 1934 he had his first article published and his case gained increasing attention with a number of intellectuals stressing his exceptional talent, his youth, and the harshness of his treatment, first by the university and later by the courts. After serving almost seven years, he was released and, in 1937, married Jean Johnson. He obtained financial and creative support from some of those who had campaigned for his release, including Langston Hughes, and had a number of stories accepted for publication with hard-boiled magazines. But Himes still faced financial hardship and eventually decided to move to Los Angeles where he hoped to obtain work as a writer in the film industry.

Los Angeles

Although the move to Los Angeles was partially the result of his difficult financial situation, Himes was extremely optimistic about his prospects in the thriving film industry. Following his discharge from prison, he had worked on the Federal Writers' Project which, although it was temporary and poorly paid, was a generally positive experience in terms of the racial attitudes he encountered. He had also published a number of stories and worked for a Cleveland newspaper, and he moved to Los Angeles believing that he had the talent and experience to be a successful screen-writer. Himes was unprepared for the racism he encountered in Los Angeles: he found the government-sponsored shipyards ruled by 'Jim Crow' practices and his brief stay at Warner Brothers ended when Jack Warner, hearing of his employment, commented that he would have 'no goddamned niggers' on his payroll. His first two novels *If He Hollers Let Him Go* (1945) and *Lonely Crusade* (1947) engage with issues relating to both racial discrimination and sexual violence. With his novels receiving a generally negative response, his marriage to Jean ended, and feeling increasingly bitter and disillusioned about the prospects for personal or racial advancement in the United States, Himes decided, in the early 1950s, to join a number of other black writers and intellectuals in exile in France.

Enter the detectives

The middle phase of Himes's writing career, which include *Cast the First Stone* (1952), *The Third Generation* (1954) and *The Primitive* (1955), are all works dealing with the impact of racial oppression, particularly in work-place situations, and the tensions inherent in mixed-race sexual relation-ships. It was during his stay in Paris that his publisher, Marcel Duhamel, suggested that he should try his hand at detective stories and, despite being middle-aged and considering the genre as probably beneath his ability, he threw himself into the work with enthusiasm. He later said that writing the Harlem Domestic series, the first novel of which he claimed to produce in just over six weeks (although he sometimes said it only took three), was the happiest experience of his life. *A Rage in Harlem* (1957) originally published as *For Love of Imabelle* and also titled *The Five-Cornered Square*, is the first work of the series, and it is well-advanced into a chaotic, horrifi-cally violent and simultaneously comical plot before the police detective partnership of Coffin Ed Johnson and Grave Digger Jones arrives on the scene. Described at their first appearance as two 'tall, loose-jointed, sloppily dressed, ordinary-looking dark-brown colored men' (Himes, 1957, p. 52), they remain throughout the series simultaneously unremarkable – and thus able to almost disappear within their community – and extraordinary, with their exploits the stuff of legend in Harlem. Working entirely within the Harlem boundaries, they are black men upholding white power structures and so occupy an ambivalent position – yet they explicitly foreground black masculinity and thus challenge the traditional landscape of the hard-boiled detective story.

In each novel Coffin and Grave Digger have to solve crimes which are violent, complex and extremely confusing, and they always approach their task with strength, endurance, courage and skill. They are clearly exceptional men and remarkable detectives with a determination to achieve as much justice as they can for the residents of Harlem. At the same time they are frequently violent towards those residents, and Coffin's and Grave Digger's place in the white power structure, which Himes presents as ultimately responsible for crime, makes their status ambivalent. As the series progresses, it becomes increasingly clear that the men, despite their abilities, cannot overcome the challenges which face their community, and the last novel in the series *Blind Man With a Pistol* finds them aging and powerless when faced with the senseless anarchy of a race riot.

By the time he wrote *Blind Man With a Pistol*, Himes had been living outside the United States for a number of years and, although his anger and bitterness at the racism he had found there was undiminished, he had no personal experience of the race riots which swept American cities in the middle and late 1960s. He remained convinced throughout his life that the route to racial harmony was through unified action for working men, of whatever race, rather than through specific projects, initiatives, or actions – including riots – which included only the black community. These beliefs, formed through his association with the Writers' Project and his links with the Communist Party in his Los Angeles years, placed him increasingly at odds with some other black intellectuals. Himes was equally clear that his main concerns in the Harlem series remained those he had addressed in his earlier works – how black masculinity and heterosexuality could be expressed within a racist society and the inevitability of violence for black men denied that expression.

Coffin and Grave Digger feature as powerful examples of an active black masculinity, yet they are clearly restricted by their race and unable to obtain access to the levers of real power or avenge their community by violence towards the white society so that they, and other men in Harlem, appear to often demonstrate their masculinity through violence towards women.

Women in Himes's detective novels

Himes's presentation of women in the Harlem Domestic series is controversial. His two detectives, unusually for the genre, are apparently happily married, although their wives play very restricted roles in the narratives. However Himes does place a large number of female characters, all either black or 'high-yellow', at the heart of their communities and the centre of his narratives. Whilst some, mainly older black women, are treated with respect, Himes's presentation of lighter-skinned women is invariably negative: they are usually seeking to seduce, betray and deceive black men. The violent treatment they receive, often at the hands of the detectives, is apparently no more than they deserve. Yet their presence, as female, non-white, characters at the centre of the narrative challenges the hard-boiled detective formula. Like the detectives themselves the 'high-yellow' woman is a boundary transgressor – her very existence proof that racial boundaries have been crossed. Her attempts to seduce black men threatens a continuation of that transgression and raises the spectre of her triumph not only over their masculinity but also their blackness.

Harlem

Coffin and Grave Digger patrol a Harlem which Himes said 'was never meant to be real' but which he did want 'to take [....] away from the white man if only in my books' (Himes, 1972, p. 126). Basing his presentation of the city on the fantastic stories he had been told in prison, he created an imagined self-contained black universe – clearly not a real urban location but a parable of the effect of a racist society on a contained population. Himes's Harlem is a chaotic, violent and dangerous place to live, but it is also incoherent and this offers its residents some protection from white authorities who find it impossible to penetrate its mysteries. The detectives, facing a multiplicity of crimes and generally bizarre behaviour, are often bemused and confused by incidents which are often both horrifically tragic and grotesquely comic, but they are more skilled than white officialdom at understanding what is happening because they understand the desperation which drives the residents. One crime list in *Cotton Comes to Harlem* includes a man who has killed his wife with an axe because she burned his breakfast, another who has inexplicably attacked a stranger with a razor, and a man dressed as a Cherokee Indian who has used a home-made tomahawk to split a white bartender's skull.

Literary success

Himes claimed to view the Coffin and Grave Digger novels purely as work for hire yet, in the series, he engaged with essentially the same material as in his first novels – the exploitation of African-Americans within the United States – but he added an absurdist landscape and a bitterly ironic humour. From the outset the series enjoyed considerable success in France where they were regarded as sociological crime novels with *For Love of Imabelle* (*Rage in Harlem*) winning the *Grand Prix* in 1958 for best detective novel of the year. During his writing of the series, Himes also produced two other novels, *Pinktoes* (1961) and *Run Man Run* (1966), both of which engaged with similar hard-boiled themes. His major writings after the Harlem series were his two autobiographical works *The Quality of Hurt* (1973) and *My Life of Absurdity* (1976). Despite the success of his work, Himes continued to experience financial hardship, at least partially because of his apparent inability to manage his money, and he was able to live fairly comfortably only because a number of patrons made various homes available to him for a period of time. This resulted in him moving frequently, living at various times in Spain, Sweden, England and Egypt.

During his time in Paris, Himes began a serious relationship with Lesley Packard, whom he eventually married after finally divorcing Jean, but he continued to have a series of relationships with white women. During a visit to see a girlfriend in Mexico in the early 1960s, he suffered a serious stroke which left him incapacitated for a number of months at a time in his life when he seemed to be obtaining some financial stability and, finally, critical recognition in the United States. In 1969 he and his wife moved to Moraira in Spain where Himes died in 1984, after spending the last years of his life working on his autobiographical works.

Himes published 17 novels, 60 short stories and two volumes of autobiography: three of the Harlem series were made into films, *Cotton Comes to Harlem* was directed by Ossie Davis in 1970 and starred Godfrey Cambridge and Raymond St. Jacques who also appeared in *Come Back Charleston Blue* (the film version of *The Heat's On*) in 1974. *A Rage in Harlem* was filmed in 1991.

Suggested reading

J. Sallis (2000) *Chester Himes: A Life* (Edinburgh: Payback Press).

R.E. Skinner (1989) *Two Guns from Harlem: The Detective Fiction of Chester Himes* (Bowling Green: Bowling Green State University Press).

S.F. Soitos (1996) *The Blues Detective: A Study of African-American Detective Fiction* (Amherst: University of Massachusetts Press).

W.W. Walters (1994) 'Limited Options: Strategic Maneuverings in Himes's Harlem' *African-American Review*, Winter 1994, 28 (4) 615–31.

Maureen Sunderland

Huggins, Roy (1914–2002)

Predominantly a screenwriter for film and television, Huggins began his career as a crime novelist in the mid-1940s. Born in Washington State, Huggins attended the University of California between 1935–41 before working as a special representative of the US Civil Service during the Second World War between the years 1941–43, and as an industrial engineer from 1943–46. He was nominated for an Emmy Award in 1968 and 1977, received the 1991 Shamus Award from the Private Eye Writers of America, the 1994 Golden Laurel Award from the Producers Guild of America and the 2002 Golden Boot Award. Huggins was first married to artist Bonnie Porter and then to actress Adele Mara and had five children from the two marriages.

The Double Take (1946) was Huggins's first novel. Influenced by Chandler, it featured the private eye Stuart Bailey who also appeared in the 1946 short stories 'Now You See It' and 'Appointment with Fear'. This novel and two short stories were all published in the *Saturday Evening Post*, while another Bailey short story, 'Death and the Skylark' (1952), appeared in *Esquire*. The three short stories of this period were collected in *77 Sunset Strip* (1959), which shared its title with the television series (1958–64) for which Huggins adapted his PI Bailey. Charged with being a communist, Huggins testified before Senator Joseph McCarthy's House Committee on Un-American Activities. Huggins claimed he had only joined the Communist party in the 1930s for its anti-fascist stance and left after the signing of the Nazi-Soviet pact in August 1939. During his testimony, Huggins named 21 other party members, and as a result, he was not blacklisted. He later hired blacklisted writers to work on several of his programmes.

Huggins published other novels but soon began writing for Hollywood, with his first film scripts *Fuller Brush Man* and *I Love Trouble* released in 1948. It was in film, and from 1955 in television, that Huggins had his greatest impact on the crime genre. Denied a share of the profits for his television series, Huggins left Warner Brothers and became Vice President of television production at 20th Century Fox in 1960, and in 1963 at Universal, where he wrote and produced many television series including *The Fugitive* (1963–67),

The Rockford Files (1974–80) and the short-lived *City of Angels* (1976). After leaving Warner Brothers, Huggins demanded full ownership of all the television concepts he authored, and this became known as the 'Huggins Contract', which was much coveted by other producers. Huggins's prolific output has sometimes appeared under the pseudonym John Thomas James, derived from the first names of his three sons to Adele Mara.

Suggested reading

D. Marc and R. J. Thompson (1995) 'Roy Huggins: Let Cooler Heads Prevail' *Prime Time, Prime Movers: From I Love Lucy to L.A. Law-America's Favorite TV Shows and the People Who Created Them* (New York: Syracuse University Press) pp. 141–52.

Chris Pak

Hughes, Dorothy B(elle) (1904–93)

Novelist, journalist and poet Dorothy B. Hughes is best known for her 14 hard-boiled/noir crime novels, the most popular of which are *Ride the Pink Horse* (1946) and *In a Lonely Place* (1947), both of which were memorably adapted for cinema at the height of the American film noir movement. *Ride the Pink Horse* (1947) starred Robert Montgomery and *In a Lonely Place* (1950) saw Humphrey Bogart in the role of Dix Steele.

Hughes was born Dorothy Belle Flanagan in Kansas City, Missouri. She studied journalism at the University of Missouri. After graduation, she worked as a journalist as well as publishing a volume of poetry, *Dark Certainty* (1931), which won the Yale Younger poets Award. She spent some time as a graduate at the University of New Mexico and Columbia University, New York, and she lived most of her adult life in Santa Fe, New Mexico, the location for several of her novels. Her journalistic style is arguably evident in her fiction, which is often direct, fast-paced and pared-down. It also has a strong theme of detached observation, on the part of the narrator and other characters, who note precise details of each other's actions and appearance. The realistic atmosphere that this detailing generates is sometimes in tension with the more stylised requirements of the noir genre, such as the name of the killer rapist 'Dix Steele' in *In a Lonely Place*.

Her first book, *The So Blue Marble* was published in 1940, a slightly fantastical crime/spy thriller. Like all of her works, it reflects contemporary America: the aftermath of the depression, World War II, and the paranoia of the McCarthy Era all inform the action of her stories. She wrote approximately one novel a year until family responsibilities effectively curtailed her literary career: she married Levi Allen Hughes Jr in 1932 and they had three children. Her final novel, *The Expendable Man*, appeared in 1963. This is considered by many to be her best work. Hughes continued her journalistic writing, however. Between 1940 and 1979, she reviewed crime novels for a number of publications, including the *Los Angeles Times* and the *New York Herald-Tribune*, and her critical biography, *Erle Stanley Gardner: The Case of the Real Perry Mason* (1978), won an Edgar Award. She was named Grand Master by the Mystery Writers of American in 1978.

As noir is stereotypically a male-dominated genre, there has been considerable focus on Hughes as a woman writing noir, and this gender issue has been a key interest of recent critical studies in her work. The Feminist Press republished *In a Lonely Place* in 2002 and *The Blackbirder* in 2004: both novels offer strong women characters, which bucked the trend for many genres at the time of their original publication. There is more to Hughes than proto-feminism, though: her work stands as classic, well-written, hardboiled crime fiction regardless of the writer's gender.

Suggested reading

S. Orr (2010) *Darkly Perfect World: Colonial Adventure, Postmodernism and American Noir* (Columbus: Ohio State University Press).

A. Villarejo (2004) 'Afterword' *The Blackbirder* by D. B. Hughes (New York: Feminist Press). pp. 209–234.

Esme Miskimmin

Keene, Day (1903/1904–69)

One of the first writers to successfully transition from pulp magazines to paperback originals, Day Keene's biography is obscure, but the recent republication of his work has led to renewed interest in his contribution to crime writing.

Born Gunard Hjerstedt in Chicago, Keene was an actor in repertory theatre in the 1920s. Keene eventually chose writing over acting, purportedly by flipping a coin, and under his real name, Hjerstedt, wrote several crime stories in the early 30s for pulp magazines, mainly *Detective Fiction Weekly*. Keene wrote for the female PI radio drama *Kitty Keene Inc* (1937–41) and for several other radio soaps including *The First Nighter*, *Behind the Camera Lines* and *Little Orphan Annie*. The first short story to appear under his pseudonym derived from his mother's maiden name Daisy Keeney was 'It Could Happen Here!' (1940), which was published in the pulp magazine *Ace G-Man Stories*. Initially prompted by an editor for a pseudonym, Keene would eventually change his name legally. Keene wrote for various pulps at the rate of two or three stories per month. His regular publishers included *Detective Tales* and *Dime Detective*. Keene also wrote an occasional westerns or jungle stories and appeared from time to time in the more prestigious *Short Stories*.

The novels

Keene published his first novel, *Framed in Guilt*, in 1949. Unlike many of his later novels, it was published in hardcover. *Framed in Guilt* is a rather traditional Hollywood novel about a successful screenwriter who is being blackmailed over a crime from his past. In *Home is the Sailor* (1952), a man punches and subsequently kills a man who has raped a beautiful blonde woman. Rather than go to the police, they decide to secretly bury the body, a decision which leads to events spiralling out of control.

Keene wrote convincingly about ordinary people who get caught in the world of crime. In his books no one is ever totally evil or corrupt, and even the best of his protagonists are faulty and obsessive. In *Who Has Wilma*

Lahtrop? (1955), Jim Lathrop is a teacher that starts receiving threats about his wife. Soon his wife disappears, and he has to track her down himself. He finds himself investigating Wilma's rather disturbed family: the novel deals with unsettling themes of sexual molestation and incest.

In *Murder on the Side* (1956) Larry Hanson, a slightly bored middle-aged man, gets a call from his secretary, claiming she has accidentally killed her ex-boyfriend, and she asks Hanson for help. Hanson, who is stuck in an unhappy marriage, sees an opportunity for adventure. Things do not turn out the way he wants or even expects them to, as is typical in noir fiction the protagonists cannot control events initiated by their weaknesses. Keene tackles the same themes and subjects as other Fawcett Gold Medal writers of the 50s, like Gil Brewer, Harry Whittington and Charles Williams. Keene's female leads are often *femme fatales*, but they are also as often victims of male sexuality and obsession. His *femmes fatales* are never purely evil. Keene wrote two novels, *Dead in Bed* (1959) and *Payola* (1960), featuring a half-Hawaiian, half-Irish private detective Johnny Aloha. Keene later abandoned the mystery genre to write more mainstream fiction. By the end of his career, he had written over 50 novels and hundreds of short stories.

Keene lived most of his active working years in Tampa, Florida, where he was acquainted with many other crime writers of the time, including Talmage Powell, John D. MacDonald and Robert Turner.

Several of Day Keene's novels were filmed in France in the 50s and 60s, most notably *Joy House* (1954). It was directed as *Les félins* by René Clement in 1964, starring Alain Delon and Jane Fonda, with a screenplay by Charles Williams. Keene's son, Albert James Hjertstedt, became the crime writer Al James.

Suggested reading

B. Crider, S. Lewis and V.A. Birch (2004) *MysteryFile.com* www.mysteryfile.com/GM_Keene/Keene.html, date accessed 9 June 2011.
J. Reilly ed. (1985) *Twentieth-Century Crime and Mystery Writers* (New York: St Martin's Press).

Juri Nummelin

Kellerman, Jonathan (1949–)

A distinguished psychologist and psychotherapist whose most well-known fictional creation is the forensic psychologist Alex Delaware, Kellerman achieved instant critical and commercial success with his first novel, *When the Bough Breaks* (1985), and since then has published at least one thriller novel every year, including 26 novels in the Delaware series.

Early life and career

Jonathan Kellerman was born 9 August 1949, in New York City. Kellerman was brought up in Los Angeles and attended UCLA graduating with a PhD in psychology at the age of 24. Some of Delaware's character biography reads closely to Kellerman's, and the author has suggested, perhaps in jest, that Delaware is a fantasy version of himself. During his studies, Kellerman worked in a variety of job roles including a stint as an editorial cartoonist, columnist, editor and freelance musician. An early indication of his literary promise came when he won the Samuel Goldwyn Writing Award for fiction at the age of 22. In 1977 Kellerman became the founding director of the Psychosocial Program Division of Oncology at Children's Hospital Los Angeles – one of the first such programmes to research the emotional and psychological aspects of paediatric cancer. Kellerman's first publications were non-fiction works in his research field. *Psychological Aspects of Childhood Cancer* appeared in 1980 followed the next year by a book written for parents *Helping the Fearful Child: A Guide to Everyday and Problem Anxieties.* Kellerman's most recent psychological study is *Savage Spawn: Reflections on Violent Children* (1999). A life-long enthusiast for guitars and rock music, Kellerman also authored *With Strings Attached: The Art and Beauty of Vintage Guitars* (2008). Kellerman is currently Clinical Professor of Paediatrics and Psychology at University of Southern California Keck School of Medicine. Kellerman is married to fellow mystery novelist Faye Kellerman with whom he has co-authored the novels *Double Homicide* (2004) and *Capital Crimes* (2006). Jonathan and Faye Kellerman have four children together, the oldest of whom, Jesse Kellerman, is also a novelist and playwright. Kellerman claims that while his medical/academic career was developing he spent 13 years attempting unsuccessfully to publish his novels. *When the Bough Breaks* was to be his last attempt at writing fiction, and if it did not see publication, Kellerman intended to abandon his ambitions of being a novelist. Completed in 1981, it was rejected by several literary agents until it was accepted by Barney Karpfinger, who would become Kellerman's agent thereafter. The novel was published in 1985, several years after it had been accepted for publication, and was an unexpected bestseller. The novel introduced the character of Alex Delaware, and the plot was closely tied to Kellerman's research field, a subject he had avoided in prior writing attempts. A corrupt psychiatrist is murdered and the only possible witness is a seven-year-old girl. Delaware must work with the girl to unravel the mystery. *When the Bough Breaks* won the Edgar Award for Best First Novel and was adapted into a highly rated NBC television film with Ted Danson in the role of Delaware, but no other Kellerman novels have ever been adapted into film.

Alex Delaware novels

Delaware is a retired child psychologist now working for the LAPD as a 'special consultant' forensic psychologist. Delaware can be highly critical about some of the pseudoscience attached to psychology and police investigation, such as criminal profiling, as well as public misconceptions about DNA profiling. Delaware is in a long-term relationship with girlfriend Robin Castagna. The couple endure many separations during which Delaware pursues other romantic relationships. Many of the novels begin in the third-person as the reader is given a glimpse of the crime which becomes central to the mystery; the novel then shifts predominantly to Delaware's first-person narration as the investigation is seen from his viewpoint, but there may be occasional brief returns to third-person to portray a scene outside of Delaware's purview. Delaware is partnered with LAPD detective Miller 'Milo' Sturgis. Sturgis often takes the lead in an investigation in terms of police work with Delaware in the more observant, analytical consultant role. However, Delaware often finds himself in dangerous situations. *Bad Love* (1994) climaxes with Delaware almost being killed when a psychopath destroys his luxurious canyon home. The second Delaware novel *Blood Test* (1986) exceeded the first in its ambitious handling of controversial subjects, as the plot deals with disturbing themes such as incest and group sex. Kellerman began writing full-time after the third Delaware novel *Over the Edge* (1987), which explored the line between genius and insanity through Delaware's back-story as a researcher for a project which examined the psychological problems faced by exceptionally gifted children. Kellerman often explores the tension between individual and institutional identity: Sturgis is a tough and resourceful detective and is open about his homosexuality, sometimes to the disapproval of his colleagues. The bulk of Delaware's income comes from private sector work independent of the LAPD. In *The Web* (1996) Kellerman takes Delaware out of LA to an exotic location, a fictitious island in Micronesia where Delaware has accepted a highly paid consultancy job. *The Web* is more preposterously plotted than any other Delaware narrative and is one of several novels which fall into more than one camp: mystery genre and psychological and physical horror. Kellerman made several visits to a state hospital for the criminally insane to research the setting of the thirteenth Kellerman novel *Monster* (1999). The novel is dedicated to the late Kenneth Millar, the crime writer who wrote under the pseudonym Ross MacDonald. Millar's key theme of webs of violence going back generations has been frequently explored in Kellerman's focus on psychologically motivated crimes. The novels often feature dark, ironic humour: *Evidence* (2009) revolves around a series of violent crimes connected to a half-built mansion in Los Angeles. In the denouement, Delaware observes a young couple who are excitedly buying the seemingly cursed house unaware of its grisly past. The latest Delaware novel *Mystery* (2011) reads as a tribute to LA's history as a perfect noir setting. The novel begins with Delaware and Robin having drinks in their favourite venue, the Fauborg Hotel, which is due to permanently close. The mystery ensues when Delaware spots a beautiful, enigmatic-looking young woman in the hotel that night who is later found murdered.

Petra Connor series and other novels

Kellerman's first novel outside of the Delaware series was *The Butcher's Theatre* (1988) set in Jerusalem and employing the Israeli Police Chief Inspector, Daniel Sharavi, as the lead protagonist. Kellerman is an Orthodox Jew and has lived in Israel several times, the first being in 1968 shortly after the Six-Day War. The narrative focuses on the hunt for a serial killer in a city where, aside from the political tensions, violent crime is rare especially in comparison to Kellerman's usual setting of LA. Sharavi would return in the Delaware novel *Survival of the Fittest* (1997) wherein Sharavi is sent to LA to work on a case. Kellerman also departed from his LA setting for *The Conspiracy Club* (2003). The setting is a monolithic, gloomy hospital in an unnamed mid-western city. The leading character is Dr Jeremy Carrier. Kellerman wanted to create a psychologist who was very different from Delaware. In a departure for Kellerman, some of the plotting resembles a modern-day attempt at the locked-room mystery. Kellerman has written several novels as spin-offs from the Delaware series. Petra Connor is a detective who first appeared in *Survival of the Fittest*. In *Billy Straight* (1998) the viewpoint alternates between Connor and the titular character, a 12–year-old runaway boy living in LA's Griffith Park where he witnesses a brutal murder. Kellerman's experience working with children adds authenticity to the narrative and buttresses his credentials as a writer who can explore controversial subjects. The novel also alludes to true crime cases, as the murder Billy witnesses is strikingly reminiscent of the O.J. Simpson murder case which sent shockwaves through LA. Kellerman has since written three more novels featuring Petra Connor. A consistent theme in Kellerman's novels is the clash of anachronistic values in contemporary culture. Kellerman often makes biblical allusions in his narratives, examining the role of religion in a secular world. In the novels *Bones* (2008) and *True Detectives* (2009), Kellerman introduces two rival detectives and half-brothers Moses Reed and Aaron Fox. Moses is Caucasian and Aaron is Black. Their mother married two policemen who died prematurely. Flashback sequences establish their unusual upbringing. The detective half-brothers are named after the two prophets and brothers of the Old Testament. *True Detectives* contains many scriptural references; one suspect is a born-again Christian who has directed the film *Saul to Paul: The Moment*. The novel contains frequent references to angels as a cultural term, and how this relates to its theological genesis. Delaware and Sturgis sometimes make appearances in the Connor novels and in *True Detectives* as mentoring characters.

Suggested reading

B. Forshaw (1999) 'Keeping it Fresh: Jonathan Kellerman' *Crime Time* http://www.crimetime.co.uk/interviews/jonathankellerman.php, date accessed 4 June 2010.

J. Kellerman (2011) *Jonathan Kellerman* http://jonathankellerman.com.

L. Lees (2002) 'Jonathan Kellerman: Tangled Web Interview' 28 February 2002, http://www.twbooks.co.uk/authors/jkinterview.html,date accessed 4 June 2010.

J. Mayberry (2009) 'True Detectives by Jonathan Kellerman' *Big Thrill* http://www.thrillerwriters.org/2009/02/true-detectives-by-jonathan-kellerman.html, date accessed 4 June 2010.

Steven Powell

King, C(harles) Daly (1895–1963)

A distinguished and unorthodox psychologist who brought a skill for creating inventively elaborate mysteries to a series of memorable novels featuring series detective Michael Lord, King's fiction, however, suffered from long technical digressions on issues such as psychological theories.

Life and career

Charles Daly King was born in New York City in 1895. He was educated at Newark Academy and Yale University, graduating Phi Beta Kappa. He served as a Lieutenant in the United States Field Artillery during the First World War. After the war, he returned to higher education gaining an MA in psychology from Columbia University in 1928 and a PhD from Yale in 1946. King wrote several books on psychology, some of which have been republished in recent years, including *Beyond Behaviorism* written under the pseudonym Robert Courtney, which was reprinted as *The Butterfly: A Symbol of Conscious Evolution* in 1996. His other books include *The Psychology of Consciousness* (1932) and the posthumously published *The States of Human Consciousness* (1963). King was interested in the ideas of George Gurdjieff and was a member of the A.R. Orage group in New York. He wrote a privately circulated manuscript on Orage, *The Oragean Vision* (1951). Aside from practicing psychology, King also spent a period of time as a partner in a cotton and woollen business and as a treasurer in an advertising agency. King's debut novel, *Obelists at Sea* (1933), featured four psychologists from different schools of thought who investigate a series of crimes. All of their solutions are proved wrong.

Michael Lord novels

With his second novel, King introduced a series character who would appear in all of his subsequent novels. Michael Lord is a special officer attached to the staff of the police commissioner of New York. King's novels focus mainly on plotting, and King reveals very little of Lord's character other than his occupation. The first two novels are *Obelists en Route* (1934) and *Obelists Fly High* (1935). King coined the term 'obelists' and the meaning changes from novel to novel. In *Obelists at Sea* it refers to 'a person of little or no value', whereas in *Obelists en Route*, it is defined as someone who harbours suspicions. According to Jon Woodsman, the shifting spurious definition of obelist alludes to the surface narrative of detective fiction wherein the reader and detective must look beneath the surface to find a deeper esoteric meaning which unravels the mystery. This definition would cohere with King's understanding of Gurdjieff. The stories themselves are exceptionally complex Golden Age style impossible crimes. The most highly regarded Lord novel is *Obelists Fly High*, a locked room mystery set aboard an airplane. The timeframe of the novel jumps backwards and forwards through an unusual application of both epilogue and prologue. In the later Lord novels, King discarded the word obelist for the alliterative titles, *Careless Corpse: A Thanatophony* (1937), *Arrogant Alibi* (1939) and *Bermuda Burial* (1941), the last of which was set on the titular island where King spent many years writing detective fiction. King's only other book in this genre was the short story anthology *The Curious Mr Tarrant* (1935). The stories feature amateur detective Trevis Tarrant and are a continuation of the baffling, complex locked room mysteries at which King excelled often combined with a horror atmosphere focusing on bizarre religious imagery. According to Michael E Grost, King may have written a seventh Michael Lord novel that was never published.

Suggested reading

J. Reilly ed. (1985) *Twentieth Century Crime and Mystery Writers* (New York: St Martin's Press).

C.D. King (1999) *The Psychology of Consciousness* (London: Routledge).

Diana Powell

Latimer, Jonathan (1906–83)

As the creator of private detective William Crane, Latimer made a significant contribution to the development of screwball comedy in mystery fiction of the 1930s, writing a series of hard-boiled romps with a hint of inspired madness. In some cases, the madness was a plot device, as Crane is introduced in the first novel *Murder in the Madhouse* (1935) as a patient being committed to an asylum.

Life and early career

Jonathan Wyatt Latimer was born in Chicago on 23 October 1906. He was educated at Mesa Ranch High School, Arizona, and then at Knox College, Galesburg, Illinois. Latimer worked a diverse set of jobs before and during his literary career: he was a reporter for the *Herald-Examiner* and then for the *Chicago Tribune* from 1929–34. He mostly covered crime stories. During his time as a reporter, he met notorious underworld figures such as Al Capone and George 'Bugs' Moran. Latimer also served as a ghost-writer for Secretary of the Interior Harold Ickes, making a significant contribution to Ickes' book on the New Deal projects *Back to Work: The Story of the P.W.A* (1935). During the Second World War, he served in the United States Navy on a destroyer assigned to convoy duty in the Atlantic and Mediterranean. Latimer married Ellen Baxter Peabody in 1937, and the union produced two sons and a daughter. His second wife was Jo Ann Hanzlik, whom he married in 1954. Latimer's screenwriting career began in the late 1930s, and his best work included scripting the memorable film noir adaptations of Dashiell Hammett's *The Glass Key* (1942) and Kenneth Fearing's *The Big Clock* (1948).

William Crane series and other novels

William 'Bill' Crane is a hard-drinking detective for the New York-based Colonel Black Detective Agency. Crane's wisecracking and alcoholism provide opportunities for slapstick and screwball humour, but these comical mishaps do not impair his deductive skills as he always solves the case eventually. The first Crane novel appeared a year after the introduction of Hammett's Nick and Nora Charles in *The Thin Man* (1934), a series with a similar screwball comedic style. Latimer followed *Murder in the Madhouse* with *Headed for a Hearse* (1936). The novel is a locked room mystery in which Crane has to prove his client did not murder his wife in order to save him from the electric chair. In *The Lady in the Morgue* (1936), Crane and his equally soused detective partners Doc and O'Malley investigate a case of switched identities. As the titles of the novels suggest, the series took the themes of madness and death as the material for black humour. Latimer ended the series after claiming he grew bored with the character. The final Crane novels were *The Dead Don't Care* (1938) and *Red Gardenias* (1939), with Crane's engagement to his assistant providing the resolution to the series. Crane was played by Preston Foster in three fairly successful film adaptations for Universal Studios in the 1930s. Latimer also wrote one novel under the pseudonym Peter Coffin, who is also the narrator and detective in *The Search for My Great Uncle's Head* (1937). Latimer wrote one novel outside the crime genre, *Dark Memory* (1940), an adventure set in Africa. Latimer's most retrospectively praised novel, *Solomon's Vineyard* (1941), features ruthless St Louis based private detective Karl Craven. The novel is far removed from the Crane series in terms of style with its explicit scenes of sex and violence, which predated the Mickey Spillane series by several years. In *Solomon's Vineyard*, Craven is hired to rescue a girl from a bizarre religious cult. The novel was released in Great Britain in 1941, but only a heavily censored version was released in the US under the title *The Fifth Grave* in 1950. The original version was finally made available in the US in the 1980s. Latimer authored two more stand-alone novels after the war, *Sinners and Shrouds* (1955) and *Black is the Fashion for Dying* (1956), which were well written but lacked the intensity and excitement of his earlier work. In his later career he wrote for television, with credits on such series as *Markham* and *Perry Mason*. Latimer died of lung cancer in La Jolla, California, in 1983.

Suggested reading

B. Brubaker (1993) *Stewards of the House: The Detective Fiction of Jonathan Latimer* (Bowling Green, OH: Bowling Green State University Press).

W.L. DeAndrea (1994) *Encyclopedia Mysteriosa* (New York: Prentice Hall).

J. Reilly ed. (1985) *Twentieth Century Crime and Mystery Writers* (New York: St Martin's Press).

Steven Powell

Lehane, Dennis (1965–)

Best known for his novels *Mystic River* (2001) and *Shutter Island* (2003), both of which were turned into major Hollywood films, Dennis Lehane came to prominence with the publication of a series of thrillers featuring the private detective duo Patrick Kenzie and Angie Gennaro. Lehane's work is notable for its use of Boston – and in particular the working-class areas of South Boston – as a setting, and for its exploration of dark subject matter such as child abuse. In the last few years, Lehane's output has included a literary novel concerning early twentieth-century Boston, a play, a book of short stories and scripts for the critically acclaimed television show *The Wire*, for which he won an Edgar Award for best teleplay. With increasing popular and critical success, Lehane has gradually built a reputation as one of the finest of contemporary American crime writers. Lehane is married to an optometrist, Dr Angela Bernardo; his first marriage to the lawyer Sheila Lawn ended in divorce. He divides his time between Florida and Boston. His work has won both the Anthony Award and the Barry Award.

Lehane was born in Boston, Massachusetts, on 4 August 1965. Both of his parents were first-generation Irish immigrants and growing up in the city in the 70s gave Lehane a sharp sense of the tensions inherent in Boston's social fabric. Lehane lived with his family in the neighbourhood of Dorchester, which was sandwiched between predominantly black Roxbury to the east and the poor working-class area of South Boston to the north. The decade was marked by race riots. Lehane has acknowledged that observing such unrest proved a formative experience for his writing; the often startling acts of violence that dot his fiction draw on his sense of the city's streets being the theatre for a brutal expression of race and class tensions. Brought up a Catholic, Lehane attended the Jesuit Boston College High School. Years after Lehane's departure, the institution was mired in a series of sex scandals in which a number of the priests that worked there were exposed as paedophiles. Although Lehane was not personally a victim of abuse, he has stated that the experience of being taught by authority figures whom he knew were not to be trusted, as well as a short post-college stint working as a counsellor with disabled and abused children, made a considerable impact upon his writing.

Kenzie and Gennaro series

Lehane attended Eckerd College in Florida, where he wrote his first novel manuscript. After graduation he revised and redrafted the manuscript and it was published as *A Drink Before the War* in 1994 and introduced Kenzie and Gennaro. Writing one novel a year, Lehane continued the series of his blue-collar detective duo in *Darkness, Take My Hand* (1996), *Sacred* (1997), *Gone, Baby, Gone* (1998) and *Prayers for Rain* (1999).

In *A Drink Before the War,* Lehane establishes the dynamics of the Kenzie-Gennaro partnership as the pair investigate the kidnapping of a black cleaning woman alleged to have stolen confidential government documents. Throughout the six novels that feature the two Dorchester natives, Lehane uses Patrick Kenzie as his first person narrator, a technique that allows him to depict the Boston ghettos with an affectionate but compelling clarity. Kenzie's voice is hip and uncompromising and yet Lehane invests the character with considerable charm: whilst at the outset of *A Drink Before the War* he comes across as a parody of a private eye, 'There was a bounce to my step, a bright twinkle in my eyes, and nary a hair out of place. All was right with the world' (Lehane, 2011, p. 3), as the series progresses the reader gains an appreciation of a fully realised character. Patrick Kenzie is a Marx Brothers fan, infatuated with Angie, loyal to the friends he grew up with, and engaged in an internal battle with the memory of an abusive father. In *Darkness Take My Hand*, Lehane uses one of his recurrent motifs – that of the dream sequence, or confessional prologue – to establish the focus of the ensuing narrative as nothing less than the violent breakdown of an insular community. Their investigations into police corruption and serial murder have serious consequences for Patrick and Angie and the novel concludes with their partnership under dire strain. Reunited by the time of the events of *Sacred*, the third Kenzie-Gennaro story involves them leaving Boston for Florida to investigate the seemingly straightforward disappearance of a rich man's daughter. As Lehane has spent many years living in Florida, his descriptions of the state's Gulf Coast carry the same authenticity as his evocative Boston settings. In the novel, Kenzie develops a growing understanding of what he holds sacred, as the title suggests, which is ironic as he and Gennaro view, with increasing disbelief, the dysfunctional wealthy family they are involved with. *Gone, Baby, Gone* – adapted into film in 2007, directed by Ben Affleck and starring Casey Affleck as Kenzie and Michelle Monaghan as Gennaro – follows the pair as they investigate the disappearance of four-year-old Amanda McCready. The trail brings them into contact with the forces of the local underworld and the police department, and their efforts to find the missing girl are confounded by the fact that the line between the legal and the illegal becomes blurred, another key Lehane trope. Bringing the case to a resolution has severe consequences for Patrick and Angie's relationship. In *Prayers for Rain*, set in a stiflingly hot Boston summer, Patrick – now working alone in Angie's absence – sets out to investigate the apparent suicide of a girl who had previously visited him requesting help months before. As he is drawn deeper into the mystery, he is pitted against the wiles of a brilliant sociopath and has to call on the resources of all his Dorchester contacts, and, following a reconciliation, all the support Angie can offer. President Bill Clinton was photographed on Air Force One with a copy of *Prayers for Rain* and this seemingly minor incident transformed Lehane's quietly impressive sales into something more spectacular. In these five novels, Kenzie is as much a vigilante as he is a detective, and the impotence of the official forces of law and order is a frequent plot and thematic point. Through the series Lehane has skillfully balanced the entertainment value expected of the genre with the literary quality readers and critics have come to associate with his work. The sixth Kenzie-Gennaro thriller, *Moonlight Mile*, was released in 2010 after Lehane had taken a break of 11 years from the series to work on other projects.

Mainstream and critical success

After five novels dissecting the professional and personal dramas of Kenzie and Gennaro, Lehane then published *Mystic River*. In a reference to the novel's temporal sweep and its unflinching portrayal of the ways tragedy leads to the unravelling of individual lives, Lehane has playfully suggested that *Mystic River* was in part inspired by too much Shakespeare and Russian literature in college. The novel concerns the fallout from a child abduction, and Lehane focuses the narrative on the different perspectives of three longstanding friends and natives of the East Buckingham area of Boston in which the story is set, creating intimately drawn characters in a novel with tragic grandeur. The novel received critical praise and was turned into an Oscar-winning film by Clint Eastwood in 2003, starring Sean Penn, Kevin Bacon, and Tim Robbins. Lehane's tendency to experiment with the conventions of the crime thriller continued with his next work, *Shutter Island*, a tale of an FBI investigation into a mental hospital situated on a remote island off the coast from Boston. This was the first of Lehane's novels not to be set in the present day, and the 1950s setting allows for the exploration of complex historical issues, such as GI involvement in World War II, the Cold War, and developments in psychiatric medicine. A film adaptation, directed by Martin Scorsese and starring Leonardo DiCaprio, was released in 2010. In 2006, Lehane published *Coronado*, a volume featuring five short stories and the titular two-act play. Lehane's most ambitious work, *The Given Day*, appeared in 2008; at over 700 pages, this was Lehane's first attempt at literary historical fiction, which took five years for him to write. Set in early twentieth-century Boston, the novel climaxes with the Boston Police strike of 1919.

Suggested reading

E. Brockes (2009) 'A Life in Writing: Dennis Lehane' *The Guardian*, 24 January 2009 http://www.guardian.co.uk/culture/2009/jan/24/dennis-lehane, date accessed 2 October 2010.

D. Lehane (2010) 'Build a solid story around a strong character: A bestselling novelist stresses that you can begin working on plot and other narrative elements only after you know your protagonist to his core' *Writer* November 2010, 123 (11) pp. 22–55.

L. Jones (2009) 'Dennis Lehane: Hard-Boiled In Boston'. *Publishers Weekly*, 21 June 2009, 246 (25) pp. 40–1.

S. McCabe (2006) 'Reconciling Violence and a Life in Literature: An Interview with Dennis Lehane' *Writer's Chronicle*, September 2006, 39 (1) pp. 8–13.

Tim Foster

Leonard, Elmore (1925–)

Celebrated, prolific author of crime fiction and western novels, who is widely considered to be one of the finest crime writers alive today.

Youth and education

Elmore Leonard was born on 11 October 1925 in New Orleans, Louisiana. His father's profession as a scout for General Motors took the family around various locations in the US, before settling them in Detroit, Michigan, a city that would go on to feature heavily in Leonard's work. A 1984 feature in *Time* magazine famously named Leonard the 'Dickens from Detroit'. In school he acquired the nickname 'Dutch' after the baseball player Dutch Leonard, a moniker he uses in his personal life to this day. After high school graduation in 1943, Leonard was drafted, serving in the US Navy during the Second World War as a Seabee in the South Pacific.

It was after his discharge from the Navy in 1946 that Leonard took the first steps towards what would prove to be his life-long career. He became an English and philosophy student at the University of Detroit, and during his studies began to write short fiction, once winning second prize in a contest. After graduating in 1950, having married his first wife Beverley Cline the previous year, he earned a living writing advertising copy in Detroit, a job he would hold down for the next decade while nurturing his nascent writing career.

Early career

Leonard's first forays into writing for money were short western stories. In the early 1950s the western genre was a popular and potentially lucrative source of income for a young writer. Leonard followed a disciplined writing regime, working on his fiction early in the morning before heading out to his job. He met with success fairly swiftly, when *Argosy* magazine bought his story 'Trail Of The Apache' for $1,000 in 1951.

In 1953 Leonard's first novel, the western *The Bounty Hunters*, was published, followed by *The Law At Randado* (1955), *Escape From Five Shadows* (1956) and *Last Stand at Saber River* aka *Lawless River* (1959). However, it was the 1953 short story 'Three-Ten to Yuma' and the 1961 Western novel *Hombre* that proved to be the significant turning points in his career. *Hombre* met with acclaim – the novel's antihero John Russell is a complex and intriguing figure – before being sold to Twentieth Century Fox for $10,000 in 1965. *Hombre* was adapted for the screen in 1967 and 'Three-Ten to Yuma' in 1957 and 2007. *Hombre* has come to be regarded as something of a classic of the western fiction genre and was voted as one of the best 25 western novels of all time by the Western Writers of America.

Move into crime fiction

It was in the mid-1960s, after a short stint writing for corporate and industrial films and while running his own advertising agency, that Leonard began to move away from the declining western genre and started to write crime fiction. However, he did not abandon the western genre altogether, publishing *Valdez Is Coming* (1970), *Forty Lashes Less One* (1972) and *Gunsights* (1979), the first of which he regards as his favourite of his own western novels. His first crime novel, *The Big Bounce* (1969) had an unorthodox publication trajectory. Rejected a total of 84 times by publishers, the manuscript was first sold for film rights for $50,000 before the novel was subsequently accepted for book publication. *The Big Bounce* contains many of the motifs that would go on to characterise Leonard's later crime novels. It is set in Michigan and its protagonist, Jack Ryan (who later returns in the 1977 novel *Unknown Man No. 89*), has several of the attributes of the typical Leonard criminal antihero, a thief down on his luck drawn into a series of elaborate double crosses and promises of a big score. There is also the presence of a dangerously psychotic supporting character, Nancy Hayes, and the undercurrent of an unconventional or mercenary approach to romance – a motif which perhaps finds its peak in the screwball relationship between Jack Foley and Karen Cisco in *Out Of Sight* (1996). Despite the generally negative reception afforded to the 1969 film adaptation starring Ryan O'Neal (a 2004 remake was also coolly received), the money acquired from selling the rights enabled Leonard to throw himself into full-time writing and screenwriting.

Later career and mainstream recognition

Throughout the 1970s Leonard wrote a series of crime novels – among them *52 Pick-Up* (1974), *Swag* (1976) *The Hunted* (1977) and *The Switch* (1978) – that steadily built him a reputation as a crime writer of the highest calibre. Leonard does not begin writing a novel with a plot outline, rather his writing first establishes a sense of place and character and the story latterly takes form improvisationally within the text. Leonard's novels are noted for their evocative milieu of locations. Detroit and South Florida are his most used settings: he has also written works set in New Orleans and Atlantic City and hires researchers to assist in building an accurate portrait of a city. Occasionally, the back-story of his novels will take in foreign locales such as the war-torn settings of the Dominican Republic in *Cat Chaser* (1982) and Rwanda in *Pagan Babies* (2000). His parallel career as a Hollywood screenwriter also afforded him financial security during this time. In May 1977 Leonard's first marriage ended in divorce. He would go on to marry Joan Shepard in September 1979, a marriage that would last until her death in 1993. In 1978, the *Detroit News* commissioned Leonard to write an article on the local police. Leonard spent over two months at the police station studying the characters who would pass through the doors everyday learning the rhythms of speech and street philosophies of different urban groups. This research directly led to the novel *City Primeval* (1980), Leonard's first to feature a police detective as protagonist.

It was the 1980s when Leonard began to receive serious recognition as one of the world's leading crime writers. At the end of the 1970s, *The Switch* had been nominated for an Edgar Award by the Mystery Writers of America (Best Original Paperback Novel), and 1981's *Split Images* was nominated in the even more prestigious Best Novel category. In 1984, in a crucial breakthrough which was to begin his rise to widespread popularity, he won the Edgar Best Novel award for *LaBrava* (1983), a kidnapping caper set in Miami that makes a number of allusions to Hollywood and the movie business. The denouement of a Leonard novel often keeps the suspense alive until the very last line, which may also, through the form of a line of dialogue or a character's inner thought, summarise the absurdity of events leading up to this point or allude to more violent events to come. *LaBrava* was followed by *Glitz* (1985), and the combination of acclaim for both novels made them bestsellers and marked Leonard's entry into the cultural mainstream, although his screenwriting included several successful films during the 1970s. It was also at this time that a feature on Leonard appeared in *Time*, this was the article that carried the Dickens comparison; sales of his fiction rose accordingly.

Leonard continued to write, releasing some of his biggest-selling and most popular novels during the late 1980s and early 1990s. *Bandits* (1987) was a robbery thriller with a rare political edge which dealt, albeit indirectly, with the Reagan-supported Contras in Nicaragua (it was later adapted into the unrecognisable and largely unloved Bruce Willis film in 2001). Other novels included the bestsellers *Killshot* (1989), *Get Shorty* (1990), *Rum Punch* (1992) and *Out Of Sight* (1996). Leonard adeptly and sympathetically portrays figures on both sides of the law or anywhere in between. Be they retired cops, ex-marines, bomb squad experts, used-car salesmen, stockbrokers, hippies, gangsters, hit-men or even psychopaths, Leonard's empathy for people is shown in his characters, who are partly hostage to events outside of their control which often naturally end in violence. In 1992 Leonard received a significant honour when the Mystery Writers of America awarded him their highest accolade, the Grand Master Award, for lifetime achievement in and advancement of the genre. Leonard has since received acclaim from writers as disparate as Stephen King and Martin Amis. In 1993, after the death of Joan Shepard, Leonard married his third wife, his former gardener Christine Kent.

The 1990s was also the decade that saw Leonard firmly established in the consciousness of non-readers of his work, thanks to a series of successful adaptations of his novels for the screen.

Screenwriting and adaptations

One of the most significant creative relationships in Leonard's life has been with Hollywood and the movie industry. This began with the first notable example of an adaptation of his work, the 1957 screen adaptation of *Three-Ten to Yuma*. After *Hombre* was filmed with Paul Newman in 1967, the following decade saw an increase in Leonard's novels being adapted for the screen and also his own burgeoning career as a screenwriter. During the 1970s and 1980s, he adapted and co-adapted a number of his own works for the cinema; examples include *The Moonshine War* (1970), *Mr Majestyk* (1974), *Stick* (1985), *52 Pick-Up* (1986) and *Cat Chaser* (1989). He was also adept at writing original screenplays for such films as *Joe Kidd* (1972) directed by John Sturges.

In the 1990s Leonard withdrew from screenplay writing, reportedly unhappy with studio interference and preferring the singular creative control afforded the novelist. However, that same decade saw a new and arguably younger audience introduced to Leonard's novels through a number of high-profile screen adaptations of his work. The films *Get Shorty* (1995), *Jackie Brown* (1997, a fairly free adaptation of *Rum Punch*) and *Out Of Sight* (1998) were all critical and commercial successes. The latter two films were directed by Quentin Tarantino and Stephen Soderbergh respectively. Tarantino's earlier *Pulp Fiction* (1994) had shown a significant Leonard influence and the film director acknowledged his debt to the author. The combination of their hip reputation and the canny casting of Hollywood actors and established stars, George Clooney and Jennifer Lopez in *Out Of Sight*, Samuel Jackson, Pam Grier and Robert De Niro in *Jackie Brown*, brought Leonard's oeuvre to the attention of a wider audience. Leonard has expressed his admiration of all three adaptations, stating that '*Get Shorty* was the first film that "got it"' (Leonard, 2011a). The Coen Brothers have also optioned the 1998 novel *Cuba Libre* for potential adaptation, and the character of Karen Cisco from *Out Of Sight* even got her own eponymous spin-off TV series in 2003.

Influences and style

Leonard has spoken openly of his admiration for the writing of Ernest Hemingway, stating in an *Armchair Detective* interview that he studied Hemingway's technique closely and regarded *For Whom the Bell Tolls* as a western. In terms of his crime fiction, Leonard's dialogue-heavy style also bears traces of the work of the crime writer George V. Higgins, whom Leonard has acknowledged as an influence, in particular Higgins's debut novel *The Friends of Eddie Coyle* (1972) which Leonard described as 'the best crime book ever written'.

Leonard's prose has a clean, lean style, incorporating street and criminal slang but never swamped by it. His famous ear for speech, whole pages are often comprised of conversation, means that his novels are driven primarily through dialogue rather than elaborate digressive authorial explanation, although his narratives are primarily composed in the third-person narrative voice. *Hombre* is a rare exception which uses first-person narration. His work is frequently blackly comic and situations can verge on the farcical, though events will sometimes take an unexpectedly serious and violent turn. His parallel career as a screenwriter has also engendered in his fiction a direct, unfussy pace without major digression, a strong sense of location, as well as an ability to transmit the essentials of a character's personality with immediacy.

Leonard has an admitted fondness for criminal and individual rules and codes in his novel, and meta-fictional codes relating to an understanding of the novels. His novel *Swag* features a character, Frank Ryan, who has a set of ten rules to facilitate a successful robbery. One of these rules suggests that one should always be polite while committing a robbery, and it is key to an understanding of the relative moral codes at play in Leonard's work and how these codes determine the novel's heroes and villains within an overarching criminal network. For example, Jack Foley in *Out Of Sight* is a convicted bank robber not above using violence to escape from prison, but his criminal code is thrown into sharp relief when confronted with a group of violent rapists and murderers who commit house robberies. Relative to this gang, Jack becomes a rogue antihero rather than a violent robber.

Leonard himself outlined ten essential rules for writing in his 2001 *New York Times* article 'Easy On The Adverbs, Exclamation Points And Especially Hooptedoodle', and these rules are also the key to understanding the construction of his fiction. The general timbre of the rules is to keep things neat, quick and lean. 'Never open a book with weather' (Leonard, 2001) is one rule, something that, ironically, his literary hero Hemingway famously did in *A Farewell to Arms*. 'Avoid detailed descriptions of characters' and 'Try to leave out the part that readers tend to skip' are other telling rules, presumably at least partly influenced by the consideration of commercial practice with which he began his career (Leonard, 2001). His final summation rule – 'If it sounds like writing, I rewrite it' and the following statement 'I can't allow what we learned in English composition to disrupt the sound and rhythm of the narrative' are a testament to his desire for a direct, accurate-sounding language that reflects the lives and speech of the characters he depicts (Leonard, 2001).

Leonard does not identify himself as a mystery writer, preferring to play up the elements of crime in his fiction. 'There is never a mystery in my books', he says. 'They are not whodunits. The reader knows as much as I do. The reader knows more than the main character does. I'm not interested in mystery. I do write crime novels. There is always a crime in my novels' (Leonard, 2011b).

Suggested reading

P.C. Challen (2000) *Get Dutch!: a biography of Elmore Leonard* (Toronto: ECW Press).
D. Geherin (1989) *Elmore Leonard* (London: Continuum),
M.H. Hayes (2010) *Elmore Leonard: His Life and Letters* (Westport: Praeger).

David Hering

Levin, Ira (1929–2007)

An expert at the suspense thriller which contained elements of gothic horror and fantasy, Ira Marvin Levin was one of the few authors in the mystery field to successfully alternate between writing plays and novels. Born in New York City on 27 August 1929, Levin was educated at Drake University in Iowa and New York University. Between the years of 1953–55, he served in the Army Signal Corps. Levin was married and divorced twice – to Gabrielle Aronsohn (1960–68) and Phyllis Finkel (1979–81) – and had three sons from his first marriage.

When still a student, Levin entered a screenwriting competition run by CBS; although he did not win, he nonetheless sold the screenplay to NBC, where it was filmed as an episode for the mystery series *Lights Out* in 1951. It was whilst he was writing for television that Levin published his first novel, the thriller *A Kiss Before Dying* (1953), which won him the 1954 Edgar Award for Best First Novel from the Mystery Writers of America. It was filmed twice, in 1956 with Robert Wagner and in 1991 with Matt Dillon. The novel establishes many of the motifs that feature in his later fiction, even those works which could be more easily categorised as horror and science fiction: female protagonists imperilled by perfidious males and a sense of the extraordinary lurking behind the mundane facade of everyday existence. A tale of a charming sociopath intent on availing himself of the Kingship family fortune by seducing the patriarch's two daughters, Dorothy and Ellen, the narrative is remarkable for the way in which Levin switches the viewpoint from criminal to victim and back again. Indeed, it is not until over halfway through the book that the reader discovers the villain's identity and just how deeply he has ingratiated himself into the family's business.

Following *A Kiss Before Dying*'s success, Levin focused his energies on writing for the stage and it would not be until 1967 that his second novel was published, *Rosemary's Baby*. The novel concerns a young pregnant woman who begins to suspect that a Satanic cult want her unborn child for a sacrifice to the Devil. Levin wrote a sequel, *Son of Rosemary* (1997), updating the events of the narrative forward to the eve of the millennium. *The Stepford*

Wives (1972) similarly addresses issues of gender relations in a suspense narrative about a young woman who moves into an idyllic Connecticut suburb and begins to suspect the submissive wives of the community may be some form of robot. *The Boys from Brazil* (1976) was his final major novel, and it concerned the efforts of Nazi war criminals trying to re-establish the Third Reich by cloning Hitler. All three novels inspired successful Hollywood adaptations. *The Stepford Wives* became something of a television and film franchise with the original film spawning a series of made for TV sequels and a cinema remake in 2004. Of his plays, *Deathtrap* (1978) proved to be his greatest success. The play, which was also adapted for film, is a comedy thriller about a past-his-prime playwright who decides to steal a manuscript from one of his promising young students and kill him.

Although there were never claims made for Levin as a literary writer, partly due to his reliance on far-fetched plots, his ability to craft thrilling page-turning fiction earned him considerable respect and financial success. He is often thought of as an author who was most influential in the fantasy and horror genre, but his importance as a crime writer lies in the way his mystery stories were combined with elements taken from a host of other genres. Ira Levin died on 12 November 2007.

Suggested reading

D. Fowler (1988) *Ira Levin* (Mercer Island, WA: Starmont House).
M. Fox (2007) 'Ira Levin of "Rosemary's Baby", dies at 78' *New York Times*, 14 November 2007, http://www.nytimes.com/2007/11/14/books/14levin.html?ref=a, date accessed 21 June 2011.

Tim Foster

Linington, Elizabeth (1921–88)

A prolific writer of over 80 novels, Elizabeth Linington was one of the first, best and most frequent writers in the still male-dominated police-procedural genre. The three separate series characters she created and her prodigious output led the critic Allen J. Hubin to describe her as 'The Queen of the Procedurals' (Penzler and Steinbrunner, 1976, p. 248).

Life and career

Born Barbara Elizabeth Linington in Aurora, Illinois, on 11 March 1921, Linington moved with her family to California as a child where they settled in Hollywood. Linington attended Herbert Hoover High School and graduated from Glendale College with a BA in 1942. Linington's first novels were historical fiction, which remained her primary interest, and her move into mystery fiction has been attributed to financial consider-ations. Her debut novel, *The Proud Man* (1955), dealt with the life of the sixteenth-century Ulster Prince Shane O'Neill. Linington believed herself to be of Welsh and Gaelic heritage and wrote from an anti-English perspec-tive, although according to William DeAndrea her descendants were most likely English. Linington wrote four more historical novels and a fifth was rejected for publication. Linington believed this was due to left-wing publishers objecting to patriotic themes in her writing. Linington was for many years an active member of the right-wing, anti-communist John Birch Society. Linington wrote *Come to Think of It* (1965) extolling the society's conservative views, but she finally left the John Birch Society when it began to develop a pro-organised religion stance. Linington had an interest in spiritualism and the occult which influenced several of her novels. *Nightmare* (1961), written under the pseudonym Anne Blaisdell, concerned an American girl on holiday who falls prey to a female religious fanatic.

Police procedurals

Linington employed several pseudonyms, usually to separate one series from another. With *Case Pending* (1960), written under the pseudonym Dell Shannon, she introduced her first and most popular series detective Lt Luis Mendoza and a large cast of supporting characters. The novels are memorable for their awareness of LA's diverse ethnic identity, Mendoza being a then rare Hispanic detective. Many of the plots of her novels were taken from real criminal cases, often through her reading of the true crime magazines *True Detective*, *Master Detective* and *Official Detective*. Linington presented detective fiction as a morality play of good versus evil often with a sympathetic portrayal of the victims of crime. Much of Linington's writing explored the characters of policemen and their complex domestic lives. In the second Mendoza novel *Ace of Spades* (1961), Linington dedicates a great deal of the narrative to Mendoza's extravagant and eccentric lifestyle. Mendoza is a scholarly gentleman detective, who after inheriting a small fortune, has developed a passion for sports cars and collecting exotic cats. Under the moniker Lesley Egan, Linington began a new series with the novel *Case Appeal* (1961). The series is based in the Glendale suburbs of Los Angeles and follows Detective Vic Varallo. Also as Egan, Linington created the series character Jesse Falkenstein, a Jewish lawyer. The two Egan-authored series would occasionally overlap. The most celebrated novel featuring Falkenstein is *Some Avenger, Rise!* (1966) where the lawyer temporarily leaves his law practice to help a detective friend from a bribery allegation. Under her own name, Linington began a series with the novel *Greenmask!* (1964). The long-running series focuses on Sergeant Ivor Maddox, a bachelor with an active love life. In the first novel, Maddox and his team use detective techniques from classic mystery novels to solve a bizarre series of murders. Linington wrote on average three books a year through a process of two months' research and then two weeks' intensive writing. Elizabeth Linington died on 5 April 1988.

Suggested reading

M. J. DeMarr (1994) 'Elizabeth Linington' *Great Women Mystery Writers: classic to contemporary*, K. Gregory Klein ed. (Westport, Conn: Greenwood Press). pp.192–6.
J. Reilly ed. (1985) *Twentieth Century Crime and Mystery Writers* (New York: St Martin's Press).

Diana Powell

Lipsky, Eleazar (1911–93)

A distinguished prosecutor, lawyer and an active member of Jewish-American organisations, Eleazar Lipsky wrote a series of novels which blended a tough action style with his intricate knowledge of the legal system.

Life and career

Eleazar Lipsky was born in New York in 1911, the middle son of Louis and Charlotte Lipsky. His father was a leader in the American Zionist movement, and his mother was an active Jewish Socialist and an admirer of Emma Goldman. Lipsky earned his BA from Columbia University and latterly attended Columbia Law School. Lipsky worked in private practice from 1934–39. In 1935 he married Hannah Kohn, and they eventually had three sons. From 1942–46 he was Assistant District Attorney of New York County. In 1946 he returned to private practice. He would continue in private practice until a few weeks prior to his death. Lipsky had some experience as a journalist before his literary career began with the novel *The Kiss of Death* in 1947. *The Kiss of Death* tells the story of a sympathetic criminal caught between the law and the underworld criminal code. It was released as a successful film noir the same year as the book, and sources indicate Twentieth Century Fox bought the rights to the novel when it was still in manuscript stage. The novel was reissued as *The Hoodlum* by Lion in 1953 and then under its original title in 1961. The film was remade as the western *The Fiend Who Walked the West* (1958) and again as *Kiss of Death* (1995) updated to a contemporary setting. Lipsky's follow-up novels were the legal thrillers *Murder One* (1948) and *The People Against O'Hara* (1950). The latter novel was successfully filmed with Spencer Tracy in the lead role. *Lincoln McKeever* (1952) was a period western examining a murder trial in the New Mexico Territory. *The Scientists* (1959) veers towards science fiction as a distinguished professor and his young research student compete for recognition in the breakthrough discovery of the fictional 'biocyn'. Lipsky wrote *Four-Time Loser* (1962) under the pseudonym Dan Lynch and provided a favourable blurb for the novel using his real name. Lipsky's final novels were *The Devil's Daughter* (1969) and *Malpractice* (1972). The latter was one of his most praised novels for its judicial procedural narrative exploring the complex legal issues which come into play when a patient sues the hospital where they received treatment.

Lipsky also wrote two plays and regularly provided scripts based on his own case files for the radio drama *Indictment* (1956–59). Like his parents before him, Lipsky was a dedicated Zionist and belonged to pro-Israel organisations such as the World Zionist Congress Court. In his writing and speeches, Lipsky was knowledgeable and supportive of a broad number of Jewish causes. In the 1970s, Lipsky moved away from crime fiction after he signed a contract with Doubleday for a three-volume fictionalised history of three generations of his family. Progress was slow as Lipsky immersed himself in the huge amounts of research that was needed. Doubleday cancelled the contract in 1981, by which time Lipsky had written 225 pages of a manuscript based on his mother's life. A legal battle ensued, and Lipsky subsequently became active in issues surrounding artist's contracts. Lipsky then made plans to write a biography of his father but he died of Leukaemia in 1993, and the project was never finished.

Suggested reading

E. Pace (1993) 'Eleazar Lipsky, 81, a Prosecutor, Lawyer, Novelist and Playwright' *New York Times*, 15 February 1993, p. 16. http://www.nytimes.com/1993/02/15/arts/ eleazar-lipsky-81-a-prosecutor-lawyer-novelist-and-playwright.html, date accessed 16 February 2011.

Lipsky Family Papers (2008) arranged by R. Miller (Boston and New York: American Jewish Historical Society) Accession Number: edsoai.705028748 http://digital. cjh.org/view/action/singleViewer.do?dvs=1322678866351~574&locale=en_ GB&VIEWER_URL=/view/action/singleViewer.do?&DELIVERY_RULE_ID=5&fram eld=1&usePid1=true&usePid2=true.

Steven Powell

Lutz, John (1939–)

A prolific mystery writer who published his first short story in *Alfred Hitchcock's Mystery Magazine* in 1966, Lutz has continuously written since then, producing a prodigious body of work including short stories, stand-alone novels, several acclaimed private investigator series novels and also mystery jigsaw puzzles.

Born in St Louis, Missouri, on 1 September 1939, Lutz's early jobs included working as a theatre usher and a Teamster warehouseman. From 1959–60 Lutz worked as a switchboard operator for the St Louis Metropolitan Police. His tasks included tracking district patrol cars while maintaining communication with beat cops and members of the public. Lutz has credited this period of his working life as giving him insights into the process of police investigation and the psychology of detectives. After a period of writing short stories, Lutz's debut novel, *The Truth of the Matter*, appeared in 1971. The lead protagonist of the piece, Lou Roebuck, is drawn into a web of increasing violence and mayhem seemingly initiated by a single lie he told. Lutz began writing full time in 1975, and it was around this period that he created the first of his several memorable private detective characters, Alo Nudger, who debuted in *Buyer Beware* (1976). Based in Lutz's hometown of St Louis, Nudger is the antidote to the hard-drinking, tough-talking private detective. As his name suggests, Nudger lacks direction and conviction: he is middle-aged with a nervous disposition and a stomach condition which forced him to leave the police. Nudger's shambolic office is above a doughnut shop, and he is hounded by a malevolent ex-wife. Lutz has written ten novels in the Nudger series and numerous short stories collected in the omnibus *The Nudger Dilemmas* (2001). The novels are rife with black comedy but also a sense of sympathy, as tragedy continually befalls the hapless Nudger and those around him. One notable title is *The Right to Sing the Blues* (1985) in which the jazz-loving Nudger travels to New Orleans to work a case for a legendary clarinettist.

Later series characters

Lutz created a series character in Fred Carver that was every bit as down-trodden as Nudger, but darker, more cynical and more violent. Carver lives and works in the fictional Florida city of Del Moray. Carver first appeared in the novel *Tropical Heat* (1986) and has appeared in nine subsequent novels. An embittered, disabled man, Carver feels constant physical pain from a gunshot wound to the leg which ended his police career. His investigative work often brings tragedy into his life, as in *Scorcher* (1987) wherein his son is murdered.

Lutz later developed the 'Night' series, featuring a different police detective in each novel working on a separate serial killer case in New York City. From the plot themes of nocturnal serial murderers in the 'Night' series, Lutz developed the Frank Quinn novels. Quinn is a disgraced ex-homicide detective, wounded and stigmatised after becoming embroiled in a conspiracy within the NYPD. In the first novel, *Darker Than Night* (2004), Quinn is brought back to the police department to assist in finding a brutal serial killer. The slow unravelling of the killer's back-story is interwoven with the narrative of the main investigation. In the following novels, Quinn sets up a detective agency specialising in the hunt for serial killers. Amongst his best work, the Quinn novels showcase Lutz's expertise at plot twists, multiple viewpoints, false endings and creating a palpable sense of dread in the portrayal of the killer's psychology. The stand-alone novels *SWF Seeks Same* (1990) and *The Ex* (1996) have been adapted into film, the former as the motion picture *Single White Female* (1992) and the latter as a HBO television film. Lutz was awarded an honorary arts and letters degree from the University of Missouri in 2007. Lutz is also a former president of the Mystery Writers of America and has received lifetime achievement awards from the Short Mystery Fiction Society and the Private Eye Writers of America.

Suggested reading

G. Powell (2002) 'Lutz for Life' *Bleeker Books.com* http://www.bleekerbooks.com /Features/LutzInterview.asp, date accessed 7 June 2011.

J. Reilly ed. (1985) *Twentieth-Century Crime and Mystery Writers* (New York: St Martin's Press).

Steven Powell

MacDonald, John D(ann) (1916–86)

Prolific author of more than 60 novels and nearly 400 works of short fiction, John D. MacDonald was one of the bestselling writers of fiction in America from 1946–86. Specialising primarily in the field of crime and suspense, his work covered a broad range of subject matter, including non-fiction, science fiction, sport stories, westerns and mainstream fiction. He is best known for the series character and protagonist of 21 novels, Travis McGee, a unique kind of private investigator whose self-designation is 'salvage expert' and who lives on a houseboat in Florida.

Born on 24 July 1916 in the small town of Sharon, Pennsylvania, MacDonald was the son of a corporate executive, a self-made man of singular focus who demanded the same discipline of his son. At the age of ten, MacDonald became ill and contracted mastoiditis, requiring surgery and a long recovery. At the same time, the family moved to Utica, New York, a city that became a stand-in for many of the fictional locales in MacDonald's novels. Bedridden for nearly a full year, MacDonald's mother spent long hours reading to him, and eventually he began to read on his own. His imagination now fired, he slowly changed from a normal, active young boy to a voracious and compulsive reader of fiction, devouring everything from Tarzan stories to the novels of Charles Dickens. He eventually made his way through most of the shelves of fiction in the Utica Public Library and, in doing so, became more and more of a withdrawn loner.

A bright student, MacDonald graduated high school at the age of 15, and then spent a year taking college preparatory classes before enrolling – at his father's insistence – at the prestigious Wharton School of Finance at the University of Pennsylvania. Unhappy there, he left after two years, took a year off and then finished his college education at Syracuse University. While at Syracuse he met a former student six years his senior, Dorothy Prentiss, an artist, art teacher and divorcee. They were married five months later and the union produced a son. Once MacDonald graduated, they moved to Boston where he did postgraduate work at the Harvard Business School, eventually earning a master's degree in business administration.

Wartime service

MacDonald embarked on a series of jobs in the business and finance industries, failing miserably in everything he tried. In 1940, at the age of 24, he was offered and accepted a commission in the United States Army, serving as a procurement officer in nearby Rochester, New York, entering at the rank of Lieutenant. Eighteen months after the United States entered the Second World War, MacDonald was transferred overseas and served for the remainder of the conflict in the China-Burma-India theatre of war. Originally assigned to procurement in India, he was transferred to Sri Lanka (then Ceylon) in 1944 to work in the Office of Strategic Services (OSS), the Army's espionage unit and the forerunner of the Central Intelligence Agency (CIA). He eventually achieved the rank of Lieutenant Colonel.

Writing fiction

It was during this long wartime separation from his wife that an unhappy MacDonald began writing fiction, after a suggestion from his wife that he do so in order to '[release some of the] unnatural constraint between you and your self-expression' (Merrill, 2000, pp. 37–8). Limited in what he could write about because of heavy military censorship, MacDonald wrote a brief short story and sent it home. Without telling him, Dorothy MacDonald typed it up in manuscript form and submitted it for publication, first to *Esquire* (they rejected it) then to *Story Magazine*, who paid $25 for the rights to publish it under the title 'Interlude in India'.

Dorothy waited until her husband returned home before telling him the news, and MacDonald was floored. 'I did not think of myself as a writer', he recalled years later, 'only one who wished he were one [...] I felt as if I were a fraud, as if I were masquerading, as if I were trying to be something that I wasn't' (Hirshberg, 1985, p. 12). He quit the army and began writing, working 80 hours a week and producing over 800,000 words without making a single sale. 'Interlude in India' was not a mystery story, and much of the early work MacDonald attempted (and later burned) was mainstream fiction, work he once characterised sarcastically as 'wonderful beautiful things about dying blind musicians [...] a lot of those words were really dreadful' (Hirshberg, 1985, p. 13). Five months after he began, he managed to sell a second story to a pulp magazine called *Detective Tales,* and his path as a writer was made clear.

Employing a work ethic that served him his entire career, MacDonald continued writing at a disciplined pace, working eight to ten hours a day, six to seven days a week. His stories began appearing in a wide variety of mainly mystery and detective pulp fiction magazines, including *Dime Detective, Doc Savage* and *Black Mask.* By the end of 1946 he had 24 stories published, 35 in 1947, 50 in 1948 and an astonishing 73 short stories and novellas in

1949. Several of these sales were to mainstream, 'slick' magazines, including *Liberty, Collier's* and *Cosmopolitan*, and MacDonald continued to produce this kind of fiction throughout his career. Also, he wrote for numerous science fiction pulp magazines, including *Super Science Stories, Astounding Science Fiction* and *Thrilling Wonder Stories*, producing over 50 such works of fiction. He wrote sports stories, family stories and even a few westerns.

Much of MacDonald's early work is that of a writer heavily influenced by his peers, and his tales of troubled war veterans returning home and attempting to re-establish themselves in society reflect a lot of the hopeless existentialism of Cornell Woolrich. Yet even in the earliest of stories one can see evidence of the hallmarks of MacDonald's prose: strong, believable characters, keen attention to detail, an observant eye for setting, and, above all, a strong sense of narrative drive, to which all other characteristics take a secondary position.

From short stories to novels

As the popularity of pulp magazines waned in the late 1940s, MacDonald began writing for the newly-emergent paperback market, one that had grown from simply reprinting cheap versions of hard cover releases to one that published original material. MacDonald's first such work was a hard-boiled mystery story titled *The Brass Cupcake* (1950), and featured an insurance investigator in the place of the traditional private detective, a practice the author would continue with variations throughout his writing career.

The author's early books included two science fiction novels (both published in hardcover) and two mainstream works (also published in hardcover), but most were crime or mystery stories, in whole or in part. Two of these novels deserve mention, for entirely different reasons.

The Damned (1952) is a multi-character novel told in the third person concerning a disparate group of travellers in Mexico stuck at a ferry crossing while awaiting its repair. Bearing more than a passing resemblance to Thornton Wilder's 1929 novel *The Bridge of San Luis Rey*, MacDonald's exploration of multiple points-of-view was a form he would continue to expand upon throughout his career. These novels, while not mysteries or crime stories, invariably have some criminal element associated with one or more of the characters. The novel was also notable for its marketing: the cover featured a quote from author Mickey Spillane, 'I wish I had written this book', who was at the time the best-selling hard-boiled mystery writer in America. The quote did much to put *The Damned* into the hands of readers, and the novel remains MacDonald's all-time bestseller.

Dead Low Tide (1953) is, stylistically, the highpoint of MacDonald's early period, and it provided a different kind of template that the author would continue to utilise throughout his career. Told in the first person, the novel is the story of an ordinary man, in this case an employee of a residential construction company, who is inadvertently swept up in a crime that he must eventually become involved with in order to exonerate himself. Drawing on Raymond Chandler and Dashiell Hammett's traditional private detectives, MacDonald adjusts the tradition by using ordinary citizens who the reader can identify with in that role. The novel was MacDonald's second to be set in Florida, his newly adopted home, and he would go on to feature the locale more and more in his work, eventually becoming known as the preeminent novelist of the state.

MacDonald's body of work from 1950 to 1963 is that of an author continually trying to improve his art and expand upon his prior successes. MacDonald wrote 41 novels before 1964, and those works, while mostly mystery and crime novels, include a wide variety of other types of fiction, including a fantasy, a comic novel, a film novelisation and novels ranging in topic from sexual obsession to the effects of marital infidelity on middle class America. But it is the mystery and suspense novels that were his strong suit: now-forgotten works with titles such as *The Price of Murder* (1957), *Soft Touch* (1958), *Deadly Welcome* (1959), *The End of the Night* (1960), and *One Monday We Killed Them All* (1961) are all excellent works of an artist at the peak of his creativity. They exhibit MacDonald's characteristic style, a spare descriptive prose that wasted no words, a sociological interest in many of the problems of modern society and a preoccupation with the psychology of evil, which the author believed was a force of nature that existed irrespective of any causation within society. All of his work exhibits a strong moral tone in a world where 'people must accept responsibility for those acts which affect the lives of others' (Hirshberg, 1985, p. 66). Evil is defeated, but never eliminated, while good struggles onward. His protagonists are often everyday middle class characters who are caught up in events not of their own making or professionals who are forced to deal with events that nearly undo them. Had MacDonald never written a series character, his other work would still be noted as exemplary within the world of mystery fiction.

Travis McGee

In 1963 MacDonald was asked by his publisher to create a series character, something that the author had refused to do several years before out of fear that it would pigeonhole him as one type of author and prevent him from publishing other kinds of fiction. MacDonald wrote three full novels, discarding the first two, before settling on a character he felt could sustain a series as well as one that he himself would enjoy writing. Travis McGee made his debut in *The Deep Blue Goodby* (1964). A beach bum living on a houseboat in Fort Lauderdale, McGee is an ex-Marine who saw action in the Korean War (making him most likely in his 30s, but his age is never specified) and who lives his life with no visible means of support. His sporadic income comes from the recovery of stolen goods, cash or other valuables, retrieved when there is no other legal means of getting them back, and for which he is paid 50% of the goods' value. McGee has no detective license to practice his calling, a profession he fell into when helping a friend. He takes cases only from people he knows or from their acquaintances. He describes himself as a man who is taking his retirement in chunks.

McGee is a uniquely self-aware American male who, through MacDonald's expertly-crafted first-person narrative, drives the strong, intricate plots while at the same time indulging in frequent asides that comment on many facets of modern society and modern man. As a fitting symbol for this most colourful of private detectives, all of the McGee novels feature a colour in the title: *A Purple Place for Dying, The Quick Red Fox, Nightmare in Pink* (all published in 1964). The author acknowledged using many of the traditional conventions of detective fiction: McGee has a friend and sidekick in Meyer, a retired economist and intellectual who is very different from the man of action McGee, but they work together well. Later imitated by crime writers such as Geoffrey Norman, James Hall and Carl Hiassen, McGee was the first of several Florida-based PIs or adventurers who finds himself in conflict with greedy developers intent on destroying areas of Southern Florida's ecological beauty for profit. MacDonald wrote the first three Travis McGee novels before the first was ever published, and then released them (all in paperback) simultaneously. They were an immediate success and were imitated by other novelists and television scriptwriters. Aside from a handful of works published after 1964, the McGee series would prove to be MacDonald's primary focus for the rest of his life. In 1973 the novels had become so popular that they began appearing first in hardcover and, without exception, appeared on most of the bestseller listings in America.

Legacy

MacDonald's works – including those outside the Travis McGee series – have been translated into many different languages and published throughout the world. The author's reputation, especially after 1970, was at a highpoint, notably among his fellow writers. Admirers of his work included Raymond Chandler, Ian Fleming, Rex Stout, Kurt Vonnegut Jr, Kingsley Amis and Stephen King. The author was the recipient of many awards throughout his lifetime, including the Benjamin Franklin Award for Fiction, the American Book Award, and the *Grand Prix de Litterature Policiere* for the French edition of his novel *A Key to the Suite* (1962). He served as the president of the Mystery Writers of America in 1962 and was awarded that organisation's Grand Master award in 1972. He received several honorary degrees from various American Universities and, for nearly 40 years, was the subject of a journal devoted exclusively to the study and appreciation of his work, the *JDM Bibliophile*.

Many of MacDonald's novels and short stories have made their way to film, with mixed results. Travis McGee has not transferred successfully to the screen, with adaptations of *Darker Than Amber* (1966) and *The Empty Copper Sea* (1978) proving underwhelming. His novel *The Executioners* (1958) was filmed twice as *Cape Fear*, the first version was directed by J. Lee Thompson and the latter by Martin Scorsese, with both versions altering the ending substantially. Several of his short stories appeared in television anthology series of the 1950s and his 1977 bestseller *Condominium* was produced as a multi-part made-for-television movie. Perhaps the most successful (certainly the most faithful) adaptation of MacDonald's work was the 1985 independent film *A Flash of Green*, directed and adapted by Victor Nunez from MacDonald's 1962 novel. It came the closest of any MacDonald film adaptation to capturing the literary qualities of the author, and MacDonald himself was one of the financial backers of the project. MacDonald's non-fiction works include *No Deadly Drug* (1968), an account of the murder trial of Dr Carl Coppolino, and *A Friendship: The Letters of Dan Rowan and John D. MacDonald, 1967–1974* (1987), an edited collection of his correspondence with his friend and comedian Dan Rowan. *Reading for Survival* (1987), a short book fashioned around a dialogue between Travis McGee and Meyer on the importance of reading which was written for the Library of Congress' Center for the Book, was published posthumously.

MacDonald died on 28 December 1986 at St Mary's Hospital in Milwaukee of complications from heart surgery. He was 70 years old.

Suggested reading

D. Geherin (1982) *John D. MacDonald* (New York: Frederick Ungar).

E. W. Hirshberg (1985) *John D. MacDonald* (Boston: Twayne Publishers).

H. Merrill (2000) *The Red Hot Typewriter: The Life and Times of John D. MacDonald* (New York: Thomas Dunne Books/ St. Martin's Minotaur).

L.D. Moore (1994) *Meditations on America: John D. MacDonald's Travis McGee Series and Other Fiction* (Bowling Green, Ohio: Bowling Green State University Popular Press).

Steve Scott

Macdonald, Ross (1915–83)

Ross Macdonald was born Kenneth Millar in Los Gatos, California, on 13 December 1915. During a highly successful and prolific writing career he published crime stories first as Kenneth Millar and then as Ken Millar, the most successful of which were *The Dark Tunnel* (1944), *Trouble Follows Me* (1946), *Blue City* (1947) and *The Three Roads* (1948). He then briefly wrote as John Macdonald, producing in 1949 *The Moving Target*, the first full-length work to feature his California private eye Lew Archer (Archer had made his first appearance in a 1946 short story *Find the Woman*). The Archer series continued with Millar writing as John Ross Macdonald: *The Drowning Pool* (1950), *The Way Some People Die* (1951), *The Ivory Grin* (1952), *Meet Me at the Morgue* (1953) and *Find a Victim* (1954). From the publication of *The Barbarous Coast* (1956) as Ross Macdonald, the pseudonym under which he became most famous, he wrote further Lew Archer novels: *The Doomsters* (1958), *The Galton Case* (1959), *The Wycherly Woman* (1961), *The Zebra-Striped Hearse* (1962), *The Chill* (1964), *The Far Side of the Dollar* (1965), *Black Money* (1966), *The Instant Enemy* (1968), *The Goodbye Look* (1969), *The Underground Man* (1971), *Sleeping Beauty* (1973) and *The Blue Hammer* (1976). A number of the earlier novels were later republished under the name Ross Macdonald and, in some cases, with changed titles (he dropped the John Macdonald and John Ross Macdonald pseudonyms to avoid confusion with fellow crime writer John D. MacDonald). In addition to the Lew Archer novels, Macdonald wrote a number of short stories, two major non-fiction works, *On Crime Writing* (1973) and *Self-Portrait, Ceaselessly Into the Past* (1981) as well as a number of academic articles of literary criticism.

Macdonald created a fictional biography for his pen-name: born in California, he spent most of his adult life there and made his adopted home town Santa Barbara (under the name Santa Teresa) the base of his most famous creation Lew Archer. In contrast, Millar's formative years were spent in Canada, originally Kitchener, Ontario, and both of his parents were Canadian. The most significant event in his childhood was the departure of his father, a writer, poet and sailor who left his wife and child in desperate financial circumstances. A combination of poverty and his mother's persistent poor health resulted in him being shifted around to various relatives and boarding schools as a child and adolescent. By the time he reached the age of 16, he claimed to have lived in about 50 different rooms. The theme of parental abandonment, particularly the loss of the father and the resulting life-long impact on the child or adolescent is central to the Lew Archer novels.

Macdonald gained some stability and a sense of purpose and worth through his participation in higher education (he attended the University of Western Ontario and then the University of Michigan where his PhD study focused on the writings of Samuel Coleridge). He married, in 1938, Margaret Sturm, who was also committed to becoming a writer and who later published crime novels as Margaret Millar. In 1939 their only daughter, Linda, was born. Linda, who died in 1970, had a number of emotional and psychological problems which caused Macdonald considerable distress and made his marriage to Margaret extremely difficult at times. Macdonald's first novel was published before the end of World War II. Having served in the Pacific as a communications officer in the American navy, Macdonald returned to Michigan to complete his PhD and concentrate on his writing. Macdonald drew on his childhood experiences and his psychoanalysis sessions (which both he and Linda underwent) for his crime writing: at the heart of the Lew Archer novels were family secrets. Macdonald examined the damage caused by those secrets and the possible positive consequences of uncovering and confronting them. This psychological unearthing replicated detective work. The act of remembering for Macdonald was part of the creative process: he described his memories – '[m]y half-suppressed Canadian years, my whole childhood and youth, rose like a corpse from the bottom of the sea to confront me' (Macdonald, 1981, p. 30). The Archer novels' central project is an engagement with the significant past to confront it and possibly assuage guilt.

Hammett, Chandler and Macdonald

Macdonald considered his Lew Archer novels as being situated in the hard-boiled tradition established by Dashiell Hammett and further developed by Raymond Chandler. He had great admiration for Hammett, taking the name Archer from Miles Archer, Sam Spade's partner in *The Maltese Falcon*. Despite feeling that Chandler was an inferior writer, Macdonald acknowledged that he had a greater influence on his own work. He described Chandler's vision as 'lack[ing] the tragic unity of Hammett's' but accepted that Chandler's isolated Los Angeles private-eye was the model for his early presentations of Lew Archer (Macdonald, 1981, p. 117). Macdonald claimed that he 'learned a great deal from Chandler' but, particularly as he enjoyed greater success, was anxious to explain that he had developed his own distinctive style – one which he considered was superior to that of Chandler (Macdonald, 1981, p. 120). Macdonald clearly marked his work, after 1957 when he wrote *The Doomsters* (1958), as 'mature' and described this novel as marking 'a fairly clean break with the Chandler tradition, which it had taken me some years to digest, and freed me to make my own approach' (Macdonald, 1981, p. 120). In particular he sought to distance himself from Chandler's presentation of Marlowe, saying that he saw 'Marlowe's voice [as] limited by his role as the hard-boiled hero', (Macdonald, 1973, p. 22) unlike '[m]y narrator Archer [who has a] wider and less rigidly stylized range of expression' (Macdonald, 1981, p. 120). Macdonald clearly considered Archer as being a more interesting and admirable creation than either Sam Spade or Philip Marlowe and the novels foreground a number of characteristics of Archer which are extremely unusual in the hard-boiled genre.

Lew Archer: compassionate frontiersman

In his working practices and physical appearance Lew Archer is firmly in accordance with the traditions of the hard-boiled genre. He operates alone, outside the official structure of the law, and with limited resources. A tall, athletic, handsome man he has seen action in World War II, served in the police force, participated in boxing and always appears fearless when confronting physical danger. In *The Galton Case* he says he is around six foot tall and weighs 190 pounds, and in *The Wycherly Woman* a female character asks him 'Are you a professional athlete? You seem to be in very good trim, for a middle-aged man' (Macdonald, 1963, p. 73). Macdonald establishes Archer as an active and powerful example of masculinity although, in the actual texts, it appears that he has moved away from direct aggressive action into a more cerebral and compassionate approach to life. He is attacked and injured much more frequently than he does damage to others: his body is powerful and yet curiously vulnerable. Whilst always trying to avoid violence, and very rarely an active participant in it he shows courage and endurance when he is attacked or threatened. He can appear unusually passive in the narratives, rarely occupying centre stage but rather functioning as a guide into, and through, Macdonald's labyrinthine plots. At times Archer, the lens through which everything is viewed, seems almost invisible to other protagonists as he sees, and hears, their most private business.

Archer operates as a secular confessional figure, a psychoanalyst, as he moves beyond the crime to uncover the motivation behind it (which will almost certainly reveal dysfunctional family relationships). The typical Archer plot involves him being hired to find someone, or something, on behalf of a wealthy family: invariably he is given only part of the information he needs because the family has secrets they are not prepared to share. The missing person, or object, leads him directly into the past and the case cannot be brought to any conclusion until he has deciphered the meaning of events which, although they appear to have been buried, have now resurfaced. These events have power because they have never been confronted and consequently lie at the heart of family deceit. He frequently recommends that those he meets, particularly the young, should seek psychiatric help and often suggests that this will be likely to have a positive outcome thus, unusually in the hard-boiled genre, many of his novels appear to have optimistic endings. Because of this Macdonald's work has at times been viewed as representing no challenge to the structure of society as he appears to reveal that crime is always individual, with causes within family histories, rather than being related to the operation of the state. However Macdonald's continual examination of wealthy or comfortably middle class families who appear outwardly to represent contented bourgeois values but are fractured and damaged by past transgressions indicates that his work has subversive elements.

Macdonald's passionate interest in, and concern for, the landscape and wildlife of Southern California and the impact of the growth of the city on that environment is reflected throughout the Archer novels. Archer moves through a landscape he observes as beautiful, but vulnerable, constantly threatened by the encroaching city and the growth of an increasingly technological, capitalist, society. Macdonald establishes Archer as not only in the tradition of the hard-boiled genre but also in an earlier tradition, of the lone frontiersman. In *The Zebra-Striped Hearse,* Archer drives 'off the highway through thickening timber' and his association with the western tracker becomes explicit: his passenger asks if Lew Archer is his real name and he replies 'Naturally not. My real name is Natty Bumppo' (Macdonald, 1962, p. 113). The link with a legendary western lone tracker at one with nature was reinforced by Macdonald on a number of occasions. Asked if Archer featured as a modern day Bumppo, Macdonald replied, 'Yes, of course...let's call him the benevolent hunter. Archer is...a descendant both socially and literally of those men. It's the western tradition' (Grogg, 1973, pp. 219–20). For Macdonald an important element of that tradition, as well as the idea of tracking and uncovering new territory, was respect for the landscape and a determination to live within it without damaging its beauty. For Macdonald the growth of the city and the increasingly technological and money-dominated society it represents threatens that beauty. The wealthy families he meets fail to find contentment because they are denying not only their individual pasts but also the western tradition and history of their nation in order to achieve short-term financial benefits.

Literary success and recognition

Macdonald enjoyed a considerable amount of success with the Lew Archer novels with his work outselling both Hammett and Chandler throughout the 1950s and 1960s. In many respects he moved the hard-boiled tradition from its heritage of engagement with working-class male readers, established from the early days of *Black Mask* magazine, to a more literary and intellectual audience who he envisaged as sharing his own interests and understanding of classical literature, myth, environmental and social change and psychoanalysis or psychiatry. Two of his novels, *The Moving Target* and *The Drowning Pool* were adapted as films, both starring Paul Newman in the role of Lew Archer. In both films, however, Archer's name was changed to Harper supposedly because Newman had enjoyed recent success as characters whose name begins with the letter 'H', although other sources indicate there were more complex legal reasons behind the name change. *The Moving Target* was filmed as *Harper* (1966) and *The Drowning Pool* under its original title in 1975. *The Underground Man*, Macdonald's most directly environmental novel, was filmed for television in 1974 starring Peter Graves as Archer. Brian Keith played the detective in a TV series broadcast in 1975 which ran for one season titled simply, *Archer*. The lack of filmic and television success for the works may be because of the relative passivity of Archer himself, in a medium which prioritises action, as well as the complex nature of the plots and their focus on psychological issues. *Harper* received mixed reviews from critics with its kitsch style and overtly comic scenes making for an entertaining film but one that held little resemblance to the original novels.

Macdonald became president of *The Mystery Writers of America* in 1965, after receiving the Silver Dagger from *The British Crime Writers Association* in 1964. In 1965 the same organisation awarded him the Gold Dagger, and in 1981 *The Private Eye Writers of America* awarded him their lifetime achievement award, The Eye. In the later years of his life, living in Santa Barbara, he became involved in both teaching and advising a wide range of students or aspiring writers on crime fiction. These activities gave him considerable personal satisfaction, not only because he seems to have genuinely enjoyed the company of young people, but also because throughout his life he appeared to seek confirmation of the significance and literary quality of his work. Macdonald's work has been acknowledged as influencing a number of other writers, including William Goldman and Michael Connelly. Sue Grafton uses his fictional town of Santa Teresa as the setting for her 'alphabet' crime novels and James Ellroy, a writer whose frenzied and violent detectives seem far removed from the cerebral and compassionate Lew Archer, has paid homage to the influence of Macdonald on his work.

The last Lew Archer novel, *The Blue Hammer,* was published in 1976. In it, Macdonald appears to depart from Archer's usual modus operandi when it seems likely he is about to embark on a long-term relationship. Throughout the novels, Archer's failed marriage to Sue, although never featuring directly in any of the works, was established as a major sadness in his life and the direct cause of his loneliness. The fact that Archer now seemed likely to settle with another woman signalled a fundamental change in his life. In the late 1970s Macdonald began suffering from what was eventually diagnosed as Alzheimer's disease. His illness had a certain tragic irony, considering his life-long interest in mental problems and psychiatry and his generally positive presentation of possible treatment. Macdonald died in Santa Barbara, which had been his home for 30 years, at the age of 67.

Suggested reading

R.B. Browne (1990) 'Ross Macdonald: Revolutionary Author and Critic; Or The Need for the Oath of Macdonald' *Journal of Popular Culture*, Winter 1990, 24 (3) 101–11.

S.R. Busch (1986). 'Ross Macdonald as Chronicler of Southern California' *South Dakota Review*, Spring 1986, 24 (1) 111–20.

S. Grogg Jr. (1973) 'Ross Macdonald: At the Edge', *Journal of Popular Culture*, Summer 1973, 7, 213–22.

J. Tutunjian (1974) 'A Conversation with Ross Macdonald', *Tamarack Review* 62, 66–85.

Maureen Sunderland

Marlowe, Dan J(ames) (1914–87)

Hard-boiled novelist, newspaper columnist and magazine writer who also wrote under the name Jaime Sandaval, Marlowe is best known for novels featuring the series character Earl Drake, and in particular for *The Name of the Game is Death* (1962).

Though quite well known in the 1960s and 1970s, by the time of his death in August 1986 (in some references the year is mistakenly dated as 1987) Dan Marlowe had fallen into relative obscurity. His life is not well documented and this, combined with a strange episode of memory loss in June 1977, has left the details of his biography uncertain.

Marlowe was born 10 July 1914 in Lowell, Massachusetts, where he was raised by two aunts following the death of his mother. According to an excellent profile by Charles Kelly, Marlowe trained as an accountant at the Bentley School of Accounting and Finance in Boston and worked as assistant manager of two Connecticut country clubs between 1934 and 1941. Marlowe held a wide variety of jobs, ranging from office manager to travelling salesman. He also claimed to have been a professional gambler. According to Kelly he was also a heavy drinker, a theatre lover and a womaniser.

Marlowe's writing career appears to have begun following the sudden death of his wife in 1956. Kelly explains that 'he walked out of his home in suburban Washington, D.C., and never went back. Never much of a drinker prior to this time, he began to indulge heavily' (Kelly, 2007). He began writing his first novel, *Doorway to Death*, in 1957, and it was published in 1959. The novel introduced the character Johnny Killain, a New York bell captain and private detective based at the Hotel Duarte, who appeared in four more novels between 1959 and 1961. However, *The Name of the Game is Death*, published in 1962, was Marlowe's first real success.

The Name of the Game is Death features Chet Arnold (in later books Earl Drake, having changed his name after plastic surgery) and his partner Bunny, who go on the run after robbing a bank in Phoenix and killing several people along the way. Arnold, who has been shot, holes up in Phoenix and Bunny escapes to Florida with the money. The book was widely praised, including by Anthony Boucher, who said it was 'tensely plotted, forcefully written, and extraordinarily effective'.

After the novel appeared, Marlowe received a phone call from Albert Nussbaum, a bank robber on the FBI's 'Most Wanted List' who praised the novel for its authenticity. After Nussbaum was captured, he was finally paroled from prison with assistance from Marlowe. Marlowe helped Nussbaum establish his writing career. Nussbaum helped Marlowe with his later books, in particular when Marlowe was recuperating from his amnesia. Nussbaum would vet Marlowe's work for accuracy in details regarding weapons, ballistics, safes, vaults and alarm systems.

The character of Earl Drake appeared in *One Endless Hour*, and then became a spy in a series of 'Operation' novels beginning with *Flashpoint* (1970), which was later published as *Operation Flashpoint*, and won the Mystery Writers of America Best Paperback Original award. In all Marlowe published around 50 novels under his own name and more under pseudonyms. He died from heart failure at home in Tarzana, California, and is buried alongside his wife in Stratford, Connecticut.

Suggested reading

C. Kelly (2007) 'Mystery Man: Dan J. Marlowe'. *Allan Guthrie's Noir Originals* http://www.allanguthrie.co.uk/pages/noir_zine/profiles/dan_j_marlowe.php, date accessed 16 September 2010.

Christopher Routledge

McBain, Ed (1926–2005)

Ed McBain was the main pseudonym of the astonishingly prolific and popular writer Evan Hunter who wrote under many aliases across all genres and in many formats, including short stories, novels, television screenplays and feature film scripts. He invented the name specifically to write police crime stories. *Cop Hater* (1956) was the first of what became 55 novels about the detectives who worked in 87th Precinct district in the imaginary American city of Isola, which is clearly New York City in all but name. With this series of novels, McBain did not create the police procedural sub-genre of crime fiction, but through the quality of writing and the novels' phenomenal success, he made the genre his own.

Early life and beginnings of literary career

McBain was born Salvatore Alberto Lombino in East Harlem (Little Italy) in New York on 15 October 1926. At school he was awarded an Arts Student League scholarship and studied Art at Cooper Union from 1943–44. He had ideas about becoming a cartoonist but towards the end of the Second World War, now aged 18, he joined the navy to avoid being drafted into the army. He was stationed in Hawaii and, once the war was over, in Japan as a radar operator on a destroyer. It was during this time that he began to read novels by authors as diverse as Ernest Hemingway, James Joyce, Dashiell Hammett and James M. Cain, amongst others, as well as pulp crime books. He began to write short stories, but his initial submissions to magazines and journals were unsuccessful.

On release from the navy, he entered Hunter College, New York, (on the GI bill) in 1946 to study literature, graduating Phi Beta Kappa in 1950. On leaving he had a number of jobs, one of them as an English teacher at a Bronx Vocational High School. It was not an experience he particularly enjoyed: the students 'didn't give a rat's ass' about literature, and he left after 17 days (Hamill, 2000, p. 67). In 1950, while working as a lobster salesman, he answered an advertisement in *The New York Times* and was hired by the

Scott Meredith Agency (Mickey Spillane was one of their clients, as were Arthur C. Clarke and P. G. Wodehouse). His day job was to asses stories from new writers for publication, but in the evenings and at weekends he began writing stories himself. He wrote science fiction, private eye stories and teenage fiction. He wrote for pulp paperbacks such as *Smashing Detective*, *Famous Detective* and *Manhunt*, and began using pseudonyms because he often had three or more stories in a single issue without the editor's knowledge. His pen names included Hunt Collins, Matt Cordell, Richard Marsten, John Abbot and Curt Cannon. In 1952, with grander literary ambitions, he legally changed his name from Lombino to Evan Hunter because he and his new agent reasoned it would be a more acceptable than his Italian name to the then ethnically conscious publishing world.

His first big success as Evan Hunter was *The Blackboard Jungle* (1954). This was a realistic portrayal of angry, difficult and rebellious teenagers and an idealist teacher in a tough city high school. His own teaching experience. together with extensive research (something that was to become a trademark of his later work), enabled him to focus on the youth of America that had been portrayed very differently, and ideally, in the media. The novel marked the arrival of the 'teenager' as a social group. Critically acclaimed and recognised as a major work, the book was a bestseller. It was made into a film in 1955 and became a controversial success due to its rock and roll soundtrack and after audiences rioted at some showings in the US and the UK.

87th Precinct novels and police procedural

In 1956, Permabooks, the paperback division of Doubleday, offered Evan Hunter a contract to produce three police mysteries. In the same year he produced *Cop Hater*, *The Mugger*, and *The Pusher*, the novels that introduced the detectives of the 87th Precinct. Fearing for his literary reputation if Evan Hunter was associated with crime paperbacks, and because he was planning to write Hunter novels at the same time as his police stories, he decided to invent a new crime writer, Ed McBain. The books were noticed by Anthony Boucher, *The New York Times'* mystery critic who thought them 'distinguished contributions to the procedural school of police stories', ('police procedural' being a term Boucher himself was credited with coining), and included the first two on his list of Best Suspense Novels of 1956 (Dove, 1985, p. 2).

The police procedural genre in the late 40s and early 50s was a new departure for crime fiction. The 30s and 40s pulp fiction writers, among them Dashiel Hammett, Raymond Chandler and later Mickey Spillane, had made their heroes tough guy private investigators with the police portrayed as either corrupt or incompetent characters in supporting roles. McBain thought that the last time a real private eye solved a murder was 'never'. Real murders were solved by the police.

McBain therefore started researching, in patrol cars, forensic laboratories, hospitals, detention cells, morgues, courts, anywhere he needed to be to verify aspects of his story. It was, however, in the squad room that an original idea came to him. The squad room itself would be a form of leading character, with every detective being a composite and vital part of the police station. There had already been novels and works in other media which resembled what is now recognised as police procedurals, such as Hillary Waugh's *Last Seen Wearing*... (1952), as well as the immensely popular radio and television series *Dragnet*, but an accurate depiction of police teams and their working practices was still an untapped source of potential literary material. The 87th Precinct series was an inspiration and forerunner to such police television dramas as *Hill Street Blues*, *NYPD Blue* and *The Shield*. The Swedish authors Maj Sjöwall and Per Wahlöö, creators of the highly regarded 'Martin Beck' procedural novels (1965–75), also acknowledged McBain as an influence on their work.

Unlike Chandler's Philip Marlowe and other charismatic private eyes, the policemen McBain created are just people coming into work every day to earn a living. They are people trying to do their job well despite the attendant frustrations, such as lack of monetary rewards, physical dangers and the psychological effect of continually dealing with the darker side of human nature. The detectives, who alternate as the main characters, are a microcosm of the ethnic mix of New York, here renamed Isola which translates as 'island' in Italian. The most regular character, Steve Carella is Italian, Meyer Meyer is Jewish, Bert Kling and Cotton Hawes are all American WASPs, Arthur Brown is black, Peter Brynes is Irish, Frankie Hernandez is Puerto Rican and there is even a Japanese detective named Takashi Fujiwara. McBain deftly trod the path between mystery fiction and social realism. 'A mystery should be exciting, believable and entertaining' McBain said. The problem was that crime is not this way in real life:

> There is no mystery in police work, nothing fits into a carefully conceived scheme. The high point is often the corpse that opens the case, there is no climatic progression, suspense is for the movies. There are only people, curiously twisted motives, small unexplained details and coincidence and the unexpected that combine to form a sequence of events. There is no mystery. There never is. (McBain, 2005, p. 59)

In the early novels, McBain gave the reader the same information about a case that the police characters had at their disposal, thus creating a shared viewpoint. The text of the novels contain official forms, autopsy reports, photographs, timetables, and lists which may or may not contain clues which the reader can analyse and digest in the same way as the detectives. The entire narrative of *Jigsaw* (1970) revolves around the deciphering of jigsaw-shaped pieces of paper. In later novels McBain revealed the villain to the reader before the police know his identity, thus changing the dynamic of the story. *He Who Hesitates* (1965) is written entirely from the point of view of the villain committing the perfect crime, and who ultimately escapes police detection. In *The Heckler* (1960), McBain introduced the 'Deaf Man' into the series, an ingenious super-villain, inspired by the character The Riddler in the Batman comics McBain used to read as a child. Deaf Man provides a break from the realism of the series, although by taunting the police with his crimes he pre-dates several real-life criminals such as the Zodiac killer in Northern California and the serial killer Heriberto Seda of New York, who also teased the police with cryptic messages. *Fuzz* (1968) is a comedy of errors as the Deaf Man's deadly puzzles make the police look inept. By contrast, McBain's novels that feature psychopathic killers – *Doll* (1965), *So Long As You Both Shall Live* (1976) and especially *Calypso* (1979) – are dark and shocking in their examination of the psychopathology of homicide. The novels are a thematic and stylistic precursor to the Hannibal Lecter series by Thomas Harris, as well as the forensic thrillers of Patricia Cornwell.

One of the main characteristics usually attributed to the police procedural is the detailed description of technical processes. McBain had a gift for this, using it to add to the drama and often to make fun of other crime genres. In *The Heckler*, the step by step reconstruction of a burnt match book from its ashes is explained in painstaking detail. Sam Grossman, the forensic genius at the laboratory, teases Carella with a hypothetical but remarkably detailed description of the unknown owner of the matchbook as though analysed from its remains, before revealing the one small clue that all of his work has actually exposed. The stories also highlight the fact that, despite all the technologies available to detectives, most crimes are in the end solved through dogged repetitive legwork and a fair amount of luck and coincidence. In *Fuzz*, the Deaf Man's plans, which have defeated the concentrated efforts of the 87th Precinct men, are inadvertently foiled by a bored patrolman wanting an ice cream.

The detectives are often taken by McBain into other cultural worlds. Several novels involve the theatre: *Ten Plus One* (1963), *Ice* (1983), *Romance* (1995) and *The Last Dance* (1999). Many of the stories have allusions to the craft of writing and other popular novelists. *Fat Ollies Book* (2003) revolves around a police crime novel that one of the detectives in the precinct is trying to get published. The open plan layout of the squad room, with all the detectives being able to informally catch bits of information about their colleague's cases, also encouraged a multiple plot style. *Hail Hail, the Gangs All Here!* (1971) has 14 separate storylines all taking place within 24 hours, where minor cases have to be dealt with alongside major ones, sometimes causing unexpected crossovers that lead to the solving of a case. McBain's skill at interweaving plot and sub-plot allowed him to have fun with different crime genres within the procedural novel. The 87th Precinct series consists of suspense thrillers, locked room mysteries, mistaken identities, puzzle pieces, psychopathic serial killers, a ghost story, crime comedies and allusions to several Sherlock Holmes plots.

Other works

At the same time as he was writing the 87th Precinct novels, McBain was also producing an enormous amount of other literary material. Ironically, as his most famous series were considered the antithesis of private investigator novels, McBain also created numerous memorable PI characters in stories and novels very much of the hard-boiled genre. Under the pseudonym Hunt Collins he wrote about milk-loving PI Guthrie Lamb in several short stories for *Famous Detective Magazine* in the early 1950s. Also as Collins, he wrote a spoof of Mickey Spillane novels for the magazine *Manhunt*, featuring Dudley Sledge in the story 'Kiss Me Dudley'. In another series written for *Manhunt*, Matt Cordell is a brutal PI who lost his investigator's licence after pistol-whipping his wife's lover. He is now an alcoholic but still working on cases. Cordell was renamed Curt Cannon in *I'm Cannon – For Hire* (1958) which was reprinted as *The Gutter and the Grave* in 2005. Benjamin Smoke is a retired detective turned private eye in the stand-alone novel *Where There's Smoke* (1975), but McBain's most long-running series outside the 87th Precinct novels featured Florida attorney Mathew Hope. Hope made his debut in *Goldilocks* (1978) and subsequently featured in 12 further novels, including *Gladly the Cross-Eyed Bear* (1996), which contains an appearance by Guthrie Lamb. All of the titles of the Hope series were taken from nursery rhymes or children's nursery stories.

As Evan Hunter, he began to write screenplays: he wrote several episodes for the television series *Alfred Hitchcock Presents,* and in 1960, he wrote the screenplay for *The Young Savages* based on his book about teenage gangs, *A Matter Of Conviction*. In 1963 Alfred Hitchcock asked him to adapt the Daphne Du Maurier short story *The Birds,* and the subsequent film was a great success. He wrote teleplays for westerns, among them, *The Chisolms* (1980) adapted from his own novel published in 1976. He wrote for *Ironside* (1968) and *Columbo* (1992–94). At the same time he produced another 18 successful novels on various social themes: *Mothers And Daughters* (1961) is concerned with the emptiness of middle class life, *Sons* (1969) with the Vietnam war, and *Love Dad* (1981) with the Hippie movement. Although many of these did receive critical acclaim, he still felt 'literary' recognition as an author was lukewarm. Ultimately, he did receive many awards, among them the Mystery Writers of America Grand Master Award in 1986 and he was the first American to be awarded the British Crime Writers Association's Diamond Dagger (1998). His 87th Precinct novel, *Money, Money, Money* (2001), won the Edgar Award for Best Novel. Eventually he became reconciled to the fact that he would probably be remembered more for his crime writing than his literary work and latterly had fun with his two personas Hunter, the serious writer, and McBain the popular crime writer. Hunter and McBain were 'photographed' together and had conversations with each other about writing. *Candyland: A Novel in Two Parts* (2001) is credited as co-authored by Hunter and McBain and mixes the two writing styles.

McBain continued with his prodigious output even after suffering a series of heart attacks. He also suffered a persistent sore throat for years which doctors were never able to successfully treat and was finally diagnosed as throat cancer in 2002. He had his larynx removed the same year and lamented that he could no longer conduct readings and converse with his fans. He had always engaged with his readers and never took his success for granted. He wrote around 100 novels as well as short stories and screenplays, and to date he has sold over a 100 million books worldwide. McBain died on 6 July 2005, at his Connecticut home. At his memorial service many tributes were paid, both from his readers in the form of emails which were read out and from a number of writers present, including Elmore Leonard and Stephen King. All stressed his wit, forthrightness and humanity as well as his literary heritage. Stephen King said 'that by successfully merging realism with genre fiction he may actually have created the kind of popular fiction that drove the best seller lists and lit up the American imagination in the years 1960–2000' (D'Ascoli, 2005). McBain was married three times, to Anita Melnick in 1949 with whom he had three sons, and to Mary Vann Finley in 1973. Both these unions ended in divorce. He married the Yugoslavian-born Dragica Dimitrijevic in 1997, and they co-authored the memoir *Let's Talk: A Story of Cancer and Love* (2005). In 2010, McBain was posthumously awarded honorary citizenship of the Italian town of Ruvo Del Monte, the birthplace of his grandfather Giuseppantonio Coppola.

Suggested reading

J.C. Carr (1983) *The Craft of Crime: Conversations with Crime Writers* (Boston: Houghton Mifflin).

G.N. Dove (1985) *The Boys From Grover Avenue: Ed McBain's 87th Precinct Novels* (Bowling Green, OH: Bowling Green State University Press).

J.Kingston. Pierce (2005) 'The Double-Man: a final farewell to novelist Ed McBain' *January Magazine*, October 2005, http://www.januarymagazine.com/features /mcbainintro.html, date accessed 6 October 2010.

Martin Lightening

McCoy, Horace (1897–1955)

Best known for *They Shoot Horses, Don't They?* (1935), Horace Stanley McCoy wrote five novels, four of them on themes such as civic corruption and moral collapse born of desperation; a sixth novel was published after his death, based on fragments of manuscript and film treatments. McCoy was among a group of writers who defined the hard-boiled style in the 1930s. McCoy also wrote many screenplays over two decades as a writer in Hollywood and had several of his novels adapted for the big screen.

Born on 14 April 1897 in the small town of Pegram, Tennessee, McCoy grew up in Nashville. Throughout his childhood, McCoy's parents were poor, though not as poor as he liked people to think. His maternal great-grandfather had founded the town of Pegram and other ancestors had been Civil War officers, but McCoy's father worked on the railroad and later as a travelling salesman. McCoy described his parents as 'book rich-money poor' (Nolan, 1985, p. 177). They moved to Dallas when McCoy was 15 years old and though he grew up an avid reader, he spent only one year (1912–13) in high school before leaving to help his father sell Jewel Brand coffee and tea.

McCoy's writing career began while he was on active service in the Air National Guard during World War I: he wrote articles for the unit's newspaper, the Romo Exhaust. He served in France from July 1918 until the end of the war as an aerial observer, a job that required lying face down in the belly of a plane taking photographs, but he also acted as radio operator, navigator, gunner and bombardier. He received the *Croix de Guerre* for bravery from the French government when he managed to bring his plane home after the pilot was killed, and he himself had been injured by two machine-gun bullets. When the war ended, McCoy became publicity manager for the 'Romo Follies', a travelling entertainment show provided for the troops.

After the war, it did not take long for McCoy to find a writing job. He moved to Dallas in 1919 and presented himself at the offices of the *Dallas Morning News* looking for work. Always blessed with considerable self-esteem, McCoy suggested he was an ex-*New York Tribune* writer and was given a job as a reporter, only to lose it again three days later when his deception was uncovered. He was then hired by the *Dallas Dispatch* but soon moved to the *Dallas Journal* as a news reporter. He transferred to the sports desk, where he stayed for ten years, until it was discovered that he had been inventing news stories. McCoy was also a popular and leading figure in the Dallas Little Theatre which he co-founded. He helped establish *The Dallasite*, a short-lived magazine along the lines of the *New Yorker*, for which he wrote theatre reviews, sports reports, and sketches of the Dallas social scene.

McCoy married Loline Sherer on 9 July 1921 and they had a son, Stanley, born in 1924. They divorced after seven years, and McCoy married a second time to a woman described in most sources as 'a Dallas socialite'. The marriage did not last long, and he was married for a third time in 1933 to Helen Vinmont, whose wealthy family disapproved of the match. They had two children, Amanda and Peter.

Fiction

By the mid-1920s McCoy had already shown himself to be a capable journalist, but he wanted to write stories and published his first, 'Brass Buttons' (1927), in *Holland's Magazine*. The same year he sold the first of 17 stories he would eventually write for *Black Mask* magazine, the most famous of the pulp magazines of the time. McCoy's magazine stories are often detective yarns or air-adventure fiction full of action, tough guy bravado and hard-boiled dialogue, but like Dashiell Hammett and Raymond Chandler, both of whom began their writing careers at *Black Mask*, they also display a style and flair that are recognisably his own. Unlike Hammett and Chandler, however, McCoy did not re-use his short stories in his novels.

McCoy had several successes as a leading man on the stage of the Dallas Little Theatre. At six feet tall and of athletic build, McCoy decided he wanted to become a professional actor and moved to Hollywood in 1931 to take up the offer of a screen test at MGM. But when that failed, he began to make a small living writing scenarios and story treatments as well as continuing to write for *Black Mask*. Most of his original ideas for scripts, including one for a movie about a marathon dance competition submitted in the early 1930s, came to nothing.

McCoy published his first novel *They Shoot Horses, Don't They?* in 1935 to mixed reviews. Like the rest of McCoy's novels, *They Shoot Horses, Don't They?* is an exposé of sorts, but it also introduced McCoy's bleak view of the value of human endeavour. The marathon dance craze that gripped small-town America at the time offered people 'free food and free bed for as long as you last and a thousand dollars if you win' (McCoy, 2000, p. 476). What the promoters of these freak shows declined to mention was that the bed would only be available for a few minutes at a time and that people would pay to watch the dancers humiliate and injure themselves.

McCoy's own disappointing experience of looking for work in the movies no doubt fed into the mood of the book, but its clear-sightedness is the work of McCoy the reporter, finding a shocking human story behind a popular entertainment. The novel's narrator, Robert, describes the desperation of 'contestants' willing to damage their health in order to get noticed by the 'Hollywood bunch'. His death-row narrative actually manages to make suicide seem preferable to the life he sees all around him. Perhaps it was not what people wanted to hear in the middle of the Great Depression: the novel failed to win widespread acclaim in the United States and only sold around 3,000 copies.

Success in Europe

The book's success in Europe – especially in France – was a different matter. French readers were already consuming American crime and mystery stories in large numbers. Writers such as Ernest Hemingway and William Faulkner were among the more 'literary' writers who were well known in France at the time, and McCoy's name was soon being mentioned alongside them as one of the most important contemporary American writers. The tough existentialist message of his first novel also led to comparisons with Jean-Paul Sartre, and McCoy was described as 'the American existentialist', though there is no evidence that McCoy read the work of the French philosopher. Both the sentiment and the death row narrative of Albert Camus' novel *The Stranger* (1942) seem to have originated in James M. Cain's *The Postman Always Rings Twice* (1934) rather than McCoy's novel, but the latter was certainly a popular favourite in France: in 1944 a French translation of McCoy's novel was published by the French Resistance.

By the mid-1930s McCoy was making headway in the film industry. He wrote screenplays for films such as *The Trail of the Lonesome Pine* (1936), *Persons in Hiding* (1939), *Gentleman Jim* (1942), the biopic of boxer James J. Corbett, and *The Lusty Men* (1952), a defining film in the career of actor Robert Mitchum. But despite these successes, McCoy remained a frustrated novelist and continued to write fiction: he published *No Pockets in a Shroud*, in 1938. This second novel is the story of an investigative journalist who goes up against corruption and a Ku Klux Klan-like fascist organisation called The Crusaders. There are clear resonances here of McCoy's own experiences as editor of *The Dallasite*, where he had made a name for himself in 1930 exposing scandals in the Dallas police department. Unlike Mike Dolan, the hero of his novel, McCoy did not actually establish the magazine for which he wrote, but he did use its pages to campaign against corruption and the 'lazy' journalists who allowed it to continue.

By the late 1930s McCoy's reputation as a serious novelist was growing, especially in Europe, where an advertisement for *No Pockets in a Shroud* featured portraits of McCoy and Hemingway side by side. But in the United

States he remained a marginal figure. *No Pockets* was released mainly in response to McCoy's success in Europe, and it did not sell well in the writer's home country. *I Should Have Stayed Home* (1938) is a Hollywood novel with a naïve protagonist named Ralph whose efforts to become a screen actor are thwarted by bad luck: his Southern drawl disqualifies him from working in the 'talkies'. The novel is a tale of sexual confusion and sadomasochism in which Ralph is dominated by an older, predatory woman. Mark Roydon Winchell identifies its central flaw: 'Ralph Carston is just too stupid to produce much reader empathy' (Winchell, 1982, p. 22). The novel is semi-autobiographical about McCoy's experiences in Hollywood and very bitter in its attitude towards the home of American cinema.

The relative lack of success of these novels and the pressure of his scriptwriting work kept McCoy away from writing fiction for the next decade. But he gradually became aware of the success of his novels outside the United States in the mid-1940s and was encouraged enough to return to fiction writing. *Kiss Tomorrow Goodbye* appeared in 1948 and is arguably his most accomplished work, though it never achieved the popularity of *They Shoot Horses*. Its portrayal of a psychopathic killer is a cut above the stock psycho-killer plots of the time, drawing on what Winchell calls 'deep-seated compulsions,' in particular a fear of castration.

Hollywood

Kiss Tomorrow Goodbye shares the dramatic, hard-edged prose style of McCoy's earlier novels, but is much more ambitious. *They Shoot Horses, Don't They?* is a simpler, more honest kind of novel, described by Winchell as a 'minor masterpiece', but *Kiss Tomorrow Goodbye* is McCoy's attempt at literary greatness and is undeservedly overlooked. Sturak notes the irony that, while McCoy had tried unsuccessfully to interest Hollywood in his earlier novels, the rights to this one, which he kept away from his studio contacts, were sold for 'a large sum.' *Kiss Tomorrow Goodbye* was adapted into a memorable film noir in 1950 with James Cagney starring as the lead character, the violent prison escapee Ralph Cotter.

McCoy had dreamed for some time of escaping Hollywood and moving back East to write. But money had always been a distraction to him, and the payment for *Kiss Tomorrow Goodbye* plus the considerable amount of money he earned for his 'potboiler' *Scalpel* (1952) was soon spent on clothes, foreign travel, and a Lincoln Continental. *Scalpel*, which he wrote with money and escape from Hollywood in mind, is a competent but uninspired story about a successful doctor and former miner who undergoes a journey of self-realisation and ends up a professor at Harvard.

By the time of its publication, McCoy was already overweight and suffering from heart trouble. He had a minor heart attack in 1948, but late in 1953 he suffered another, this time more serious. He did not write again until 1955.

That year he submitted the first 46 pages of a new novel, *The Hard-Rock Man*, to his agent and was also working on a movie treatment of early short stories. *The Hard-Rock Man* was completed after his death as *Corruption City* in 1959 and is credited as McCoy's, but his contribution was not significant. McCoy died suddenly at home on 15 December 1955, from a third heart attack. Despite the success of *Scalpel*, he died in semi-obscurity and with very little money. His widow had to sell his books to pay for the funeral. An obituary appeared in the *New York Times* on 17 December 1955.

Although McCoy has six novels credited to him, 30 screenplays, many short stories, movie treatments and investigative journalism, his reputation in Europe always exceeded his appreciation in the United States. It was 14 years after his death that his best-known work, *They Shoot Horses, Don't They?* became a film, directed by Sydney Pollack and starring Jane Fonda in the role of Gloria. *No Pockets in a Shroud* was adapted into a French film in 1974 directed by Jean-Pierre Mocky.

Suggested reading

J.T. Sturak (1966) *The Life and Writings of Horace McCoy*, 1897–1955, PhD (University of California, Los Angeles).
M.R. Winchell (1982) *Horace McCoy* (Boise, Idaho: Boise State University).

Christopher Routledge

McGivern, William P(eter) (1922–82)

An experienced genre writer who found a distinct style with his exploration of moral themes, McGivern covered the full breadth and diversity of crime fiction including homicide investigations, espionage, political corruption as well as key genre characters such as private detectives, crooked policemen and psychopaths in over 20 novels.

Life and career

William Peter McGivern was born in Chicago on 6 December 1922, and grew up in Mobile, Alabama. He began writing short fiction in the 1940s which appeared in publications such as *Amazing Stories* and *Short Stories*. His writing career was interrupted by the Second World War during which McGivern served as a Line Sergeant in the US Army. He received the Soldiers' Medal for jumping on a bombed tanker and rescuing its crew by opening the valves to release the gas inside. His experiences formed the basis of his later novel *Soldiers of '44* (1979). After the war, but before his return to the US, McGivern studied at the University of Birmingham in the UK. In 1948 he married fellow writer Maureen Daly, and they would have two children. McGivern worked as a police reporter for the *Philadelphia Bulletin* from 1946–48 and as a reviewer for *Evening Bulletin* from 1949–51 by which time his first novels were being published.

Novels and writing range

With his debut novel *But Death Runs Faster* (1948), McGivern takes a self-reverential look at the crime pulps, as the story concerns the murder of the associate editor of a pulp detective magazine. The narrator is the editor and one of the suspects in the mystery. McGivern followed this with several hard-boiled style novels *Heaven Ran Last* (1949), *Very Cold for May* (1950), *Shield for Murder* (1951) and *Blondes Die Young* (1952); the latter of which was written under the pseudonym Bill Peters and featured ruthless private detective Bill Canalli who prays to God that he will get to punish the criminals before the police find them. McGivern's best novels of the 1950s dealt with the theme of police corruption. In *The Big Heat* (1953), the tough but honest detective Dave Bannion is driven to vigilantism when an act of retaliation by the criminals he is investigating leads to personal tragedy. The story was originally serialised in the *Saturday Evening Post* and was turned into a gritty film noir directed by Fritz Lang with one notorious scene wherein a gangster, played by Lee Marvin, throws boiling hot coffee in his girlfriend's face. McGivern's next great police novel was *Rogue Cop* (1954). It is a story with biblical parallels as the leading characters are two policeman brothers, one is honest and the other is on the take. McGivern explores the familiar themes of morality, here with a religious underpinning, as Katherine Restiano writes of the corrupt cop, 'a man who has given up on the principle of two fathers – one his own, now deceased father, a former policeman; the other, God the Father' (Reilly, 1985, p. 632).

The tense clash between cultural values reappears in *Odds Against Tomorrow* (1957) in which a Caucasian man and a black man involved in a bank robbery together engage in a battle of survival complicated by bigotry and prejudice. The novel was made into another memorable film noir starring Harry Belafonte and Robert Ryan. In the 1960s and 1970s McGivern's novels became less frequent as he wrote increasingly for film and television, including scripts for the detective series *Banyon* and *Kojak*. With the later novels he continued to prove his versatility as a writer: *Caprifoil* (1972) is an espionage thriller, and *Night of the Juggler* (1975) a psychological chase thriller. McGivern spent many years travelling through Europe and Africa with his family, which inspired the memoir, *Mention my Name in Mombasa: the unscheduled adventures of an American family abroad* (1958), co-written with his wife. William P. McGivern died on 18 November 1982. His final novel, *A Matter of Honor*, was completed by Maureen Daly and released in 1984.

Suggested reading

P. Liukkonen (2008) 'William P(eter) McGivern (1922–1982)' *Books and Writers* http://kirjasto.sci.fi/mcgivern.htm, date accessed 15 July 2011

W.P. McGivern and M. Daly (1958) Mention my name in Mombasa: the unscheduled adventures of an American family abroad (New York, Dodd, Mead).

J. Reilly ed. (1985) *Twentieth-Century Crime and Mystery Writers* (New York: St Martin's Press).

Steven Powell

Millar, Margaret (1915–94)

Canadian-American Margaret Millar was one of the most important crime writers of the 1950s and 1960s, whose works stands as amongst the best and most original novels of the noir genre. Despite the consistently high quality of her writing, Millar never achieved the same level of commercial success as some of her contemporaries, and her books are largely out of print today.

Margaret Ellis Millar (nee Sturm) was born on 5 February 1915 in Kitchener, Ontario, Canada. She was educated at the Kitchener-Waterloo Collegiate Institute from 1929–33 and studied in the University of Toronto from 1933 to 1936 majoring in Classics and contributing stories to the university's literary magazine. She married Kenneth Millar, who was later to become the crime novelist and creator of the acclaimed Lew Archer series under the pseudonym Ross Macdonald, in 1938. Margaret Millar published her first novel a few years before Kenneth Millar, and to avoid confusion and competition her husband decided to use a pseudonym in his books. Throughout her career Margaret Millar remained somewhat in the shadow of her husband's success, but she was a revered crime writer in her own right.

Early career

Millar's first two novels, *The Invisible Worm* (1941) and *The Weak-Eyed Bat* (1942), differ somewhat from her later works, as they are more in the vein of the Golden Age mysteries than Millar's later psychological crime novels. The two books also feature a series protagonist, although Millar would never write a long-running series. The lead character is the rather whimsical psychiatrist detective Paul Prye. Prye assists the Toronto detective Inspector Sands, who by contrast is dour and lonely. Sands appears as the lead character in two of Millar's later novels, *Wall of Eyes* (1943) and *The Iron Gates* (1945). The latter of which was Millar's first real success with a narrative that merged several bizarre and grisly plot points into a psychological puzzle which maintains the suspense right until the very end.

Many of Millar's early novels are set in her country of birth, Canada. *Fire Will Freeze* (1944) is set in the snowy background of a ski resort. The driver of the bus taking people to the resort disappears during a snowstorm, and the passengers take shelter in a large house where tensions reach breaking point when strange things start to happen. Millar also displayed a flair for political commentary as the novel features a character modelled after Canadian fascist leader, Adrien Arcand. Millar returned to the Canadian landscape in *An Air That Kills* (1957), where the country terrain provides the backdrop for a tale of a disintegrating marriage complicated by an unexpected death.

Do Evil In Return (1950) is perhaps the best crime novel of Millar's early career. In it, Millar handles the controversial and delicate theme of abortion. Doctor Charlotte Keating receives a patient, who asks the doctor to perform a then-illegal abortion. Keating refuses, but starts digging into the matter when the girl is found drowned, and Keating is left in a dangerous position with blackmailers and the police. Alongside these crime novels Millar also wrote three mainstream novels, *Experiment in Springtime* (1947), *The Cannibal Heart* (1949), *Wives and Lovers* (1954), and one children's book, *It's All In the Family* (1948).

Millar's greatest novels

Throughout her career Millar usually wrote about distorted minds: people who have lost the perspective of everyday life and its restrictions. Millar's characters are loners, hermits, bored and alienated housewives or young women, who have lost their interest in the world. In this respect, she is one of the greatest female noir writers of the late 40s, 50s and 60s for her compelling psychological portraits. Millar is also rooted in the second generation of hard-boiled crime writers of which her husband was master during the same period, and she could merge crime fiction with the literary aspects of her work with relative ease. British crime writer and critic H. R. F. Keating wrote of Millar: '[Millar's] are books that tingle with uneasy suspense, dart with quiet wit and produce gaspingly surprise endings which at the same time carry with them a doomed inevitability' (Keating, 1994).

Millar differed from her contemporary Patricia Highsmith, in that Millar does not share Highsmith's misanthropy and pessimistic world-view. Millar is always on the side of the weak, and when tragedy occurs in her work it is with a degree of pathos. Even her sociopathic manipulators are victims. In this Millar shares the same traits as her husband, Ross Macdonald.

As Millar did not write long series, there is no defining fictional character in her literary career, although she did create several memorable private detectives. In *A Stranger In My Grave* (1960) the Mexican-American Steve Piñata is asked to investigate a most unusual and unsettling case: a young woman called Daisy Harker keeps seeing dreams of her own tombstone and finally she sees one in clear daylight. The solution lies in the past, with webs of intrigue going back through generations of family secrets. *A Stranger In My Grave* is one of Millar's novels most rooted in noir depicting double identities, strange dreams and hallucinations. Millar steps into the dark psychological realm of a Cornell Woolrich novel, but with clarity and steadiness. Millar's work often explores feminist themes, and in her mature career her lead characters are almost always women. The men stand somewhere outside the women's life. The husband of Daisy Harker is not interested in his wife's troubles, pushing them away by saying they are only dreams. Millar also handles the theme of a struggle between mother and daughter candidly but delicately.

The Listening Walls (1959) begins with two young American women travelling in Mexico. Suddenly, one of the women jumps from the hotel window, killing herself. The brother of the deceased woman hires a private eye to look into the case. The private eye in question, Elmer Dodd, is somewhat reminiscent of Lew Archer. He has previously worked a lot of different jobs, from carpenter to Bible salesman, and started out as a private eye only in his 40s.

One of Millar's most acclaimed novels is *How Like an Angel* (1962). The lead character is Las Vegas gambler, freelance security man and private detective, Joe Quinn. He is down on his luck when he meets a member of a reclusive religious community called The True Believers. Sister Blessing persuades Quinn to search for a man named Patrick O'Gorman. The missing persons case has been a plot device of hundreds, if not thousands, of prior detective novels but Millar's puts a unique spin on proceedings. During Quinn's investigation he becomes involved with O'Gorman's widow Martha. The final twist is one of the most shocking in the history of crime literature, and it comes just in the novels last lines, maximising their effect. *How Like an Angel* shows what a crime novel can do at its best, balancing an entertaining and thrilling narrative with social and psychological insight. Millar seems to foresee the rise of underground culture and the alternative lifestyle communities of the 60s. Her depiction of these communities, and their need to withdraw from society, is sympathetic and believable. The True Believers are outsiders in the commercial society, just as Joe Quinn is an outsider of a different kind: the cynical detective with a bleak existentialist outlook. The novel contains memorable hard-boiled dialogue: when one character accuses Joe Quinn of being a suspicious type, he replies: 'By nature, training, experience and observation, yes' (Millar, 1962, p. 48).

Beast in View (1955) is another of Millar's finest works. The novel shares the same themes of double identities with *A Stranger in My Grave*, but is more of a thriller than the later novel. Miss Clarvoe is a recluse living in a hotel. She receives a threatening phone call from a female stranger. Clarvoe asks the man taking care of her savings, Paul Blackshear, to look into the matter. The surprising twist ending has been much imitated since and helps to make the complicated series of events seem very plausible. The book is marred only by the dated depiction of homosexuals as weak and wicked by nature. *Beast in View* deservedly won the Edgar Award for best novel in 1956. It was filmed twice for television, first in 1964 for the *Alfred Hitchcock Hour* and then in 1986 for *Alfred Hitchcock Presents*.

One of Millar's central themes is also the idea of the child locked within an adult's body. Thus the abortion plot in *Do Evil In Return* has added poignancy. The child inside a grown woman's body appears also in *Beast in View*, in which Miss Clarvoe remembers and still suffers from her parents' cruel comments on her reclusiveness and loneliness. The constant verbal abuse leads to serious mental trouble in later years.

The psychology of the characters is the foreground of Millar's novels. They are clearly Freudian, as befits a writer who rose to eminence in the 50s, the era of Freudian pop psychology and psychoanalysis. In this respect, Millar's occasional use of Mexico as a setting carries weighty symbolism. Although as she lived in Southern California and set her novels there, Mexico may have just proved useful as an occasional setting as it did for many Los Angeles based crime writers, but its frequent, ominous appearance in her works adds substance to the psychological issues. *The Listening Walls* starts with a death in a Mexico hotel, Steve Piñata in *A Stranger in My Grave* is half-Mexican, Tom Aragon tries to find a missing person in Tijuana in *Ask For Me Tomorrow* (1976), as he does in *The Murder of Miranda* (1979). *Beast in View* takes place partly in Mexico, with the rest of the novel set in the suburbs and downtown of Los Angeles. One of Miss Clarvoe's lies involves Mexico. Thus, Mexico is often a false refuge for Millar's characters, the place where Americans try go get away from their troubles, but end up only finding sexual love and death competing with each other.

Millar's last novels

In her later career Millar produced several novels which did not rise to the level of her classic works. A good example is *Ask For Me Tomorrow* (1976), which is also one of her most traditional crime novels. The hero of the book is a young lawyer named Tom Aragon, who is called to help in the search for a missing husband. The writing richly evokes the US and Mexican settings, especially the poor wasteland of Baja California. Millar draws memorable portraits of people living in destitution and their struggle to survive. Millar was particularly skilled at depicting Americans trying to find the American Dream, to rise from rags to riches, and the abandonment of values in doing so. The Edgar nominated *Beyond This Point Are Monsters* (1970) includes a vivid portrayal of Chicano culture in the San Diego area in a tale of the aftermath of a disappearance which points to a probable murder.

Ask For Me Tomorrow was followed by *The Murder of Miranda*, which also stars Tom Aragon. The last of the three Tom Aragon novels, *Mermaid* (1982), is about Aragon searching for a runaway girl from a wealthy West Coast family.

Millar's last novel was *Spider Webs* (1986), a courtroom drama of a murder trial. Millar wrote only a handful of short stories, and they were all collected in the book, *The Couple Next Door*, posthumously published in 2004 and edited by Tom Nolan. Inspector Sands plays the lead in the titular story, which was first published in the *Ellery Queen's Mystery Magazine* in 1954. Millar published her memoir *The Birds and the Beasts Were There* in 1968. Millar resided in Santa Barbara, California for much of her life, where she and her husband were active in the conservation movement. Millar's daughter Linda died of a brain haemorrhage in 1970, and the author did not publish another novel for six years. In the last years of his life Ross Macdonald's health was failing, and he was eventually diagnosed with Alzheimer's disease. Millar died on 26 March 1994, over ten years after the death of her husband in 1983.

Suggested reading

W. Grimes (1994) 'Margaret Millar Is Dead at 79; Wrote Psychological Mysteries' *New York Times*, 29 March 1994, p. D22.

T. Nolan (2004) 'Introduction' *The Couple Next Door* by M. Millar (Norfolk, VA: Crippen & Landru).

T. Nolan (2001) 'Ross Macdonald and Margaret Millar: Partners in Crime' *Mystery Reader's Journal, Partners in Crime II*, 17.3 http://www.mysteryreaders.org/Issues /Partners2.html

Themed issue Margaret Millar, *Clues: A Journal of Detection* 25.3 (Spring 2007).

Juri Nummelin

Mosley, Walter (1952–)

A prolific and diverse writer, Walter Ellis Mosley has produced over 30 novels, including four crime fiction series featuring, respectively, Ezekiel (Easy) Rawlins, Socrates Fortlow, Fearless Jones and Leonid McGill. In addition he has written science fiction novels, politically inspired non-fiction, a young-adult novel, a graphic novel, two works which he has categorised as 'erotica' and a number of other works of fiction. His first play *The Fall of Heaven* was premiered in Cincinnati in January 2010. Mosley began writing seriously at the age of 34, after apparently struggling to decide which career to pursue, and claims to have written every day since then. He is best known for the Easy Rawlins series which begins with *Devil in a Blue Dress* (1990) followed by *A Red Death* (1992), *White Butterfly* (1992), *Black Betty* (1994), *A Little Yellow Dog* (1996), *Bad Boy Brawly Brown* (2002), *Little Scarlet* (2004), *Cinnamon Kiss* (2005) and *Blonde Faith* (2008). The series also includes a prequel, *Gone Fishin'* (1997), and a collection of short stories *Six Easy* Pieces (2003).

In locating his Easy Rawlins' series in Los Angeles in the immediate post-war years, Mosley was revisiting the time and place of his formative years. He was born in Watts, Los Angeles, in 1952 to Ella Mosley (nee Slatkin), a white woman of Polish Jewish extraction, and Leroy Mosley, an African-American originally from Louisiana. As well as family histories containing racial atrocities, his parents had direct experience of racial oppression and prejudice. Although mixed marriages were legal in California, no-one would provide them with a licence, and they were unable to marry until after Mosley's birth. His father had worked in a clerical capacity during World War II in the segregated American military and had, therefore, experienced both the demeaning treatment accorded to African-Americans in restricting them to menial clerical tasks and the contempt for their supposed cowardice which resulted from their exclusion from front-line fighting. Mosley ascribed his father's experiences to Rawlins and documented his bitterness at the treatment of African-American soldiers who had struggled to be allowed to fight in the front line but who, even when they conducted themselves heroically, were then still the victims of racial discrimination in the post-war world.

Mosley's parents made financial sacrifices in order to send their only child to a private African-American day school (Victory Baptist) and were able to relocate to a more affluent western suburb of Los Angeles in the early 1960s. Mosley described his background as non-political but also as being deeply shaped by the racial conflicts around him, particularly the Watts riots of the 1960s. Although he appeared to avoid political controversy in the early years of his career, in recent times he has become more outspoken about racial and political issues. In 1997, as a bestselling writer, he rejected a sizeable advance from a large publisher in order to place his Rawlins' prequel *Gone Fishin'* with the minor independent publisher Black Classic Press which was run by a former member of the Black Panthers. His home background stimulated and encouraged him in reading and storytelling, and he has described his father as a 'black Socrates' whose storytelling with his LA-based Southern friends were the source of many of the incidents he incorporated into his narratives of Easy Rawlins and Socrates Fortlow.

Encouraged by his parents to be ambitious as well as imaginative, he first studied liberal arts and then computer science before taking time out from his work with an oil company to study creative writing. One of his tutors was Edna O'Brien who not only praised his work but encouraged him to appreciate, for the first time, that his rich racial heritage and background could be a significant resource for fiction. Mosley has repeatedly stressed the importance of his parents, and their experiences and heritage, in his writing. In 1987 he married Joy Kellman, a choreographer and dancer, from whom he separated in 1997: they divorced in 2001.

Literary success: the Easy Rawlins novels

In 1992 the Democratic presidential candidate, Bill Clinton, during an interview about his personal reading and influences, described Mosley as one of his favourite writers. Clinton's comment was immensely significant for Mosley, immediately gaining him recognition with the American public and, crucially, enabling him to obtain a breakthrough into an extensive white readership and thus into the bestselling category. At that stage Mosley had published only two of the Easy Rawlins' books, and Clinton's praise, as well as having a major impact on the sales of those works, created a demand for further works in the series. The resulting fame did bring Mosley some criticism from black scholars who felt that Clinton's endorsement confirmed the view that the character of Rawlins was potentially too passive and non-threatening to white society, a criticism sharpened by Mosley's own apparent unwillingness at this stage of his career to be outspoken on racial issues.

Mosley has commented, 'I kind of took on the job of doing the type of hard-boiled fiction that originated with Dashiell Hammett, Raymond

Chandler, and Ross Macdonald', and Easy Rawlins's first appearance makes clear both Mosley's awareness of Chandler's legacy and his determination to challenge it (Mudge, 2001). Rawlins, as a private detective working in post-war Los Angeles, enters a literary landscape rendered iconic by Chandler's Philip Marlowe novels. The opening scene of *Devil in a Blue Dress* explicitly revisits the opening of Chandler's *Farewell, My Lovely* (1940) when Marlowe follows Moose Molloy, searching for his fiancée Velma, into what he clearly views as the alien environment of an exclusively black bar. Mosley reverses the viewpoint as Rawlins, sitting with the black clientele, watches a white man enter the bar to seek help in tracing a mysterious woman whose fiancée is searching for her. For Rawlins, and the other drinkers, it is the white visitor who appears alien and, as the series progresses, Mosley reveals his project to reclaim and celebrate the hidden history of a community whose strength and diversity is absent from Chandler's narratives. Rawlins moves through a post-war landscape within which he is an integral element of that community, with friends, enemies and acquaintances featuring in almost every narrative.

Characters who are significant throughout the series are Rawlins' psycho-pathic sidekick and alter-ego Raymond (Mouse) Alexander; the brilliant but unreliable Jackson Blue, and the women with whom Rawlins forms relationships, in particular his wife, Regina, and his lovers Etta-Mae Harris and Bonnie Shay. These, and others, are part of a web of contacts within the black community and, at different points, they support, threaten, sustain and betray him, but it is always clear that Rawlins cannot function in isolation; he needs his contacts in order to carry out his role. As the series unfolds Rawlins observes the impact of major events, such as the assassination of President Kennedy and the race riots in the Los Angeles suburb of Watts, from the perspective of his immediate neighbours: members of a community dominated by the experience of racial discrimination and marked by frequent violence. The titles of the Rawlins' novels make clear the centrality of the issue of colour and also the importance of women. Rawlins has a number of sexual relationships or encounters, many of them explicitly described. A further very unusual feature of Rawlins, as a hard-boiled detective, is his role as a father with prime responsibility for the care of two children, one of whom is only a baby when he finds her. The children, Jesus and Feather, are both of mixed race and unrelated to Rawlins or to each other. Despite the fact that Rawlins never officially adopts either of them, they are the most constant and significant relationships in his life.

Treading a fine line between the law and criminal society, Rawlins's ambitions are to achieve a life which accords with many of the most traditional ideals of American society, seeking a stable home and family life, financial security and respectability. He is a reluctant detective, forced by a combination of his own precarious position in society and his desire for respectability to undertake his assignments. His first venture into detection arises because, having been dismissed from his post for refusing to accept a racial insult, he needs money to pay his mortgage. Although the outcome of his investigation should make him financially secure, it actually leaves him vulnerable to further pressure, which leads to his subsequent adventures. Despite his best intentions, Rawlins is repeatedly thwarted in his search for economic and educational advancement, and he becomes increasingly disillusioned, embittered and dangerous as the series progresses.

Mosley's other crime stories

The central theme of the Rawlins' series is racial oppression, with the private detective struggling to assert an active and moral black masculinity denied by authority. The same ideas are explored in the Socrates Fortlow series, *Always Outnumbered, Always Outgunned* (1997), *Walkin' the Dog* (1999) and *The Right Mistake* (2008); the Fearless Jones mysteries, *Fearless Jones* (2001), *Fear Itself* (2003) and *Fear of the Dark* (2006), and the two novels featuring Leonid McGill *The Long Fall* (2009) and *Known to Evil* (2010). Mosley's work repeatedly engages with ideas of 'passing' and the complexities of a racially diverse heritage and society and the trajectory of his crime fiction appears to be towards an increasingly pessimistic vision of the prospects for racial progress and harmony.

Socrates Fortlow is, like Rawlins, a resident of the Los Angeles suburb of Watts where he has settled after his release from prison. Fortlow has served 27 years for murder and, despite being hardened and embittered by his prison experiences, he is determined to try to live a moral life in a world which seems to repeatedly conspire to draw him back into violence. As signalled by his name, he is not content to just exist, although his circumstances make even existence a struggle, as he is forced to make his home in a derelict space between buildings. Fortlow wants to confront major philosophical questions, in particular with regard to the nature and implications of violence. Whereas the early works in the Rawlins' series foreground a man who believes that he can make progress despite racial discrimination, if he only works hard and obeys the rules of society, Fortlow knows from the outset that he has little or no realistic prospect of improving his life in material terms, and his struggle is to understand his position in the world and how an individual can, within the world in which he finds himself, live a moral life.

The Fearless Jones series of novels also feature a protagonist, Paris Minton, who wants to make a quiet success of his life but who is somehow thrust into violence. Minton runs a shabby second-hand book shop selling library cast-offs which manages to only just provide him with an adequate income. Like Mosley's other protagonists, he somehow becomes entangled with a beautiful and mysterious woman with the result that his shop is destroyed and he finds himself with only one possible avenue – to pay the bail money for his friend Fearless Jones so that they can try to find out who is responsible. The two protagonists, the peaceable book-loving Minton and the almost mythically dangerous Jones echo the roles of Rawlins and Mouse. Like Fortlow and Rawlins, Minton has to try to negotiate the racially divided city of Los Angeles whilst facing danger and violence, but Mosley places his most recent private detective, Leonid McGill, in Manhattan, and also introduces some other interesting developments in his character. McGill, unlike Mosley's other protagonists, appears at times to have 'made it' in terms of financial security, but the complexity of his life and the 'bad things' he has done make it clear from the outset that any peaceful solutions are unlikely. The McGill stories are possibly Mosley's most complex in terms of the number of characters and the intricacies of plot, and they also contain a number of humorous incidents – albeit of a rather dark nature.

Two of Mosley's works, *Devil in a Blue Dress* and *Always Outnumbered, Always Outgunned*, have been filmed. *Devil in a Blue Dress*, directed by Carl Franklin in 1995, starred Denzel Washington as Easy Rawlins, Jennifer Beals as Daphne Monet and Don Cheadle as Mouse Alexander. The film was well received critically and was nominated for a number of awards, with Cheadle's performance particularly praised. Despite the presence of a major star, however, the production faced the substantial difficulty of making a film entirely based in the black community, but featuring a handful of white characters, a commercial success. *Always Outnumbered Always Outgunned*, directed for television by Michael Apted and starring Laurence Fishburne and Daniel Williams, also faced this problem and was less successful.

Mosley has become an incredibly successful bestselling author with the great majority of his sales, despite his other writings, continuing to come from his crime fiction work. In recent years he has taken a more openly political stance, particularly in relation to America's involvement in the war in Iraq, and has also taken a more active role in causes related to racial advancement, making clear that he believes many of the challenges presented in his fictional narratives continue to face black men in America.

Suggested reading

Berger, Roger (1997) '"The black dick": Race, Sexuality, and Discourse in the L.A. Novels of Walter Mosley' *African-American Review* 31 (2) 281–91.

O.E. Brady (2011) *Conversations with Walter Mosley* (Jackson: University of Mississippi).

O.E. Brady and D.C. Maus eds. (2008) *Finding a Way Home: a Critical Assessment of Walter Mosley's Fiction* (Jackson: University of Mississippi).

Mason, Jr. Theodore O. (1992) 'Walter Mosley's Easy Rawlins: The Detective and Afro-American Fiction' *The Kenyon Review*, Fall 1992, 14 (4) 173–83.

Maureen Sunderland

Muller, Marcia (1944–)

One of the first authors to create a contemporary female private detective series character, Marcia Muller liberated female shamuses from their limited, male-dependent roles and made them fully fledged PIs through her character Sharon McCone. Muller has clarified that she is not the first woman author to write a female PI – P.D. James' Cordelia Grey predates McCone – but she did help redefine the image of the female PI, paving the way for her peers Sara Paretsky and Sue Grafton to create other female detectives. Muller also experimented with the race of the PI: Sharon McCone is one-eighth Native American (Shoshone) and art curator and amateur sleuth Elena Oliverez is Latino. A prolific writer who has published up to three novels a year, Muller has authored over 30 novels, three of which were co-written with her second husband and fellow crime writer Bill Pronzini, seven short story collections (two with Pronzini), as well as edited 12 anthologies with Pronzini, one of which, *Lady on the Case* (1988), was also co-edited with Martin H. Greenberg. She has also stepped outside crime fiction to write a collection of western short stories, *Time of the Wolves* (2003). She has been awarded the Private Eye Writers of America Lifetime Achievement Award, The Eye, in 1993 and the Anthony Award for *Wolf in the Shadows* (1993). Named Grand Master by the Mystery Writers of America in 2005, she received the Shamus Hardcover Novel Award for *Locked In* (2009) and the Shamus Short Story Award for 'Final Resting Place' (1991).

Life and career

Born in Detroit, Michigan, on 28 September 1944, Muller graduated from the University of Michigan with a BA in English (1966) and an MA in journalism (1971). Her creative writing professor told her to switch to journalism because she had nothing to say, but Muller found that as a journalist she had a tendency to embellish her source material: 'I was always putting quotes into people's mouths' (Muller, 1998). Muller was married to naval officer Frederick T. Gilson from 1967 to 1981. Muller married Bill Pronzini in 1992. Between 1967 and 1969 she worked as a merchandising supervisor for *Sunset Magazine*; her colleagues at *Sunset* would inspire Muller's physical description of PI Sharon McCone. Muller worked as an interviewer for University of Michigan Institute of Social Research (1971–73), a position that enlarged her understanding of the San Francisco Bay Area and would aid her in researching her novels. Muller held a variety of jobs including proposal writer, freight forwarder and secretary before opening Invisible Ink in 1979, an editorial services firm, with then unpublished crime author Julie Smith. Muller became a full-time writer in 1983.

Sharon McCone series and other works

With *Edwin of the Iron Shoes* (1977) Muller launched 30-year-old PI Sharon McCone, whose name was an amalgam of Muller's college roommate and a former director of the CIA John McCone. The novel would establish McCone as a level-headed investigator and a modern woman who is not immune to the charms of men. Licensed by the State of California and operating in San Francisco, McCone is a staff investigator for All Souls Legal Co-operative firm. The plotting is relatively plausible with a murder in an antique shop being the catalyst of investigation in *Edwin of the Iron Shoes*. For over 30 years, McCone has been the subject of 28 novels and two short-story collections. In the later novels, McCone sets up her own detective agency and there is a greater narrative emphasis on her personal life, with an ever-expanding series of supporting characters.

The McCone series is regarded as an optimistic depiction of the social outcomes of feminism, as it propagates the idea that gender could be removed as an issue in the workplace. Aside from this feminist ideal, Muller also has her characters express socially or politically liberal views: McCone employs an openly homosexual man in her agency; she expresses disgust over the lack of government funding for the homeless; and the Bush administration's perceived abuse of power is criticised in *Coming Back* (2010). Muller's later novels also place a male character in the typically female role of office assistant. As McCone is a techno-phobe, her computer-literate nephew steps in to do research for her.

Of her recent work, *Locked In* (2009) pushed new boundaries by disabling McCone. Shot by an armed intruder, McCone has locked-in syndrome, the inability to communicate, but she has not lost the ability to reason or the motivation to find her shooter. Thus, the story moves on with her colleagues doing the legwork and leaving McCone to ruminate over the details and crack the case.

Aside from the McCone novels, Muller has also created the series characters Elena Oliverez, art security expert Joanna Stark, and a series of novels loosely connected by their setting, the fictitious Soledad County, California. Novels in the Soledad County series include *Cyanide Wells* (2003), in which a man is accused of his wife's murder only to find out she is alive 14 years later, and *Point Deception* (2001), wherein feelings of guilt associated with a mass murder case early in a female deputy sheriff's career return when a series of new murders occur. Of the short series involving art curator Elena Oliverez, *Beyond the Grave* (1986), co-authored with Bill Pronzini, is the best and most ambitious. The text alternates between Muller's and Pronzini's protagonists (John Quincannon) and between their respective time periods (Oliverez in the 1980s with Quincannon in 1894). Finding a note Quincannon left in an old chest, Oliverez hopes to discover the treasure Quincannon was unable to unearth. Pronzini's and Muller's other collaborations include the crossover novel *Double* (1984), in which Muller pairs McCone with Pronzini's Nameless Detective, and *The Lighthouse* (1987) a non-series novel. Muller's series character Joanna Stark, a security consultant to museums and art galleries, was introduced in *The Cavalier in White* (1986) and like Oliverez was the subject of three novels in the 1980s. Stark's story is dominated by her clashes with Parducci, an art thief who is also the father of her child.

Suggested reading

A.N. Howe and C.A. Jackson (2008) *Marcia Muller and the Female Private Eye: Essays on the Novels That Defined a Subgenre* (Jefferson, NC ; London: McFarland).
B.C. Plummer (1994) 'Marcia Muller' *Great Women Mystery Writers: classic to contemporary*, K. Gregory Klein ed. (Westport, Conn: Greenwood Press). pp. 244–8.
J. Reilly ed. (1985) *Twentieth-Century Crime and Mystery Writers* (New York: St Martin's Press).

Diana Powell

Nebel, Frederick (1903–67)

Born in Staten Island, New York, 'Louis' Frederick Nebel left school at 15 and began working as a dockhand and valet before moving to Canada to work on his great-uncle's homestead. Nebel's experience with the wilderness informed his frequent contributions to the western pulps *North West Stories* and *Lariat*, but in 1926 he published his first *Black Mask* story 'The Breaks of the Game' and soon became, along with his good friend Dashiell Hammett, one of the established contributors to that pulp magazine. After marrying Dorothy Blank in 1930, Nebel moved to St Louis, the location of much of his fiction, and in 1934 to Connecticut, where he began writing for the slicks. In 1937 his son Christopher Nebel was born. Suffering from high blood pressure in the late 1950s, Nebel moved to Laguna Beach, California, where his health continued to decline. Nebel died from a cerebral haemorrhage in 1967.

Nebel also wrote under the pseudonyms Grimes Hill, Lewis Nebel and Eric Lewis. He published his first novel, *Sleeper's East*, in 1933, and it later became the basis of the film *Sleeper's West* (1941). He wrote only two other novels, *But Not the End* (1934) and *Fifty Roads to Town* (1936). Nebel was one of the early practitioners of hard-boiled detective stories who could combine humour with gritty and realistic character portrayals without descending into parody. However, this quality would not always survive in the transition to the big screen. The hard-boiled novel *Fifty Roads to Town* was adapted into a comedy film of the same name starring Don Ameche in 1937. Nebel sold the rights to his popular MacBride and Kennedy stories, which featured the policeman Captain Steve MacBride and the alcoholic reporter Kennedy and disassociated himself from the subsequent cinema adaptations, which spiralled into a series of nine films. In these films, Kennedy is remodelled as the wisecracking newswoman 'Torchy' Blaine, who harboured romantic intentions for MacBride and pursued him throughout all nine films. The first five MacBride and Kennedy stories appeared in the anthology *The Black Lizard Big Book of Pulps* (2007). Another notable series character was Dick Donahue of the Inter-State Detective Agency, modelled on Hammett's Sam

Spade. Six stories featuring Donahue appear in the collection *Six Deadly Dames* (1950). In the 1930s Nebel began contributing to *Dime Detective* with his series character Jack Cardigan, the hard-boiled Irish detective of the Cosmos Detective Agency. Six of these stories are collected in *The Adventures of Cardigan* (1988). Nebel stopped writing hard-boiled and mystery fiction for the pulps in favour of romantic stories for the slicks in 1937, but in 1956 made a brief return to mystery writing by publishing six short stories in *Ellery Queen's Mystery Magazine*.

Suggested reading

K. Harper (2000) 'Frederick Nebel (1903–1967)' *Dictionary of Literary Biography: American Hard-Boiled Crime Writers*, G. P. Anderson and J.B. Anderson eds. vol 226 (Detroit: The Gale Group) 283–88.

H. Lessing and K. B. Smith (n.d.) 'Frederick Nebel' *The Thrilling Detective* http://www.thrillingdetective.com/trivia/nebel.html., date accessed 8 September 2011.

W.F. Nolan (1985) 'Behind the Mask: Frederick Nebel' *The Black Mask Boys*. (New York: Mysterious Press).pp. 152–57.

Chris Pak

Neely, Barbara (1941–)

African-American novelist and creator of the Blanche White series, whose debut novel, *Blanche on the Lam*, won the Agatha, the Anthony and the Macavity awards as well as the Go On Girl! Book Club award for a debut novel.

Life and career

BarbaraNeely (the author does not separate her forename and surname) was born in Lebanon, Pennsylvania, in 1941. Lebanon was then a small, predominately Dutch community. Neely attended a Catholic Elementary School and was both the only child in her class to speak English fluently and the only African-American student. In 1971, Neely began studying for a master's degree in urban and regional planning at the University of Pittsburgh. Neely has had a long and distinguished career in community activism and the public sector. One of her first activist roles was organising a community-based home for ex-convict women in the Shady Side suburb of Pittsburgh. This program was met with fierce opposition by local residents, but Neely persevered and it was deemed a success. Neely has also acted as a branch director of the Young Women's Christian Association, worked for the Institute of Social Research and was Executive Director of Women for Economic Justice. Neely is the former host of the award-winning Massachusetts public affairs radio program *Commonwealth Journal*. Neely was also a radio producer for Africa News Service. For her life-long commitment to activism, Neely has received the Community Works Social Action Award for Leadership and Activism for Women's Rights and Economic Justice and the Fighting for Women's Voices Award from the Coalition for Basic Human Needs.

Beginning of literary career

Neely began her literary career by writing short stories. Her first published short story 'Passing the Word' appeared in *Essence* in 1981. Neely then moved to North Carolina, to what would become the setting of the first Blanche novels. Her short stories continued to appear in such publications as *Things That Divide Us, Speaking for Ourselves, Constellations* and *Literature: Reading and Writing the Human Experience.* Neely's debut novel would not appear until 1992, but she credits her inspiration to write and develop her writing from short stories into novels from an incident in 1978 where she saw an elderly woman dance in front of a band. The woman pointed at members of the audience as she danced and when she pointed at Neely the future novelist felt called to begin a writing career lest the opportunity passed. Neely was working on a manuscript she dreamed would become 'the great African American novel' when she started to develop the character of Blanche, who would fit in a comical and engaging narrative about race and class. During this time, she was contacted by an editor and agent who wanted her to work on a longer project than short stories. Neely mentioned the two ideas she was working on, and both responded that she should develop the Blanche character. Although the tone of the Blanche novels would often veer towards comedy, Neely would not shy away from social issues such as racism, classism, misogyny and political corruption.

Blanche White

Blanche on the Lam (1992) introduces Blanche White, a financially struggling black domestic worker from Farleigh, North Carolina, who begins the novel being sentenced to 30 days' jail time and restitution after being found guilty of passing bad cheques. Blanche quietly escapes through the courtroom toilet window and seeks refuge as the housekeeper of a wealthy local white family. There, Blanche begins to investigate the dark secrets of the family. When several people die in mysterious circumstances, Blanche is convinced that there is a murderer within the family. It falls on Blanche to unmask the murderer before she too becomes a victim.

Blanche White is in early middle-age, has a somewhat plump but sexually attractive appearance, and possesses a feisty but quick-witted temperament. Her name ironically means to whiten, or in a sense, double-white, but she can be quite dogmatic about black culture and often feels antagonism towards whites. She frequently experiences racism from Caucasians (and occasionally fellow blacks). Her back-story includes being raped by a white employer. She quietly spits at a Confederate Civil War monument every time she passes it. She is irreligious, regarding Christianity as a slave's religion; however, she does practice ancestor worship, seeking guidance from dead relatives during difficult times. She laments 'darkies disease', blacks who try to emulate white culture and are ashamed of their own heritage, whilst she is mocking of whites who try imitate blacks. A quote from the second novel in the series, *Blanche Among the Talented Tenth* (1994), neatly defines her attachment to black culture: 'She couldn't make the leap to wanting to step out of the talk, walk, music, food and feeling of being black that the white world often imitated but never really understood. She realized how small a part her complexion played in what it meant to her to be black' (Neely, 1995, p. 20) However, Blanche's attitude towards black society is complex and not uncritical. She deplores the homophobia and misogyny found in the lyrics of black rap artists. Blanche has a strong moral sense, becoming the guardian of her nephew and niece after her sister dies of cancer, although she is not afraid to flout social conventions: she has never married her long-term on-again off-again lover despite his many proposals. Neely identifies herself as a feminist writer, and Blanche as a feminist character. The novels explore perceptions of female beauty as personified by Blanche in her unorthodox, by societal standards, body size and figure. The Blanche novels could be read as satirising the stereotype of the fiercely loyal but overly dependent black maid in a Southern household, deluded into thinking she is loved as a family member. In her first novel, Neely references Butterfly McQueen who played Prissy in the film version of *Gone With the Wind* (1939), in a performance that typified this kind of loyal but naive maid. Due to her tendency to be continually finding and fleeing trouble, Blanche leads a perpetually nomadic lifestyle, becoming embroiled in violent intrigue wherever she goes and assuming the role of amateur sleuth. Her strength of character is described towards the end of *Blanche on the Lam*, 'She will always be a woman who has fought for her life and won. She's capable of negotiating enemy territory – even without a reference from her most recent employer' (Neely, 1992, p. 215). After events in the first novel force her to leave North Carolina, Blanche moves to Boston, but the second novel takes place at an exclusive all-black resort in Maine. The title is taken from the essay 'The Talented Tenth' by the Black intellectual W.E.B. Du Bois which first appeared in *The Negro Problem* (1903), and just as the first novel was critical of the racism prevalent in white society in the Deep South, the follow-up novel makes several criticisms of the black upper-middle class of New England. In the third novel, *Blanche Cleans Up* (1998), Blanche begins working as the cook-housekeeper for a family headed by a Boston Brahmin politician. Similarly to the first novel, each family member carries a secret, personal tragedy. Blanche has to solve the mystery when a series of deaths all seem to link back to the family home. In the fourth and to-date latest novel in the series, *Blanche Passes Go* (2000), the housekeeper–cum-detective returns to Farleigh, North Carolina and begins to plot her revenge against David Palmer, her former employer who once raped her (an event alluded to in the first novel).

Suggested reading

K. Lampley and N. Manis (2007) 'Barbara Neely: Life and Work' *Penn State Africana Research Center* http://arc.psu.edu/pablackwriters/the-writers/barbara-neely, date accessed 25 April 2011.

D. Witt (2000) 'Detecting Bodies: Barbara Neely's Domestic Sleuth and the Trope of the (In)Visible Woman' *Recovering the Black Female Body: Self Representations by African-American Women*, M. Bennett and V. D. Dickerson. eds. (New Brunswick: Rutgers University Press) pp. 165–94.

Steven Powell

Nolan, William F(rancis) (1928–)

Mystery writer predominantly active in science fiction, fantasy and horror who has also published under the pseudonyms Frank Anmar and F.E. Edwards. Born in Kansas City, Missouri, Nolan was educated at Kansas City Art Institute and then, after moving to California in the late 1940s, at San Diego State College. Nolan moved to Los Angeles in 1953 where he joined the Southern California Group, along with writers Ray Bradbury, Charles Beaumont and Richard Matheson. He was an active member of the Los Angeles Science Fantasy Society (LASFS), where he also met Leigh Brackett and Fredric Brown. Nolan was awarded the Edgar Allan Poe Award from the Mystery Writers of America for Best Paperback Original in 1971 for *Space for Hire*.

Nolan has written over 750 short stories, magazine and newspaper articles, 80 books (13 of which are novels) and 16 television and film scripts, for such films as *The Kansas City Massacre* (1975) and *Sky Heist* (1975). His crime writing has often crossed genre boundaries with science fiction and fantasy. *Space For Hire* (1971) inaugurated the Sam Space series, which includes *Look Out for Space* (1985) and the short story collections *Three for Space* (1992), *Far Out* (2004) and *Seven for Space* (2008). Sam Space is a private eye on Mars, and the series parodies many science fiction and hard-boiled genre conventions. Space's name is a play on Sam Spade, Dashiell Hammett's tough private detective in *The Maltese Falcon* (1930).

Two other notable series are the Logan's Run and the Black Mask series. In the Black Mask series, *The Black Mask Murders* (1994), *The Marble Orchard* (1996) and *Sharks Never Sleep* (1998), iconic crime writers Dashiell Hammett, Raymond Chandler and Erle Stanley Gardner, all of whom contributed to *the Black Mask* magazine, appear as the leading characters of each novel respectively. The ongoing Logan's Run series, currently comprising *Logan's Run* (1967), *Logan's World* (1977), *Logan's Search* (1980) (coll. *Logan: A Trilogy* 1986) and *Logan's Return* (2001), has spawned comic book and game franchises. *Logan's Run* was adapted for film in 1976 (Dir. Michael Anderson) and as a television series in 1977. A remake of *Logan's Run* is in development and has been planned for release in 2012. In *Logan's Run* (co-authored with George Clayton Johnson), the hero Logan is a Sandman, a member of the law enforcement class in a dystopic society. Logan is charged with tracking and eliminating those who attempt to 'run', to escape from their ageist society which demands people are killed once they reach a certain age, only to turn renegade and run himself.

Two collections of Nolan's short stories, *Impact-20* (1963) and *Dark Universe* (2001), offer a representative spread of his fiction. Nolan has also written scholarly and biographical works on Hammett, Bradbury and western writer Max Brand. Works on Hammett include *Dashiell Hammett: A Casebook* (1969), *Hammett: A Life at the Edge* (1983), *A Life Beyond Thursday* (2004) and the stage play *Dash* (2004).

Suggested reading

B. Clarke and J. Hopkins (1988) *The Work of William F. Nolan: An Annotated Bibliography & Guide*. (San Bernardino, CA: Borgo Press).

Chris Pak

Paretsky, Sara (1947–)

Crime writer and civil activist Sara Paretsky is best known for her 14 novels featuring the tough-talking, feminist private eye, V. I. Warshawski. The fifteenth book in the series, *Breakdown*, is due for publication in 2012. She has also written a collection of short stories featuring Warshawski, *Windy City Blues* (1995) and two non-genre novels, *Ghost Country* (1998), a mystical tale which draws on the social disparities of Chicago society, and *Bleeding Kansas* (2008), a family saga based in the Kaw River Valley. She has edited two volumes of mystery fiction by women writers, *Women on the Case* (1996) and *Sisters on the Case* (2007). Her non-fiction work, *Writing in an Age of Silence* (2007) is an autobiographical work that explores her writing and the role of the writer in relation to American society and politics, especially in the wake of 9/11. She is also a regular contributor to the *New York Times*, *The Guardian*, and the *Chicago Tribune*.

Paretsky was born in Ames, Iowa, and grew up near Lawrence, Kansas. She graduated from the University of Kansas in 1967 with a BA in Political Science and went on to gain an MBA and a PhD from the University of Chicago (1977). After graduating she remained in Chicago, working for several large insurance companies, an experience that she has drawn from in her fictional representations of the corporate world. Paretsky now lives on Chicago's South Side with her husband, Courtenay, and her passion for the city is integral to her crime writing. The novels are detailed in their presentation of Chicago's topography and history but her 'mapping' of the city is also historical, cultural and psychological.

V.I. Warshawski series

Paretsky's first novel, *Indemnity Only* (1983), introduced the character of 'V. I.' (Victoria Iphigenia – 'Vic' to her friends) Warshawski and established many of the features of style and theme that continue throughout the series. Stylistically, the hard-boiled tone is evident from the beginning with its tough-talking detective first-person narration and its setting, in and around the 'mean streets' of south Chicago where the urban decay is all too evident: 'Away from the lake the city was quieter. The South Loop, with no entertainment beyond a few peepshows and the city lockup, was deserted – a drunk weaving uncertainly down the street was my only companion' (Paretsky, 1987, p. 1). The reference to 'peepshows' perhaps echoes an earlier era, belonging more to the vocabulary of Chandler, and is one of many nods to the ancestry of Paretsky's writing. The title's allusion to James M. Cain's *Double Indemnity* (serialised 1936, published in novel form 1943), simultaneously shows Paretsky's deliberate placement of her writing within a genre and her rejection of its largely patriarchal history and traditions. The narrative contains echoes of the classic hard-boiled style, but V. I. breaks the mould of the female character in the American crime-writing that precedes her: she is neither *femme fatale* nor victim.

Gender is an inevitable theme in crime stories that posit a female detective. Ten years earlier, Warshawski's British counterpart, Cordelia Gray, was battling prejudice in P.D. James' *An Unsuitable Job for a Woman* (1972), and Paretsky's detective also faces direct opposition to her career choice: she is questioned as to her ability to emotionally or physically do her job and provoked by assumptions that she would be better off doing a more 'suitable' job for a woman – looking after a husband and children. Warshawski has, in fact, been married, but split from her husband because 'he saw [her] independence as a challenge, and when he couldn't break it down, he got angry' (Paretsky, 1987, p. 141). She carefully and deliberately labels herself as 'feminist', and her gender-politics closely reflect those of her creator. Writing initially at the height of America's second wave of feminism, and actively involved in the women's rights movement, there was always going to be a feminist or female-focused agenda to Paretsky's writing. As an undergraduate, Paretsky chaired Kansas University's first Commission on the Status of Women, and in 1986, she co-founded 'Sisters in Crime', an organisation that supports women crime writers and seeks 'to promote the professional development and the advancement of women crime writers to achieve equality in the industry'.

V. I. Warshawski's back-story establishes her active engagement in the women's rights movement as a student, graduate barrister and private investigator. In *Indemnity Only*, she returns to the University of Chicago, where she studied and infiltrates a meeting of 'University Women United', which, she observes is more than there was when she was an undergraduate 'when even women radicals treated women's liberation as a dirty phrase' (Paretsky, 1987, p. 47). Warshawski rejects attempts by men to infantalise or feminise her. When a male character addresses her '[...] you are a girl and things may get heavy', she responds, 'I'm a woman, Mr Thayer, and I can look out for myself' (Paretsky, 1987, p. 47). Paretsky also deliberately re-appropriates traditionally male-centred language by describing the new State of Illinois Building as 'one of the worst monstrosities known to woman' (Paretsky,

1988, p. 163). Warshawski's overt politicising of gender has perhaps been tempered over the three decades that she has been detecting, but it remains integral to her characterisation.

Warshawski's cultural identity is equally important. She is the daughter of a Polish-immigrant father and Italian-immigrant mother, and grew up in working-class, south side Chicago. The European-American status of the character allows Paretsky to explore issues of culture and race, often in relation to poverty and prejudice, throughout her novels. At the beginning of *Bitter Medicine* (1987), for example, V. I. finds herself in 'Friendship Five' hospital accompanying Consuelo Hernandez, a pregnant 16-year-old in premature labour. The hospital assumes that she is 'some Mexican girl' who cannot pay, and consequently stall their treatment of her. V. I. observes that 'Americans have never been very understanding of poverty, but since Reagan was elected it's become a crime almost as bad as child-molesting', an overtly political statement that is typical of her character (Paretsky, 1988, p. 11). V. I. Warshawski has a highly developed sense of political and social injustice and her investigations usually find her on the side of the underdog, often working for little or no money. Often the wrong doers are within large, nameless corporations or wealthy families, the representatives of which are nearly always white and male.

Paretsky gives her character a careful, sustained back-story, emphasising the wider theme of the past in the novels. The significance of past events is an inevitable part of the detective genre, as it informs and generates the events of the investigation, but the past in the Warshawski novels extends beyond that pertaining to V. I.'s current case to her personal history and to the history of Chicago and wider America. The figures of V. I. Warshawski's parents, both dead, ghost every investigation, as she imagines her policeman father's response to her chosen career, and hears her opera-singer mother's voice urging her to be more compassionate or hard-working. The story of Warshawski's own life and that of her immigrant parents (and therefore by extension a wider social narrative) is developed with each publication.

Warshawski arguably mythologises her family and the incidents in their American story, such as her mother and father's relationship. She has a particularly idealised view of her father, a former Chicago police officer, whom she sees as above the corruption which is rife in the police department. In keeping with Paretsky's constant evolution of her character, however, *Hardball* (2009) details Warshawski's reassessment of her father in the light of her investigations, when she is forced to acknowledge his concealment of police brutality in a case 40 years ago. The result is a more difficult, but realistic construction of the man she has set on a pedestal in previous novels.

Family is a key theme throughout the Warshawski series, and many of the familial relationships are portrayed as dysfunctional, for example the

Thayer family in *Indemnity Only*, where the father's corrupt dealings result in the death of the son, the Messenger family in *Tunnel Vision* (1993), whose despotic patriarch rapes his teenage daughter, and the various wealthy, long-established families in *Blacklist* (2003), whose complex and incestuous secrets are contained within the now-decaying mansions, a symbol of the corruption and decline of Chicago's 'elite'. Warshawski's own family is similarly fragmented and problematic. Although her parents are dead, she has various uncles, aunts and cousins who either generate or appear in her investigations, such as in *Deadlock* (1984) where she investigates the death of her cousin, 'Boom-Boom', or in *Killing Orders* (1985) where her mother's bitter and estranged sister asks her to clear her of charges of embezzlement. None of her extended family is close to Warshawski; indeed, many of them actively reject her and her chosen profession.

Despite the absence of a permanent partner or close family, V. I. has a tight-knit support network. This is largely female, with the exception of Mr Contreras, her tough elderly neighbour whose interference in her life and investigations exasperates her, although she regards him with genuine affection, and he saves her life in *Toxic Shock* (1988, published as *Blood Shot* in America). Warshawski explains her choice of friends in *Indemnity Only*: 'I have some close women friends, because I don't feel they're trying to take over my turf. But with men, it always seems, or often seems, as though I'm having to fight to maintain who I am' (Paretsky, 1987, p. 141). The most significant member of Warshawski's adoptive female 'family' is Charlotte ('Lotty') Herschel, a doctor who is older than V. I. whom V. I. turns to in times of need. Herschel is another strong female character with a burdened past and a definite social conscience: she is a Jewish refugee from the Second World War. A survivor of persecution whose family died in the concentration camps, Herschel has an innate distrust of authority. She runs a clinic in a deprived part of Chicago where, amongst other medical services, she performs abortions, a contentious subject in Paretsky's novels. Warshawski is inevitably outspoken about her pro-choice stance, for example going under the pseudonym of 'Rosemary Jiminez' in *Bitter Medicine*: 'the first woman killed from a back-alley abortion after the state cut off public-aid funds for poor women' (Paretsky, 1988, p. 163). There are various other strong, independent women friends who feature as secondary, sometimes recurrent characters in the novels, such as Carol Alvarado, Lotty's nurse, and Mary-Louise Neely, a one-time police officer who briefly becomes Warshawski's partner in detection. The relationship with Neely breaks down in *Hard Time* (1999) when Neely's foster children are threatened by the investigation. As in much crime fiction, the role of detective is often incompatible with close personal relationships, and Warshawski pushes hers to the limits. Her friendship with Herschel is tested many times, and the events of *Total Recall* (2001) damage their friendship almost beyond repair.

The job also, inevitably, interferes with any potential romantic relationships:

> it's not an easy job to combine with marriage. It's only intermittently demanding, but when I'm hot after something, I don't want to be distracted by the thought of someone at home stewing because he doesn't know what to do about dinner. Or fussing at me because Earl Smeissen beat me up. (Paretsky, 1987, p. 142)

The tension between detection and personal life seems exacerbated by gender, but Warshawski has several short and long-term relationships during the course of the series. There are a few, brief sexual encounters in which Paretsky presents her character as having the same level of sexual appetite and liberation as her male counterparts. The most notable long-term relationships, both of which span several books, are with Conrad Rawlings, a black police officer, and Morrell, a journalist whose exploits in warzones seem to, temporarily at least, give him the equality and understanding that is needed to sustain a relationship with V. I. Warshawski. Inevitably, however, these relationships end due to her job.

Warshawski's attitude to her work is hard-line dedication, and this is compounded by a clear sense of justice, although Paretsky presents a morally complex world for her detective to function in, where the crimes are intricate and multiple and each stage of the investigation reveals a new layer of corruption. To work within this world, Warshawski cannot be entirely inflexible. Although she is clearly on the side of 'right' and 'justice' and neither 'tarnished nor afraid', meeting Chandler's requirements of the fictional detective (with the obvious exception of being a woman), like many other fictional detectives she is no stranger to breaking and entering or practicing near-illegal forms of deception. She is judgmental and judged, experiences violence and acts violently, but perhaps gives more compassion than she expects for herself.

Despite the serious and brutal nature of the investigations, and the necessary toughness that renders her essentially alone, Warshawski's characterisation has a lighter side, often comprising of traits she shares with her creator. There is the mildly humorous acknowledgement of her poor housekeeping: 'I stacked my dishes by the sink and eyed them thoughtfully: one more day and I'd have to wash them', and her love of Johnnie Walker Black Label and good steak, all traits which are perhaps intended to underscore an absence of 'femininity' in Paretsky's detective but which also make her likeably human (Paretsky, 1987, p. 10). On her website, Paretsky admits to sharing the untidiness and acknowledges other semi-autobiographical elements to V. I., such as running, singing, and supporting the Chicago Cubs. She also owns a golden retriever, the breed of dog that Warshawski 'inherits' at the end of *Bitter Medicine*.

Sara Paretsky has won a number of awards including the *Ms. Magazine* 'Woman of the Year Award' in 1987 for her work with Sisters in Crime, the Cartier Diamond Dagger Award for lifetime achievement from British Crime Writers and the British Crime Writers Gold Dagger Award for *Blacklist* in 2004.

Suggested reading

M. Effron (2010) 'Sara Paretsky' in *A Companion to Crime Fiction*, C. J. Rzepka and L. Horsley eds. (Oxford: Blackwell) pp. 523–30.
S. Paretsky (2011) *Sarah Paretsky* http://www.saraparetsky.com
S. Paretsky (2009) *Writing in an Age of Silence* (New York: Verso).

Esme Miskimmin

Parker, Robert B(rown) (1932–2010)

Revising the classic American hard-boiled private eye for the socially progressive 1970s, Parker created Spenser, an alternately violent and vulnerable, wise-cracking, gourmet-cooking, and literature-quoting sleuth, whose popularity in more than three dozen books led to multiple television adaptations. Spenser's residency in Boston, Massachusetts – far from the Manhattan or Los Angeles beats of so many of his predecessors – helped foment the regional spread of literary gumshoes. Parker later launched two additional crime-fiction series, tried his hand at westerns and young-adult novels, and completed Raymond Chandler's final unfinished manuscript, *Poodle Springs*. In 2002, the Mystery Writers of America recognized Parker's contributions to crime fiction by presenting him with its Grand Master Award.

Born in Springfield, Massachusetts, on 17 September 1932, Parker was the roughneck son of what he called 'a semi dysfunctional Irish Catholic mother, and a kind Yankee father' – a telephone company executive – 'who used up many of his emotional energies keeping my mother from flying apart' (Parker, 1993). Parker's interest in detective fiction began at age 14, when he stumbled across a 1940 novel titled *Mr. Marlow Stops for Brandy*, by John Bentley, and then went looking for another Marlow story, only to find Chandler's *The Big Sleep* (1939). He attended Colby College in Waterville, Maine, graduating with a degree in English in 1954, and then joined the army (1954–56), which shipped him off to post-war Korea where he served as a radio operator. Soon after his return home, Parker married Joan Hall, a Boston-area native whom he had met and fallen in love with during a freshman dance at Colby in 1950.

Parker earned a master's degree in English from Boston University in 1957, then undertook a variety of jobs, including technical writer and group leader at Raytheon Corporation, copy writer and editor for the Prudential Insurance Company, and co-owner of a small advertising agency. In 1962, Parker went back to Boston University for his PhD, which he hoped would help him win a tenured college professor's job and more leisure time in which to write. In 1968, he joined the English faculty at Northeastern University, and stayed there until he resigned on 1 January 1979, to become a full-time author. Parker was awarded his PhD in 1971. His dissertation depicted the detectives fashioned by Chandler, Dashiell Hammett, and Ross Macdonald as modern-day versions of literature's frontier heroes, men who although they no longer needed to tame the wilderness, employed their strengths and virtues to defy civilisation's often-corrupting values.

Earning his author stripes

He started writing his first novel, *The Godwulf Manuscript*, in the same year he received his PhD. The book introduced Spenser, a thirty-seven-year-old former Massachusetts State Police trooper, assigned to the Suffolk County District Attorney's office, who having been dismissed for 'insubordination' becomes a Boston private eye. At over six-foot-tall and 195 pounds, the ex-heavyweight boxer, weightlifter, and Korean War veteran could manage dangerous confrontations, which proved useful, since his sardonic wit and impatience with pomposity often angered those around him – his clients as frequently as anyone else. Spenser, though, claimed a soft side as well, largely borrowed from his inventor. Like Parker, who had briefly been *Boston* magazine's dining-out columnist, the PI was an excellent cook. Also like Parker, who had resigned from his college fraternity because it forbade African-American membership, Spenser abhorred racism. Both creator and character trusted in psychotherapy, bore a lingering eye for pretty women, loved baseball and dogs, and had what David Geherin called a 'profound sympathy for life's victims and a particular fondness for the young' (Geherin, 1980, p. 10).

Parker christened his protagonist in honour of the sixteenth century English poet Edmund Spenser, and originally gave him the first name David, the same as his elder son (b. 1959). However, the author worried that this would upset his younger child, Daniel (b. 1963), so he eventually combed through the manuscript of his debut novel and crossed out all references to Spenser's first name, leaving him with only a single moniker.

The Godwulf Manuscript (1973) had Spenser searching for a priceless medieval document that belonged to a Boston university library, and connecting that theft to drug trafficking and a college student's murder. While the story owed much to Chandler, especially in terms of dialogue and Spenser's casting as a knight errant, Parker probably endowed his own hero with more of a private life in several chapters than Chandler gave Philip Marlowe over seven novels. He went further in *God Save the Child* (1974), which found Spenser hired to find a missing teenage boy. In *Godwulf* the PI gleefully engaged in sex not only with his client, but with her 20-year-old daughter, but in this sequel he confined his romancing to a school guidance counsellor named Susan Silverman. Harvard-educated, Jewish, and divorced, Susan Silverman (née Hirsch) – who, later in the series, would receive a PhD in clinical psychology – became the love of Spenser's life, though their relationship was not without its problems (such as a difficult separation and a disastrous experiment in living together). Once more, Parker mined his own life for these twists. He and his wife, a professor of child psychology, split up in 1982 after their sons left home. They entered therapy, and two years later reunited for what they called their 'second marriage,' buying a Victorian house in Cambridge, Massachusetts, but living on separate floors and pursuing their individual interests on their own schedules.

While Spenser's long-time relationship with Susan Silverman was unusual for a detective series, his association with Hawk, a smart-mouthed ex-fighter and former freelance leg-breaker, became the standard by which later sidekicks were measured. Tall, bald, brawny, and proudly black, with a loyal streak as wide as Spenser's but a more results-oriented moral code, Hawk made his entrance into this series in the Edgar Award-winning *Promised Land* (1977) and stayed on, acting variously as the gumshoe's bodyguard and backup. Although Spenser called the flashy-dressing Hawk 'a bad man', they were friends, even two sides of the same coin: '[I]f I were black and Hawk were white', Spenser once explained, 'then he'd be me and I'd be him' (Parker, 2009, p. 302).

Branching out

Criticism of Parker's efforts rose with his renown. Benjamin DeMott found the disconnection between Spenser's asserted sensitivity and his frequent, remorseless beatings of foes jarring, an attempt 'to pass off butchery as decency, and brutality as cultivation' (DeMott, 1985, p. 18). As the series grew in overly familiar patterns, Carl Hoffman encouraged Parker to shake things up by making Spenser 'responsible for the death of Susan Silverman, having his obsession with "honorable behavior" lead somehow to her murder' (Hoffman, 1983, p. 142). The author disregarded this advice.

Parker's books were commercially successful, and several Spenser novels rank among the best of the genre. These include *Looking for Rachel Wallace* (1980) in which the PI tries to protect a radical lesbian feminist author, who objects to his belligerence and 'preening male arrogance'; *Early Autumn* (1981) which has Spenser 'saving' a teenage boy from his dysfunctional parents, then taking him into the Maine woods to teach him skills he needs to live on his own; and *Taming a Seahorse* (1986) wherein the PI hopes to rescue a 20-year-old prostitute he placed in an exclusive brothel from her new lover-pimp. The novels were popular enough to inspire an ABC-TV drama, *Spenser: For Hire* (1985–88), which starred Robert Urich, with Avery Brooks as the menacing but magnetic Hawk. Seven further small-screen films were made from Parker's books, four of which (beginning with *Ceremony*, 1993) also placed Urich in the title role; the remaining adaptations starred Joe Mantegna as the Boston sleuth.

Beyond the Spenser series, Parker and his wife wrote *Three Weeks in Spring* (1978), a non-fiction account of her battle with breast cancer. Separately, he penned the stand-alone thriller *Wilderness* (1979), as well as a roman à clef romance titled *Love and Glory* (1983). Notable amongst his works of historical fiction are the police-family saga *All Our Yesterdays* (1994), and the baseball novel *Double Play* (2004), about a quondam marine hired in 1947 to defend the Brooklyn Dodgers' new black baseball star, Jackie Robinson, after the player starts receiving death threats. Parker was chosen by Raymond Chandler's estate to compose *Poodle Springs* (1989), the completion of a Marlowe novel Chandler abandoned prior to his death in 1959. Parker went on to produce *Perchance to Dream* (1991), a sequel to *The Big Sleep*. In later years, he dabbled in westerns, such as *Gunman's Rhapsody*, a 2001 novel based on Wyatt Earp's life, and in young-adult novels, such as *Chasing the Bear* (2009), which developed Spenser's back-story by focusing on his childhood. He also undertook two more detective series. The first, beginning with *Night Passage* (1997), focused on Jesse Stone, an alcoholic former LAPD homicide detective, who signs on as police chief in the fictional small town of Paradise, Massachusetts. The actor and former *Magnum, P.I.* star Tom Selleck later portrayed Stone in a succession of television movies. In *Family Honor* (1999), Parker introduced sexy Boston shamus Sonya Joan 'Sunny' Randall, a character developed at the behest of actress Helen Hunt, who hoped to play the protagonist on screen, but the project never came to fruition.

Parker died on 18 January 2010, in the same way he had lived so much of his adult life: sitting at his desk at home, working on another novel.

Suggested reading

J.C. Carr (1983) *The Craft of Crime: Conversations with Crime Writers* (Boston: Houghton Mifflin).

D. James and E. Foxwell (2005) *The Robert B. Parker Companion* (New York: Berkley Prime Crime).

D. Geherin (1980) *Sons of Sam Spade: The Private Eye Novel in the '70s* (New York: Frederick Unger).

O. Penzler ed. (2009) *The Lineup: The World's Greatest Crime Writers Tell the Inside Story of Their Greatest Detectives* (New York: Little, Brown).

J. Kingston Pierce

Pelecanos, George (1957–)

At the age of 39, after publishing five novels, George Pelecanos was on the point of giving up writing. He had been called 'the best kept secret in crime fiction – maybe all fiction' by Michael Connolly, but although his sales had been enough to keep his publisher interested in the next novel they were not nearly enough to support a family. He had a demanding job during the day and could only write in the evening, which he felt was compromising his time with his children. He planned to test the waters with one more novel, which eventually became *King Suckerman* (1997). The novel was accepted for publication by Little Brown & Co and Pelecanos secured a two-book deal for $90,000 and subsequently the film rights were sold. He could now write full time, and Pelecanos' reputation would grow to the extent that he is now one of the most commercially and critically successful of contemporary American crime novelists.

Early life and background

George Pelecanos was born in Washington DC on 18 February 1957. His father, Peter Pelecanos, was born in Greece and came to the US as an infant. Peter Pelecanos served in the US marines during the Second World War and saw action in the Philippines. On his return to the US, he opened the Jefferson Coffee Shop: a lunch counter and take-out restaurant in downtown Washington mostly serving the white collar workers of Washington's political and business community. When he was eight years old, George Pelecanos moved with his family to Silver Spring, Maryland, where he still resides to this day. By the age of 11, George Pelecanos was helping out in his father's business during the holidays, mainly delivering orders on foot to the many offices in the area. Although the customers were mostly Caucasians, his father's employees were black. It was in this working-class environment that he began to learn of race and class issues, loyalty and friendship as well as struggle and depression. The opening of his novel *The Turnaround* (2008), is a semi-biographical account of this time. At school Pelecanos became something of a rebellious teenager. He always had part-time work though, mostly as a stock boy working in music and electrical retail stores for pocket money. Later he enrolled on a film course at the University of Maryland, College Park, graduating in 1980. On the course he took a class in hard-boiled fiction, and through the influence of his tutor Charles C. Mish, he became an enthusiastic reader of crime novels. Raymond Chandler's *The Lady in the Lake* (1943) made a significant impression according to Pelecanos: 'it blew my doors off' (Cornwell, 2001).

From there he discovered the work of Dashiell Hammett, Ross Macdonald, David Goodis and many others including the later generation of crime writers Elmore Leonard, James Crumley, Newton Thorburg and Ken Nunn.

When his father had a heart attack, he left college early and took on the running of the lunch counter for his family. When his father returned, he drifted through a number of regular jobs to pay the bills: working in bars, selling shoes in an upmarket woman's shoe shop and selling television sets and other electrical appliances. By night he was still living a wild lifestyle and was part of the post-Vietnam punk rock generation. In 1985 he married Emily Hawk and began to ease off the fast living, and by 1989 he was manager of a number of electrical retail shops. Pelecanos and his wife have three adopted children, two sons from Brazil and a daughter from Guatemala. He was still reading crime novels and had for some years been dreaming of writing one himself. His wife encouraged him to write a novel. When it was finished, he sent the manuscript to St Martin's Press, but he did not receive a reply. Undeterred, he began to write a second book.

By this time he was working for Circle Films, a company run by Ted and Jim Pedas who owned a chain of cinemas as well as a film production company. A year later he was contacted by an editor at St Martin's Press keen to publish his book and apologising for the long delay. Pelecanos' debut novel *A Firing Offense* was published in 1992, and Pelecanos was to write another five novels before he became a full-time author. However, at the same time he was also achieving success in his film production career. Over the course of ten years he progressed from script reader to producer and distributor, working with filmmakers such as the Coen brothers on *Miller's Crossing* (1990) and *Barton Fink* (1991), with Robert Young on *Caught* (1996) and with Susan Skoog on *Whatever* (1998).

The novels

Although firmly rooted in the crime genre, Pelecanos' novels offer such a detailed, realistic depiction of their settings and characters that they collectively amount to a modern social history of Washington DC, with a strong focus on the immigrant and black communities largely ignored by the media. As someone who lived in the city for many years, Pelecanos' writing reflects the changes he observed on the streets, as well as changes in his personal life.

In *A Firing Offence*, Pelecanos introduced series character and first person narrator Nick Stefanos, the advertising manager of the electrical retail company 'Nutty Nathan's' who becomes a reluctant investigator. In *Nick's Trip* (1993), he has become a licensed private investigator who works part time as a barman, and in *Down by the River Where The Dead Men Go* (1995), he has become a PI knight-errant, dealing out retribution. Stefanos, however, is rather too fond of booze and drugs. He is tough and charming, and his work often leads to sex and violence, but he is gradually losing control. In 1994, Pelecanos published his first stand-alone novel *Shoedog* (1994) where he experimented for the first time in writing in the third person. His 'cool' main character is a drifter returning to Washington DC after a 17-year absence and ends up as the driver on a liquor store heist. Such a noir character is inevitably and inexorably drawn to a violent end.

In his essay 'The Writing Life' (2003), Pelecanos describes how on a trip to Brazil in 1993 he first saw real third-world poverty: children starving and dying on the street, looking as though they would actually commit murder to get food. This experience changed his world-view and, subsequently, his writing plans. He now wanted to write with more ambition about his own city and its ignored communities. He had also been impressed by Richard Price's novel *Clockers* (1992) which dealt with murder and drugs on an African-American housing project in a fictitious New Jersey city. Pelecanos would try to incorporate the history of DC's forgotten areas, as well as some of

> the local issues facing the working class: the endangerment of the city's youth, sub-par schools, racism, drugs corruption, illegal guns, the importance of family, the responsibility of parenthood, and the struggle to find some kind of spirituality in a violent world. (Pelecanos, 2003)

The DC quartet, as the novels became known, were the first to show signs of his new literary ambitions. Written again in the third person they chart the history of Washington DC in the overlooked communities in places such as Park View and Georgia Avenue from the 1930s to the 1950s, through the lives of a large group of characters. *The Big Blowdown* (1996) deals with the Italian and Greek immigrant communities of the 1950s in a narrative that follows Nick Stefanos' grandfather and father and their brushes with organised crime. Pelecanos has proved adept at moving his characters from one series to another at specific points in the novels.

In *King Suckerman* (1997), he introduces Marcus Clay, a black Vietnam veteran, and his Greek-American friend Dimitri Karras. The pair go on to appear in *The Sweet Forever* (1998) and *Shame The Devil* (2000). The novels follow them from their carefree 20s to their 40s, by which time Marcus is running several record stores. Of intrinsic importance to the novels are multiple pop-culture and music references, which form a soundtrack to the narrative and change accordingly as the characters move through the time-frame of the series.

In 2001 he started another series of books with the protagonist Derek Strange. Strange is a black middle-aged ex-policeman who now runs his own detective agency, Strange Investigations. In the first novel *Right As Rain* (2001), Strange is hired by the mother of a black police officer who was killed in a shooting by a white police officer. Pelecanos explores America's race issues in all their complexity as Strange becomes close to the now former policeman who is plagued with guilt over the shooting which an official investigation dubbed 'Right as Rain'. Strange returned in *Hell To Pay* (2002), *Soul Circus* (2003) and as a young policeman in the race riots of 1968 in a prequel to the series *Hard Revolution* (2004).

In the Nick Stefanos novels, the main character had been to some extent Pelecanos' alter-ego, with many of the settings drawing on the author's varied work experience. In the DC quartet and the Derek Steange novels, however, Pelecanos produced main characters who moved outside his realm of experience. Pelecanos began to conduct more extensive research, spending time in libraries researching DC history. He spent time with police officers, followed cases with the homicide division, met probation officers, ex-offenders, members of Narcotics Anonymous and The Humane Society. He began to go into prisons and young offenders institutions to talk about his books and, after some initial disinterest, he began to get feedback from prisoners telling him about their lives. Pelecanos' novels did not become social tracts. They remained suspenseful crime stories with well-drawn characters. Often graphically violent, Pelecanos' novels were also tender and witty. His work is noted for its muscular writing style, thrilling dialogue, an acute sense of dialect and a documentary-camera viewpoint of the people and the city. Many of the novels feature car journeys where the demographics and land-scape of Washington are detailed with cartographic precision. The music on car radios and the cars themselves are described with the same level of detail that Pelecanos gives to the mapping of the city.

Pelecanos was a writer and latterly producer on 17 episodes of *The Wire*. The series, created by journalist and author David Simon, followed the fortunes of characters on both sides of the law caught up in the war on drugs in deprived areas of Baltimore, Maryland, which were not dissimilar to the communities of Washington DC that Pelecanos had written about. The series, which ran to five seasons from 2002 to 2008, won multiple awards and was critically acclaimed. During this time, he also published four stand-alone novels. *Drama City* (2005) features an ex-con working as a dog warden and trying to stay out of trouble, but feeling that he has to cross the line and use violence to stop a teenage killer. *The Night Gardener* (2006) is a police mystery loosely based on the Freeway Phantom murder case. The novel moves from a murder scene in 1985 to one in 2005, which suggests the return of a serial killer tracing the implications of this re-emergence for police involved in the initial, now-forgotten case. *The Turnaround* (2008) has another of Pelecanos' recurring themes: how acts of bravado can suddenly escalate into major incidents which change lives forever. Three white teenagers drive into the isolated black neighbourhood of Heathrow Heights in Washington DC. The driver of the car shouts racist abuse and throws a cherry pie at one of the locals, which quickly escalates into a fight wherein one person is left dead. Pelecanos moves the narrative to years later to examine how the incident has ruined peoples' lives: the survivors are now adults living in an America divided and drained of confidence by the Iraq and Afghanistan wars. The story was based on a real violent racial incident which occurred in DC in the 1970s and was also partially inspired by a personal incident from Pelecanos' teenage years when he accidently shot a friend in the face and missed killing him by inches. Pelecanos has since toiled with the guilt that accompanies causing such an accident, which he claims haunts him every day, as well as the knowledge that things might have been very much worse, and his own life would have been irrevocably changed. *The Way Home* (2009) returns to the theme of father–son relationships which has featured in a number of his novels. A son from a good home gradually falls into bad behaviour and criminal acts despite his parents support and ends up in juvenile prison. After his release, he works successfully for several years in his father's carpet-laying business. One day he finds a bag of money. He tries to do the right thing, but temptation gets the better of him and he, his friends and his father are gradually dragged into a series of events that inevitably leads to a violent, doom-laden conclusion.

His recent work includes co-writing the Second World War television series *The Pacific*, produced by Steven Spielberg and Tom Hanks and another television series with David Simon, *Treme* which is set in New Orleans after Hurricane Katrina. He has also edited two editions of short stories for the *DC Noir* anthologies. Pelecanos' latest novel *The Cut* (2011) is something of a return to his roots, as it introduces Iraq war veteran turned private investigator Spero Lucas.

Suggested reading

G. Pelecanos (2010) 'Biography' *George Pelecanos* http://www.hachettebookgroup.com/features/georgepelecanos/bio/, date accessed 14 April 2011.
Anon. (2011) 'Maryland Author Biographies' *University of Maryland Libraries* http://lib.guides.umd.edu/content.php?pid=179706&sid=1511841, date accessed 16 April 2011.
A. Raphael (2008) 'Murder he wrote' *The Observer*, 27 July 2008, http://www.guardian.co.uk/media/2008/jul/27/television.books.culture, date accessed 16 April 2011.

Martin Lightening

Poe, Edgar Allan (1809–49)

A writer of short stories, poetry, criticism, philosophical treatises and scientific theories, who was named 'the undisputed father of the detective story' by Julian Symons (Symons, 1985, p. 35). While others may lay similarly contested claim to having inaugurated the genre, Poe can certainly be said to have condensed the major generic features into a structure and form later adopted and developed by Charles Dickens, Wilkie Collins, Emile Gaboriau, Arthur Conan Doyle, and G.K. Chesterton, among others. If Poe did not invent detective fiction out of nothing, then in his three 'tales of ratiocination', published in the 1840s, he at least demonstrated for the first time its power and possibilities.

Edgar Poe was born in Boston on 19 January 1809. His father David, and mother, Elizabeth Hopkins Poe, were both actors whose working lives were spent travelling between theatres in the cities of the East coast of the United States. They died while Poe was still a child, first his father, probably in 1810, and then his mother the following year. Poe's childhood was a troubled and unhappy one, but even as a boy he showed a precocious ability with language, read widely, and wrote poetry. After the death of his parents, he went to live with John Allan, a Scottish tobacco merchant in Richmond, Virginia, and his wife, Frances. The Allans brought him up as their son and raised him in the hope that he would take over the family business. Poe took Allan as his middle name. When the Allans temporarily relocated to England, between 1815 and 1820, Poe attended at the Manor School in Stoke Newington. Poe's memories of his schooldays in England later formed the setting for the psychological horror story 'William Wilson' (1843).

Allan later supported Poe when he attended the University of Virginia, in 1826–27, but disowned him when Poe ran up gambling debts and was expelled from the university. Allan is said to have turned away creditors for a year afterwards. The rift with Allan affected Poe profoundly, not the least because he had to support himself financially. He joined the US Army under the name Edgar A. Perry in 1827, but he had also begun to write, and the same year he self-published the collection *Tamerlane and Other Poems* by 'A Bostonian'.

Following the death of Frances Allan, Poe and his mentor John Allan were, for a short time, reconciled, and with Allan's help Poe was admitted to West Point Military Academy. Poe's determination to emulate his literary hero, Lord Byron, and his anger at the discovery that Allan had remarried without telling him, meant that he spent only eight months at West Point before being dishonourably discharged for neglect of military duty. He moved to Baltimore, where he lodged with Maria Clemm, his father's sister.

Although still in his 20s, Poe was already establishing himself as an influential and talented magazine editor and writer. He began working at the *Southern Literary Messenger* in 1835 and remained there for two years. His stories, book reviews, and editorial oversight raised the circulation of the *Messenger* from 500 to 3,500 copies in two years. In 1836 he married his cousin, Virginia Clemm, who was then just 13 years old. The marriage seems to have been a happy one, and it was in these early years that Poe produced some of his best-known work, including his only novel, *The Narrative of Arthur Gordon Pym of Nantucket* (1838), a collection of early tales, *Tales of the Grotesque and the Arabesque* (1839), and two of his three 'tales of ratiocination': 'The Murders in the Rue Morgue' (1841) and 'The Mystery of Marie Rogêt' (1842).

Poe was a skilled and successful magazine editor and, for a while, a literary celebrity. His abilities as a writer are best represented in the twenty-first century by his *Tales of Mystery and Imagination* (1908), a comprehensive collection of short stories featuring strange, quasi-supernatural events, horrific situations and psychological disturbances. Along with a handful of poems, notably 'The Raven', these tales define Poe as one of the foremost American Gothic writers and arguably the country's most influential exponent and theorist of the short story as a form. Among the most significant developments to emerge from the *Tales*, was Poe's early experimentation with detective fiction.

Crime and detective fiction

Although Poe is often described as a writer of tales of horror, crime, imaginary crime, and guilt the pursuit of the solution to mysteries is at the heart of many of his stories. There are acts of violence, in 'The Black Cat' and 'William Wilson'; poisonings, in 'Ligeia' (1838); premature burial, in 'The Fall of the House of Usher' (1839); and concealed guilt, in 'The Tell-Tale Heart'. Dorothy L. Sayers cites 'Thou Art the Man' (1844), a story about a missing corpse and a false accusation of murder, as an example of the fusion of detection and horror that became Poe's contribution to detective fiction (1946: 73). 'Thou Art the Man' is perhaps a development towards what might now be called a thriller, with its emphasis on personal obsession rather than detection as such. However, it is also more light-hearted and humorous than the earlier 'tales of ratiocination'. Maurice S. Lee points out in his essay on Poe in the *Blackwell Companion to Crime Fiction* (2010), that it is in Poe's detective stories that we enjoy his 'most sustained narratives of crime and revelation' and argues that the detective stories can be seen as Poe's 'greatest literary achievement' (Lee, 2010, p. 369).

In the three 'tales of ratiocination' –'The Murders in the Rue Morgue' (1841), 'The Mystery of Marie Rogêt' (1842), and 'The Purloined Letter' (1845) – Poe created a detective in whom the combination of imagination and rational method made him capable of solving any mystery. His investigator – the word 'detective' was not used as an adjective until 1843, nor as a noun until 1850 – C. Auguste Dupin is a prototype for the 'great detective' of later stories by writers such as Arthur Conan Doyle. In fact in *A Study in Scarlet* (1887), Sherlock Holmes makes a point of comparing himself with Dupin and finding the latter wanting in 'analytical genius'.

Notwithstanding Holmes's assessment of him as 'showy and superficial', Dupin's rational method endows him with powers of understanding and insight that might seem omniscient, and yet, when explained, appear entirely natural. Furthermore, Dupin's deductive rigour is tempered by mystical and bohemian tendencies which also surface in Holmes. Dupin's strangeness leads the narrator of 'The Murders in the Rue Morgue' to describe their life together in terms of madness, and eccentricity. The pair close the shutters in the morning and spend the day reading and conversing before 'roaming far and wide' after nightfall:

> It was a freak of fancy in my friend (for what else shall I call it?) to be enamored of the Night for her own sake; and into this *bizarrerie*, as into all his others, I quietly fell; giving myself up to his wild whims with perfect *abandon* ... (Poe, 2006, p. 182)
>
> Dupin can be seen as in some ways a product of Poe's early Byronic fantasies: intelligent and assured but mysterious and introspective. Sayers's argument that Poe combined the genres of detection and horror can be extended to the level of character, where Poe's interest is also in duality. At the beginning of 'The Murders in the Rue Morgue' the narrator is amused 'with the fancy of a double Dupin –the creative and the resolvent.' (Poe, 2006, p. 182)

The Murders in the Rue Morgue

Poe was a commercial writer, whose output of stories was driven by the need to earn a living, and whose tendency towards the sensational, the grotesque, and the Gothic, reflected contemporary popular tastes. The rationality of Dupin similarly reflected a growing popular belief in the idea of a rational universe, building on an Enlightenment view that mysteries could be explained by careful observation and scientific method.

Of Poe's three stories of ratiocination, it is in the first, 'The Murders in the Rue Morgue', that the principles of detective fiction are laid down most clearly: unexplained deaths, a locked room puzzle, the presentation and gathering of evidence, and a detective who impresses onlookers and readers alike with the superiority of his methods and intellectual prowess. Other generic tropes introduced in this story include the detective's less intellectual but still formidable narrator-sidekick who shares the readers' awe at the detective's analytical brilliance, and the closure of the case, and the story, with an explanation of events that by now seems obvious and incontrovertible.

Poe's stories, and the detective stories that followed them, grew from experiences of urbanisation brought about by the industrial revolution in Europe. European cities in the 1840s were growing rapidly, swelled by incomers from surrounding regions; communities and families were separated, and powerful bureaucratic structures, most notably the police, took their place in maintaining order and managing the practicalities of life. It is significant that Poe set all three of his ratiocinative tales in Paris, rather than the United States, even going so far as to relocate the real case of the murder of Mary Rogers in New York, across the Atlantic. Paris, a city by then greatly in need of modernisation, satisfied Poe's need for an exotic, unfamiliar Gothic setting, while allowing him to play upon homegrown fears of anonymity, alienation, and underlying urban dangers.

'The Murders in the Rue Morgue' brings together an apartment house in which the inhabitants live quiet, anonymous lives – where people are indistinguishable from one another, even to the extent that their language cannot be identified – and the existence of an animalistic 'criminal' act so far outside their experience and expectations that its possibility occurs to nobody but Dupin. In this respect the story reflects an urban sensibility in which the individual operates in an environment entirely built and regulated, and in which disturbances, though not uncommon, can be explained and perhaps even obviated by careful planning. This story, in common with other stories in which horror derives from the extremes of experience, introduces an element of chaos to an otherwise ordered setting.

The Mystery of Marie Rogêt, and The Purloined Letter

Besides the overt detective tales, other stories point towards the future of detective fiction. 'The Gold Bug' (1843), for which Poe won a prize in the Dollar Newspaper competition, involves the deciphering of a code, while 'The Man of the Crowd' (1840) describes a flâneur familiar to readers of Baudelaire and a loose prototype for American detectives such as Sam Spade and Philip Marlowe. Poe's interest in writing tales of ratiocination went beyond mere storytelling, however: Dupin's rational analytic method became a theoretical and philosophical position which Poe promoted in the second tale of ratiocination, 'The Mystery of Marie Rogêt'.

Poe's interest in ratiocination, and in cryptology, combined with the success in America and Europe, of 'The Murders in the Rue Morgue', led him to take a risk with his next story. Beginning with the mysterious death of Mary Rogers, whose body was found in the Hudson River in New York City in 1841, Poe hoped to show how ratiocination could help solve real-life crimes. Poe set his story in Paris, and it appeared in three instalments in *Snowden's Ladies Companion* in the winter of 1842–3. His 'solution' was that the victim was killed by a jealous lover, but as Maurice S. Lee explains, Poe's conclusions turned out to be false: Mary Rogers died following an abortion operation, a revelation that emerged before the final instalment of the story was published. Even the creative Dupin failed to envisage such a solution.

Despite its failure to solve the real crime, 'The Mystery of Marie Rogêt' is an accomplished tale in which Dupin further establishes himself as a prototype for the observant, analytical Great Detective. In the third tale of ratiocination, 'The Purloined Letter', the problem is rather different, involving as it does a missing letter and a blackmail plot. As in the earlier stories, the plodding logic of the police contrasts with the imaginative, inductive reasoning of Dupin but is magnified by the emphasis Poe places on the number of times, and the thoroughness with which, the police search the apartment in where the letter is apparently hidden. Dupin exhorts them to look again, confident that their limited frame of reference will not lead them to it; only he, with his intuition and creative genius, can see what is hidden in plain view.

Poe's three groundbreaking tales of ratiocination established many of the tropes and generic features of the detective story, which became highly popular in the decades that followed. But while Dupin has become famous for his 'ratiocinative' method, it is Poe's blending of aspects of the sensation story, Gothic and other elements with detection that makes the stories so compelling and influential. Poe's exploration of psychology, as in 'The Purloined Letter', where Dupin's knowledge of the police chief's mental attitude helps him understand what the police are failing to see, as well as his approach to puzzles, codes, and illusions, take his stories beyond detection itself and into more modern notions of motive, profiling, and the science of forensics. Poe's thoughts on the ratiocinative method are outlined and theorised in his prose poem *Eureka* (1848).

Despite his success with these three stories, Poe's magazine work was intermittent, and after his wife became ill in 1842, he grew increasingly erratic, both in his writing and in his personal life. Until her death in 1847, Poe's wife was an invalid, and after she died he never really recovered. Poe died in Baltimore on 7 October 1849. Although his death has often been attributed to drunkenness – it is widely believed he was found in a Baltimore gutter after a drinking spree a few days prior to his death – the actual cause has been the subject of much speculation, ranging from a brain tumour to cholera, even to murder.

Suggested reading

P.H. Bellas (1995) Poe, *Master of Macabre* (Baltimore: Xavier).
E.W. Carlson, ed. (1996), *A Companion to Poe Studies* (Westport, CT: Greenwood).
F.S. Frank and A. Magistrale (1997) *The Poe Encyclopedia* (Westport, CT: Greenwood).
M.S. Lee (2010) 'Edgar Allan Poe (1840–1849)' C. Rzepka and L. Horsley eds. *A Companion to Crime Fiction* (London: Wiley-Blackwell) pp. 369–80.
K. Silverman (1992) *Edgar A. Poe: Mournful and Never-Ending Remembrance* (London: Wiedenfeld and Nicholson).

Christopher Routledge

Post, Melville Davisson (1869–1930)

Post is the creator of the well-known series character Uncle Abner, a Virginian squire and detective from the post-revolutionary period in American history. Besides being a prolific and highly paid writer of short stories for the burgeoning magazine market of the early twentieth century, Post was also a lawyer and Democrat campaigner.

Melville Davisson Post was born 19 April 1869 (some sources erroneously state 1871) in Harrison County in rural West Virginia. His father Ira Carper Post was a wealthy farmer; his mother was Florence May (Davisson). He attended West Virginia University, graduating in 1892 with a law degree. He began writing and publishing stories while working as a criminal and corporate lawyer. By the time of his marriage to Anne Bloomfield Gamble Schoolfield in 1903, he was successful enough to abandon his law career to write full time. After the death of their only child, Ira, he and his wife travelled in Europe. They later owned and ran a stable for polo ponies.

Post created several series characters, including Sir Henry Marquis, an English police chief, Monsieur Jonquelle, a Parisian policeman, and Randolph Mason, a crooked lawyer who uses his intricate knowledge of the law to help criminals escape prosecution through legal loopholes. Mason appeared in Post's first collection of stories in 1896, but it is Uncle Abner for whom Post is most widely known. Uncle Abner's ability to solve mysteries by spotting logical inconsistencies or obscure clues has seen him placed alongside Dupin and Holmes as a 'great detective', but in many ways he resembles the stern, silent, authoritative moral heroes of the western tradition.

The Uncle Abner stories are set in Jeffersonian-era Western Virginia, in the area that later became part of West Virginia, where Post lived. Operating in the absence of an official police force, backwoodsman Uncle Abner applies his own brand of forceful character and profound religious conviction to investigating crime. He is notable for his strong moral purpose, informed by rigorous Bible study, and his belief in 'the justice of God'. The Uncle Abner stories appeared in several collections, including *Uncle Abner: Master of Mysteries* (1918). Randolph Mason features in *The Strange Schemes of*

Randolph Mason (1896), and *The Man of Last Resort* (1897), Sir Henry Marquis in *The Sleuth of St James Square* (1920), and Monsieur Jonquelle in *Monsieur Jonquelle, Prefect of Police of Paris* (1923).

Post was a highly skilled storyteller and has sometimes been described as a successor to Edgar Allan Poe. William Faulkner studied his stories while writing the 'Uncle Gavin' stories in *Knight's Gambit* (1949). Post pioneered the idea that mystery stories did not need the solution explained at the end. Instead the solution is delivered as part of the story, a technique common in late twentieth-century detective fiction.

Post died in Harrison County, West Virginia, where he was born and had lived most of his life. In some accounts he died after falling from a horse, but his death certificate records long-term illness as the primary cause.

Suggested reading

C.A. Norton (1973) *Melville Davisson Post: Man of Many Mysteries* (Bowling Green OH: Popular Press).

Christopher Routledge

Prather, Richard S(cott) (1921–2007)

Prolific American mystery novelist who created the phenomenally successful Shell Scott private eye series, which numbered 41 books. The Scott series, comprised mostly of novels and a few short story collections, sold over 40 million copies. Richard Scott Prather was born on 9 September 1921, in Santa Ana, California. During the Second World War, Prather served in the United States Merchant Marines as a fireman, oiler and engineer from 1942 to 1945. The year the war ended, Prather married Tina Yager, a marriage that lasted 58 years until Tina's death in 2004. Prather worked as Chief Civilian Clerk at March Air Force Base in Riverside, California, from 1945 to 1949, eventually leaving his position to pursue his writing career. After becoming a client of the renowned literary agent Scott Meredith, Prather moved with his wife to Laguna Beach where he developed his intensive work schedule of up to, and sometimes exceeding, 17 hours of writing per day, seven days a week.

Shell Scott Series

Sheldon 'Shell' Scott made his first appearance in Prather's debut novel *Case of the Vanishing Beauty* (1950). An ex-marine with bright white hair, a perpetual tan and gaudy dress sense, Scott is by his own admission unusual in appearance, even ugly, but this does not stop him being seemingly irresistible to beautiful women whom he refers to as his 'tomatoes'. *The Cheim Manuscript* (1969) ends with Scott hurriedly making his way to a threesome with two sexually enticing women. Innuendo, screwball and slapstick humour were common throughout the series. *Strip for Murder* (1956) is set in a nudist colony. *The Wailing Frail* (1956) begins with Scott being greeted by a naked woman at her front door. The penultimate novel *The Amber Effect* (1986) begins with Scott finding a beautiful naked woman at his front door. Each novel is written in a first-person prose style which playfully engages the reader. From *The Kubla Khan Caper*: 'You want to know why? You don't, huh? Well, I'll tell you anyway!' (Prather, 1988, p. 39). Scott's narration gently mocked the preposterous storylines, and the PI's violent, unorthodox methods exasperated but still earned the grudging respect of his contacts in the LAPD. Scott had no great intellect as a detective, but neither did he have the angst that is usually associated with a private eye. Instead, he has a zestful love of life. Prather wrote relatively few novels outside the Scott series: *Lie Down, Killer* (1952) and *The Peddler* (1963) are among them. He occasionally wrote under the pseudonyms David Knight and Douglas Ring. Prather collaborated with Stephen Marlowe on the crossover novel *Double in Trouble* (1959), in which Scott works with Marlowe's Washington DC-based PI Chet Drum. Prather also edited *The Comfortable Coffin* (1960), an acclaimed anthology of comic-crime stories. Despite his prodigious output, Prather took a ten-year break from writing in 1975 after a disagreement with his publisher, Pocket Books, led him to sue them. He spent his time away from writing living off his considerable royalties and cultivating avocados. The final Shell Scott novel, *Shellshock*, appeared in 1987. Richard S. Prather died in his sleep at his Sedona, Arizona home on 14 February 2007.

Suggested reading

M. Carlson (2007) 'Richard S Prather: Thriller writer from a world of sex, violence, Caddys and "frails"' *The Guardian,* 29 March 2007, http://www.guardian.co.uk /news/2007/mar/29/guardianobituaries.books, date accessed 24 September 2011.

J. Reilly ed. (1985) *Twentieth-Century Crime and Mystery Writers* (New York: St Martin's Press).

Steven Powell

Pronzini, Bill (1943–)

Prolific in his contributions to crime, suspense, and western fiction, Pronzini has produced some three dozen novels starring his Nameless Detective, an even larger number of non-series works, and close to 200 short stories and novellas. He has also edited or co-edited more than 100 fiction anthologies. For his efforts, Pronzini has won an array of commendations, including three Shamus Awards, France's *Grand Prix de la Littérature Policière*, the Mystery Writers of America's 2008 Grand Master Award and the 1987 Private Eye Writers of America's lifetime achievement award, The Eye.

William John Pronzini was born on 13 April 1943, in Petaluma, California. Pronzini began writing mysteries as a schoolboy. After two years of junior college, he took a string of jobs including newspaper reporter, plumbing supply salesman and civilian guard with the U.S. Marshal's Office, which gave him enough financial stability to pursue his writing ambitions. He sold his first fiction to *Shell Scott Mystery Magazine* in 1966, and in 1971 his debut novel, a stand-alone called *The Stalker*, was published. But it was his second novel, *The Snatch* (1971) that set the course for Pronzini's career. The story featured Nameless, a character previously introduced in a 1968 short story – a lonely, modest, out-of-shape but tenacious San Francisco gumshoe in his late 40s, who served in Army Intelligence during World War II and clocked 15 years as a detective with the San Francisco Police before going private. Succeeding entries in the series have become less conventional, as its protagonist has grown older and more emotionally developed facing challenges to his health, a cancer scare in *Blowback* (1977), and changes to his independence, his first marriage to long-time girlfriend Kerry Wade is followed by fatherhood in his 60s. Pronzini calls Nameless 'my alter ego', while noting that the peeper is 'more courageous and gentlemanly, but I have a better sense of humor' (Pronzini, 2006). In recent books, Nameless has slid into semi-retirement, still taking cases but turning over more responsibilities to his junior partners – a young black woman named Tamara Corbin, and Jake Runyon, a former Seattle homicide cop and widower.

Early in his career, Pronzini ghost-wrote private detective Mike Shayne novelettes under the name of Shayne's creator, Brett Halliday, and composed other books as 'Jack Foxx' and 'Alex Saxon'. He has since collaborated on crime works with authors such as Collin Wilcox, John Lutz, and Marcia Muller – who is also his third wife (they married in 1992) and the creator of series sleuth Sharon McCone. Pronzini and Muller joined forces on novels such as *Double* (1984), starring both Nameless and McCone, and *Beyond the Grave* (1986), in which Muller's modern-day protagonist Elena Oliverez solves a mystery from the century-old case notes of John Quincannon, Pronzini's frequent short-story protagonist, an 1890s Secret Service agent turned San Francisco detective. Pronzini co-authored, with Jeffrey Wallmann, *Day of the Moon* (1983) about a troubleshooter named Flagg, who is hired as a private detective of sorts by a West Coast crime syndicate. In his non-series novels, Pronzini has explored the breadth and diversity of crime fiction, as in the suspense novel *Snowbound* (1974) set entirely in a California mountain town which is cut off from the outside world during a heavy storm. Other stand-alone novels include the domestic-abuse thriller *In an Evil Time* (2001) and *Blue Lonesome* (1995), about a lonely accountant who becomes obsessed with a woman he barely knew after he learns she has committed suicide.

In addition to his fiction, Pronzini – an avid pulp magazine collector like Nameless –has published two critical studies of 'bad' mystery yarns, *Gun in Cheek* (1982) and *Son of Gun in Cheek* (1987), and one of the 'worst' in western fiction, *Sixgun in Cheek* (1990). He served as the first president of the Private Eye Writers of America (1982–83).

Suggested reading

M. Ashley, ed. (2002) *The Mammoth Encyclopedia of Modern Crime Fiction* (New York: Carroll & Graf).

B.F. Murphy (1999) *The Encyclopedia of Murder and Mystery* (New York: St. Martin's Minotaur).

A. Shechter (2006) 'Interview: Marcia Muller and Bill Pronzini,' *Library Journal*, 15 July 2006 http://www.freetrialzone.com/lj/ljinprintcurrentissue/866599–403/marcia_muller_amp_bill_pronzini.html.csp., date accessed 15 July 2011.

J. Kingston Pierce

Queen, Ellery (pseudonym of Manfred B[ennington] Lee, 1905–71, and Frederic Dannay, 1905–82)

Using the name of their original protagonist – New York mystery writer and detective Ellery Queen – as their joint pseudonym, cousins Lee and Dannay spent more than four decades developing one of the most successful and beloved crime-fiction series of all time. While the character Ellery Queen inspired radio, film and television projects, as well as comic books and board games, his creators extended the Queen brand further by editing short-story anthologies, writing true-crime essays, and launching a magazine that helped to popularise mystery fiction and which remains the leading periodical of its kind. Critical appreciation for Lee and Dannay's work has declined somewhat over the years; but in 1951, their reputation was strong enough that critic Anthony Boucher declared, 'Ellery Queen *is* the American detective story' (Boucher, 1951, p. 11).

Lee and Dannay were born in a tenement district of Brooklyn, New York, Lee on 11 January 1905 and Dannay on 20 October 1905. Coming from Russian Jewish immigrant families, and hoping to better assimilate into the American culture, they both later changed their names – Manford Lepofsky becoming Manfred B. Lee and Daniel Nathan transforming himself into Frederic Dannay. Together they attended the historic Boys' High School (now Boys and Girls High School). Lee went on to New York University, where between studies he led a jazz band. Meanwhile, Dannay took painting courses at the Art Students League of New York.

The cousins were early crime-fiction enthusiasts and aspired to literary careers, but it would not be until 1928 – when Lee was employed as a film industry publicist and Dannay served as a copy writer and art director with an advertising agency – that they collaborated on their first novel. Responding to a mystery-writing contest that offered $7,500 in prize money, and was co-sponsored by *McClure's* magazine and J.B. Lippincott & Co. (Arthur Conan Doyle's initial U.S. publisher), they concocted *The Roman Hat Mystery*. Essentially a locked-room mystery about the bizarre murder of a crooked lawyer in a crowded theatre, the story introduced young bibliophile Ellery Queen and his New York City policeman father, Inspector Richard

Queen. As the competition required entrants to use aliases, Lee and Dannay took on their character's moniker, hoping it would make them more noticeable. Shortly after the cousins were told they had won, *McClure's* was sold and its new executives gave the prize instead to *Murder Yet to Come*, by Isabel Briggs Myers (co-inventor of the Myers-Briggs personality test). Fortunately, publisher Frederick A. Stokes took on *The Roman Hat Mystery*, releasing it in 1929. The novel proved popular enough that Lee and Dannay composed the first of what would eventually be almost three dozen sequels, *The French Powder Mystery* (1930). They took up full-time writing in 1931.

The evolution of Ellery Queen as a character

The character of amateur detective Ellery Queen evolved over the decades. To begin with he was a tall, slender, foppish Harvard graduate, 'a sartorial cliché, dressed in tweeds, wearing pince-nez, and carrying a walking stick'. Blessed with 'an independent income from a maternal uncle', and seeking a life of leisure and learning, he tended toward superciliousness and was given to lecturing others from the lofty pedestal of his deductive reasoning. William L. DeAndrea dubbed him 'a junior edition Philo Vance', an apt assessment, since Ellery's creators had modelled him on S.S. Van Dine's *bon vivant* detective (DeAndrea, 1994, p. 292). Manfred Lee was blunter still, calling the early Ellery 'probably the biggest prig that ever came down the pike' (Nivens and Greenburg, 1985, p. xi). What saved Ellery in readers' eyes was his loving relationship with his father, whose homicide investigations supplied the younger man with material for his fiction. Richard Queen was a 'small, withered, rather mild-appearing old gentleman', gray-topped and moustached, who walked with a stoop (Queen, 1932, p. 12). A widower, though he later remarried in *House of Brass* (1968), the inspector shared a book-lined apartment with Ellery on Manhattan's West 87th Street, the top floor of a three-family brownstone. In the early stories, the address was maintained by Djuna, a cheerful, teenage, gypsy-blooded orphan, who worshipped the inspector and his son, and operated as their 'man-of-work, general factotum, errand boy, valet, and mascot' (Queen, 1932, p. 106). However, the houseboy disappeared from the series after *The Spanish Cape Mystery* (1935).

Djuna's departure was part of a larger shift in the Queen canon. The opening nine novels – all featuring nationalities in their titles – were intricate 'fair-play' mysteries that literally challenged readers, not long before their solutions were revealed, to figure out the answers for themselves. But beginning with *Halfway House* (1936), Lee and Dannay simplified their plots, blended in human-interest elements, and redefined Ellery Queen as less all-knowing, more fallible, and more of a romantic and philosopher than before. The result was an increasingly character-driven series that saw the character of Ellery harder at work than he had been as a mystery novelist.

Ellery and his father became able to outwit antagonists without each other's assistance, and the intellectual hero was transported to locales beyond New York City. Three novels – *The Devil to Pay* (1938), *The Four of Hearts* (1938) and *The Origin of Evil* (1951) – were set in Hollywood, where Ellery tackled homicide cases as well as screenwriting, the latter of which Lee and Dannay also experimented with, unsuccessfully, in the 1930s. Four other novels, starting with the psychologically complex family tragedy, *Calamity Town* (1942), took place in an ostensibly serene hamlet called Wrightsville.

With Dannay conceiving the plots and characters, and Lee detailing the stories, the cousins produced Ellery Queen mysteries that rank among the best books of the genre. They include *Calamity Town* and *The Devil to Pay* as well as the unexpected-body-in-a-casket puzzler, *The Greek Coffin Mystery* (1932), the religion-tinged *Ten Days' Wonder* (1948), and an early serial-killer thriller, *Cat of Many Tails* (1949). In addition, the authors created four whodunits, beginning with 1932's *The Tragedy of X*, under a second nom de plume, 'Barnaby Ross', and featuring amateur sleuth Drury Lane, a former Shakespearean actor who was forced to retire due to deafness. During the early 1930s, Lee and Dannay took to the national lecture circuit as 'Ellery Queen' and 'Barnaby Ross' respectively, wearing black masks and challenging each other to solve confounding but well-rehearsed mysteries. Not until 1936 were the novelists' true identities finally revealed.

Expanding the queen influence

After conceding their struggle to become Hollywood screenwriters, the cousins turned their energies to new endeavours. In 1938 Dannay assembled the first of what would be many Queen-edited short-story anthologies. Three years later, he and Lee founded *Ellery Queen's Mystery Magazine*, a digest that Dannay went on to edit for the next four decades. *EQMM* helped launch many writing careers, and to this day is the longest-running US mystery-fiction magazine still being published.

In 1939 the pair launched *The Adventures of Ellery Queen*, a radio drama series that ran in various incarnations on the CBS, NBC, and ABC networks between 1939 and 1948. Most of the episodes were scripted by Lee and Dannay, or later by Lee and other wordsmiths, such as Anthony Boucher. By the late 1930s, Ellery Queen was also becoming a movie-theatre fixture, having been introduced to audiences in a 1935 film adaptation of *The Spanish Cape Mystery*. Nine Queen pictures were shot, most starring either Ralph Bellamy or William Gargan, the last of the bunch being 1942's *Enemy Agents Meet Ellery Queen*. The character made the leap to television in 1950, in the first of four Queen series: two were titled *The Adventures of Ellery Queen* (1950–52 and 1954–56), a third called *The Further Adventures of Ellery Queen* (1958–59), and finally *Ellery Queen* (1975–76). The last – and finest –adaptation starred Jim Hutton as a brilliant but absentminded Ellery, and David

Wayne as his crusty, tenacious father. Set back in the 1940s, it was produced by long-time Ellery Queen fans William Link and Richard Levinson.

Lee and Dannay received the Grand Master Award in 1961 from the Mystery Writers of America. However, by that time their partnership had grown contentious. *The Finishing Stroke* (1958) was reportedly intended as their swan song, but not long after it saw print, they decided to keep publishing with help from ghost writers. They had already hired anonymous writers on a series of 'Ellery Queen Jr' juvenile mysteries, which resurrected Djuna in the role of boy sleuth. Now they lent their byline to authors such as Charles Runyon, Richard Deming and Talmage Powell, who – under Dannay's editorship – wrote crime novels without the character of Ellery Queen or any pretence of capturing the cousins' style. When Lee suffered writer's block in the early 1960s, Dannay turned to novelists Theodore Sturgeon and Avram Davidson, who (without being credited) converted his outlines for new Ellery Queen tales into such completed works as *The Player on the Other Side* (1963) and *The Fourth Side of the Triangle* (1965). The third-party collaborations, and how they raised questions in readers' minds about the provenance of all the Queen novels, are often cited – along with the artificial complexity of the cousins' plots – as cause for the subsequent waning of Lee and Dannay's literary reputation.

Following a series of heart attacks, Manfred Lee died on 3 April 1971, not long after the cousins welcomed the publication of their last Queen novel, *A Fine and Private Place*. Frederic Dannay subsequently stopped writing fiction, but continued to edit his magazine until shortly before he passed away on 3 September 1982.

Suggested reading

A. Boucher (1951) *Ellery Queen: A Double Profile* (New York: Little Brown).

R. Lee (1975) 'Dad and Cousin Fred Entered a Contest...', *TV Guide*, 11 October 1975, pp. 21–23.

C. Akers-Jordan (1998) 'Ellery Queen: Forgotten Master Detective' Master of Liberal Studies, University of Michigan-Flint http://spruce.flint.umich.edu/~cakers/EQThesis.pdf

Ellery Queen: A Website of Detection (1999) http://neptune.spaceports.com/~queen/index.html, date accessed 22 October 2011.

J. Kingston Pierce

Reeve, Arthur B(enjamin) (1880–1936)

One of the first crime writers to employ the forensic devices of finger printing, ballistics, lie detectors and blood analysis in his scientific detection stories featuring Craig Kennedy, Reeve also introduced psychoanalysis as a tool for criminal investigations almost 20 years before Freud's theories gained popularity.

Reeve was born in Patchogue, Long Island on 15 October 1880 but grew up in Brooklyn. Reeve graduated from Princeton in 1903 and then attended New York Law School. Reeve married Margaret Allen Smith in 1906, and they had two sons and one daughter. Instead of practicing law, Reeve turned to journalism, working as an assistant editor for *Public Opinion* (1906), as a writer for *Survey* (1907) and an editor for *Our Own Times* (1906–10) before going freelance. Reeve would cover the Lindbergh baby's kidnapper's trial and the unsolved murder of director and actor William Desmond Taylor. The bulk of Reeve's Craig Kennedy short stories were published in *Cosmopolitan*, but Reeve also published in *The Popular Magazine, Detective Story Magazine, Country Gentleman, Boy's Life, Everybody's Magazine, Flynn's World Man Hunters, Complete Detective Novel Magazine, Dime Detective, Popular Detective, Scientific Detective, Detective Fiction Weekly* and *Weird Tales*. From 1912 to 1920, Reeve enjoyed popular success in Britain and America. Although he had no formal criminologist training, Reeve was approached by the US government during World War I to create a scientific laboratory in Washington DC dedicated to the fight against espionage and crime. The laboratory was considered the most advanced in the world at that time and a model for later crime laboratories.

Reeve was an astute businessman who repackaged his work between novels, screenplays and short stories: six of his novels were based on his screenplays. Reeve wrote 18 novels, 16 screenplays and published 12 short story collections. Most of these focused on his scientific sleuth Craig Kennedy; however, there were several exceptions: *Guy Garrick* (1914), *Constance Dunlap: Woman Detective* (1916), *The Master Mystery* (1919) co-authored with John W. Grey and *The Mystery Mind* (1920). Harry Houdini starred in Reeve's *The Master*

Mystery (1920), a film serial (with 15 episodes) co-written with Charles Logue. *The Exploits of Elaine* (1914) (14 episodes), in which the Elaine of the title is repeatedly rescued by Craig Kennedy, was one of his most successful screenplay serials.

Craig Kennedy series

Reeve's most famous creation was undoubtedly Craig Kennedy, a Professor of Chemistry at Columbia University, who along with his newspaper reporter friend Walter Jameson would solve crimes the police deemed unsolvable. Reeve was inspired by a series of articles he wrote on scientific crime solving as a journalist, and his stories focus more on the technical aspects of solving the crime than on character development and narrative. Aside from advising the police, a role which Reeve outlined as belonging to academics in *The Silent Bullet* (1912), Kennedy also comes to the aid of friends and others. Dubbed the 'American Sherlock Holmes', Kennedy's and Jameson's relationship differs from Holmes's and Watson's in that Jameson stands to profit from accompanying Kennedy, their investigations turn up criminals that are more sexually deviant, and Jameson contributes to the investigation through his newspaper connections. Jameson also narrates most of the stories. The popularity of Reeve's character Kennedy was such that the author stood in for photos of the character, as Mickey Spillane would later do for Mike Hammer, although there was little physical resemblance.

Arthur B. Reeve died on 9 August 1936. In 1952, *Craig Kennedy, Criminologist*, a TV show based on Reeve's character, was aired for one season. Since then, Reeve's critical reputation has been steadily declining to the point of obscurity, but his work stands as an entertaining testament to the scientific detective of the Golden Age.

Suggested reading

W.L. DeAndrea (1994) *Encyclopedia Mysteriosa* (New York: Macmillan).
J. Reilly, ed. (1985) *Twentieth Century Crime and Mystery Writers* (New York: St Martin's Press).

Diana Powell

Rinehart, Mary Roberts (1876–1958)

Mary Roberts Rinehart is best known for her novel *The Circular Staircase* (1908) as well as the Miss Pinkerton series, the 'Tish' stories and the play *The Bat* (1920), which would be adapted into two films and was cited by Batman creator Bob Kane as one of the inspirations for the comic book caped crusader. The parodic cliché of crime fiction, 'The butler did it', is sometimes considered to have originated with Rinehart's *The Door* (1930), although the phrase never actually appears in the novel. Many of Rinehart's novels, especially her early works such as *The Circular Staircase*, can be identified as early examples of the 'Had-I-But-Known' tradition of crime fiction, which refers to a technique in which a character, often the first-person narrator, draws out the plot's action through misunderstandings and incorrect assumptions. The character usually ends up lamenting 'had she but known' that terrible things would happen she would have acted differently. During a career that spanned more than 50 years, Rinehart wrote 54 novels, five plays, an autobiography, travelogues and many short stories. Rinehart was for a period of time the highest-earning American author.

Early years

Rinehart was the first of two daughters born to Thomas Roberts and Cornelia Roberts (nee Gilleland) in Pittsburgh, Pennsylvania – some sources state Allegheny as Allegheny City was absorbed into Pittsburgh in 1907. The Roberts family struggled financially throughout Rinehart's childhood, and Rinehart's father, a failed inventor, committed suicide in 1895. Rinehart first published her writing at the age of 15, when she sold two short stories to the *Pittsburgh Press*. Rinehart attended school in Pittsburgh, and upon her graduation enrolled in the Pittsburgh Training School for Nurses. Rinehart's experiences as a nurse inform her work, notably in novels *K* (1915) and *The Doctor* (1936) as well as short stories such as 'The Buckled Bag' (1914) and 'Locked Doors' (1914). The protagonist of the two stories is a nurse named

Hilda Adams who does undercover investigative work under the name Miss Pinkerton.

While training to be a nurse, Rinehart met a physician named Stanley Marshall Rinehart, whom she married in 1896 after finishing nursing school. Following her marriage, Rinehart worked with her husband in his medical practice. The couple would have three children, Stanley Jr, Alan and Frederick. Though she had been dabbling in writing during her spare time, Roberts began pursuing her career seriously after she and her husband lost a substantial amount of money in the stock-market crash of 1904. Her efforts met with success, and her first short story, 'His Other Self', was published in the magazine *Munsey's* in 1904.

Professional success

Rinehart's first serial, *The Man in Lower 10*, was sold to the magazine *All-Story* in 1905 for the then-large sum of 400 dollars. In 1908, Rinehart sold the manuscripts for *The Man in Lower 10*, *The Circular Staircase* and *The Mystery of 1122* to the publishing company Bobbs-Merrill. Though it was chronologically her first novel-length work, *The Man in Lower 10* was published as a novel in 1909 after *The Circular Staircase*. It would be the first American crime novel to become a bestseller.

The Circular Staircase, which had previously been published in 1907 as a serial in the magazine *All-Story*, was released as Rinehart's first novel in 1908. The plot of *The Circular Staircase* introduces spinster Rachel Innes, who rents a summer house in the country at the encouragement of her niece and nephew. The strange occurrences at the house, including ghostly manifestations and the discovery of a secret room, give the novel a gothic tone, though all is explained at the novel's conclusion as originating from a prosaic case of embezzlement, fraud and murder. The 'Had-I-But-Known' style was well suited to serials as it raised suspense from one instalment to the next. The protagonist of such stories must always be an emotionally sympathetic character the reader trusts and connects with and thus feels a sense of terror at the growing danger. However, the first-person narrator is partly omniscient, knowing what will come next, and reassuring the reader that all will be revealed. The stories can also be violent, although not in the hard-boiled sense, with one murder followed by a series of additional murders. Innes is not the primary detective figure, but her character is a capable, logical middle-aged woman whose observations are taken seriously by the police. The self-deprecating remarks the character often makes about being an 'elderly spinster' who has no business being involved in the unfolding murder investigation serve to highlight her competence when contrasted with her behaviour. As the first-person narrator of the story, Innes demonstrates that she in fact has a healthy opinion of her own abilities: she justifies telling her own version of the story by calling the newspaper accounts 'garbled and incomplete – one of them mentioned [her] but once, and then only as the tenant at the time the thing happened' (Rinehart, 1908, p. 10). Innes is the first of several of Rinehart's positive depictions of middle-aged spinsters who are adept, self-possessed and independent.

After her initial success with writing and publishing, Rinehart became fascinated with the theatre and determined to turn her hand to writing plays. In 1906, her play *The Double Life*, based on an earlier short story about a man with amnesia, opened in New York, but the play received lacklustre reviews and had only a short run before closing. Rinehart's 1909 comedy *Seven Days* would prove to be far more successful, running for 397 performances.

In 1910, the first of Rinehart's well-known 'Tish' stories, 'That Awful Night', was published in *The Saturday Evening Post*. Miss Letitia Carberry, 'Tish', is an adventurous spinster who embarks on daring exploits with her friends, fellow spinsters Lizzie and Aggie. The stories are humorous, but they depict an empowering image of older single women in the spirit of Rinehart's other characters Miss Pinkerton and *The Circular Staircase*'s Rachel Innes.

Rinehart travelled to Europe in 1915 as a war correspondent for *The Saturday Evening Post*, visiting Belgium and England, where she would interview King Albert of Belgium as well as Winston Churchill and Queen Mary of Teck, and touring hospitals along the lines. Upon her return, Rinehart visited the American West, writing two travelogues about her journey through Glacier National Park in Montana. She would return to Europe in 1918, and her experiences on the front led her to write the novel *The Amazing Interlude* (1918), about a young woman who leaves her home in Pennsylvania in order to volunteer for the Red Cross in Belgium during the First World War.

In 1920, Rinehart's stage adaptation of *The Circular Staircase*, called *The Bat*, opened on Broadway. The play's plot was changed from the novel by the addition of a mysterious villain called 'The Bat'. The play was enormously successful, running for two years and being adapted for two films, *The Bat* (1926) and *The Bat Whispers* (1930).

Later years

Rinehart's writing gave her and her family financial security, and she eventually owned homes in New York, Washington, D.C. and Bar Harbor, Maine. Rinehart's husband Stanley died in 1932. In 1935, Rinehart moved to New York City, where she and her sons started a publishing company, Farrar and Rinehart, which would publish most of her work for the rest of her life.

Rinehart was diagnosed with breast cancer in 1936 which was successfully treated after she underwent a radical mastectomy. At the time, breast cancer was a taboo subject and Rinehart decided to help raise public awareness of the disease. In 1947, Rinehart sat for an interview entitled 'I Had Cancer' for the *Ladies Home Journal* in which she discussed her experience with cancer and encouraged other women to conduct regular breast examinations. She was one of the first American women to speak publicly about the disease.

Rinehart's later career was notable for suspense novels such as *The Swimming Pool* (1952) and *The Frightened Wife* (1953). In 1954, Rinehart received a Special Edgar Award from the Mystery Writers of America. Rinehart died in New York City on 22 September 1958.

Suggested reading

J. Cohn (1980) *Improbable Fiction: The Life of Mary Roberts Rinehart* (Pittsburgh: University of Pittsburgh Press).
M.R. Rinehart (1931) *My Story* (New York: Farrar and Rinehart).

Megan Hoffman

Sallis, James (1944–)

Although best known for his crime novels featuring the enigmatic private detective Lew Griffin, one of the most daringly original fictional PIs ever created, James Sallis is a prolific author, whose work spans the genres of biography, criticism, poetry and fiction.

Early life and career

Sallis was born on 21 December 1944, in Helena, Arkansas, a quiet town on the banks of the Mississippi River. From 1962 to 1964, he attended Tulane University in New Orleans, which was also the alma mater of his elder brother, John, now an eminent philosopher. It was while at Tulane that Sallis first considered the possibility of making a living as a writer. After dropping out of Tulane, Sallis lived for a while in Iowa and then moved to London and later Paris. In London he edited the science fiction magazine *New Worlds* with Michael Moorcock. Initially, his writing output was confined to poetry and short stories, which formed the basis of his first book, *A Few Last Words*, published in 1968. Sallis continued to publish short fiction throughout the 1970s, while also editing various anthologies. A talented multi-instrumentalist, Sallis later branched out into musicology, editing several books on jazz, *Jazz Guitars: An Anthology* (1984) and *The Guitar in Jazz* (1996), while also making an occasional living as a music teacher. In addition to his creative and critical oeuvre, Sallis has built a reputation as a talented translator, rendering works by authors as diverse as Raymond Queneau, Pablo Neruda and Boris Pasternak into English. While he has devoted the bulk of his career to writing, Sallis is also a trained respiratory therapist and has worked in intensive care units across the US. On the legal issues surrounding American healthcare, Sallis expressed his anger at the Bush administration's interference with the Terri Schiavo case. He is currently based in Phoenix, Arizona, where he lives with his wife, Karyn, and teaches creative writing at Phoenix College. The variety of roles Sallis has held parallels the diversity possible within a single identity of many of his characters, including his most famous creation Lew Griffin.

The Lew Griffin series

Sallis made his first foray into crime fiction in 1992 with *The Long Legged Fly*. Set in New Orleans, the novel introduces his series protagonist, Lew Griffin, a functioning alcoholic and amateur private detective, who also, self-referentially, writes detective fiction in his spare time. Griffin's elusive identity is the enduring enigma of the series. He is variously and at times simultaneously an alcoholic, violent thug, private detective, literature instructor and novelist. The reader can come to many different plausible conclusions as to who Griffin is, which of course may be very different to the author's perception of the character. The opening novel's structure is akin to four self-contained novellas of four missing persons cases at four different points in Griffin's life – beginning with him killing a man in an oil field in 1964 and ending in 1990 when his life is almost over. Although Sallis is Caucasian, Griffin is black, and Sallis's work is often compared to African-American writers such as Walter Mosley and Chester Himes, the latter of whom Sallis wrote a biography: *Chester Himes: A Life*, in 2000. Sallis also wrote a study of Himes and several other American crime writers in *Difficult Lives: Jim Thompson, David Goodis, Chester Himes* (1993). Sallis's novels have been widely praised for their authenticity in portraying the black experience in America, and Griffin is a complex and convincingly depicted character. For several years, Sallis struggled with alcoholism and this informed his composition of Griffin's drinking problem, although he maintains he is very different from the character. As all of the novels are relating past events, there is extensive meditation on the nature of time, memory and identity. Since his inception, Griffin has featured in five more novels: *Moth* (1993), *Black Hornet* (1996), *Eye of the Cricket* (1997), *Bluebottle* (1999) and *Ghost of a Flea* (2000). In *Eye of the Cricket*, the ongoing mystery of Griffin's true self is further complicated with a surreal take on the traditional detective fiction theme of doubling: a vagrant arrives at a local hospital carrying nothing but a copy of one of Griffin's books and claiming to be the author. The action of the Griffin novels frequently hinges upon cases involving missing persons, including Griffin's own son, David. However, these cases often go unresolved and carry over from one novel to the next. Thus, the series can be read in publication sequence as one long novel, perhaps written by Griffin himself, with the last lines of one book becoming the opening lines of another that Griffin is apparently writing. Griffin has written several novels featuring a character called Lew Griffin, an inventive and abstract meta-fictional device of the novels which explores the relationship between fiction and reality. The denouement of the to-date final novel of the series, *Ghost of a Flea*, contains another twist which forces the reader to re-evaluate the meaning of the entire series. Sallis's texts refuse to be confined by narrative convention and regularly jump back and forth in their timeframe, as though events themselves exist outside of a comprehensible narrative. By side-stepping linear storytelling and moving away from neat, conclusive endings, Sallis brings a genuinely subversive and deconstructive element to the genre, focusing on the milieu of detective fiction as opposed to plotting.

Other projects

The Lew Griffin series is renowned for its high quality of writing and literary allusions, but Sallis has also written a more directly literary, avant-garde novel in *Renderings* (1995), which is about an artist reflecting on life and death. His novel *Death Will Have Your Eyes* (1997) is a post-Cold War spy thriller about a former agent of an elite corps group called out of his peaceful retirement to track down a fellow member of the corps who has gone rogue. With *Cypress Grove* (2003), Sallis introduced a new series detective known only as Turner. Turner is a former cop and ex-convict living in a remote cabin near Cripple Creek, Tennessee – a setting loosely inspired by Sallis's rural upbringing. The county sheriff enlists his help in a murder case. Both titles in the Turner series are taken from the names of country songs. In the sequel *Cripple Creek* (2006) Turner is now a deputy sheriff. As with much of Sallis's fiction, the back-story to Turner is as important, if not more, than the novel's present investigation, although ultimately Sallis's character's core identity appears to be unknowable. While his innovative approach has been praised by many critics, Sallis remains, for the most part, a cult writer whose work has yet to attain widespread readership. However, Sallis's work may be on the brink of wider commercial success as Nicholas Winding Refn has directed a film adaptation of the Sallis novel *Drive* (2005) which was released in 2011. Sallis's novel concerns an unnamed protagonist who alternates as a Hollywood stunt driver and getaway driver in armed robberies. At the time of writing, Sallis has several projects in various stages of development: he has written the bulk of a manuscript for a novel provisionally titled 'Bottomfeeders' about a cop killer, and he has also researched the life of Gilles de Rais, the French commander under Joan of Arc who was also a notorious paedophile and serial killer, for a potential novel.

Suggested reading

P. Duncan (1997) *The Third Degree: crime writers in conversation* (Harpenden: No Exit Press) pp. 156–73.

C. McDonald (2009) 'James Sallis' *Rogue Males: conversations and confrontations about the writing life* (Madison, WI: Bleak House) pp. 237–66.
J. Sallis (2011) *The James Sallis Web Pages* www.jamessallis.com.

Susan Massey
Steven Powell

Schuyler, George S(amuel) (1895–1977)

African-American journalist and social commentator noted for his complex and evolving political views: a radical left-winger in the 1920s and 30s, Schuyler became a far-right conservative after the Second World War, an apologist of the McCarthyite witchhunts and a trenchant critic of the Civil Rights movement. His contribution to crime fiction rests in a series of stories serialised in the *Pittsburgh Courier* and latterly published as the novel *Black Empire* in 1993.

Early life and heritage

George Samuel Schuyler claimed to have been born 25 February 1895, in Providence, Rhode Island, although in his biography of Schuyler, Oscar R. Williams suggests that, as no birth certificate exists, and as the US census of 1900 lists his birthplace as New York City, and the census of 1910 as Massachusetts, Schuyler may have been adopted – which also may explain why he was dark skinned and his parents were mixed race. Convinced the military was the best opportunity of self-advancement for black Americans, Schuyler dropped out of high school at the age of 17 to join the army. Schuyler served in the army for six years, rising to the rank of first lieutenant. His military career was somewhat haphazard: he was briefly discharged before reenlisting in 1915, and finally deserted in 1918 after an incident in which a Greek immigrant refused to shine his shoes. Schuyler stayed in San Diego before surrendering himself to the authorities after around three months in hiding. He was sentenced to five years' imprisonment but served only nine months at Castle Williams Military Prison at Governor's Island in New York. Schuyler saw and experienced racist abuse during his military career, which hardened his opposition to the Jim Crow laws. In 1921 Schuyler joined the Socialist Party of Syracuse, New York. In 1923, he began his journalistic career writing for the magazine the *Messenger*, and in 1924 he began a column for the African-American newspaper *Pittsburgh Courier* for which he would continue to write during the next 40 years.

Literary career and *Black Empire*

Schuyler's first novel *Black No More* (1931) was a science fiction fantasy in which an African-American scientist devises a process which transforms blacks into Caucasians. As more and more black people undergo this change, the racial and economic inequality in the United States becomes increasingly apparent and problematic. Schuyler followed this with *Slaves Today: A Story of Liberia* (also released in 1931) which told the story of a young Liberian couple whose lives are destroyed by the system of domestic slavery. Schuyler had visited Liberia to research the novel, and despite a favourable critical reception, it would be the last novel he wrote that would be published in his lifetime. In the early 1930s, Schuyler was a prolific writer of pulp fiction, often employing pseudonyms such as Rachel Call and Samuel I. Brooks. His output included hundreds of serialised stories, which appeared in a weekly column in the *Courier* and were usually revenge fantasies involving blacks resorting to vigilante justice against their cruel white oppressors. Serials Schuyler wrote during this period include *Devil Town: An Enthralling Story of Tropical Africa* (June–July 1933), *Golden Gods: A Story of Love, Intrigue and Adventure in African Jungles* (December 1933–February 1934), and *The Beast of Bradhurst Avenue: A Gripping Tale of Adventure in the Heart of Harlem* (March–May 1934). *The Ethiopian Murder Mystery* and *Revolt in Ethiopia* concerned black Americans becoming embroiled in the Ethiopian struggle against the invasion by fascist Italy in 1935 and were latterly published in the collection *Ethiopian Stories* (1995). However, Schuyler's most acclaimed contribution to crime fiction is regarded as the 1936–38 serials *The Black Internationale* and *Black Empire*, both published posthumously as the novel *Black Empire* in 1993. The plot of *Black Empire* is thin and haphazard and takes second place to the elaborate action scenes. In the afterword to the 1993 republication of *Black Empire*, the editors Robert A. Hill and R. Kent Rasmussen claim Schuyler most likely invented the plot with each episode and had not planned the narrative in advance. Carl Slater, a black journalist for the fictitious newspaper the *Harlem Blade*, witnesses the murder of a white woman by the debonair Dr Belsidus. Forced to choose between death at the hands of Belsidus or joining Belsidus' mysterious organisation, the Black Internationale, Slater chooses the latter and soon becomes part of Belsidus' fiendish, ingenious scheme to achieve pan-Africanism and subjugate the white colonial powers to a new black superpower. Slater finds himself in many death-defying scenarios, facing cannibals, armies of plague-carrying rats, bizarre religions, spies and weapons of mass destruction. Schuyler was skilled at interweaving political ideas with different literary styles. The cunning and enigmatic Dr Belsidus is reminiscent of Sax Rohmer's arch-villain Fu Manchu, whereas the newspaperman Slater is a character typical of the emergent hard-boiled school of crime writing. Some elements of the narrative appear prophetic in regards to the coming devastation wrought in the Second World War, but at other times *Black Empire* is a barbed satire on various black cultural movements, such as the Harlem Renaissance and the Back to Africa movement.

Later life and family tragedy

Schuyler's political and social views moved further to the right with each passing year. He defended the anti-communist witchhunts of Senator Joseph McCarthy, resigning from the anti-Communist American Committee for Cultural Freedom as he felt too many of its members were critical of McCarthy. Schuyler campaigned for Republican candidate Senator Barry Goldwater in the 1964 presidential election and made many personal attacks on Martin Luther King Jr and the Southern Christian Leadership Conference's tactics of civil disobedience in the Civil Rights Movement. His final column for the *Courier* appeared in 1966 after he was finally forced out when his unabated criticisms of King became too problematic for the newspaper. By this time his work was already predominantly featured in conservative publications, such as a syndicated column for the North American Newspaper Alliance. He became a member of the ultra-conservative John Birch Society in 1965. His memoir *Black and Conservative* was released in 1966. Schuyler married Josephine Lewis Codgell in 1928, a white Texan heiress, and the union produced a daughter, Phillipa Schuyler (b. 1931), who became a music prodigy and highly acclaimed pianist. Phillippa Schuyler died in a helicopter crash during a tour of Vietnam in 1967. Overcome with grief, Josephine Codgell committed suicide in 1969. George S. Schuyler died at the age of 82 on 31 August 1977, while in hospital in New York.

Suggested reading

O.R. Williams (1967) *George S. Schuyler: Portrait of a Black Conservative* (Knoxville: University of Tennessee Press).

G. Schuyler (1966) *Black and Conservative: the autobiography of George Schuyler* (New Rochelle, NY: Arlington House).

Steven Powell

Shore, Viola Brothers (1890–1970)

Viola Brothers Shore is best known for writing screenplays such as *Blond Cheat* (1938) and *Breakfast for Two* (1937), but she also produced two well-regarded crime novels, *The Beauty-Mask Murder* (1930) and *Murder on the Glass Floor* (1933). Both feature Gwynn Leith, a capable woman amateur detective, and her husband, Colin Keats, who acts as Leith's sidekick. In addition to writing crime fiction and screenplays, Shore worked as a free-lance journalist and wrote short stories, plays, titles for silent films and a biography, *Stage Struck John Golden* (1930).

Shore was born in New York City to Dr Abram Brothers and Minnie Brothers (nee Epstein). She was educated first in public schools and then at Normal College in New York City. Shore left school at 16 hoping to become a violinist but was unsuccessful and instead attended business school. She married engineer William Shore in 1912 and they started an electrical contracting business. Shore's only child, Wilma, was born in 1913. Shore divorced William in 1926 and married Henry Braxton in 1931. Shore was building a career as a screenwriter, and she and Braxton moved to Hollywood only to divorce in 1933.

Shore's experience with writing for the theatre and screen served her well when she turned her hand to crime fiction, as her two novels and short stories are carried by their engaging dialogue. One of her best short stories was 'The Mackenzie Case' (1934), which again featured Leith and was repub-lished in *101 Years' Entertainment: The Great Detective Stories 1841–1941* (1941), edited by Ellery Queen. Shore's Gwynn Leith and Colin Keats stories signifi-cantly play with the conventions of the genre by placing a young, attractive married woman in the 'great detective' role traditionally assigned to a male character and casting the sleuth's husband as her unenlightened sidekick and chronicler of her exploits. Keats is even referred to as Leith's 'Watson'. Shore's enjoyment in rethinking the crime genre's gender stereotypes is also evident in a Sherlock Holmes pastiche written for *Ellery Queen's Mystery Magazine* called 'A Case of Facsimile' (1948) in which 'Shirley Holmes' and 'Jean Watson' solve a case with 'Samantha Spade', 'Regina Fortune', 'Nerissa

Wolfe' and 'Elsie Queen' – all feminised versions of well-known detective characters.

Shore did not achieve long-term success in Hollywood. While working as a screenwriter, she had become active in the League of American Writers, an anti-fascist organisation closely associated with the Communist Party. She was also the membership director of the Sacco-Vanzetti Club of the Communist Political Association. Due to her involvement in the Communist Party, Shore was investigated by the House Un-American Activities Committee and was subsequently blacklisted. In 1939, Shore married union activist Haskoll Gleichman; they divorced in 1945. Shore moved back to New York City in 1954 and began to teach writing at New York University. She died in New York City on 27 March 1970.

Suggested reading

Anon (1970) 'Viola Shore Wrote Stories and Movies' *The New York Times*, 31 March 1970, p. 41.

F.D. Bzowski (1992) *American Women Playwrights, 1900–1930: A Checklist* (Westport, CT; London: Greenwood Press).

B. O'Sullivan (1997) 'Shore, Viola Brothers, 1890–1970' *Jewish Women in America: An Historical Encyclopedia*, Vol. 2: M-Z. P. E. Hyman and D. Dash Moore, eds. (New York: Routledge).

Megan Hoffman

Slim, Iceberg (1918–92)

Iceberg Slim, born Robert Lee Maupin and also known as Robert Beck, was an African-American author of fiction and non-fiction works on the life of street hustlers, prostitutes and pimps.

Born in Chicago, he spent his childhood moving around Illinois with his mother after they were abandoned by his father. Despite moving from one deprived neighbourhood to the next, and their lack of prospects, his mother worked hard to support them both. Slim briefly attended the Tuskegee Institute in the 1930s at the same time as Ralph Ellison (whose time there was fictionalised in his novel *Invisible Man* (1952)), although the two were not acquainted. Slim reportedly had an IQ of 175, which was measured during one of his stints in prison.

Career as a pimp

In his late teenage years he moved to Chicago's South Side where, fascinated by the underworld culture, he turned to hustling and pimping. He adopted the name Iceberg Slim as a reference to the cool and emotionless attitude necessary to make it as a successful street pimp. In his memoir, the origin of the name is specifically attributed to an incident where he supposedly took a bullet through his hat without flinching.

Slim served a number of stretches of varying length in prison, including time at the notoriously harsh Leavenworth prison. During his penultimate 'bit' he managed to escape, and returned to pimping for several years as a fugitive before being recaptured. It was during this final stint in prison, the majority of which was spent in solitary confinement, that Slim decided to give up pimping, become a law-abiding citizen and start a family.

After he left a life of crime, he dropped the 'Iceberg' moniker and wished to be known as Robert Beck (although he retained Iceberg Slim as his pen name). In the early 1960s, a time that also saw the death of his beloved mother, he met and started a family with Betty Shue, who took the name

Betty Mae Beck as his common law wife, although in his memoir he refers to his wife as Catherine.

Pimp

Slim's best known and most influential book is *Pimp: The Story of My Life* (1967), a memoir of his life growing up in and around Chicago and his rise through the city's underworld as a successful pimp from the 1930s to the 1960s. The book covers his life from birth to his mid-40s, when he underwent the change of heart about his profession during his final gruelling term in solitary confinement.

Pimp, like all of Slim's work, is a brutally uncompromising portrait of an underworld society where violence and misogyny are commonplace, and its relationship to the more mainstream African-American literature of the early and mid-twentieth century is an interesting one. As a ghetto narrative it provides a potent contrast to the more ostensibly 'literary' undertakings of Richard Wright, James Baldwin and Ralph Ellison. However, on closer inspection, Slim's technique is actually surprisingly close to some of the more critically established African-American novelists. Despite the relentless violence and horror of the subject matter, Slim's voice is allusive and often even poetic, with skilful use of simile and an effortless incorporation of street slang (Slim incorporated a glossary into some editions of the book). This lyrical tone, coupled with a thriller-style narrative pace, helps propel the reader through relentless scenes of violence and misery that may otherwise prove too overwhelming in their intensity. Slim's writing possessed a keen, visceral sense of environment, and draws continuous attention to the differences in texture and even odour between the life of the street hustler and the successful pimp.

Pimp also uses musical motifs for historical and emotional context. While Ralph Ellison uses jazz as both scene and structure for the narrative of *Invisible Man*, Slim frequently employs the slow, mournful blues of Billie Holiday – even the notorious suicide ballad 'Gloomy Sunday' is present here. This undertone of sadness and despair actually underpins the narrative more strongly than a cursory reading would suggest. Slim's childhood is represented in the book as a horrifying cycle of sexual and physical abuse (the former beginning at the age of three) and the manner in which the narrative is written – as a cautionary tale from the perspective of the older family man – suggests that the life of a pimp is a lonely one and should be avoided by young men with similarly deprived upbringings.

Slim's work does not shy away from the racial and economic hierarchies of the time. While not patterned explicitly as a socially conscious journey in the same way as Wright's or Ellison's fictional accounts, the narrative of *Pimp* still finds time for digressions on the American economy and the racial history of the country. On one occasion Sweet Jones, Slim's powerful pimp mentor, tells his protégé how the wartime economy will affect prostitution in the US. Sweet later digresses about the history of African-American pimping, a trade he believes has its roots in the immediate aftermath of slavery and the realisation among freed slaves that old hierarchies were still in existence.

Pimp was an extraordinary critical and commercial success. Within five years of release it had sold around two million copies, making Slim one of the most successful and widely read African-American authors in the US (ultimately over six million copies of his books were sold during his lifetime). In a 1973 interview with *The Washington Post*, when questioned about his motivations to write he stated that 'most of all I should like to prove to the world, to dispel the myth that street niggers are devoid of intellect. You know that's a myth. They think we are devoid of wit' (West, 1973).

Later writing career and influence

After the success of *Pimp*, Slim continued to publish works of fiction and non-fiction. His best known novels are *Trick Baby* (1967) and *Long White Con* (1977), two hard-boiled crime stories featuring the character of White Folks, a light-skinned black man, and detailing his hustling against the backdrop of Chicago's South Side. In 1973 a film adaptation of *Trick Baby* was released in cinemas. After the success of *The Godfather* (1972) *Pimp* was optioned for a screen adaptation, but the material was ultimately decided to be too contentious (rumours persist of an imminent adaptation). Other novels – *Mama Black Widow* (1969), *Death Wish: A Story of the Mafia* (1977), *Doom Fox* (published posthumously in 1998) – retained the focus on street life and gang warfare. A collection of personal recollections, *The Naked Soul of Iceberg Slim*, was also released in 1971. In 1976, he released a record called *Reflections*, featuring spoken-word stories by Slim set to music.

In the 1970s, Iceberg Slim's position as a representative of the street hustling and pimping cultures brought him into conflict with militant movements like the Black Panthers, though he was hugely influential on a generation of African-American artists, not only writers such as Donald Goines but also musicians, with rappers Ice-T and Ice Cube stating their admiration for his work. Ice-T wrote an introduction to later editions of *Pimp*. Slim's influence is also evident in the Blaxploitation cinema genre that rose to prominence in the 1970s, with its tales of street life, drugs and gangsters, these films in turn also influencing mainstream television with characters like *Starsky and Hutch's* Huggy Bear, played by Antonio Fargas, a veteran of Blaxploitation cinema. Latterly, Blaxploitation influenced the work of Quentin Tarantino, who brought the pimp and gangster style and motifs of Slim's work to a new audience in films such as *Pulp Fiction* (1994) and particularly *Jackie Brown* (1997).

Robert Beck died on 28 April 1992 of complications arising from diabetes.

Suggested reading

I. Slim (1996) *Pimp: The Story Of My Life* (London: Canongate).
W.L. Van Deburg (1997) *Black Camelot: African-American Culture Heroes in Their Times, 1960–1980* (Chicago: University of Chicago Press).

David Hering

Spillane, Mickey (1918–2006)

One of the most important post-war crime writers of the hard-boiled style, Mickey Spillane achieved unprecedented commercial success with the creation of his signature private detective Mike Hammer. Yet, Spillane was also the most critically reviled crime writer of his generation as a consequence of the hyperbolic misogyny and sadistically violent tendencies of the Hammer character. Spillane places Hammer in a much more uncompromisingly brutal society than most private detectives are forced to inhabit. Perhaps this is because, through Spillane's use of first-person narrative, Hammer appears more self-righteous than his predecessors, and unlike some of them, Hammer is not lacking in a system of moral justification, however flawed. The author Max Allan Collins has described Spillane's hero as compelled by morality: 'Hammer is a moral man who chooses (as he sees it) a necessary amoral route' (Collins, 1984, p. 14).

Early life and the Hammer novels

Born in Brooklyn, New York, on 9 March 1918, Spillane was the only child of John, an Irish-American bartender from a Catholic background, and Anne, a Protestant. Spillane was raised with no particular religious background, but his parents' differing heritage led him to be baptised Frank Michael Spillane in a Catholic church and Frank Morrison Spillane in a Protestant church. Raised in Elizabeth, New Jersey, Spillane worked a variety of jobs as a young man. He received training at Kansas State Teachers College, worked as a salesman at the department store Gimbel's Basement and began writing short stories for pulp magazines under a variety of pseudonyms, including Frank Morrison. Spillane enlisted in the Army Air Corps during the Second World War and spent most of his military service as a pilot instructor in Greenwood, Mississippi. Spillane also claimed to have worked with federal agents in helping to break up a narcotics ring. After the war, Spillane conceived a comic strip series character: private detective Mike Danger. The comic strip never came to fruition, but Danger was a clear literary precursor to Spillane's most famous creation, Mike Hammer. Spillane's first novel *I, the Jury* (1947) took him about a fortnight to write (the exact number of days differs according to the source) and was released to only moderate success in the hardcover edition but immediate commercial success in the paperback edition. Spillane is said to have written the novel because he needed $1,000 to buy materials to build a house. The novel hinged on a rather conventional plot for the crime genre: Mike Hammer sets out to avenge the murder of a friend and fellow war veteran. For Hammer, there are no ethical limitations on his quest, and he feels fully justified in embarking on a course of violent vigilante retribution. As the title suggests, Hammer is self-appointed judge, jury and executioner. Following *I, the Jury*, Spillane wrote six more Hammer novels between 1947 and 1953: *My Gun is Quick* (1950), *Vengeance is Mine!* (1950), *The Big Kill* (1951), *The Long Wait* (1951), *One Lonely Night* (1951) and *Kiss Me, Deadly* (1952). Spillane's frequent use of personal pronouns in novel titles alludes to Hammer's individuality, self-justification and harsh enforcement of simple moral rules. As his name implies, Hammer's enactment of justice is swift, blunt and lacking in subtlety. Spillane's novels often featured plot twists that reveal the guilty party is a woman, often a woman who Hammer has been romantically involved with. Hammer is just as ruthless with ex-lovers and other females as he is with their male counterparts. *I, the Jury* famously ends with Hammer's dying fiancée, and as it happens a murderess, asking him how he could be so ruthless after he has shot her. Hammer's response forms the last sentence of the novel: 'It was easy' (Spillane, 1947, p. 174). Spillane was especially skilled at withholding vital plot details until the very last sentence or even the last word of the novel. *Vengeance is Mine!* is a strong example of this technique with the novel ending with a startling twist. The critical reaction to Hammer's casual misogyny was extremely negative and only exacerbated by his immense popularity. The psychiatrist Dr Fredric Wertham accused Spillane of fomenting teenage delinquency, an ironic criticism as the novels essentially propagate a socially conservative philosophy. Many of Spillane's readers were war veterans who saw Hammer as symbolic of their values in an age of increasing moral relativism. The Hammer character was not beyond introspection and doubt: *One Lonely Night* features an imaginary conversation which takes place in Hammer's mind between himself and a liberal-minded judge who had previously chastised him in court, with the detective forced to justify his actions. The depiction of violence in the Hammer novels is undeniably graphic. In *One Lonely Night,* Hammer is relentless in his pursuit of undercover communist agents and traitors in respectable American society: he singlehandedly kills dozens of them with a machine gun in one scene. Some of Spillane's views were endorsed by the novelist and founder of the philosophy of objectivism Ayn Rand. Rand admired Spillane for his anti-communism and Spillane regarded *Atlas Shrugged* as one of his favourite novels. Lee Horsley argues that Hammer acts out of 'McCarthyite paranoia', although the main villain of *One Lonely Knight* is a thinly disguised version of Senator Joseph McCarthy (Horsley, 2005, p. 90).

Hammer's use of violence is sadistic and motivated by moral disgust: in *Kiss Me, Deadly*, he kills a suspect who appears to be a beautiful woman but it transpires that she possesses a physically deformed and hideously ugly body which mirrors her moral character. Although Hammer is unhesitant about using violence against women when he feels they are deserving of rough justice, every instance scars his conscience, and there are several references to him being haunted by the times he has killed a woman. It was a shock to Spillane's fans when he abruptly stopped writing Hammer novels after leaving the character presumably dying in a burning building at the end of *Kiss Me, Deadly*. It has been suggested that Spillane's 1951 conversion to the Jehovah's Witnesses persuaded him to stop writing violent tales. It would be nine years before Spillane wrote another Mike Hammer novel, but he would not spend those years idly. In the interim he travelled with a circus act where he worked as a trampoline artist and was shot out of a cannon, and he was an enthusiastic practitioner of stock car racing, fencing, flying and diving. Literary works produced during this period include the adventure novel *The Deep* (1961), the title of which Peter Benchley would borrow with Spillane's permission for one of his own novels. Mike Hammer would return in *The Girl Hunters* (1962) to popular acclaim. *The Girl Hunters* would begin a new trend in Hammer novels: the violence was toned down and Spillane's writing became more polished. However, due to these changes Spillane's writing began to lose the original seven Hammer novels' sense of visceral excitement. The appearance of Hammer novels would become increasingly sporadic, with Hammer literally coming out of a coma for the later novel *Black Alley* (1996). Spillane kept the Hammer series chronologically consistent, and Hammer grows increasingly elderly, and the stories more ludicrous, as a result. Several Hammer novels have been published posthumously. Spillane's personal friend and leading Spillane scholar Max Allan Collins has worked towards completing Spillane's unfinished manuscripts. *The Goliath Bone* (2008) featured Hammer pitted against Islamic terrorists in post 9/11 New York. Spillane was motivated to resurrect Hammer as a viable hero in the War on Terrorism, but the novel is littered with humorous references to Hammer's advanced age (he would be at least in his eighties), and the story is too implausible as a result. However, *The Goliath Bone* was soon followed by *The Big Bang* (2010), *Kiss Her Goodbye* (2011) and *Lady, Go Die!* (2012). Of the Hammer novels that were adapted for the screen, Robert Aldrich's 1955 adaptation of *Kiss Me, Deadly* is the only Mike Hammer film to receive high critical acclaim. Screenwriter A.I. Bezzerides regarded Spillane's novel with contempt and was not faithful to the material, much to Spillane's displeasure, adding an apocalyptic climax which symbolised the coming end of the film noir era. Stacy Keach played

Mike Hammer in two successful made–for-television films and a subsequent series.

Mike Hammer as private-eye

The back-story of Mike Hammer is, like the basic formula of each Hammer novel, slight and unchanging. Hammer is a former serviceman who served in the Pacific campaign during the Second World War and saw frequent combat. It is possible that the horrors of armed conflict had desensitised Hammer to violence, but Hammer seems to have enjoyed his wartime experiences and had difficulty readjusting to society. Hammer is also an ex-cop with the New York Police Department, and although his reasons for leaving are never made clear, his unorthodox investigation methods are a likely cause. His most loyal friend is his police contact Pat Chambers, who informally calls upon Hammer's expertise in difficult cases. Chambers is a reserved character who does not always approve of Hammer's methods but appreciates the results. Hammer also has an enemy in the unnamed District Attorney who will do anything to undermine him. In each novel, Hammer depends upon his loyal and beautiful secretary Velda. Velda is hopelessly in love with Hammer, but although he is aware of this, he never reciprocates the emotion in the first seven novels and has frequent affairs with beautiful women. Hammer's feelings for Velda grow in later books as she displays increasing resourcefulness and bravery in assisting him in his investigations. They finally consummate their relationship in *The Snake* (1964) and then have a very long engagement, not marrying until *The Goliath Bone* in 2008. Each Hammer novel is narrated by the private detective in the first-person, and as a consequence, very little is known about Hammer's physical appearance. Although he considers himself to be ugly, he is certainly physically imposing and is able to seduce beautiful women with apparent ease. In many ways Mike Hammer seems to be a hyperbolic endpoint to the hard-boiled private eye, it seems appropriate then that Spillane's largest single inspiration in creating Hammer was Carroll John Daly's violent PI Race Williams, one of the very first hard-boiled detectives who made his debut in a *Black Mask* story in 1923.

Disappointed with previous film adaptations of the Hammer novels – the outrageous depictions of violence and colourful, stereotypical characterisations did not transfer well to the moody, existentialist tone of film noir – Spillane produced and starred as Mike Hammer in the 1963 adaptation of *The Girl Hunters*. Spillane also posed as Hammer on the cover of paperback editions of the novels and played a composite of himself and Mike Hammer in a long-running and humorous series of commercials for Miller Lite Beer. In his superlative study of the author *One Lonely Knight: Mickey Spillane's Mike Hammer* (1984), Collins argues that Spillane embraced Hammer as his literary alter-ego, despite the clear differences in their character, as a response to the

314 Spillane, Mickey (1918–2006)

overwhelmingly negative critical reaction to the novels. Whatever effect the criticism had on Spillane, he eschewed literary pretensions, famously stating, 'I'm a commercial writer, not an "author"' (Johnston, 1952, p. 86). Indeed, Spillane's appearances as Hammer were an effective publicity device in that he developed an affable, quasi-celebrity persona which mitigated much of the critical opprobrium previously directed at him.

Personal life and other projects

In the mid-60s, Spillane created another series character, Tiger Mann, who was the hero in four novels: *Day of the Guns* (1964), *Bloody Sunrise* (1965), *The Death Dealers* (1965) and *The By-Pass Control* (1966). Spillane was inspired by the success of Ian Fleming's James Bond series to create Tiger Mann, but unlike Bond, Mann works for an independent right-wing organisation based in New York where all the novels are set. The Tiger Mann series had its admirers, but as with so much of Spillane's work, the outright lack of plausibility undermined the novel's ability to be enjoyed as fantasy. Spillane made another surprising departure from the private detective genre with the young adult novel, *The Day the Sea Rolled Back,* published in 1979. It won a Junior Literary Guild Award and was followed by *The Ship That Never Was* (1982). Spillane married Mary Ann Pearce in 1945 and they had four children. The couple were divorced in 1962. Spillane wed the actress Sherri (Selma) Malinou in 1965, and they enjoyed a rather high celebrity profile. Ms Malinou would appear naked on the cover of the novels *The Erection Set* (1972) and *The Last Cop Out* (1973), the former of which was Spillane's most ambitious novel, a sprawling attempt at a Harold Robbins-style melodrama and a rare excursion into third-person narrative. *The Erection Set* was the first American novel to feature nudity on the dust jacket of a hardcover edition. Spillane was separated from his wife for much of the latter part of their marriage, during which he pursued a quiet life in the small town of Murrell's Inlet, South Carolina. Murrell's Inlet, which was nearly destroyed in Hurricane Hugo in 1989, would be his home for the rest of his life. In 1983, Spillane divorced his second wife and later that year married Jane Johnson, a former beauty queen turned fitness teacher. Spillane died at the age of 88 in 2006.

Suggested reading

J.K. Van Dover (1984) *Murder in the Millions: Erle Stanley Gardener, Mickey Spillane, Ian Fleming* (New York, Ungar).

M.A. Collins and J.L. Traylor (1984) *One Lonely Knight: Mickey Spillane's Mike Hammer* (Bowling Green: Bowling Green University Popular Press).

Steven Powell

Stout, Rex (1886–1975)

Rex Todhunter Stout was born 1 December 1886, in Noblesville, Indiana, the sixth child of nine born to a Quaker family. Soon after his birth, the parents, John Wallace Stout and Lucetta Elizabeth Todhunter Stout, moved the family to Kansas. His father was a teacher and encouraged him to read, especially the Bible which, according to his family, he had read twice from cover to cover by the age of four. Stout was a gifted student: at 13 he was the spelling bee champion of the State of Kansas. He attended the Topeka High School in Kansas, and then the University of Kansas, Lawrence.

An active life

Between 1906 and 1908, Stout served in the US Navy as Yeoman on President Theodore Roosevelt's official yacht, the U.S.S. Mayflower. Stout travelled and took on many different jobs, in six different states, while at the same time writing poems and stories for various magazines. Between 1916 and 1927 he worked as an office boy, store clerk, bookkeeper and hotel manager.

In 1916, along with one of his brothers, he invented a school banking system. The system was adopted in 400 cities across the US, and Stout became rich enough to travel around Europe. However, he lost the money he had made with his school banking system in the Great Depression. He married Fay Kennedy in 1916, but they divorced in 1932, and he married Pola Weinbach Hoffman later that year. Pola was born in Stry, Poland, and studied fabric design in Vienna. The marriage lasted until Stout's death, and they had two daughters together.

Stout's literary career began when he started writing romance, detective and adventure stories for pulp magazines such as *All-Story Magazine* and *All-Story Weekly*. In 1927, he became a full-time writer. While staying in Paris in 1929, he wrote his debut novel *How Like A God*. Although practically forgotten today, this bizarre psychological tale gives some indication of Stout's nascent literary talent as he deftly mixes the main narrative with a seemingly unrelated short story and switches between third and second

315

person narration. He would then write a political thriller, *The President Vanishes* (1934), which was published anonymously as a method to raise speculation and interest in the book. It was adapted into film the same year, directed by William Wellman, and Stout considered the film superior to his own work.

Nero Wolfe and Archie Goodwin

After his return to the US, Stout, an admirer of Arthur Conan Doyle's Sherlock Holmes stories, created the characters of Nero Wolfe and Archie Goodwin, who were to be the protagonists of 46 novels and many short stories. In 1934, *Fer-de-lance*, their first adventure, was published.

Nero Wolfe is an obese private investigator who relies on his assistant Archie Goodwin, a charming womaniser, to do all the legwork, even picking up the phone. Wolfe is so overweight that he can hardly cross his legs and needs especially strong chairs to support him. He hardly ever leaves home, but solves all the mysteries brought to him by his clients by letting Goodwin investigate. When all the elements he needs are collected, he proffers the solution. His main passion is his orchid garden. He has a greenhouse on the roof of his building and maintains strict hours for taking care of his flowers. Wolfe lives in a luxurious brownstone residence on West 35th Street, Manhattan. He keeps a fairly regular schedule and is a man of habit. The characters do not age and Stout, according to his biographer John McAleer, stated Wolfe was 56. At first, Wolfe was born in Montenegro, but due to protests from *The American Magazine*, his place of birth was latterly referenced as the US. Stout himself had never been to Montenegro but had enjoyed reading Louis Adamic's book *The Native's Return*. The novels *Over My Dead Body* (1940) and *The Black Mountain* (1954) explore Wolfe's Montenegrin heritage. In the latter novel Wolfe returns to his native country to investigate the murder of a friend. Wolfe is interested in fine cuisine, which he enjoys in copious amounts. He also enjoys good wine and brandy. Unlike Goodwin, Wolfe does not care much for the company of women, is reticent when it comes to physical contact with anyone and dislikes shaking hands. Wolfe is misanthropic, lazy and temperamental. He claims to take on cases strictly for financial reasons. He conducts his interviews at home, and sends Goodwin out when he needs information brought to him.

Archie Goodwin is the narrator of the stories. He was born in Ohio. Humorous and charming, Goodwin lives at the same residence as Wolfe and is his friend despite the sharp contrasts in their personalities. Unlike other detective fiction sidekicks, Goodwin is in some regards the main protagonist of the stories as he is also a detective in his own right: his verbatim memory, his bravery and his quick-thinking make him more than an admiring second. Goodwin possesses most of the traits of a typical hard-boiled detective. He has a sarcastic wit and he loves the company of beautiful women;

however, he deviates from the stereotype as his drink of choice is milk. The Nero Wolfe novels are noted for their humour, their quirky but believable characters and their clever storylines. Aside from Wolfe and Goodwin there are a regular cast of enduring supporting characters including Fritz Brenner, an exceptional Swiss cook who Wolfe keeps very busy, Theodore Hortsmann who looks after Wolfe's beloved orchids and Saul Panzer, a private detective who assists in the investigations.

Until 1966, Rex Stout regularly wrote at least one Nero Wolfe story a year, with the exception of the war years 1941–45. His prolific output slowed down after 1966, but Stout continued writing until his death. His last novel, *A Family Affair,* came out a few weeks before his death in 1975, and features a rare downbeat ending. Stout was a Liberal patriot, and the then unravelling Watergate scandal imbued the novel with a prevailing sense of melancholia.

During the Second World War, he wrote less fiction and joined the Fight for Freedom organisation to write propaganda. He hosted three radio shows every week and, as chairman of the Writers' War Board, coordinated American writers in the war effort. In 1944 Stout became the first chair of the Society for the Prevention of World War III, which lobbied for very strict peace conditions for Germany. However, Stout's anti-German rhetoric began to look dated after the war, with the US focusing more on combating the spread of communism.

After the war, apart from writing detective fiction, he owned a farm at High Meadows in Brewster, New York State. He also served as President of the Authors Guild and of the Mystery Writers of America. He was a close friend of P.G. Wodehouse, and Wodehouse wrote the foreword to John McAleer's Edgar-winning 1977 biography of Stout.

During the McCarthy era, Stout, who was an active liberal, ignored a subpoena from the House of Un-American Activities Committee. Stout presented himself as a strict anti-communist in his opinions regarding the Vietnam War and the Soviet Union. Stout's anti-communism can be readily discerned in the Nero Wolfe mystery *The Second Confession* (1949). However, Stout was also critical of J. Edgar Hoover, writing a thinly veiled critique of his leadership of the FBI in the Wolfe mystery *The Doorbell Rang* (1965). Stout created several other memorable private detectives. Tecumseh Fox, a dapper detective living on a farm in New York State, appeared in three novels – *Double for Death* (1939), *Bad for Business* (1940) and *The Broken Vase* (1941) – the first of which Stout considered one of the finest detective stories he ever wrote. The stand-alone novel *Alphabet Hicks* (1941, reissued as *The Sound of Murder* in 1965) features disgraced lawyer turned taxi driver and amateur private eye Alfred 'Alphabet' Hicks. In his 1937 novel *Hand in Glove*, Stout invented the female private investigator, Theolinda 'Dol' Bonner, who was later to reappear in several Wolfe stories. Bonner was one of the first female private detectives, and through her creation

Stout paved the way for the numerous contemporary female investigators in crime fiction.

In 1959, Stout was presented with the Mystery Writers of America Grand Master Award. After Stout's death, the Nero Wolfe series was continued in seven novels written by Robert Goldsborough and published between 1986 and 1994. There have been many radio, television and cinema adaptations of the Wolfe series of varying quality and limited success. The recent *A Nero Wolfe Mystery* (2001–02) starring Maury Chaykin as Wolfe and Timothy Hutton as Archie Goodwin garnered critical acclaim and high ratings.

Suggested reading

W.S. Baring Gould (1969) *Nero Wolfe of West Thirty-Fifth Street: The Life and Times of America's Largest Detective* (New York: Viking).

J.J. McAleer (1979) *Rex Stout: A Biography* (Boston: Little, Brown).

J.K. Van Dover (1991) *Three At Wolfe's Door* (New York: Bantham, 1995).

Delphine Cingal

Thompson, Jim (1906–77)

Author of more than 30 novels, a large number of short stories and newspaper articles, as well as Hollywood and television scripts, James Myers 'Jim' Thompson is best known for his pulp novels featuring criminal psychopaths. Although he enjoyed some success during his lifetime, at the time of his death none of his works were in print in the United States. However, Thompson's reputation has steadily increased in recent years. His best known novels, including *The Killer Inside Me* (1952), *Savage Night* (1953), *A Hell of a Woman* (1954), *After Dark, My Sweet* (1955), *The Grifters* (1963) and *Pop. 1280* (1964) are now celebrated as masterpieces of the noir genre.

The re-evaluation of Thompson's work resulted, in the 1990s, in a number of his novels being adapted as films: *A Swell Looking Babe* (1954) filmed as *Hit Me* in 1996; *After Dark, My Sweet* filmed in 1990 *The Kill-Off* (1957, filmed in 1989); *The Getaway* (1959, filmed twice, 1972 and 1994) and, most successfully, *The Grifters* directed by Stephen Frears and released in 1990 which enjoyed both popular and critical acclaim. Earlier adaptations of his work had been less successful with Hollywood apparently unable to entirely embrace Thompson's bleak vision.

Although Thompson's early life was undoubtedly eventful, his accounts of his childhood and youth added drama for effect: he liked to explain that he was born in Anadarko, Oklahoma, in the town jailhouse – without always adding that his father was the sheriff and the family lived on the premises. Equally, although Thompson was clearly a precocious writing talent, the story that he had his first fiction published when he was only 14 – a claim which, if he did not originate, he certainly did not discourage – appears to be without foundation. His father, known as 'Big Jim', certainly did have a colourful life: as town sheriff he gained a reputation for decisive and dangerous actions to combat crime, but he was also suspected of embezzlement and eventually had to flee to Mexico to escape prosecution. He later suffered a mental breakdown and was institutionalized for many years prior to his death.

Thompson appears to have been obsessed with his father's character – his intellectual ability, which was far superior to those around him, the demands of his work, his cavalier risk-taking and careless parenting – and the numerous adventures and escapades of his varied life. The shadow of 'Big Jim' can be found in Thompson's portrayal of erratic, dangerous and criminally insane men who, perhaps feeling themselves to be superior to others, have no concern for, or even concept of, the emotions and lives of their victims.

Early years

Thompson began writing as a teenager and, whilst attending college during the day, spent about two years in the early 1920s in a low-paid job as a hotel bellboy in Fort Worth, Texas. He soon learned how to supplement his income through criminal means by catering to the needs of the clientele – procuring alcohol, prostitutes and drugs for those prepared to pay. His experiences from this period, when he became familiar with the local gangsters and their establishments, provided material for his later novels. A further legacy of these years was the beginning of his life-long dependency on alcohol: he claimed that constant drinking enabled him to stay awake through the night shift after his day in college. He also found that alcohol made him more confident and fluent in dealing with his older, and sometimes dangerous, associates. However his lifestyle soon took its toll and, aged 19, he was admitted to hospital with 'nervous exhaustion' and tuberculosis.

In the years following his release from hospital (1926), Thompson tried a number of ventures. Despite the fact that his father had apparently appropriated most of his savings whilst Thompson was hospitalised, they set up an unsuccessful independent oil company together, and Thompson also tried to earn a living from his writing. The Great Depression was approaching, however, and finding work was difficult – the next few years saw Thompson leading an itinerant life with a succession of poorly paid casual jobs.

In 1931 Thompson married Alberta Hesse and in the next few years became involved in the New Deal-funded Oklahoma Federal Writers' Project. Thompson later published some freelance stories and contracted newspaper articles. In the mid-30s, like many others in the Writers' Project, he became a member of the Communist Party. During this time, he also had a number of short stories published, mainly in true crime magazines. His unsettled lifestyle meant that he had lived in a number of small towns in Oklahoma, Texas and Nebraska and had, on occasions, been arrested and had short periods of imprisonment, mainly for drunkenness and vagrancy. All these experiences became material for the major works of hard-boiled noir, which he began in the early 1940s. Like other members of the Writers' Project, he relocated to California hoping to find work in the thriving film industry.

The 1940s

Although Thompson initially failed to find work in Hollywood, he did gain regular employment in the aircraft industry. His communist associations, however, resulted in an investigation by the FBI which threatened his new-found stability. In the early 1940s he published his first novels, *Now And On Earth* (1942), set in an airplane manufacturing plant during World War II and *Heed The Thunder* (1946), a western following the fortunes of the fictitious Fargo clan in early twentieth-century Nebraska. Both novels, although they received some good reviews, sold few copies. Thompson was also now suffering major health problems as a result of his alcoholism. In 1946, after being repeatedly hospitalised with alcohol-related problems, he suffered his second major physical and mental collapse. His drinking also exacerbated his financial problems. By the end of the 1940s, his health had improved and he had regular employment as a reporter. His first financially successful novel, *Nothing More Than Murder* was published in 1949.

The 1950s and the major works

Thompson's most prolific period as a writer was the early 50s. Noting that crime thrillers brought a good financial return, he produced 12 in under three years. The first of these, and probably his best known work, *The Killer Inside Me*, engaged with the themes and landscape which he would return to throughout the rest of his writing career. The main protagonist, Lou Ford, appears to be merely a fairly incompetent, lazy, small-town sheriff with a deadpan sense of humour. In reality he is an extremely intelligent psychopath who describes his desire to kill as *the sickness*. The world of seedy, incestuous small towns where the law is powerful, but justice non-existent, became the landscape of Thompson's work. In his towns everyone knows the history and secrets of everyone else and, unlike the idyllic version of pastoral America being sold by Hollywood, family life is a bleak delusion and deranged and calculating killers indistinguishable from ordinary citizens.

In addition to *The Killer Inside Me*, Thompson's creative burst of the early 1950s produced some of his other major works, notably *After Dark, My Sweet* and *Savage Night* – one of the most original and unsettling hard-boiled crime novels, which includes masculine fear and hatred of women's sexuality. Despite good sales in the paperback market, his alcoholism ensured that his financial problems persisted, and he remained plagued by ill-health. His work had been encouraged by his association with Lion Books and its sympathetic editor, Arnold Hano. But by the end of the 1950s, Lion had moved out of the noir crime market and a dejected Thompson again increased his alcohol consumption, leading to his first stroke in 1959. After his partial recovery, he continued writing, but at a slower pace, and also obtained work writing for television. In the early 1960s *The Grifters* and, particularly, *Pop.*

1280, which again featured a deceptively dull psychopathic sheriff, showed that his work remained just as powerful.

The last years

When repeated strokes left Thompson unable to write, he began refusing food. After a long and harrowing illness, he died in 1977. His last years had been more comfortable financially due to his association with television and the film industry, but he repeatedly lapsed into heavy drinking and gained a reputation for unreliability and his writings' decline in quality. He wrote the screenplays for the Stanley Kubrick film *The Killing* (1956) and *Paths of Glory* (1957). He also made a cameo appearance in the 1975 adaptation of Chandler's *Farewell, My Lovely*. His reputation was well established in France, where he had always sold well, but he was out of favour in the United States and the film adaptations of his work were creatively disappointing. It was the 1980s before the importance of his work began to be fully recognised.

Suggested reading

M.J. McCauley (1991) *Jim Thompson: Sleep with the Devil* (New York: Mysterious Press).

R. Polito (1995) *Savage Art: A Biography of Jim Thompson* (New York: Alfred A. Knopf).

J. Sallis (1993) *Difficult Lives: Jim Thompson, David Goodis, Chester Himes* (New York: Gryphon Books).

C. Waring (2010) *Cigarettes and Alcohol: The Extraordinary Life of Jim Thompson* http://crimetime.co.uk/features/jim thompson accessed 30/04/2010, date accessed 21 June 2011.

Maureen Sunderland

Tidyman, Ernest Ralph (1928–84)

Following a 25-year newspaper career, Tidyman began writing both fiction and non-fiction books in the mid-60s. He achieved instant success with *Shaft* (1970), his first novel in a series that featured tough, but cool, African-American private eye John Shaft, which spawned several film adaptations and a television series. Tidyman was also successful as a screenwriter, winning the Academy Award for Best Adapted Screenplay for his work on *The French Connection* (1971).

Tidyman was born in Cleveland, Ohio, on 1 January 1928. The son of a long-time police reporter for *The Plain Dealer*, Tidyman dropped out of school at 14 and won his own police-reporting job. After serving in the US Army (1946–48), he returned to newspapers, working as an editor at *The Plain Dealer* before moving to such dailies as the *New York Post* and finally the *New York Times*, for which he edited foreign news and served as an assistant women's editor.

His first serious attempt at novel-composition produced *Flower Power* (1968), the inauspicious tale of a teenage girl who flees her Arkansas home for San Francisco's Haight-Ashbury district, where she is quickly initiated into the world of hippies, drugs and recreational sex. Tidyman followed the novel with a non-fiction work, *The Anzio Death Trap* (1968), an account of the controversial Allied assault during the Italian campaign of the Second World War. He later wrote the true-crime books *Dummy* (1974) and *Big Bucks* (1982), and several non-series novels including *Line of Duty* (1974), set in the Cleveland Police Department.

However, it was Tidyman's *Shaft* (1970) that earned him his greatest literary acclaim. It introduced the then 28-year-old John Shaft: a Harlem-born product of foster homes, juvenile-delinquency arrests and bloody combat experiences in the Vietnam War. After returning to New York City, Shaft worked for two years with a confidential investigations agency before opening his own office in then-seedy Times Square. At six feet tall, 190 pounds, with a 'French-roast coffee' complexion, the sharp-dressing Shaft was as irresistible to women as he was lethal to the murderers, kidnappers, and mobsters who crossed him. There are seven Shaft novels, two of which inspired movies *Shaft* (1971) and *Shaft's Big Score* (1972) starring Richard Roundtree. The 1973 sequel, *Shaft in Africa*, was not based on any of Tidyman's books. While the films retained the PIs slick patter, street smarts, anger, and fierce pride in his black heritage, they expunged his less admirable traits, notably his homophobia, anti-Semitism and view of women as little more than sex-objects. A 1973–74 CBS-TV version of *Shaft*, also starring Roundtree, went still further, toning down the gumshoe's language and exchanging his black leather outfits for double-knit pants and sweater vests. Roundtree reprised his role in *Shaft* (2000), although the film focused on John Shaft's namesake nephew, an NYPD detective turned private eye played by Samuel L. Jackson.

Tidyman picked up an Edgar Award for his *Shaft* screenplay. He later wrote the screenplays for *Shaft's Big Score* (1972), *High Plains Drifter* (1973) and such television movies as *To Kill a Cop* (1978, based on Robert Daley's 1976 novel). For creating the character of Shaft – the first truly credible black PI since Ed Lacy's Touissant Moore (*Room to Swing*, 1957) – the National Association for the Advancement of Colored People made Tidyman one of the few Caucasian recipients of its NAACP Image Award. Ernest Tidyman died following complications from a perforated ulcer on 14 July 1984, during a visit to London. He left behind four children and his fourth wife, Motown soul singer Chris Clark.

Suggested reading

W.L. DeAndrea (1994) *Encyclopedia Mysteriosa* (New York: Macmillan).
Anon (1984) 'Ernest R. Tidyman, Screen writer, dies at 56' *The New York Times* 16 July 1984, p. B-11.

J. Kingston Pierce

Treat, Lawrence (1903–88)

One of the key originators of the police procedural, Treat wrote a series of novels which shifted the narrative focus away from a single private detective towards a more authentic ensemble of characters working within a police department. The drama stems from both the personal lives of the policemen and the genuine methods of police investigation. Treat's output was prolific, and he continued writing into old age.

Early life and police procedural novels

Treat was born Lawrence Arthur Goldstone in New York City on 21 December 1903. Treat attended Dartmouth College and Columbia University, graduating with a Law degree in 1927. He practiced law before moving to Paris where he started writing mystery fiction. His first book was a collection of mystery picture puzzles *Bringing Sherlock Home* (1930). Upon his return to the United States, Treat's output was prodigious. He wrote over 300 short stories in his career. Treat's debut novel *Run Far, Run Fast* (1937) was published under the name Lawrence A. Goldstone, but all of his subsequent novels would be published as Treat. With his second novel *B as in Banshee* (1940), Treat introduced his first series character, criminologist Carl Wayward. The Wayward novels are a forgettable precursor to Treat's classic procedural narratives. The four Wayward novels are most notable for Treat's introduction of an alphabetical title system. The other novels in the series are *D as in Dead* (1940), *H as in Hangman* (1942) and *O as in Omen* (1943). This system was memorably imitated by Sue Grafton in the 'Alphabet series' of novels featuring private investigator Kinsey Millhone. With *V as in Victim* (1945), Treat began a new series and established the formula for the police procedural novel. The series follows three main characters, Mitch Taylor, Jub Freeman and Bill Decker in the New York Police Department. All are engaged in different fields of police detection and all three men are of very different character. Jub Freeman works as a scientist in the police laboratory and is methodical and meticulous. Homicide Lieutenant Bill Decker is the paternal detective, tough, competent but also emotionally understanding when the job calls for it. Mitch Taylor is the most vulnerable and changing of the three characters. He is anxious about providing for his wife, but his increasing greed leads to him being demoted in *The Big Shot* (1951). The final novel in the series was *Lady, Drop Dead* (1960). Treat researched the novels thoroughly, spending time at police stations in order to maintain accuracy in the details of police work. Treat denied he was the father of police procedurals: his work was overshadowed by the success of *Dragnet*, the radio and television drama which dramatised cases of the LAPD and did more to popularise the sub-genre. *V as in Victim* preceded the radio debut of *Dragnet* by four years.

Later life

Treat taught mystery writing at both universities and public schools. In 1945 he became a founder member and later President of the Mystery Writers of America. Treat was the winner of three Edgar Awards. In his later career, Treat found success with his 'Crime and Puzzlement' book series wherein young readers are invited to solve mysteries through clues in the illustrations and accompanying notes. Treat's penultimate book, *You're The Jury* (1993) co-written with his brother-in-law Judge Norbert Ehrenfreund, was aimed predominantly at educating teenagers about the judicial system. It allowed the reader to take the perspective of jury members in 12 documented cases and presented questions testing their knowledge of the case. At the end of each chapter it is revealed how the actual jury decided. Treat married Rose Ehrenfreund in 1943. They lived on Martha's Vineyard for many years, and it is where Treat died on 7 January 1988, at the age of 93.

Suggested reading

J. Reilly ed. (1985) *Twentieth Century Crime and Mystery Writers* (New York: St Martin's Press).
Anon (1989) 'Lawrence Treat, 94, Prolific Mystery Writer' *The New York Times* http://www.nytimes.com/1998/01/16/books/lawrence-treat-94-prolific-mystery-writer.html, date accessed 5 February 2011.

Diana Powell

Van Dine, S.S. (1888–1939)

Under the pseudonym S.S. Van Dine, Willard Huntingdon Wright was one of the most popular writers of detective fiction in the 1920s and 1930s. His immensely popular Detective Philo Vance's clue-puzzlers are widely seen as representative of the Golden Age of detective fiction in the United States, where they were followed, and to some extent emulated, by the Ellery Queen series, Rex Stout, and others. Wright was also a critic, writing on art and literature for the *Los Angeles Times*. He also published a 'literary' novel, *The Man of Promise* (1916). As a critic of detective fiction, Wright/Van Dine is known for his widely reprinted 'Twenty Rules for Writing Detective Stories', and for his introductory essay in the anthology *The World's Great Detective Stories* (1928).

Willard Huntingdon Wright was born in Charlottesville, Virginia, on 15 October 1888, into a relatively well-off, middle class family. Wright's father, Archibald Davenport Wright, and his mother Annie (Van Vranken) Wright, fostered an atmosphere of scholarship and an interest in the arts among their children. Wright studied at St Vincent College and Pomona College in California, before entering Harvard University, where he dropped out before graduation. Like his younger brother Stanton Macdonald-Wright, who became an artist and pioneer of stop motion colour animation, Wright studied art and art history, attending art schools in Munich and Paris.

On returning from Europe, Wright became an art critic for the *Los Angeles Times* in 1907, the same year he married Katharine Belle Boynton, with whom he had one daughter. They divorced in 1930, and Wright married portrait painter Eleanor Pulapaugh. He became editor-in-chief of the New York magazine *Smart Set* in 1912 and collaborated with H.L. Mencken and George Jean Nathan on *Europe after 8:15* (1913). His first novel, *The Man of Promise*, appeared in 1916. In this period Wright was establishing himself as a writer of serious, even scholarly books, including *What Nietzsche Taught* (1915), a commentary on the work of the German philosopher, Friedrich Nietzsche.

Perhaps more interesting, in the light of his later forays into crime fiction and the Americanisation of the classical 'English' detective story was *Misinforming a Nation* (1917) a polemical book attacking the English parochialism of the eleventh edition of the *Encyclopaedia Britannica*. At the time, *Britannica* was almost ubiquitous in the homes of middle class Americans, and Wright argued, with some justification, that its English bias had the effect of undermining the confidence of Americans in their own nation. He describes the encyclopaedia as an example of England's 'intellectual colonization of America' (Wright, 1917, p. 1) and, noting the collusion of major American institutions in this 'cultural extension' he argued, 'an Englishman, if he seeks favours, needs little more than proof of his nationality, whereas an American must give evidence of his worth' (Wright, 1917, p. 1).

In 1923, after many years of exhausting work as a journalist and editor, Wright had a nervous breakdown, possibly brought on, as John Loughery suggests, by an addiction to cocaine. Wright was not a wealthy man, and his literary works had not sold well, so it would not have been easy for him to be confined to bed, and instructed to avoid stress and excitement, for two years. To relieve the boredom, he eventually read over 2,000 detective stories and came to the conclusion that he could do better.

Hoping to keep his 'highbrow' reputation separate from his 'lowbrow' detective fiction he adopted the pseudonym 'S.S. Van Dine', a combination of the abbreviation for 'Steam Ship' and a name that is reminiscent of his mother's maiden name.

Philo Vance

Writing as S.S. Van Dine, Wright worked fast, and the first mystery featuring dilettante detective Philo Vance, *The Benson Murder Case*, was published in 1926. In submitting his ideas to publisher Scribner's, Wright was both methodical and highly confident. According to the *Encyclopedia of Mystery and Detection* (1976), he initially submitted three 10,000-word outlines to the revered editor Maxwell Perkins, who was at that time working with Ernest Hemingway, F. Scott Fitzgerald, and other major literary figures of the period. Wright envisaged his detective stories appealing to a well-educated audience, and Scribner's appeared to agree; all three outlines were accepted.

Wright's view of the detective story was that it should be a puzzle set within strict parameters, which he later outlined in his 'Twenty Rules for Writing Detective Stories'. While this meant his stories became increasingly repetitive and unconvincing as the series went on, it also gave him a backdrop in front of which his charismatic detective could perform. Stephen Knight, in *The Cambridge Companion to Crime Fiction*, describes Philo Vance as 'an archetypal East Coast American Europhile' (Knight, 2003, p. 83). Vance is an intellectual snob, who believes his learning makes him superior to those he investigates.

This was nothing new, of course; Great Detectives from Poe's Dupin onwards have distinguished themselves by their intellectual superiority. But Philo Vance goes further, looking down on the limitations of those around him in a patronising way. Wright shared Vance's flaws as much as he did his brilliance. Both author and character were intellectually arrogant and overly fond of excessive spending and luxurious living. As Ogden Nash commented, 'Philo Vance needs a kick in the pance.'

Philo Vance is intellectual, arrogant, aloof, and like Sherlock Holmes before him, skilled and knowledgeable in many surprising things, including fencing, Chinese art, and Latin. The novels contained footnotes which furthered the intellectual discussion on esoteric subjects, and in the early books at least, were often integral to the plot. Wright had made a deliberate decision to write popular books, but some critics were not convinced of his sincerity. In a letter to Hardwick Mosley on 5 January 1957, Raymond Chandler criticised writers who 'deliberately aimed at a wide public', arguing that 'it always shows' (MacShane, 1983, p. 415). He names Wright as one example of a mystery writer who had done so, adding 'and what drivel *he* wrote'. Chandler further mocked Wright's detective, and the 'classical' detective fiction he represented. In his famous essay on the subject, 'The Simple Art of Murder', Chandler describes Vance as 'probably the most asinine character in detective fiction' (Chandler, 1995, p. 985).

Nevertheless, the novels sold very well, and Julian Symons, who rated the third (*The Greene Murder Case*, 1928) and fourth (*The Bishop Murder Case*, 1929) books the best of the series, found reasons to praise them above the novels of Dorothy L. Sayers. Comparing Philo Vance with Sayers's aristocratic creation, Symons describes Vance as 'Wimsey's American cousin' (Symons, 1985, p. 102), but finds Vance's erudition more convincing than Wimsey's, and, despite the intrusive footnotes, is happy to accept his knowledge as intrinsic to the investigation: 'the best of the Van Dine stories are models of construction. Utterly remote from real life, they remain fascinating by strict adherence to the rules of their own dotty logic, and through their creator's self-absorbed immersion in his own work' (Symons, 1985, p. 103).

Twenty rules of detective fiction

As Symons says, the Van Dine stories disregard everything but the puzzle and the detective, and embody the Golden Age of detective fiction. Wright's fascination with creating stories based on a rigid structure led him to write his much-referenced 'Twenty Rules for Writing Detective Stories', which appeared in *American Magazine* in September 1928.

If the Van Dine novels are archetypes for the Golden Age detective story, the 'Twenty Rules' are the blueprint. Building on Ronald Knox's 'Detective Story Decalogue', Wright begins by saying: 'The detective story is a kind of intellectual game. It is more – it is a sporting event.' When Howard Haycraft reprinted the 'Twenty Rules' in his anthology *The Art of the Mystery Story* (1946) he suggested that 'at least Nos. 3, 7, 16, and 19 would need to be liberalised or greatly modified to win any very wide acceptance today' (Haycraft, 1946, p. 189). By then, of course, the tough private eye had taken over from the erudite amateur, and scientific detection had lost out to the wisecrack and the gun.

The success of the Van Dine novels made Wright a wealthy man. The novels were serialised, made into radio plays, and many films. By the late 1930s, despite the growing popularity of the hard-boiled detective story, Van Dine and Philo Vance were household names. And while the quality of the books themselves is widely considered to have declined as the series went on, Philo Vance remained one of the most popular fictional detectives. Although Wright made a great deal of money from his novels, he seemed able to spend it at almost the same rate as it came in, and he left very little in his estate.

Wright died on 11 April 1939, by which time his style of detective story had long been superseded by the private eye novels that dominated American crime and detective fiction in the 1930s and 1940s. Despite his relatively short period of popularity, however, Wright is more than a footnote in the history of the genre. His novels reinvented the predominantly English clue-puzzler in an American setting and social sphere, and introduced one of the most colourful detective characters. His 'Twenty Rules' have remained a curiosity for historians of the inter-war Golden Age of detective fiction.

Suggested reading

Knight, Stephen (2003) 'The Golden Age' in *The Cambridge Companion to Crime Fiction* (Cambridge: Cambridge University Press) pp. 77–94.
Loughery, John (1992) *Alias S.S. Van Dine*. (New York: Knopf).

Christopher Routledge

Wambaugh, Joseph (1937–)

Former Los Angeles police officer Joseph Wambaugh has excelled in two fields of crime writing during his long literary career, producing cynical and realistic depictions of police work which also evoke a blackly comic sense of the absurd and true crime studies of notorious cases. Wambaugh followed in the footsteps of his friend and mentor Truman Capote as one of the most distinguished practitioners of the non-fiction novel.

Early life and police career

Joseph Aloysius Wambaugh Jr was born on 22 January 1937, the only child of Anne (Malloy) Wambaugh and Joseph Aloysius Wambaugh Sr. His father was a small town Police Chief who, like his son years later, would leave the police to pursue a different career, in his case as a steelworker. The Wambaugh family moved to California, and in 1954 the young Wambaugh joined the Marine Corps. His experiences would give him rich material for use in his later novels, as it was Wambaugh's first experience of a rigidly structured, discipline-driven state institution which shared similarities with the Los Angeles Police Department that he would later work for. In his novels, many of Wambaugh's characters have military experience prior to joining the police. Wambaugh was discharged from the Marines in 1957. In 1955, Wambaugh married Dee Allsup, and the couple would have three children. They settled in Ontario, California, where Wambaugh worked at the Kaiser steel mill whilst attending college part-time, majoring in English. Wambaugh received his associate degree from Chaffey College, Alta Loma, California, in 1958 and his bachelor's degree from California State College in 1960. The same year, Wambaugh joined the LAPD as a patrolman. Over the course of his 14-year police career, he would eventually rise to the rank of Detective Sergeant. Wambaugh's early literary ambitions were modest, later stating in an interview that he would have been proud enough to have one short story published. However, his first novel *The New Centurions*

(1970) would become a bestseller, and its controversial depiction of police work would compromise his position in the LAPD.

Novels and film and television adaptations

The New Centurions follows the first five years of the careers of three very different policemen climaxing in the apocalyptic street violence of the Watts riots of 1965. The novel sparked controversy in its depiction of a neutered police force, which reflected American society in its tentativeness to prosecute certain organisations breaking the law, such as elements of the Civil Rights Movement. *The New Centurions* posits this weakness as leading to the decline of law and order as evidenced in the Watts riots. But Wambaugh was not wholly uncritical of the LAPD, and the then Police Chief Ed Davis put pressure on the publishers to amend the manuscript and excise references to the 'Policeman's Discount', which refers to police officers regularly obtaining free meals, cigarettes and liquor at local stops throughout the city. Neither Wambaugh nor the publishers gave way to the pressure and the manuscript went unchanged. Wambaugh's second novel *The Blue Knight* (1972) focuses on Bumper Moran, a chronically glutinous beat cop three days from retirement. *The Blue Knight* was turned into an Emmy Award-winning television film starring William Holden as Moran, and a television series, which ran for two seasons, with George Kennedy in the role. Wambaugh retired from the LAPD in 1974, partly as his literary celebrity was beginning to interfere with his police work. In 1975 Wambaugh published his most critically acclaimed novel, *The Choirboys*. As with his previous use of titles, Centurions and Knights, the word Choirboys is employed with heavy irony. A group of ten police officers indulge in bouts of heavy drinking and occasional group sex with groupies after nightwatch duty, which they euphemistically describe as 'choir practice'. Wambaugh's conservatism is evident throughout the narrative, as the police consistently lament the suspicion they are viewed with by outside agents such as lawyers, judges and citizen activists who constantly hinder police work. An adaptation of *The Choirboys* was filmed by Robert Aldrich in 1977: Wambaugh had written the script, but it was changed without Wambaugh's consent to include a revised, upbeat ending. Wambaugh successfully sued Universal Studios to have his name removed from the credits and was paid one million dollars in an out-of-court settlement for the residual rights. In his fourth novel, *The Black Marble* (1978), Wambaugh devotes a large amount of the narrative to satirising the lifestyle of the upper-class of Southern California. The film adaptation directed by Harold Becker won an Edgar Award for Best Motion Picture. *The Glitter Dome* (1981) deals with the pornographic film industry. *The Delta Star* (1983) would be the last novel which Wambaugh would set in Los Angeles for more than two decades.

Non-fiction novels and the Jay C. Smith controversy

Wambaugh's first true-crime book was *The Onion Field*. Published while he was still a policeman in 1973, *The Onion Field* meticulously recreated the kidnapping and murder of police officer Ian Campbell in an onion field in Bakersfield north of Los Angeles. The suspense of the kidnapping, and the escape of Campbell's partner officer Karl Hettinger, is followed by a detailed and scathing account of the repeatedly delayed trial process of the two kidnappers Jimmy Lee Smith and Gregory Powell. Wambaugh also draws a sympathetic portrayal of Hettinger, who suffered from severe depression as a consequence of the case. His police career gradually fell apart partly due to allegations of cowardice by his colleagues for surrendering his gun during the kidnapping. For *The Onion Field,* Wambaugh received a special Edgar Award for nonfiction. Wambaugh wrote the screenplay for the film adaptation of *The Onion Field*, and it was directed by Harold Becker in 1979. *The Onion Field* was one of the most acclaimed non-fiction novels to be published after Truman Capote's *In Cold Blood*, and it was heavily influenced by Capote's use of journalism, biography and novelistic narrative. Wambaugh knew Capote personally and even appeared in a comedic 'roast' tribute to him on *The Dean Martin Show* in 1974. Wambaugh's second non-fiction work, *Lines and Shadows*, chronicles the short-lived Border Crime Task Force, which was part of the San Diego Task Force, between 1976 and 1978. Again, the themes of Wambaugh's non-fiction work echo his novels as the police are portrayed as men with chaotic personal lives who are thus compelled to try and impose order on society. *The Blooding* is Wambaugh's only book set outside of California, with Wambaugh exchanging the frenetic urban setting of LA for the quaint English villages of Narborough and Enderby in his account of the first murderer convicted through the technique of DNA profiling. Wambaugh's most recent true crime book to date is *Fire Lover: a True Story* (2002), an account of former fire captain and arson investigator John Leonard Orr who was responsible for a series of arson attacks in LA throughout the 1980s and 90s that claimed four lives. In the late 1970s, Wambaugh was contacted by convicted killer Jeffrey MacDonald. MacDonald was a former Army medical doctor convicted of murdering his pregnant wife and two daughters. MacDonald protested his innocence and wanted Wambaugh to write his story. Wambaugh declined MacDonald's offer and wrote back to him: 'You should understand that I would not think of writing your story. It would be my story. Just as *The Onion Field* was my story and *In Cold Blood* is Capote's story' (Malcolm, 1990, p. 29). Wambaugh had shrewdly avoided controversy with this decision as the author who did agree to write MacDonald's story, Joe McGuinness, was heavily criticised for befriending MacDonald by writing him letters proclaiming his innocence, but then portrayed him as an adulterous psychopath in his book, *Fatal Vision* (1983). Wambaugh, however, would similarly become embroiled in controversy with *Echoes in the Darkness* (1987), an account of the murder of Susan Reinert and her two children and the subsequent trial of Jay C. Smith, Principal of Upper Merion Area High School, Pennsylvania, where Reinert worked as an English teacher. Wambaugh allegedly paid police investigators on the case $50,000 on the condition that Smith be arrested. Wambaugh later admitted, 'I didn't think the book would work until something happened to Smith' (Noe, 2011). Smith was found guilty and sentenced to death. After spending six years on Death Row, his conviction was overturned by the Pennsylvania Supreme Court for prosecutorial misconduct. Wambaugh has remained unapologetic about his actions in the case and upon Smith's death in 2009 remarked: 'I do not celebrate the death of any man, but Satan does' (Martin, 2009).

Later novels

Wambaugh returned to fiction and to the LA setting with the novel *Hollywood Station* (2006). This was followed by *Hollywood Crows* (2008), *Hollywood Moon* (2009) and *Hollywood Hills* (2010). In the preface to the first novel in the series, Wambaugh thanked fellow LA crime novelist James Ellroy for urging him to return to his LA roots. The series also marked a return to Wambaugh's early style of blackly comic realism and conservative-leaning social commentary, as the first novel in particular was critical of restrictions placed upon the LAPD in the aftermath of the Rampart scandal.

Suggested reading

J.K. Dover Centurions (1995) *Centurions, Knights, and Other Cops: The Police Novels of Joseph Wambaugh* (San Bernardino, CA: Brownstone Books).
W. Marling (2009) 'Joseph Wambaugh' *Detnovel.com* http://www.detnovel.com /Wambaugh.html, date accessed 30 June 2011.

Steven Powell

Wells, Carolyn (1862–1942)

Carolyn Wells is best known for her series of crime novels featuring Fleming Stone, a methodical, seemingly all-knowing gentleman detective in the tradition of Sherlock Holmes. Wells was a prolific writer who produced poetry, humour and children's books as well as crime fiction. She is also known for writing *The Technique of the Mystery Story* (1913), which is significant for being one of the first works to attempt to set out the 'rules' of the crime genre, both as an instruction manual for aspiring writers and a critical study of the genre.

Wells was born on 18 June 1869 in Rahway, New Jersey. The eldest of four children of William E. and Anna Wells (nee Woodruff), when Wells was six years old, she contracted scarlet fever, which left her almost totally deaf for the rest of her life. After graduating at the top of her high school class, Wells began to work for the Rahway Library Association, eventually becoming librarian of the Rahway Public Library. During the 1890s, Wells began to write humorous verse that was published in magazines such as *Punch*, *Bookman* and the *Saturday Evening Post*. Wells' first book, a collection of charades entitled *At the Sign of the Sphinx*, appeared in 1896. It was followed in 1899 by both *The Jingle Book*, a collection of humorous poetry for children, and *The Story of Betty*, the first in a series of novels for girls. In 1918, Wells married Hadwin Houghton, of the Houghton family known for founding the Houghton-Mifflin publishing company. Their marriage lasted only a year, as Houghton died in 1919. After her husband's death, Wells continued to live and write in New York City, where they had moved at the beginning of their marriage.

Wells became interested in crime fiction after being introduced to the stories of American crime novelist Anna Katherine Green and soon began to concentrate on the genre, though she still wrote poetry and humour. *The Clue*, Wells' first crime novel and the first in her Fleming Stone series, appeared in 1909. Stone usually appears in the last third of the novel, called in to solve an impossible crime which has left the police and everyone else baffled. In 1913, Wells published *The Technique of the Mystery Story*, which examines the genre's form and the components of an effective detective story using examples from successful crime novels. Between 1909 and 1942, Wells produced 82 crime novels, 61 of which are part of the Fleming Stone series. Wells' other detectives include Kenneth Carlisle, a former silent movie actor, and the psychic detective Pennington (Penny) Wise and his assistant Zizi. Wells wrote the novel *The Disappearance of Kimball Webb* (1920) under the pseudonym Rowland Wright. Wells died in New York City on 26 March 1942.

Suggested reading

C.J. Davis and K. West (1996) *Women Writers in the United States: A Timeline of Literary, Cultural, and Social History* (New York: Oxford University Press).

S. Fishinger (1996) 'Carolyn Wells, 1862–1942' *Past and Promise: Lives of New Jersey Women*, ed. J. N. Burstyn (Syracuse: Syracuse University Press).

Megan Hoffman

Westlake, Donald E(dwin) (1933–2008)

Westlake was born in Brooklyn, New York, the city in which much of his fiction is set. He began writing in his teens, and he eventually would be published under an array of pseudonyms including Richard Stark, Tucker Coe, Samuel Holt and Edwin West. He attended three colleges in New York, but did not graduate, and spent two and a half years in the US Air Force during the 1950s. Westlake was eventually awarded a doctorate of letters in 1996 from SUNY Binghamton, formerly Harpur College. He sold his first short story, the science fiction piece 'Or Give Me Death' in 1954, and his first crime story 'The Blonde Lieutenant' in 1957, before moving back to New York City in 1959. Westlake worked at a literary agency while writing part time and, by 1960, had begun writing full time. He was the recipient of three Edgar Awards bestowed by The Mystery Writers of America: the 1968 Best Novel award for *God Save the Mark*, the 1990 award for Best Short Story for 'Too Many Crooks', and the 1991 Best Motion Picture Screenplay for his adaptation of Jim Thompson's *The Grifters*. In 1993, he was named Grand Master by the same organisation.

Westlake was a long-time friend of mystery writer Lawrence Block, with whom he sometimes worked as a writing partner. He also collaborated with novelist and screenwriter Brian Garfield and the writer Justin Scott. Westlake's books feature many in-jokes referencing his friends and colleagues. Westlake's novel *Drowned Hopes* (1992) shares a chapter with Joe Gores' *32 Cadillacs* (1992). Westlake was married three times: following his marriages to Nedra Henderson and Sandra Foley, he married the non-fiction writer Abigail Adams. He had four sons, Sean, Steven, Paul and Tod Westlake, along with two stepdaughters, Adrienne Adams and Katherine Adams, and a stepson, Patrick Adams. Westlake died of a heart attack while on vacation in Mexico in 2008.

Writing

Westlake wrote prolifically under several pseudonyms for a variety of literary markets; apart from his mystery writing, he wrote erotica, science fiction and westerns. He had an aversion to electric typewriters and computers and preferred to write using a portable mechanical typewriter. His first novel, *The Mercenaries* (1960), was nominated for an Edgar Award and was later republished as *The Cutie* (2009). In this novel, the protagonist Clay is charged by his mobster boss, Ed Ganolese, to investigate a murder that the police have attributed to Clay's acquaintance, the heroin junkie Billy-Billy Cantell. The novel is notable for what would become an on-going theme of Westlake's career: the inner workings of an internally consistent criminal underworld independent of the conventions of legitimate society.

As Richard Stark, Westlake wrote 16 'Parker' novels between 1962 and 1974, taking up the series again in 1997. Beginning with *The Hunter* (1962), these novels featured the exploits of the professional hard-boiled thief Parker and his various accomplices. Westlake intentionally avoided giving any redeeming qualities to this ruthless character. *The Hunter* is a revenge story in which the double crossed Parker hunts down and assassinates his former accomplices. In *The Outfit* (1963), Parker and his associates take on the local mob, while Parker attempts to settle a vendetta between himself and the mob boss Bronson. In *Slayground* (1971), Parker finds himself trapped on the amusement park Fun Island and surrounded by the local syndicate, who go in after him to claim the money that Parker and his associates had taken during an armoured car heist. *Dirty Money* (2008), the last Parker novel, deals with the world of money laundering. Parker attempts to draw an income from the marked bills that he obtained in a previous failed armoured car heist in *Nobody Runs Forever* (2004). Westlake's Parker series shows the strong influence of Dashiell Hammett, and Westlake has also claimed Peter Rabe and Vladimir Nabokov as other important influences on his writing. Their narrative strategies, the way in which they left 'all emotion completely unstated in a book that's totally about emotion' and '[l]et physical description of the surface suggest the storms within' strongly influenced Westlake's hard-boiled style (Ardai, 2009).

Westlake began a series of novels under his own name which ran from 1970 to 2009 and which featured the character John Archibald Dortmunder, the first novel of which was *The Hot Rock* (1970). *The Hot Rock* introduced the master planner Dortmunder and his partner in crime Andy Kelp. The novel also established a narrative pattern: Kelp would entice Dortmunder with a new caper in each novel, much to Dortmunder's initial reluctance. The ensuing narrative trajectory would involve a series of increasingly threatening comedic mishaps that would eventually be resolved at the novels' climax. Like the Parker novels, Dortmunder would plan a new heist and recruit a team to execute it. In *The Hot Rock* the heist revolves around the theft of an emerald worth half a million dollars. Westlake originally intended for *The Hot Rock* to feature Parker but, because this novel tended toward a more comic outlook, he separated it from the hard-boiled Parker series. In *Jimmy the Kid* (1974), Kelp suggests a kidnapping based on the plot of an imaginary Parker novel, 'Child Heist'. Richard Stark makes a brief cameo appearance in *Jimmy the Kid*, while Kelp suggests that Dortmunder would appreciate this novel for its protagonist. *Jimmy the Kid* escalates the frequency of Westlake's allusions to his other pseudonymous work and to popular culture, including other forms of genre fiction and cinema.

Westlake wrote the mystery novels *Kinds of Love, Kinds of Death* (1966), *Murder Among Children* (1967), *Wax Apple* (1970), *A Jade in Aries* (1970) and *Don't Lie to Me* (1972) under the pseudonym Tucker Coe, all of which featured his series character the disgraced ex-cop turned private eye Mitch Tobin. As Samuel Holt he wrote the mystery novels *One of Us is Wrong* (1986), *I Know a Trick Worth Two of That* (1986), *What I Tell You Three Times is False* (1987) and *The Fourth Dimension is Death* (1989), all featuring the series character Sam Holt. Notable stand-alone novels include *Pity Him Afterwards* (1965), in which the protagonist is the psychopathic madman Robert Ellington who escapes from a lunatic asylum. Ellington's ability to adopt other identities allows him to take an acting job and escape detection; his sense of identity continues to blur and adds to the uncertainty and oneiric quality of the text. *The Ax* (1997) features a paper industry executive, Burke Devore, who turns to murder after being made redundant; he runs classified adverts for jobs in order to identify and murder his competition and so increase his chances of being hired.

Television and film

Many of Westlake's novels have been adapted for film. Westlake's novel *The Hunter* was adapted as the gripping, somewhat abstract noir *Point Blank* in 1967 and less successfully as *Payback* in 1999. In 1968 his novel *The Seventh* was filmed as *The Split* which was released in the same year. *The Busy Body* (1967), *The Hot Rock* (1972), *Cops and Robbers* (1973), *Bank Shot* (1974), *The Outfit* (1973), *Slayground* (1983), *Why Me?* (1990) and *What's the Worst That Could Happen?* (2001) were all filmed under the original novel titles. *The Ax* was adapted as the critically acclaimed European film *Le Couperet* (2005). *Jimmy the Kid* was adapted as *Come ti Rapisco il Pupo* (1976) in Italy and under its original title in both America (1982) and Germany (1998). *Two Much!* was filmed in France as *Le Jumeau* (1984) and a second adaptation, which retained the novel title, was directed by Fernando Trueba and released in 1995.

Westlake was nominated for an Academy Award for Best Adapted Screenplay for *The Grifters*. He also wrote the screenplay *The Stepfather* (1987), the teleplay for *Fatal Confession* (1987) and an initial rejected script for the James Bond film *Tomorrow Never Dies* (1997).

Suggested reading

M. Dunne (1987) 'The Comic Capers of Donald Westlake' *Comic Crime*, E. F. Bargainnier, ed. (Ohio: Bowling Green University Popular Press). pp. 168–80.

T.L. Matthews, ed. (2005) 'Westlake, Donald', in *Contemporary Authors: New Revision Series*, vol 137 (Farmington Hills, MI: Thomson Gale). pp. 407–14.

D. Westlake (2008) 'An Interview with Donald Westlake: Author of the Parker Novels', *University of Chicago Press* http://www.press.uchicago.edu/Misc/Chicago/westlake_interview.html, date accessed 8 September 2011.

Chris Pak

Whitfield, Raoul (1896–1945)

A prolific *Black Mask* pioneer, Raoul Falconia Whitfield was born in New York and lived in the Philippines with his father, a US Territorial Government bureaucrat posted in Manila. Whitfield was the nephew of Scottish-American philanthropist Andrew Carnegie; his family's privileged position allowed him to visit Japan, China and other locations before he returned to the US in 1916 to recover from a period of ill health. He worked as a silent cinema actor in California before enlisting in World War I, eventually serving as a pilot in France. Whitfield later drew upon his experiences as a pilot to write air-adventure tales for *Battle Stories*. On his return, he worked briefly at his family's steel business but soon gave that up to begin writing for the *Pittsburgh Post* in 1919. At some point he changed his middle name from 'Falconia' to the more well-known 'Fauconnier'. Whitfield married fellow reporter Prudence Ann Smith in 1923 and later moved to Florida in 1926 or 1927 to begin full time writing. After divorcing Prudence, he moved to Los Angeles in 1933, married Emily Davies Vanderbilt Thayer in the same year and his output of writing soon dwindled; the couple broke up in 1935 and Thayer committed suicide, leaving Whitfield with a small fortune. He married Lois Bell in 1935 but divorced her in 1942; a year later she committed suicide. By 1944, Whitfield had become destitute, and he died of tuberculosis in 1945.

Whitfield published his first short story in 1924, although it was not until 1926 that his first *Black Mask* short story, 'Scotty Troubles Trouble', appeared. His 'Crime Breeder' series was published in *Black Mask* from 1929–30 and featured his series character, the ex-convict Mel Ourney. These stories later became the basis for his first novel *Green Ice* (1930), which garnered praise from, among others, his colleague and friend Dashiell Hammett. His other novels, *Death in a Bowl* (1931), *Five* (1931), *The Virgin Kills* (1932) and *Killer's Carnival* (1932) would not be as successful. Due to his prolific output, Whitfield also wrote under the pseudonyms Ramon Decolta and Temple Field. As Decolta, he penned the stories that featured the Filipino detective Jo Gar, of Manila. Many of the Gar tales appeared in *Black Mask* from

1930–33. Eighteen of these 'Island Investigator' stories were collected in *Jo Gar's Casebook* (2002), including 'Death in the Pasig' (1930) and 'Climbing Death' (1932). His other series characters were Donald Free, a fallen-from-grace government agent turned private eye on which the film *Private Detective 62* (1933) starring William Powell was based. Whitfield also wrote stories featuring cynical PI Ben Jardinn.

Suggested reading

E.R. Hagemann (1980) 'Raoul F. Whitfield, A Star with the *Mask*', in *The Armchair Detective*, 13 (3) 179–84.

D. Ivison (2000) 'Raoul Whitfield (1898–1945)' *Dictionary of Literary Biography: American Hard-Boiled Crime Writers*, vol. 226.G. P. Anderson and Julie B. Anderson, eds. (Detroit: The Gale Group). 329–35.

W.F. Nolan (1985) 'Behind the Mask: Raoul Whitfield' *The Black Mask Boys* (New York: The Mysterious Press). 129–35.

P. Ruber and V.A. Berch (2002) 'Raoul Whitfield: Black Mask's Forgotten Man' *Black Mask Magazine* http://www.blackmaskmagazine.com/bm_17.html, date accessed 28 February 2011.

Chris Pak

Willeford, Charles (1919–88)

Best known for the 'Hoke Moseley' detective series, which were published towards the end of his life, Charles Ray Willeford was a prolific writer, publishing almost 20 novels, three volumes of poetry, a number of collections of short stories and at least seven substantial works of non-fiction. He also regularly contributed to newspapers, for a long period to the *Miami Herald*, and, in the early 1960s, he became one of the editors of *Alfred Hitchcock's Mystery Magazine*.

After his first publication *Proletarian Laughter* (1948), a book of poetry, Willeford produced his debut novel *The High Priest of California* in 1953 followed fairly rapidly by further crime stories: *Pick-Up* (1955), *Wild Wives* (1956) and the racially controversial *The Black Mass of Brother Springer* (originally published as *Honey Gal* in 1958). In the next four years Willeford produced six further novels, but after *Cockfighter* (1962), it was nine years before he published again, with two works appearing in 1971. Over the next 13 years he produced relatively little original crime writing, apparently concentrating more on his poetry and non-fiction until, in 1984, the first Hoke Moseley novel *Miami Blues* was published to critical and popular acclaim followed by the other works in the series: *New Hope for the Dead* (1985) *Sideswipe* (1987), *The Way We Die Now* (1988) and the unpublished 'Grimhaven'.

Willeford adapted *The High Priest of California* into a play – although it was never produced in the full version in his lifetime – and wrote the screenplay for the film adaptation of *Cockfighter*, directed by Monte Hellman in 1974. Two further film adaptations of his novels appeared after his death: *Miami Blues*, directed by George Armitage in 1990, and *The Woman Chaser*, directed by Robinson Devor in 1999.

The early years

Born in Little Rock, Arkansas, Willeford was an orphan before he was eight years old: his father died of tuberculosis in 1922 – after which he moved with his mother to Los Angeles to be closer to his grandmother – and his mother died, also of tuberculosis, in 1927. Willeford lived with his grand-mother for the next five years but, at the age of 13, he decided to leave Los Angeles, adopt another age and identity, and join the army of out-of-work hobos drifting around the country seeking employment or a permanent place to stay during the years of the Great Depression.

In 1935 he was accepted into the United States Army, following a brief stint with the California National Guard, and for the next 20 years the armed forces would provide the most stable structure for his life. Although he left the forces a number of times, he always re-enlisted and, before finally leaving in 1956, he was a decorated war hero who had become a tank commander and fought at the Battle of the Bulge. Part of his military career included time served in the United States Air Force and he left the USAF in the rank of Master Sergeant. Outside of his army experiences, he had attempted to obtain educational qualifications but his lack of any formal education at an earlier age meant that, when he did leave the forces, he was at a disadvantage to find regular employment.

By 1956, however, his writing career was beginning to take shape and his personal life appeared more settled. *Proletarian Laughter* was published towards the end of his marriage to Lara Bell Fridley – married in 1942, they divorced in 1949 – and it was after his second marriage, to Mary Jo Norton in 1952, that he began producing the crime novels from which he hoped, after leaving the forces, that he would be able to earn a comfortable living.

Life after the military

From his teenage years travelling on rail cars around the southern United States and throughout his military career, Willeford had been used to a peripatetic lifestyle and, after leaving the military, he apparently found it difficult to settle to one occupation. Although, as a result, he had an unsettled and financially precarious existence for a few years, he also used his experiences, as an actor, radio host, boxer, blacksmith and horse trainer – together with his varied experiences of casual work before and during his military career – as source material for his novels, short stories and the many anecdotes with which he entertained his friends. He finally managed to obtain the college education that he had always desired and, after achieving a master's degree from the University of Miami in 1964, he was employed, first by the University and later by an associate college, as a teacher of literature and philosophy – a position he retained until 1985.

The work

Willeford's crime novels are original, unsettling and challenging. His first work, *The High Priest of California,* introduces some of his unusual themes:

the main protagonist, Haxby, appears nothing more than an unprinci-
pled and shallow salesman entirely driven by the desire to obtain more
modern consumer goods, but Haxby is also obsessed with modern culture
and indulges in random violence. As a result, he commits violent acts and
then returns to his home, an apparent temple to mass consumerism, where
he is transported by listening to complex modern music, reading Kafka or
attempting to re-write Joyce's *Ulysses* in order to make it more accessible to
the common reader.

The Black Mass of Brother Springer raises issues which are in many ways
even more challenging, as recognised at the time by his publisher's refusal
to use either of Willeford's original suggestions for titles – when 'Black Mass'
was rejected, he proposed 'Nigger Lover'. The plot concerns a drifter who for
cynical reasons becomes pastor of an African-American church. He makes
'one mistake' (to accept a black woman's offer of sex in a public cinema
and, when the lights are unexpectedly switched on, they are seen by almost
the entire town) and, as a result, is forced to abandon not only the town
but apparently all his hopes for the rest of his life. The novel was unusual
in its engagement with the world of racial segregation and civil rights, but
Willeford had, in his second novel *Pick-Up*, also used race in an unsettling
way. Having made no mention of racial issues throughout the book, the
narrator describes himself, in the final words of the novel, as 'a tall, lonely
Negro' thus challenging the likely perceptions of the reader who would
most likely have assumed the character was white.

Willeford's continued concern with all of the issues surrounding class and
culture, as evidenced in his first title *Proletarian Laughter*, sees him repeatedly engaging with the position of so-called 'high culture', and particularly difficult modernist representations of it. Willeford's novels consider
the lives of the masses living in what he saw as an increasingly crass and
consumerist society. In his works of the late 1950s and early 1960s this also
becomes a concern with the implications, especially for white men, of living
in a racially mixed society.

Later years

In 1976 Willeford and his second wife divorced and, in 1981, he married his
third wife, Betsy Poller, with whom he remained until his death in 1988.
For the second time his remarriage seemed to coincide with a new direction
in his writing and, in 1984, he published the first of his most successful
works, the Hoke Moseley series. Set in Miami, the Hoke Moseley series have
been credited with elevating Miami as a crime fiction location to rival Los
Angeles. Moseley is a middle-aged, divorced and semi-autobiographical
character somewhat unnerved and perplexed by the rapid social change
engulfing Florida following events such as the Mariel Boat Lift in 1980 and
the resulting waves of Cuban immigration.

346   *Willeford, Charles (1919–88)*

Although the Moseley series features crime and dialogue which is in many ways typical of the hard-boiled genre, they are clearly original in the way in which the plot appears to be less important than the central characters. The Moseley characters are always slightly odd and are apparently unaware of the way in which their language or behaviour may make them unusual. There is a considerable amount of deadpan humour in the way they observe, and are observed by, others.

Willeford's success with the Moseley series finally ensured his financial stability, but it came very near to the end of his life: he received a major advance for *The Way We Die Now* but, shortly after its publication, he died in Miami of a heart attack.

Suggested reading

W. Haut (1995) *Pulp Culture: Hard-boiled Fiction and the Cold War* (London: Serpent's Tail).

W. Haut (1999) *Neon Noir: Contemporary American Crime Fiction* (London: Serpent's Tail).

L. Horsley (2005) *Twentieth-Century Crime Fiction* (Oxford: Oxford University Press).

S. McCann (2000) *Gumshoe America: Hard-boiled Crime Fiction and the Rise and Fall of New Deal Liberalism* (Durham: Duke University Press).

Maureen Sunderland

Williams, Charles (1909–75)

Although he began his writing career in middle-age, and he did not achieve lasting success during his lifetime, Charles Williams has since received deserved critical attention. His 20 novels, which depict ambiguous characters and remote settings, do not fit easily into any crime sub-genre but are generally regarded as noir fiction.

Life

Williams was born in San Angelo, Texas, on 13 August 1909. He attended Brownsville High School up to tenth grade. He joined the United States Merchant Marines in 1929 and served as a Radio Operator before he left to marry Lasca Foster in 1939. Their marriage produced a daughter. He then worked as a Radio Inspector for Radiomarine Corporation in Galveston, Texas, until 1942. Williams then moved to Washington State where he worked as an Electronics Inspector at Puget Sound Navy Yard. From 1946 to 1950 he worked as a Radio Inspector for Mackay Company in San Francisco.

Novels

Williams's literary career began with the novel *Hill Girl* (1951), which sold over a million copies and established the backwoods or small-town setting of his early work. *Hill Girl* was followed by *Big City Girl* and *River Girl* (also in 1951) all of which were published as paperback originals for Gold Medal Books, a publisher who championed Williams's short pulp novel style. Lee Horsley credits Williams as one of several 1950s novelists, alongside Charles Willeford and Jim Thompson, who reimagined the *femme fatale* as comparatively heroic and triumphing over an amoral male protagonist. In *Hell Hath No Fury* (1953) it is through the first-person narration of Harry Madox that the reader sees Dolores Harshaw, the faithless wife of Madox's employer. Madox views Dolores as little more than a nymphomaniac worth the occasional sexual liaison. Meanwhile he commits several crimes in the small-town Texas setting and pursues the younger Gloria Harper, for whom he has more loving, tender feelings. But Dolores is able to outwit Madox, reducing him to his and her 'level' in a darkly cynical ending which renders the alpha-male emasculated precisely by making him superficially respectable. In *A Touch of Death* (1953) the narrator, Lee Scarborough, is driven quite literally insane by the *femme fatale* figure, Mrs Madelon Butler. He ends the novel in a lunatic asylum oblivious to how and why she has outmanoeuvred him. If Mickey Spillane's Mike Hammer novels were shocking in their portrayal of Hammer's brutal, misogynistic moral code, Williams's 1950s novels more realistically portray cold-hearted characters in a world devoid of any moral code. In *The Big Bite* (1957) the male and female protagonists destroy one another, but only the *femme fatale* elicits sympathy in her cleverness and foresight.

A change in direction

With his eighth novel, *Scorpion Reef* (1955), Williams developed a nautical theme and high-seas setting which would become dominant in his later career. In *Aground* (1960), Williams introduced the character of John Ingram, an experienced sailor and charter captain, who rescues the beautiful Rae Osborne from two modern-day pirates lurking aboard her beached yacht. In the more celebrated sequel *Dead Calm* (1963), Ingram and Rae are on their honeymoon, sailing in the Pacific, when they rescue a young man from a sinking ship. Suspicion of the stranger grows and a battle for survival ensues. Williams used his extensive knowledge of sailing to create a claustrophobic and realistic atmosphere in the novels. Ingram is more of a straightforward hero than Williams's previous protagonists, and he does possess a strong moral code. Tension is evoked in nature's indifference to human needs, and Ingram is one of the few characters with enough sailing knowledge to stay alive at sea. Williams's only Edgar nominated novel *And the Deep Blue Sea* (1971) features a large cast of characters held hostage on a ship with a burning cargo. Williams also wrote the comic novels *The Diamond Bikini* (1956) and *Uncle Sagamore and his Girls* (1959). By the mid-60s Williams's novels were beginning to have less critical and commercial success as pulp novels were in decline. His wife died from cancer in 1972, and his final novel *Man on a Leash* (1973) received a lukewarm response. Williams committed suicide in his Los Angeles apartment in April 1975. Many of Williams's novels have been adapted into films. Orson Welles attempted to film *Dead Calm* as 'The Deep' (1970) but the project was never finished. The novel was finally filmed by Phillip Noyce, with its original title, and released in 1989. *The Long Saturday Night* (1962) was adapted as *Vivement Dimanche! (aka Confidentially Yours* (1983)) which was François Truffaut's last film. *Hell Hath No Fury* was adapted as *The Hot Spot* (1990) directed by Dennis Hopper.

Suggested reading

J. Reilly ed. (1985) *Twentieth-Century Crime and Mystery Writers* (New York: St Martin's Press).

H. Migoya (2001) *La Tormenta Y La Calma Hernan Migoya* (Barcelona: Glenat).

Steven Powell

Woolrich, Cornell (1903–68)

Cornell Woolrich's dark crime novels sold well in the 1940s and 1950s, but have not had lasting success. He is now almost unknown outside specialist circles, but his books were nevertheless staples of Hollywood filmmaking in the 1940s and 1950s. His work has been adapted by film directors as diverse as Alfred Hitchcock, François Truffaut and Robert Siodmak. Amongst the most famous adaptations of Woolrich's work was Alfred Hitchcock's *Rear Window* (1954) taken from the 1942 short story 'It Had to Be Murder'. Woolrich combined the Gothic sensibility of Edgar Allan Poe, with the dark, urban setting of hard-boiled crime fiction to create what has been called 'paranoid noir'. Perhaps because he often wrote under a pseudonym, Woolrich's name is not widely known. Many of his books are out of print, but their titles have a familiar and evocative ring nonetheless: *The Bride Wore Black* (1940), *Phantom Lady* (1942), *Night Has a Thousand Eyes* (1945), *I Married a Dead Man* (1948). As a *Black Mask* writer he was an early influence, along with Dashiell Hammett, Raymond Chandler, and Horace McCoy, on the development of hard-boiled crime fiction, and is often credited with inventing the noir sensibility. Through the many adaptations of his work he is a significant figure in the popularity of film noir in the 1940s and 1950s.

Life and career

Cornell George Hopley-Woolrich was born in New York City on 4 December 1903. His father was a civil engineer, and after his parents separated, Woolrich spent some time living with him in Mexico, where one of his hobbies was collecting spent bullet cartridges in the street. However, he idolised his mother, Claire Attalie Woolrich, and from the age of 12 he lived with her in New York City. In 1921 he went to Columbia University where he studied journalism, but illness left him bedridden for six weeks, during which time he wrote a romantic novel, *Cover Charge* (1926). Encouraged by the success of this novel, he dropped out of college. His second novel,

Children of the Ritz (1927), won a $10,000 prize and was produced as a film by First National Pictures in 1929.

Having moved to Hollywood to work on the script for *Children of the Ritz*, in 1930 Woolrich married Gloria Blackton, the daughter of a movie producer. The marriage did not last long. Within a few months they separated, probably because Blackton discovered Woolrich's secret homosexuality, and the marriage was annulled, apparently unconsummated, in 1933. Woolrich, who seems to have enjoyed patrolling the docks dressed in a sailor's uniform trying to pick up men, returned to New York where he moved in with his mother. They lived together at the Hotel Marseilles until her death in 1957; after his own death, eleven years later, Woolrich was buried with her in the same vault.

Woolrich became something of a recluse, doing much of his writing in the corner of the hotel room, while his mother sat watching. He was an alcoholic and rarely left the hotel. Following his return to New York, Woolrich began writing stories for the pulp publishers, including *Black Mask* and *Story* magazine, ultimately publishing over 250 short mystery stories. He won an Edgar Award in 1950 for his contribution to the RKO movie *The Window*.

It was in the 1940s that Woolrich produced his best work, in particular the run of 'Black' novels, so-called because they have the word 'black' in the title, beginning with *The Bride Wore Black* (1940). In common with many of Woolrich's plots, *The Bride Wore Black* involves a race against time. Here a bride, whose husband is shot dead on their wedding day, pursues the gunmen seeking vengeance. Partly because publisher Simon and Schuster 'owned' the Cornell Woolrich name, many of his best novels were written under the names William Irish and George Hopley.

The first William Irish novel, *Phantom Lady* (1942), tells the story of a man convicted and sentenced to death for killing his wife and of the race to find a woman who can provide an alibi. A film adaptation of *Phantom Lady* was made by the famous film noir director Robert Siodmak; it was his first noir feature. In 1943, Raymond Chandler wrote to Alfred A. Knopf about having read *Phantom Lady,* and described Woolrich as 'one of the oldest hands in the detective fiction business. He is known in the trade as an idea writer, liking the tour de force, and not much of a character man. I think his stuff is very readable, but leaves no warmth behind it' (Hinney and MacShane, 2000, p. 33).

Woolrich was a difficult man, uncomfortable in company, and he could be irascible and bitter. His stories express a world-view that is cynical and pessimistic about human nature. Although homosexuality is never explicitly mentioned in his work, Charles Krinsky notes in his entry for *glbtq* that in novels such as *The Bride Wore Black* and *I Married a Dead Man* (1948), love and family life fail to provide security, safety, or fulfilling relationships. In a Woolrich novel, malice and revenge are the primary motivating forces; lives are blighted by despair and paranoia. It is because of this that Woolrich has been described as an originator of 'paranoid noir', loosely defined by Philip Simpson as stories of a 'persecuted victim, caught up in a deterministic world in which the standard rules have suddenly changed for the worse' (Simpson, 2010, p. 192). *Night Has a Thousand Eyes* (1945), written as George Hopley, is perhaps the archetypal novel of this type.

Woolrich, whose diabetes and alcoholism left him disabled, became increasingly embittered. He alienated most of his friends and acquaintances and spent the final decade of his life almost entirely alone. In early 1968 an untreated foot infection caused by over-tight shoes developed into gangrene and led to the partial amputation of his leg. When he died in September that year, Woolrich left his entire estate of around $1 million dollars to Columbia University, where the Claire Woolrich scholarships, named after his mother, continue to support students in journalism and writing.

Suggested reading

C. Krinsky (2010) *glbtq: An Encyclopedia of Gay, Lesbian, Bisexual, Transgender, and Queer Culture.* http://www.glbtq.com/literature/woolrich_c.html, date accessed 7 October 2010.

F. M. Nevins (1988) *Cornell Woolrich: First You Dream, Then You Die.* (New York: Mysterious Press).

P. Simpson (2010) 'Noir and the Psycho Killer' *A Companion to Crime Fiction* C. J. Rzepka and L. Horsley, eds. (Oxford: Wiley-Blackwell) pp. 187–97.

Christopher Routledge

Bibliography

Abbott, M.E. (2002) *The Street was Mine: White Masculinity in Hard-boiled Fiction and Film Noir* (New York: Palgrave Macmillan).

Anon (1966) 'Books: Short Notices: April 29, 1966' *Time Magazine*, 29 April 1966. http://www.time.com/time/magazine/article/0,9171,835472,00.html,date accessed 19 October 2010.

Anon (1982) 'Milestones' *Time Magazine*, 10 May 1982. http://www.time.com/time /magazine/article/0,9171,925399,00.html,date accessed 11 May 2011.

Auster, P. (1998) *Hand to mouth: a chronicle of early failure* (London: Faber).

Baldwin, J. *The Cross of Redemption: Uncollected Writings*, Kenan, R. ed. (New York, Pantheon, 2010)

Blotner, J. (1991) *Faulkner: A Biography*. (New York: Vintage Books).

Borde, R. and Chaumeton, É. (1955) 'Towards a Definition of Film Noir' In: A. Silver and J. Ursini (2006) *Film Noir Reader* (New York: Limelight)

Boucher, A. (1951) *Ellery Queen: A Double Profile*. (Boston: Little Brown).

Bruccoli, M. J. and Makala, J. (2006) *George V. Higgins a Retrospective Exhibition* (Thomas Cooper Library: University of South Carolina) 06567 University Publications 10/06

Brunsdale, M.M. (2010) *Icons of Mystery and Crime Detection: From Sleuths to Superheroes* (Santa Barbara: Greenwood).

Bunker, E. (1999) *Mr Blue: Memoirs of a Renegade* (Harpenden, No Exit Press).

Burke, J.L. (2002) *The Neon Rain* (New York: Simon & Schuster)

Cain, J.M. (1969) *Cain X 3: The Postman Always Rings Twice, Mildred Pierce, and Double Indemnity,* intro Wolfe, T. (New York, Knopf).

Cain, J.M. (1982) *James M. Cain: Four Complete Novels* (New York: Avenel Books)

Cain, P. (2004) *Fast One* (Harpenden: No Exit Press).

Carr, J.D. (2002) *The Hollow Man* (London: Orion).

Cassuto, L. (2009) *Hard-Boiled Sentimentality: The Secret History of American Crime Stories* (New York: Columbia University Press).

Chandler, R. (1995) 'The Simple Art of Murder' *Later Novels & Other Writings* (New York : Library of America). pp. 977–92.

Chandler, R. (2000a) *The Big Sleep* in *The Big Sleep and Other Novels* (London: Penguin Books in association with Hamish Hamilton). pp. 1–164.

Chandler, R. (2000b) *Farewell, My Lovely* in *The Big Sleep and Other Novels* (London: Penguin Books in association with Hamish Hamilton). pp. 165–366.

Collins, M.A. and Traylor, J. L. (1984) *One Lonely Knight: Mickey Spillane's Mike Hammer* (Bowling Green: Bowling Green University Popular Press).

Cornwell, A. (2001) 'Hard Boiled-Heaven' http://www.twbooks.co.uk/crimescene /pelecanosinterviewbc.htm

Crosby, S. (2010) 'Early American crime writing' In: C.R. Nickerson ed. *The Cambridge Companion to American Crime Fiction* (New York: Cambridge University Press)

Crumley, J. (1988) *The Last Good Kiss* (New York: Vintage Books).

DeAndrea, W. L. (1994) *Encyclopedia Mysteriosa* (New York: Macmillan).

D'Ascoli, P. (2005) 'Living the Literary Life' *Fairfield County Times*, 28 November 2005, on *Ed McBain* http://www.edmcbain.com/Newsdesk.asp?id=465, date accessed 4 September 2011.

Décharné, M. 'Introduction' *Fast One* by Cain, P. (Harpenden: No Exit Press). pp. 7–12.

DeMott, B. (1985) 'Tough Guys Can't Write' *New England Monthly*, September, 18–21.

DeSilva, B. (2000) 'Get Out of Jail Free: in George V. Higgins's novel, mobsters have a sweet deal with the feds' *New York Times*, 20 Aug 2000. p. BR15.

Dove, G.N. (1985) *The Boys From Grover Avenue* 1985 (Bowling Green, OH: Bowling Green State University Press).

Ellroy, J. (1995) *American Tabloid* (New York: Knopf).

Ellroy, J. (2009) *Blood's a Rover* (New York: Knopf).

Ellroy, J. (1987) *The Black Dahlia* (New York: Warner).

Ellroy, J. (1981) *Brown's Requiem* (New York: Perennial).

Ellroy, J. (1997) *My Dark Places* (London : Arrow).

Evonovich, J. (2011) *Janet Evonovich* http://www.evanovich.com

Friedman, K. (1994) *Elvis, Jesus and Coca Cola* (London: Faber and Faber).

Friedman, K. (2000) *When the Cat's Away* (New York: Vandam Press).

Futrelle, J. (1912) 'Inscription' *My Lady's Garter* (Chicago: Rand McNally).

Futrelle, J. (2004) *The Problem of a Dressing Room* (Whitefish, Montana: Kessinger Publishing).

Gardner, E.S. (1978) *The Case of the Velvet Claws* in *A Perry Mason Omnibus* (New York: W. Morrow).

Gardner, E.S. (1937) *The Case of the Lame Canary* (New York: Morrow).

Gardner, E. S. (1939) *The Bigger They Come* (New York: Morrow).

Geherin, D. (1980) *Sons of Sam Spade: The Private Eye Novel in the '70s* (New York: Frederick Unger Publishing).

Green, D.G. (2009) 'John Dickson Carr: Explaining the Inexplicable' *Mysterynet.com* http://www.mysterynet.com/books/testimony/carr/, date accessed 4 August 2011.

Grogg, S. Jr. (1973) 'Ross Macdonald: At the Edge', *Journal of Popular Culture*, Summer 1973, 7, 213–22.

Gruber, F. (1967) *The Pulp Jungle* (Los Angles: Sherbourne Press).

Hamill, P. (2000) 'The Poet of Pulp: How Ed McBain invented the cop-squad drama' *The New Yorker*, 10 January 2000. pp. 62–7.

Haycraft, H. (1946) *The Art of the Mystery Story* (New York: Simon and Schuster).

Hiaasen, C. (1995) 'Introduction' *A Purple Place for Dying*, MacDonald, J.D. (New York: Fawcett Crest).

Hiney, T. and MacShane, F., eds. (2000) *The Raymond Chandler Papers: Selected Letters and Nonfiction, 1909–1959* (New York: Grove Press).

Higgins, G.V. (1972) *The Friends of Eddie Coyle* (New York: Knopf).

Highsmith, P. (2001) *Plotting and Writing Suspense Fiction* (London: St Martin's Press).

Himes, C. (1957) *For Love of Imabelle* (New York: Fawcett).

Himes, C. (1972) My Life of Absurdity (New York: Doubleday).

Hirshberg, E. W. (1985) *John D. MacDonald* (Boston: Twayne Publishers).

Hoffman, C. (1983) 'Spenser: The Illusion of Knighthood' *The Armchair Detective*, Spring, 131–43.

Hogan, R. (2012) 'The Beatrice Interview: 1995' *Conversations with James Ellroy* Powell, S. ed. (Jackson: University Press of Mississippi). pp. 53–60.

Hoopes, R. (1982) *Cain* (New York: Holt, Rinehart and Winston).

Horsley, L. (2009) *The Noir Thriller* (Basingstoke: Palgrave Macmillan).

Horsley, L. (2005) *Twentieth Century Crime Fiction* (Oxford: Oxford University Press).

Hughes, D. B. (1978) *Erle Stanley Gardner: The Case of the Real Perry Mason* (New York: William Morrow).

Hughes, L. (1976) 'Reflections on the Renaissance and Art for a New Day' *Voices from the Harlem Renaissance*, Huggins, N.I. ed. (Oxford: Oxford University Press). pp. 367–81.

Jakubowski, M. (2005) 'The Perfect Crime' *The Guardian*, 29 October 2005 http://www.guardian.co.uk/books/2005/oct/29/featuresreviews.guardianreview32,date accessed 15 August 2011.

Johnston, R.W. (1952) 'Death's fair-haired boy' *Life*, 23 June 1952, p. 86.

Keating, H.R.F. (1994) 'Obituary: Margaret Millar' *The Independent*, 31 March 1994 http://www.independent.co.uk/news/people/obituary-margaret-millar-1432676.html, date accessed 28 June 2011.

Knight, S. (2003) 'The Golden Age' *The Cambridge Companion to Crime Fiction* (Cambridge: Cambridge University Press). pp. 77–94.

Krebs, A. (1975) 'Erle Stanley Gardner, the Author of Perry Mason Mystery Novels' *Popular Culture*, D. M. White ed. (New York: New York Times). pp. 32–4.

Lee, M. S. (2010) 'Edgar Allan Poe (1840–1849)' *A Companion to Crime Fiction* Rzepka, C. and Horsley, L. eds. (London: Wiley-Blackwell). pp. 369–80.

Lehane, D. (2011) *A Drink Before the War* (New York: Harper Collins).

Leonard, E. (2001)'Writers on Writing; Easy on the Adverbs, Exclamation Points and Especially the Hooptedoodle' *New York Times*, 16 July 2001, http://www.nytimes.com/2001/07/16/arts/writers-writing-easy-adverbs-exclamation-points-especially-hooptedoodle.html?pagewanted=all&src=pm, date accessed 18 June 2011.

Leonard, E. (2011a) 'Frequently Asked Questions' *The Official Elmore Leonard Website* http://www.elmoreleonard.com/index.php?/faq/youve_said_that_you_were_most_happy_with_three_movies_made_from_your_work_w/, date accessed 2 October 2010.

Leonard, E. (2011b) 'Frequently Asked Questions' *The Official Elmore Leonard Website* http://www.elmoreleonard.com/index.php?/faq/are_you_a_mystery_writer/, date accessed 2 October 2010.

Macdonald, R. (1973) *On Crime Writing* (Santa Barbara: Capra Press).

Macdonald, R. (1981) *Self-portrait, Ceaselessly into the Past*, Sipper, R.B. ed. (Santa Barbara: Capra Press).

Macdonald, R. (1963) *The Wycherly Woman* (New York: Bantham).

Macdonald, R. (1962) *The Zebra-Striped Hearse* (New York, Knopf).

Mackenzie, S. (1999) 'The Searcher' *The Guardian*, 29 May 1999, http://www.guardian.co.uk/lifeandstyle/1999/may/29/paulauster, date accessed 14 June 2011.

MacShane, F., ed. (1983) *The Selected Letters of Raymond Chandler* (London: Macmillan).

Madden, D. ed.,(1968) *Tough Guy Writers of the 30s* (Carbondale, Illinois: Southern Illinois University Press).

Malraux, A. (1952) 'A Preface for Faulkner's Sanctuary' *Yale French Studies*, 10. 92–4

Marling, W. (2009) 'W.R. (William Ripley) Burnett' *DetNovel.com* http://www.detnovel.com/Burnett.html, date accessed 11 May 2011.

Mate, K. and Mulligan, P. (1986) *Backstory 1: Interviews with Screenwriters of Hollywood's Golden Age* (Berkely: University of California Press).

Martin, B. (2009) ' Jay C. Smith, Convict Later Freed in Murder Case Dies at 80' *New York Times*, 15 May 2009, http://www.nytimes.com/2009/05/15/us/15smith.html?_r=1&scp=1&sq=Jay%20C.%20Smith&st=cse, date accessed 8 July 2011.

McBain, E. (2005) *The Empty Hours: three 87th precinct mysteries* (Waterville, ME: Thorndike Press; Bath, England: Chivers).

McBride, J. (1982) *Hawks on Hawks* (Berkeley: University of California Press).

McCann, S. (2010) 'The Hard-boiled Novel' *The Cambridge Companion to American Crime Fiction* Nickerson, C.R., ed. (Cambridge; New York: Cambridge University Press). pp. 42–57.

McCoy, H. (2000) 'They Shoot Horses Don't They' *The Literature of California: Native American Beginnings to 1945* J. Hicks, J. D. Houston, M.H. Kingston and A. Young eds. (Berkely: University of California Press). pp. 471–9.

Merrill, H. (2000) *The Red Hot Typewriter: The Life and Times of John D. MacDonald* (New York: Thomas Dunne Books/ St. Martin's Minotaur).

Millar, M. (1962) *How Like An Angel* (New York, Random House).

Mudge, A. (2001) 'New Crime Fiction with a Twist from Noir Master Walter Mosley' *BookPage Interview* http://www.FirstPerson/bookpage, date accessed 19 June 2008.

Muller, M. (1998) 'Interview with Marcia Muller' *Book Browse* http://www.bookbrowse.com/author_interviews/full/index.cfm/author_number/669/marcia-muller,date accessed 24 April 2011.

Neely, B. (1995) *Blanche Among the Talented Tenth* (New York: Penguin Books).

Neely, B. (1992) *Blanche on the Lam* (New York: St. Martin's Press).

Nevins, F.M. Jr. and Greenberg, M. H., eds (1985) *The Best of Ellery Queen: Four decades of stories from the mystery masters* (New York: Beaufort Books).

Noe, A. (2011) 'The Main Line Murders: Smith Protested His Innocence Until His Death' *Tru Crime* http://www.trutv.com/library/crime/notorious_murders/classics/mainline_murders/smith-protested-his-innocence-until-his-death.html,   date accessed 15 February 2011.

Nolan, W. F. (1985) *The Black Mask Boys: Masters in the Hard-boiled School of Detective Fiction* (New York: Mysterious Press).

Oates, J. C. (1968) 'Man Under Sentence of Death: The Novels of James M. Cain' Madden, D. ed., *Tough Guy Writers of the 30s* (Carbondale, Illinois: Southern Illinois University Press). pp. 110–28.

Paretsky, S. (1987) *Indemnity Only* (New York: Random House).

Paretsky, S. (1988) *Bitter Medicine* (New York: Ballantine).

Parker, R.B. (1993) 'Letter to J.B. Putnam's Sons Offering Background Information' (30 September 1993) *Robert B. Parker Facebook Page* https://www.facebook.com/media/set/?set=a.152648871421177.33963.151856144833783&type=1, date accessed 24 September 2011.

Parker, R.B. (2009) 'Spencer by Robert Parker' *The Lineup: The World's Greatest Crime Writers Tell the Inside Story of Their Greatest Detectives* (New York: Little, Brown). p. 302

Pelecanos, G.P. (2003) 'The Writing Life: an essay' *Orion Publishing Group* http://www.orionbooks.co.uk/promotions/tv-book-club/george-pelecanos-the-writing-life, date accessed 5 April 2011.

Penzler, O. (1976) 'Interview with Robert Bloch' *The Unofficial Robert Bloch Website* http://mgpfeff.home.sprynet.com/penzler_interview1.html, date accessed 14 September 2010.

Penzler, O. and Steinbrunner, C. (1976) *Encyclopedia of Mystery and Detection*, (New York: McGraw Hill).

Pierce, J. K. (1999) 'Killers, Cover-ups and Max Allen Collins' *January Magazine*, September 1999, http://januarymagazine.com/profiles/collins.html,date accessed 18 May 2011.

Pierce, J.K. (2010) '*Sweet Wild Wench* by William Campbell Gault' *Killer Covers* http://killercoversoftheweek.blogspot.com/2010/05/sweet-wild-wench-by-william-campbell.html, date accessed 20 November 2011.

Poe, E.A. (2006) *The Works of Edgar Allan Poe*, Volume 1 (Amazon Digital Services).
Powell, S. (2012) 'Coda for Crime Fiction' *Conversations with James Ellroy* Powell, S., ed. (Jackson: University Press of Mississippi). pp. 169–75.
Prather, R.S. (1988)*The Kubla Khan Caper* (New York: TOR).
Pronzini, B. (2008) 'Bill Pronzini on William Campbell Gault' *Mystery File* http://mysteryfile.com/blog/?p=848, date accessed 9 February 2011.
Queen, E. (1932) *The Ellery Queen Omnibus: The Roman Hat Mystery; The French Powder Mystery; The Egyptian Cross Mystery* (New York : Grosset & Dunlap).
Reilly, J., ed. (1985) *Twentieth Century Crime and Mystery Writers* (New York: St Martin's Press).
Richards, L.L. (2002) '*January* Interview with Carl Hiaasen' http://januarymagazine.com/profiles/hiaasen.html, date accessed 15 October 2011.
Rinehart, M.R. (1908) *The Circular Staircase* (New York: Review of Reviews).
Shechter, A. (2006) 'Interview: Marcia Muller and Bill Pronzini' *Library Journal*, 15 July 2006, http://www.freetrialzone.com/lj/ljinprintcurrentissue/866599–403/marcia_muller_amp_bill_pronzini.html.csp., date accessed 27 February 2011.
Simpson, P. (2010) 'Noir and the Psycho Killer' *A Companion to Crime Fiction* C. J. Rzepka and L. Horsley, eds. (Oxford: Wiley-Blackwell). pp. 187–97.
Smith, K.B. (n.d.) 'Authors and Creators: Max Allan Collins' *The Thrilling Detective* http://www.thrillingdetective.com/trivia/mac.html, date accessed 6 December 2011.
Spillane, M. (2011) 'A Carroll John Daly Fan Letter' *The Vintage Library* http://www.vintagelibrary.com/pulpfiction/authors/Carroll-John-Daly-Fan-Letter.php, date accessed 8 September 2011.
Spillane, M. (1947) *I, the Jury* (New York: E. P. Dutton).
Steinbrunner, C. and Penzler, O. (1976) *Encyclopedia of Mystery and Detection* (New York: McGraw-Hill).
Symons, J. (1972) *Bloody Murder: From the Detective Story to the Crime Novel* (London: Viking).
Van Dine, S.S. (2000) 'Twenty Rules for Writing Detective Stories' *Gaslight* http://gaslight.mtroyal.ca/vandine.htm, date accessed 5 September 2011.
Walker, P. (1974) 'Paul Walker Interviews Robert Bloch' *The Unofficial Robert Bloch Website* http://mgpfeff.home.sprynet.com/interview_walker.html, date accessed 3 September 2010.
West, H.I. (1973) 'Sweet Talk, Hustle and Muscle' *Popsubculture* http://www.popsubculture.com/pop/bio_project/sub/iceberg_slim.2.html, date accessed 7 July 2011.
Winchell, M. R. (1982) *Horace McCoy*. (Boise, Idaho: Boise State University).
Wright, W. H. (1917) *Misinforming a Nation*. (New York: B.W. Huebsch).

Suggested Reading

Abbott, M.E. (2011) *Megan Abbott* http://meganabbott.com/index.html

Abbott, M.E. (2009) 'Megan Abbott: An Email Conversation with Rebecca Godfrey' in *Barnes and Noble Review,* http://bnreview.barnesandnoble.com/t5/Interview /Megan-Abbott/ba-p/1202, date accessed 20 July 2011.

Abbott, M.E. (2002) *The Street Was Mine* (New York: Palgrave Macmillan).

Adrian, J. (1999) 'Obituary: George V. Higgins's *Independent,* 10 November 1999 http://www.independent.co.uk/arts-entertainment/obituary-george-v-higgins-1124755.html

Adrian, J. (1999) 'Obituary: Howard Browne' *The Independent,* 15 November 1999 http://www.independent.co.uk/arts-entertainment/obituary-howard-browne-1126255.html, date accessed 4 June 2010.

Akers-Jordan, C. (1998) 'Ellery Queen: Forgotten Master Detective' Master of Liberal Studies, University of Michigan-Flint http://spruce.flint.umich.edu/~cakers /EQThesis.pdf

Anon (1956) 'Browne Leaves Ziff-Davis for Hollywood'. *Fantasy Times,* 247(3), May 1956.

Anon (1984) 'Ernest R. Tidyman, Screen writer, dies at 56' *The New York Times* 16 July 1984, p. B-11.

Anon (1989) 'Lawrence Treat, 94, Prolific Mystery Writer' *The New York Times* http://www.nytimes.com/1998/01/16/books/lawrence-treat-94-prolific-mystery-writer.html, date accessed 5 February 2011.

Anon. (2011) 'Maryland Author Biographies' *University of Maryland Libraries* http://lib.guides.umd.edu/content.php?pid=179706&sid=1511841, date accessed 16 April 2011.

Anon. (1987)'Vera Caspary, Screenwriter and Novelist' *The New York Times,* June 17, 1987 http://www.nytimes.com/1987/06/17/obituaries/vera-caspary-screenwriter-and-novelist.html, date accessed 8 September 2011.

Anon (1970) 'Viola Shore Wrote Stories and Movies' *The New York Times,* 31 March 1970, p. 41.

Apostolou, J.L. (2001) 'Norbert Davis: Profile of a Pulp Writer' *Black Mask Magazine. com* http://www.blackmaskmagazine.com/bm_03.html, date accessed 29 October 2010.

Ashley, M., ed. (2002) *The Mammoth Encyclopedia of Modern Crime Fiction* (New York: Carroll & Graf).

Auster, P. (1998) *Hand to Mouth: a chronicle of early failure* (London: Faber).

Baring Gould, W.S. (1969) *Nero Wolfe of West Thirty-Fifth Street: The Life and Times of America's Largest Private Detective* (New York: Viking).

Barone, D. (1995) *Beyond the Red Notebook: Essays on Paul Auster* (Philadelphia: University of Pennsylvania Press).

Bellas, P.H. (1995) *Poe, Master of Macabre* (Baltimore: Xavier).

Berger, Roger (1997) '"The black dick': Race, Sexuality, and Discourse in the L.A. Novels of Walter Mosley' *African-American Review* 31(2) 281–291.

Bertens, J.W. and D'haen, T. (2001) 'On the Ball' *Contemporary American Crime Fiction,* (Hampshire: Palgrave). pp. 122–24.

Bloch, R. (1993) *Once Around the Bloch: An Unauthorized Autobiography* (New York: TOR).

Block, L. (1990) 'Lawrence Block', *Contemporary Authors Autobiography Series*, 11 (Detroit: Gale).

Block, L. (2009) *Step By Step: a Pedestrian Memoir* (New York: William Morrow).

Block, L. and Bulow, E. (1995) *After Hours: Conversations with Lawrence Block* (Albuquerque, University of New Mexico).

Blotner, J. (1991) *Faulkner: A Biography* (New York: Vintage Books).

Bogue, B. (2006) *James Lee Burke and the Soul of Dave Robicheaux: A Critical Study of the Crime Fiction Series* (Jefferson, NC: McFarland).

Boucher, A. (1951) *Ellery Queen: A Double Profile* (New York: Little Brown).

Brackett, L. (2001) 'From *The Big Sleep* to *The Long Goodbye*' *The Big Book of Noir*. E. Gorman, L. Server and M. H. Greenberg, eds. (New York: Carroll and Graf) pp. 137 – 142.

Brady O.E. (2011) *Conversations with Walter Mosley* (Jackson: University of Mississippi).

Brady, O.E. and Maus, D.C. eds. (2008) *Finding a Way Home: a Critical Assessment of Walter Mosley's Fiction* (Jackson: University of Mississippi)

Brewer, V.M.L. (2010) 'Notes on Gil Brewer' *Gil Brewer, noir fiction writer* http://www.gilbrewer.com/notesverlaine.htm, date accessed 28 September 2009.

Brockes, E. (2009) 'A Life in Writing: Dennis Lehane' *The Guardian*, 24 January 2009 http://www.guardian.co.uk/culture/2009/jan/24/dennis-lehane, date accessed 2 October 2010.

Browne, R. B. (1990) 'Ross Macdonald: Revolutionary Author and Critic; or the Need for the Oath of Macdonald' *Journal of Popular Culture*, Winter 1990, 24(3) 101–111.

Brubaker, B. (1993) *Stewards of the House: The Detective Fiction of Jonathan Latimer* (Bowling Green, OH: Bowling Green State University Press).

Bunker, E. (1999) *Mr Blue: Memoirs of a Renegade* (Harpenden: No Exit Press).

Burke, J.L. (2004) *James Lee Burke.com* http://jamesleeburke.coml

Busch, S.R. (1986). 'Ross Macdonald as Chronicler of Southern California' *South Dakota Review*, Spring 1986, 24 (1) 111–120.

Bzowski, F.D. (1992) *American Women Playwrights, 1900–1930: A Checklist* (Westport, CT; London: Greenwood Press).

Carr, J.C. (1983) *The Craft of Crime: Conversations with Crime Writers* (Boston: Houghton Mifflin)

Carr, J.L. (1986) *Leigh Brackett: American Writer*. (Polk City, Iowa: C. Drumm).

Carlson, E.W., ed. (1996) *A Companion to Poe Studies* (Westport, CT: Greenwood).

Carlson, M. (2007) 'Richard S Prather: Thriller writer from a world of sex, violence, caddys and 'frails'' *The Guardian*, 29 March 2007, http://www.guardian.co.uk/news/2007/mar/29/guardianobituaries.books, date accessed 24 September 2011.

Carruthers, S.L. (1998) ''The Manchurian Candidate' (1962) and the Cold War Brainwashing Scare'. *Historical Journal of Film, Radio and Television* 18 (1) 75–94.

Clarke, B. and Hopkins, J. (1988) *The Work of William F. Nolan: An Annotated Bibliography & Guide* (San Bernardino, CA: Borgo Press).

Clarke, G. (1988) *Capote: A Biography* (New York: Simon and Schuster).

Chandler, R. (1950) *The Simple Art of Murder* (London: Hamish Hamilton).

Challen, P.C. (2000) *Get Dutch!: a biography of Elmore Leonard* (Toronto: ECW Press).

Coben, H. (2011) *The Official Harlan Coben Website*. http://www.harlancoben.com/index.html, date accessed 15 March 2011.

Cohn, J. (1980) *Improbable Fiction: The Life of Mary Roberts Rinehart* (Pittsburgh: University of Pittsburgh Press).

Collins, M.A. and Traylor, J. L. (1984) *One Lonely Knight: Mickey Spillane's Mike Hammer* (Bowling Green: Bowling Green University Popular Press).

Connelly, M. (2011) *Michael Connelly* http://www.michaelconnelly.com

Cornwell, P. (2011) *Patricia Cornwell* http://www.patriciacornwell.com/

Cowley, J. (2006) 'Creator of a Monstrous Hit' *Observer*, 19 November 2006 http://www.guardian.co.uk/books/2006/nov/19/fiction.thomasharris, date accessed 5 November 2010.

Crider, B., Lewis, S. and Birch, V.A. (2004) *MysteryFile.com* www.mysteryfile.com /GM_Keene/Keene.html, date accessed 9 June 2011.

Cypert, R. (2005) *America's Agatha Christie: Mignon Good Eberhart, Her Life and Works* (Selinsgrove, PA : Susquehanna University Press).

D'haen, T. (2009) 'Plum's the Girl! Janet Evanovich and the Empowerment of Ms Common America' *Investigating Identities: Questions of Identity in Contemporary International Crime Fiction.* M. Krajenbrink and K.M. Quinn eds. (Amsterdam: Rodophi).

Davis, C.J. and West, K. (1996) *Women Writers in the United States: A Timeline of Literary, Cultural, and Social History* (New York: Oxford University Press).

'Davis Grubb' *West Virginia Wesleyan College, Annie Merner Pfeiffer Library* http://www.wvwc.edu/library/wv_authors/authors/a_grubb.htm, date accessed 19 October 2010.

DeAndrea, W.L. (1994) *Encyclopedia Mysteriosa* (New York: Macmillan).

Décharné, M. 'Introduction' *Fast One* by Cain, P. (Harpenden: No Exit Press). pp. 7–12.

DeMarr, M. J. (1994) 'Elizabeth Linington' *Great Women Mystery Writers: classic to contemporary*, K. Gregory Klein ed. (Westport, Conn: Greenwood Press). pp. 192–6.

Dove, G.N. (1985) *The Boys From Grover Avenue: Ed McBain's 87th Precinct Novels* (Bowling Green, OH: Bowling Green State University Press).

Dover, J.K. (1995) *Centurions, Knights, and Other Cops: The Police Novels of Joseph Wambaugh* (San Bernardino, CA: Brownstone Books).

Duncan, P. (1997) *The Third Degree: crime writers in conversation* (Harpenden: No Exit Press) pp. 156–173.

Dunne, M. (1987)'The Comic Capers of Donald Westlake' *Comic Crime*, E. F. Bargainnier, ed. (Ohio: Bowling Green University Popular Press). pp. 168–180.

Effron, M. (2010) 'Sara Paretsky' in *A Companion to Crime Fiction*, C. J. Rzepka and L. Horsley eds. (Oxford: Blackwell,) pp. 523–530.

Ellery Queen: A Website of Detection (1999) http://neptune.spaceports.com/~queen /index.html, date accessed 22 October 2011.

Emrys, A.B. *Wilkie Collins, Vera Caspary and the Evolution of the Casebook Novel* (Jefferson, NC: McFarland, 2011).

Falk, B. (2007) 'Leigh Brackett: Much More than the Queen of Space Opera!' http://www.bewilderingstories.com/issue250/brackett1.html, date accessed 21 June 2011.

Fisher, R. (1987) *The Short Fiction of Rudolph Fisher*, ed. Margaret Perry (New York: Greenwood Press).

Fishinger, S. (1996) 'Carolyn Wells, 1862–1942' *Past and Promise: Lives of New Jersey Women*, ed. J. N. Burstyn (Syracuse: Syracuse University Press).

Flügge, A.M. (2010) *James Ellroy and the Novel of Obsession* (Trier: Wissenschaftlicher Verlag Trier)

Forshaw, B. (1999) 'Keeping it Fresh: Jonathan Kellerman' *Crime Time* http://www.crimetime.co.uk/interviews/jonathankellerman.php, date accessed 4 June 2010.

Fowler, D. (1988) *Ira Levin* (Mercer Island, WA: Starmont House).

Fox, M. (2007) 'Ira Levin of 'Rosemary's Baby,' dies at 78' *New York Times*, 14 November 2007, http://www.nytimes.com/2007/11/14/books/14levin.html?ref=a, date accessed 21 June 2011.

Fox, M. (2008) 'James Crumley, Crime Novelist, Is Dead at 68' *The New York Times*, 19 September 2008 http://www.nytimes.com/2008/09/20/books/20crumley.html, date accessed 5 June 2011.

Frank, F.S. and Magistrale, A. (1997) *The Poe Encyclopedia* (Westport, CT: Greenwood).

Friedman, K. (2011) *Kinky Friedman* www.kinkyfriedman.com

Garnier, P. (1984) *Goodis, la vie en noir et blanc: biographie* (Paris : Editions du Seuil).

Geherin, D. (1989) *Elmore Leonard* (London: Continuum).

Geherin, D. (1982) *John D. MacDonald* (New York: Frederick Ungar).

Geherin, D. (1986) 'Max Latin: Norbert Davis's *The American Private Eye: The Image in Fiction* (New York: Frederick Ungar) pp. 50–5.

Geherin, D. (1980) *Sons of Sam Spade: The Private Eye Novel in the '70s.* (New York: Frederick Unger).

Goodis, D. *Shooting Pool with David Goodis* http://www.davidgoodis.com

Gorman, E.(1998) 'Forgotten Writers: Gil Brewers' *The Big Book of Noir*, L. Server, E. Gorman and M.H. Greenberg eds. (New York: Carroll and Graf), p. 191.

Greene, D.G. (2009) 'John Dickson Carr: Explaining the Inexplicable' *Mysterynet.com* http://www.mysterynet.com/books/testimony/carr/, date accessed 4 August 2011.

Greene, D.G. (1995) *John Dickson Carr: The Man Who Explained Miracles* (New York: Otto Penzler Books).

Gregoriou, C. (2007) *Deviance in Contemporary Crime Fiction* (Houndmills, Basingstoke: Palgrave Macmillan).

Grimes, W. (1994) 'Margaret Millar Is Dead at 79; Wrote Psychological Mysteries' *New York Times*, 29 March 1994, p. D22.

Grogg, S. Jr. (1973) 'Ross Macdonald: At the Edge', *Journal of Popular Culture*, Summer 1973, 7, 213–222.

Gruber, F. (1967) *The Pulp Jungle* (Los Angeles: Sherbourne Press).

Gussow, M. (1996) 'Mignon Eberhart, Novelist, 97; Blended Mystery and Romance' *New York Times*, October 9. p. D19.

Gussow, M. (1996) 'Richard Condon, Political Novelist, Dies at 81' *The New York Times* April 1996, http://www.nytimes.com/1996/04/10/nyregion/richard-condon-political-novelist-dies-at-81.html, accessed 30 April 2011.

Hagemann, E.R. (1980) 'Raoul F. Whitfield, A Star with the *Mask*', in *The Armchair Detective*, 13 (3). 179 – 84.

Hamilton, I. (1990). *Writers in Hollywood* (London: Heinemann).

Hammett, J. (2001) *Dashiell Hammett: a daughter remembers*, R. Layman and J. M. Rivett eds. (New York: Carroll &Graf).

Harper, K. (2000) 'Frederick Nebel (1903–1967)' *Dictionary of Literary Biography: American Hard-Boiled Crime Writers*, G. P. Anderson and J.B. Anderson eds. vol 226 (Detroit: The Gale Group). 283 – 288.

Haut, W. (1999) *Neon Noir: Contemporary American Crime Fiction* (London: Serpent's Tail, 1999).

Haut, W. (1995) *Pulp Culture: Hard-boiled Fiction and the Cold War* (London: Serpent's Tail).

Hayes, M.H. (2010) *Elmore Leonard: His Life and Letters* (Westport: Praeger).

Heising, W.J. (1999) *Detecting Women 2: A Readers Guide and Checklist for Mystery Series Written by Women* (Dearborn, MI: Purple Moon Press).

Henry, O.L. (1996) 'Rudolph Fisher: An Evaluation' *The Harlem Renaissance, 1920–1940*, 6, C. D. Wintz ed. (New York: Garland Publishing). pp. 447–53.

Hiaasen, C. (n.d.) *Carl Hiaasen* http://www.carlhiaasen.com

Hillerman, T. (2002) *Seldom Disappointed* (New York: Harper).

Hiney, T. (1997) *Raymond Chandler: A Biography* (London: Random House).

Hiney, T. and MacShane, F. eds.(2000) *The Raymond Chandler Papers: Selected Letters and Non-Fiction, 1909–1959* (London: Hamish Hamilton).

Hirshberg, E. W. (1985) *John D. MacDonald* (Boston: Twayne Publishers).

Holley, J. (2008) 'Tony Hillerman, 83; Penned Navajo Series' *The Washington Post*, 28 October 2008 http://www.washingtonpost.com/wp-dyn/content/story/2008/10/28/ST2008102801372.html, date accessed 1 October 2010.

Hoopes, R. (1982) *Cain* (New York; Holt, Rinehart and Winston).

Horsley, L. (2009) *The Noir Thriller* (Basingstoke: Palgrave Macmillan).

Horsley, L. (2005) *Twentieth-Century Crime Fiction* (Oxford: Oxford University Press).

Howe, A.N. and Jackson, C.A. (2008) *Marcia Muller and the Female Private Eye: Essays on the Novels That Defined a Subgenre* (Jefferson, NC ; London: McFarland)

Hughes, D.B. (1978) *Erle Stanley Gardner: The Case of the Real Perry Mason* (New York: William Morrow).

Ivison, D. (2000) 'Raoul Whitfield (1898–1945)' *Dictionary of Literary Biography: American Hard-Boiled Crime Writers*, vol. 226.G. P. Anderson and Julie B. Anderson, eds. (Detroit: The Gale Group). 329 – 35.

Jacobson, M.F. and González, G. (2006) *What Have They Built You to Do? The Manchurian Candidate and Cold War America* (Minneapolis: University of Minnesota Press).

James, D. and Foxwell, E. (2005) *The Robert B. Parker Companion* (New York: Berkley Prime Crime).

Johnson, D. (1984) *The Life of Dashiell Hammett* (London: Chatto and Windus); also published as (1983) *Dashiell Hammett: A Life* (New York: Random House).

Jones, L. (2009) 'Dennis Lehane: Hard-Boiled In Boston'. *Publishers Weekly*, 21 June 2009, 246 (25) pp. 40–1.

Joshi, S.T. (1990) *John Dickson Carr: A Critical Study.* (Bowling Green, Ohio: Bowling Green University Popular Press).

Kaufman, N.H. and Kay, C.M. (1997) *G is for Grafton : the World of Kinsey Millhone.* New York : Henry Holt).

Kauffmann, R.W. 'Jacques Futrelle: A Tribute from Reginald Wright Kauffmann' *New York Times,* 12 May 1912 p. BR290.

Keeble, R. and Wheeler, S. (2007) *The Journalistic Imagination: Literary Journalists from Defoe to Capote and Carter* (London and New York: Routledge).

Kellerman, J. (2011) *Jonathan Kellerman* http://jonathankellerman.com.

Kelly, C. (2007) 'Mystery Man: Dan J. Marlowe'. *Allan Guthrie's Noir Originals* http://www.allanguthrie.co.uk/pages/noir_zine/profiles/dan_j_marlowe.php, date accessed 16 September 2010.

Kifner, J. (1999) 'George V. Higgins, 59, Author of Dialogue-Rich Crime Novels' *New York Times* 09 Nov 1999, p. C29.

King, C.D. (1999) *The Psychology of Consciousness* (London: Routledge).

Knight, S. 'The Golden Age' in *The Cambridge Companion to Crime Fiction*. Cambridge: Cambridge University Press, 2003. pp. 77–94.

Konigsburg, E. (2007) 'Paperback Writer', *The Atlantic* (July / August 2007) http://www.theatlantic.com/magazine/archive/2007/07/paperback-writer/5988/, date accessed 12 March 2011.

Krebs, A. 'Truman Capote Is Dead at 59; Novelist of Style and Clarity: Truman Capote, Writer of Style and Clarity, Dies' *The New York Times*, 26 August 1984, p. 1, p. 42.

Krinsky, C. (2010) *glbtq: An Encyclopedia of Gay, Lesbian, Bisexual, Transgender, and Queer Culture.* http://www.glbtq.com/literature/woolrich_c.html, date accessed 7 October 2010.

Lampley, K. and Manis. N. (2007) 'Barbara Neely: Life and Work' *Penn State Africana Research Centre* http://arc.psu.edu/pablackwriters/the-writers/barbara-neely, date accessed 25 April 2011.

Latker, L. (2010) *Shamus Town.* http://homepage.mac.com/llatker/,date accessed 2 November 2010.

Layman, R. (1981) *Shadow Man: The Life of Dashiell Hammett* (New York: Harcourt Brace Jovanovich).

Lee, M.S. (2010) 'Edgar Allan Poe (1840–1849)' C. Rzepka and L. Horsley eds. *A Companion to Crime Fiction* (London: Wiley-Blackwell) pp. 369–380.

Lee, R. (1975) 'Dad and Cousin Fred Entered a Contest. ...', *TV Guide*, 11 October 1975, pp. 21–23.

Lees, L. (2002) 'Jonathan Kellerman: Tangled Web Interview' 28 February 2002, http://www.twbooks.co.uk/authors/jkinterview.html,date accessed 4 June 2010.

Lehane, D. (2010)'Build a solid story around a strong character: A bestselling novelist stresses that you can begin working on plot and other narrative elements only after you know your protagonist to his core' *Writer* November 2010, 123(11). 22–55.

Lessing, H. and Smith, K. B. (n.d.) 'Frederick Nebel' *The Thrilling Detective* http://www.thrillingdetective.com/trivia/nebel.html., date accessed 8 September 2011

Levendorf, K. and Stoyer, D. 'Harry Bosch' *Thrilling Detective* http://www.thrilling-detective.com/eyes/bosch.html, date accessed 27 June 2011.

Lindsay, E.B. (2007) 'Janet Evanovich (1943-)' *Great Women Mystery Writers.* (Westport, Conn: Greenwood Press).

Lipsky Family Papers (2008) arranged by R. Miller (Boston and New York: American Jewish Historical Society) Accession Number: edsoai.705028748 http://digital.cjh.org/view/action/singleViewer.do?dvs=1322678866351~574&locale=en_GB&VIEWER_URL=/view/action/singleViewer.do?&DELIVERY_RULE_ID=5&frameId=1&usePid1=true&usePid2=true

Liukkonen, P. (2008)'George V(incent) Higgins (1939–1999)' *Books and Writers* http://kirjasto.sci.fi/higg.htm, date accessed 5 October 2011.

Liukkonen, P. (2008) 'Jacques Futrelle (1875–1912)' *Books and Writers* http://kirjasto.sci.fi/futrell.htm, date accessed 9 July 2011.

Liukkonen, P. (2008) 'William P(eter) McGivern(1922–1982)' *Books and Writers* http://kirjasto.sci.fi/mcgivern.htm, date accessed 15 July 2011

Loughery, John. *Alias S.S. Van Dine.* New York: Knopf (1992).

Madden, D. (1970) *James M. Cain* (Boston: Twayne Publishers).

Marc, D. and Thompson, R.J. (1995) 'Roy Huggins: Let Cooler Heads Prevail' *Prime Time, Prime Movers: From I Love Lucy to L.A. Law-America's Favorite TV Shows and the People Who Created Them* (New York: Syracuse University Press) pp. 141–52.

Marling, W. (2009) 'Joseph Wambaugh' *Detnovel.com* http://www.detnovel.com/Wambaugh.html, date accessed 30 June 2011.

Marling, W. (2009) 'Paul Cain' *Detnovel.com* http://www.detnovel.com/CainPaul.html, date accessed 23 May 2010.

Marling, W. (2009) 'W.R. (William Ripley) Burnett' *DetNovel.com* http://www.detnovel.com/Burnett.html, date accessed 11 May 2011.

Mason, T.O. Jr. (1992) 'Walter Mosley's Easy Rawlins: The Detective and Afro-American Fiction' *The Kenyon Review*, Fall 1992, 14 (4) 173–183.

Mate, K. and Mulligan. P. *Backstory 1: Interviews with Screenwriters of Hollywood's Golden Age* (contains an interview with Burnett). University of California Press, 1986.

Matthews, T. L., ed. (2005) 'Westlake, Donald', in *Contemporary Authors: New Revision Series*, vol 137 (Farmington Hills, MI: Thomson Gale). pp. 407–414.

Mawer, N. (2004) *A Critical Study of the Fiction of Patricia Highsmith: From the Psychological to the Political* (Lewiston, New York: Edwin Mellen Press).

Mayberry, J. (2009)' True Detectives by Jonathan Kellerman' *Big Thrill* http://www.thrillerwriters.org/2009/02/true-detectives-by-jonathan-kellerman.html, date accessed 4 June 2010.

McAleer, J. J. (1979) *Rex Stout: A Biography* (Boston: Little, Brown).

McCabe, S. (2006) 'Reconciling Violence and a Life in Literature: An Interview with Dennis Lehane' *Writer's Chronicle*, September 2006, 39 (1) pp. 8–13.

McCann, S. (2000) *Gumshoe America: Hard-Boiled Crime Fiction and the Rise and Fall of New Deal Liberalism* (Durham: Duke University Press).

McCauley, M. J. (1991) *Jim Thompson: Sleep with the Devil* (New York: Mysterious Press).

McDonald, C. (2009) 'James Crumley: The Right Madness' *Rogue Males: Conversations and Confrontations about the Writing Life* (Madison, WI: Bleak House). pp. 7–20.

McDonald, C. (2009) 'James Sallis's *Rogue Males: Conversations and Confrontations about the Writing Life* (Madison: WI: Bleak House).pp. 237–266.

McGivern, W.P. and Daly, M. (1958) *Mention my Name in Mombasa: the unscheduled adventures of an American family abroad* (New York, Dodd, Mead).

McGovern, M. and Friedman, K. (1999) *Eat, Drink, and Be Kinky: A Feast of Wit and Fabulous Recipes for Fans of Kinky Friedman* (New York: Simon & Schuster).

McNamara, E. (1992) *'Laura' as Novel, Film and Myth* (Lewiston, NY: Edwin Mellen Press).

McShane, F. (1976) *The Life of Raymond Chandler* (London: Jonathan Cape)

Merrill, H. (2000) *The Red Hot Typewriter: The Life and Times of John D. MacDonald* (New York: Thomas Dunne Books/ St. Martin's Minotaur).

Mertz, S. (1979) 'W. T. Ballard: An Interview' http://www.blackmaskmagazine.com/ballard.html, date accessed 5 May 2011.

Migoya, H. (2001) *La Tormenta Y La Calma Hernan Migoya* (Barcelona: Glenat).

Minter, D. (1980) *William Faulkner: His Life and Work* (Baltimore: MD, Johns Hopkins University Press).

Mizejewski, L. (2004) *Hard-boiled & High Heeled: the woman detective in popular culture* (New York: Routledge).

Moore, L.D. (1994) *Meditations on America: John D. MacDonald's Travis McGee Series and Other Fiction* (Bowling Green, Ohio: Bowling Green State University Popular Press).

Murphy, B. F. (1999) *The Encyclopedia of Murder and Mystery.* (New York: St Martin's Minotaur).

Nealon, C. (2001). *Foundlings: Lesbian and Gay Historical Emotion Before Stonewall* (Durham, NC: Duke University Press).

Nelson, C. (n.d) 'Kenneth Fearing' *Modern American Poetry* http://www.english.illinois.edu/maps/poets/a_f/fearing/fearing.htm, date accessed 22 February 2011.

Nevins, F.M. (1988) *Cornell Woolrich: First You Dream, Then You Die.* (New York: Mysterious Press).

Nevins, F.M. and Greenberg, M.H. eds. (1985) *Carnival of Crime: The Best Mystery Stories of Fredric Brown* (Carbondale: Southern Illinois University Press).

Nolan, T. (2004)'Introduction' *The Couple Next Door* by M. Millar (Norfolk, VA: Crippen & Landru).

Nolan, T. (2001)'Ross Macdonald and Margaret Millar: Partners in Crime' *Mystery Reader's Journal, Partners in Crime II*, 17:3 http://www.mysteryreaders.org/Issues /Partners2.html *CLUES: A Journal of Detection* 25.3 (Spring 2007).

Nolan, W.F. (1985) *The Black Mask Boys: Masters in the Hard-boiled School of Detective Fiction*. (New York: William Morrow).

Nolan, W.F. (1985) 'Behind the Mask: Frederick Nebel' *The Black Mask Boys*. (New York: Mysterious Press).pp. 152 – 157.

Nolan, W.F. (1985) 'Behind the Mask: Raoul Whitfield' *The Black Mask Boys* (New York: The Mysterious Press). pp. 129 – 35.

Nolan, W.F. (2002) 'Collecting Howard Browne' *Firsts: The Book Collectors Magazine*, 12 (8), October 2002.

Nolan, W.F. (1969) *Dashiell Hammett: A Casebook* (Santa Barbara: McNally and Loftin).

Norton, C.A. (1973) *Melville Davisson Post: Man of Many Mysteries* (Bowling Green OH: Popular Press).

O'Sullivan, B. (1997) 'Shore, Viola Brothers, 1890–1970' *Jewish Women in America: An Historical Encyclopedia*, Vol. 2: M-Z. P. E. Hyman and D. Dash Moore, eds. (New York: Routledge).

Oates, J.C. (1968) 'Man Under Sentence of Death: The Novels of James M. Cain,' D. Madden, ed., *Tough Guy Writers of the 30s* (Carbondale, Illinois: Southern Illinois University Press).pp. 110–28.

Orr, S. (2010) *Darkly Perfect World: Colonial Adventure, Postmodernism and American Noir* (Columbus: Ohio State University Press).

Pace, E. (1993) 'Eleazar Lipsky, 81, a Prosecutor, Lawyer, Novelist and Playwright' *New York Times*, 15 February 1993, p. 16. http://www.nytimes.com/1993/02/15/arts /eleazar-lipsky-81-a-prosecutor-lawyer-novelist-and-playwright.html, date accessed 16 February 2011.

Paretsky, S. (2011) *Sarah Paretsky* http://www.saraparetsky.com

Paretsky, S. (2009) *Writing in an Age of Silence* (New York: Verso).

Pelecanos, G. (2010) 'Biography' *George Pelecanos* http://www.hachettebookgroup. com/features/georgepelecanos/bio/, date accessed 14 April 2011.

Penzler, O. ed. (2009) *The Lineup: The World's Greatest Crime Writers Tell the Inside Story of Their Greatest Detectives* (New York: Little, Brown).

Pierce, J.K. (2005) 'The Double-Man: a final farewell to novelist Ed McBain' *January Magazine*, October 2005, http://www.januarymagazine.com/features/mcbainintro. html, date accessed 6 October 2010.

Pierce, J.K. (2010) 'A High Point for Hammer,' *The Rap Sheet*, 17 May 2010, http: //therapsheet.blogspot.com/2010/05/high-point-for-hammer.html, date accessed 19 May 2011.

Pierce, J. K. (1999) 'Killers, Cover-ups and Max Allan Collins' *January Magazine*, September 1999, http://januarymagazine.com/profiles/collins.html,date accessed 18 May 2011.

Plummer, B.C. (1994) 'Marcia Muller' *Great Women Mystery Writers: classic to contemporary*, K. Gregory Klein ed. (Westport, Conn: Greenwood Press). pp. 244–8.

Polito, R. (1995) *Savage Art: A Biography of Jim Thompson* (New York: Alfred A. Knopf).

Powell, G. (2002) 'Lutz for Life' *Bleeker Books.com* http://www.bleekerbooks.com /Features/LutzInterview.asp, date accessed 7 June 2011.

Powell, S. (2012) *Conversations with James Ellroy* (Jackson: University Press of Mississippi).

Pronzini, B. (1992) 'Some Words About William Campbell Gault' *Dead Pigeon* by W. C. Gault. (New York: Carroll & Graf Publishers).

Raphael, A. (2008) 'Murder he wrote' *The Observer*, 27 July 2008, http://www.guardian.co.uk/media/2008/jul/27/television.books.culture, date accessed 16 April 2011

Reilly, J.M. (1996) *Tony Hillerman: A Critical Companion (Critical Companions to Popular Writers* (Westport, CT: Greenwood Press).

Reilly, J. M., ed. (1985) *Twentieth-Century Crime and Mystery Writers* (New York: St Martin's Press)

Richards, L.L. (2002) *'January* Interview with Carl Hiaasen' http://januarymagazine.com/profiles/hiaasen.html, date accessed 15 October 2011.

Rinehart, M.R. (1931) *My Story* (New York: Farrar and Rinehart).

Ruber, P. and Berch, V. A. (2002) 'Raoul Whitfield: Black Mask's Forgotten Man' *Black Mask Magazine* http://www.blackmaskmagazine.com/bm_17.html, date accessed 28 February 2011.

Ryley, R.M. (1994) 'Introduction' *Kenneth Fearing: Complete Poems*. R. M. Ryley, ed. (Orono, ME: The National Poetry Foundation) pp. xlix-lxi.

Sallis, J. (2000) *Chester Himes: A Life* (Edinburgh: Payback Press).

Sallis, J. (1993) *Difficult lives: Jim Thompson, David Goodis, Chester Himes* (Brooklyn, NY: Gryphon).

Sallis, J. (2011) *The James Sallis Web Pages* www.jamessallis.com

Schenkar, J. (2009) *The Talented Miss Highsmith: The Secret Life and Serious Art of Patricia Highsmith* (London: St Martin's Press).

Schuyler, G. (1966) *Black and Conservative: the autobiography of George Schuyler* (New Rochelle, NY: Arlington House).

Seabrook, J. (1993) *Martians and Misplaced Cues: The Life and Work of Fredric Brown* (Bowling Green, OH: Bowling Green State University Popular Press).

Server, L. (2002) 'Davis, Norbert' *Encyclopedia of Pulp Fiction Writers: The Essential Guide to More Than 200 Pulp Pioneers and Mass-market Masters* (New York: Facts on File, Inc.) pp. 77–9.

Sexton, D. (2001) *The Strange World of Thomas Harris* (London: Short Books).

Shechter, A. (2006) 'Interview: Marcia Muller and Bill Pronzini,' *Library Journal*, 15 July 2006 http://www.freetrialzone.com/lj/ljinprintcurrentissue/866599–403/marcia_muller_amp_bill_pronzini.html.csp, date accessed 15 July 2011.

Silverman, K. (1992) *Edgar A. Poe: Mournful and Never-Ending Remembrance* (London: Wiedenfeld and Nicholson).

Simpson, P. (2010) 'Noir and the Psycho Killer' *A Companion to Crime Fiction* C. J. Rzepka and L. Horsley, eds. (Oxford: Wiley-Blackwell). pp. 187–197.

Skinner, R.E. (1989) *Two Guns from Harlem: The Detective Fiction of Chester Himes* (Bowling Green: Bowling Green State University Press).

Sky, M. (2007) *Twilight Tales: Ann Bannon's Lesbian Pulp Series 'The Beebo Brinker Chronicles'* Ph.D. (Ottowa: Library and Archives Canada).

Slim, I. (1996) *Pimp: The Story Of My Life* (London: Canongate)

Smith, K. B. (n.d.) 'Authors and Creators: Erle Stanley Gardner,' by Kevin Burton Smith, *The Thrilling Detective*, http://www.thrillingdetective.com/trivia/gardner.html

Smith, K.B. (nd) 'Authors and Creators: Max Allan Collins' *The Thrilling Detective* http://www.thrillingdetective.com/trivia/mac.html, date accessed 6 December 2011.

Smith, K.B. (2011) 'Lawrence Block' *Thrilling Detective* http://www.thrillingdetective. com/trivia/block.html, date accessed 22 September 2010.

Soitos, S.F. (1996) *The Blues Detective: A Study of African-American Detective Fiction* (Amherst: University of Massachusetts Press).

Spellman, M. 'W.R. Burnett: American Realist' *Shots: Crime and Thriller Ezine* http://www.shotsmag.co.uk/feature_view.aspx?FEATURE_ID=118, date accessed 11 May 2011.

Stephens, C.P. (1992) *A Checklist of Fredric Brown.* (New York: Ultramarine Publishing Company).

Stryker, S. (2001) *Queer Pulp: Perverted Passions from the Golden Age of the Paperback.* (San Francisco: Chronicle Books).

Sturak, J.T. (1966) *The Life and Writings of Horace McCoy, 1897–1955,* PhD (University of California, Los Angeles)...

Swires, S. (1991) 'Leigh Brackett: Journeyman Plumber' *Backstory 2: Interviews with Screenwriters of the 1940s and 1950s,* P. McGilligan ed. (Berkeley: University of California Press). pp. 15 – 26.

Traylor, J.L. (1985) *Hollywood Troubleshooter: W. T. Ballard's Bill Lennox stories* (Bowling Green, Ohio: University Popular Press).

Tutunjian, J. (1974) 'A Conversation with Ross Macdonald', *Tamarack Review 62,* 66–85.

Van Deburg, W. L. (1997) *Black Camelot: African-American Culture Heroes in Their Times, 1960–1980* (Chicago: University of Chicago Press).

Van Dover, J.K. ed.(1995) *The Critical Response to Raymond Chandler* (Westport, Conn.: Greenwood Press).

Van Dover, J. K. (1984) *Murder in the Millions: Erle Stanley Gardner, Mickey Spillane, Ian Fleming* (New York, Ungar).

Van Dover, J. K. (1991) *Three At Wolfe's Door* (New York: Bantham, 1995).

Villarejo, A. (2004) 'Afterword' *The Blackbirder* by D. B. Hughes (New York: Feminist Press). pp. 209–234.

Waldmeier, J.J. and Waldmeier, J.C. eds. (1999) *The Critical Response to Truman Capote* (Westport, CT: Greenwood Press).

Walters, W.W. (1994) 'Limited Options: Strategic Maneuverings in Himes's Harlem' *African-American Review,* Winter 1994, 28(4) 615–631.

Waring, C. (2011) 'Born Under a Bad Sign: the Life of Edward Bunker' http://www.crimetime.co.uk/features/edwardbunker.php, date accessed 5 November 2011.

Waring, C. (2010) *Cigarettes and Alcohol: The Extraordinary Life of Jim Thompson* http://crimetime.co.uk/features/jim thompson accessed 30/04/2010, date accessed 21 June 2011.

Weinman, S. (2009) 'Closing in on the Letter Z' *L.A. Times,* 17 December http://www.latimes.com/entertainment/news/la-et-sue-grafton17-2009dec17,0,3603461.story, date accessed 7 July 2011.

Welch, J. (1980) *Davis Grubb: A vision of Appalachia,* PhD, Carnegie-Mellon University.

Westlake, D. (2008) 'An Interview with Donald Westlake: Author of the Parker Novels', *University of Chicago Press* http://www.press.uchicago.edu/Misc/Chicago/westlake_interview.html, date accessed 8 September 2011.

Williams, O.R. (1967) *George S. Schuyler: Portrait of a Black Conservative* (Knoxville: University of Tennessee Press).

Wilson, A. (2003) *Beautiful Shadow: A Life of Patricia Highsmith* (London: Bloomsbury).

Winchell, M.R. (1982) *Horace McCoy* (Boise, Idaho: Boise State University).

Witt, D. (2000) 'Detecting Bodies: Barbara Neely's Domestic Sleuth and the Trope of the (In)Visible Woman' *Recovering the Black Female Body: Self Representations by African-American Women*, M. Bennett and V. D. Dickerson. eds. (New Brunswick: Rutgers University Press). pp. 165–194.

Wolfe, P. (2005) *Like Hot Knives to the Brain: James Ellroy's Search for Himself* (Lanham: Lexington Books).

Wolfe, T. (1969) 'Introduction' in Cain, J.M. *Cain X 3: The Postman Always Rings Twice, Mildred Pierce, and Double Indemnity* (New York: Knopf)

Index